The Country Village Christmas Show

Cathy Lake is a women's fiction writer who lives with her family and three dogs in beautiful South Wales. She writes uplifting stories about strong women, family, friendship, love, community and overcoming obstacles.

The Country Village Christmas Show

CATHY LAKE

ZAFFRE

First published in the UK in 2020 by
ZAFFRE
An imprint of Bonnier Books UK
80–81 Wimpole St, London W1G 9RE
Owned by Bonnier Books
Sveavägen 56, Stockholm, Sweden

This is a work of fiction. Names, places, events and
incidents are either the products of the author's
imagination or used fictitiously. Any resemblance to
actual persons, living or dead, or actual
events is purely coincidental.

A CIP catalogue record for this book is
available from the British Library.

ISBN: 978–1–83877–269–7

Also available as an ebook and in audio

3 5 7 9 10 8 6 4 2

Typeset by IDSUK (Data Connection) Ltd
Printed and bound in Great Britain by Clays Ltd, Elcograf S.p.A.

Zaffre is an imprint of Bonnier Books UK
www.bonnierbooks.co.uk

For my husband and children, with love always

Chapter 1

'Look at me, Mum!'

Clare Greene's heart fluttered. She turned, expecting to see her son, but instead her gaze fell on the empty space in the back garden where the swing used to be. The house and garden were full of ghosts and, as she made her way round one final time, she was being assaulted by memories and voices from the past.

Closing her eyes, Clare could picture her son, Kyle, swinging high, remember her anxiety that he'd fall off and hurt himself. But his laughter as he'd soared through the air and the joy on his face as he'd called to her, keen to garner her approval, had made the fear worth it. Her ex-husband, Jason, had taken the swing down years ago, but it had stood there for a decade, from the time Kyle was seven, and he'd had so much fun on it. Kyle was twenty-one now and at university in Bath studying performing arts – a grown man and no longer her little boy.

A cold wind whipped around the garden, tugging at her coat, and she shivered. Time had passed so quickly: she was forty-five and often felt that her life had passed her by, that she had practically sleepwalked through the days. If only it were possible to have some of that time back to savour the good times . . .

Her heart lurched and she pressed a hand to her chest. Looking down, her eyes found her wedding ring. As difficult as it would be, she really needed to take it off. Jason had removed his when the divorce was finalised, sighing at the white mark that remained on his finger. Just like the emotional scars left by the end of their marriage, it would take some time for physical marks like that to go.

She trudged back up the garden to the semi-detached house, went in through the French doors and closed them behind her, lifting the handle slightly until it clicked, then turned the key. There was a knack to locking these doors. They should have had them fixed years ago, but it was one of a list of jobs that had never been done and now it would be someone else's problem. But the new owners would also have so much to enjoy here. Clare had loved her home and was sad to leave it, but she knew it was time, even though her throat tightened as she realised she would never walk on the lush green lawn again, never sit on the patio as she savoured her morning coffee, never listen to the jazz drifting from next door on sunny afternoons. Her fragrant roses would be tended to by someone else, the shed would house the tools and bikes of others, and the birds that flocked to the feeders would become accustomed to different humans.

Slipping out of her garden shoes and into her plimsolls, she made her way through the open-plan kitchen diner with its large fireplace and driftwood mantelpiece, her soft rubber soles seemed strangely noisy on the wooden boards, the sound echoing around the empty house, making it feel as though she had company. The furniture had been moved into storage and the clothes and belongings she couldn't bear to part with, such as Kyle's baby photo albums, from a time when people had actually printed photographs, were packed in her treasured Mini Countryman, the remaining finance on it cleared with some of her half of the house sale. The car had seemed to groan under the extra weight but she felt compelled to take them with her.

She passed the lounge where she had given birth to Kyle three weeks before his due date, taken by surprise as she'd thought the pains were practice contractions. He'd slid out onto the rug, red and furious at his early arrival. Kyle's entry into the world had been dramatic and he hadn't changed a bit; he still enjoyed being the centre of attention. Clare had been just twenty-four then, so young and innocent, convinced that life had plenty to offer and that she was destined for something special, even though she hadn't had a clue what that something would be.

How things changed.

In the hallway, where the October sun streamed through the window above the door, she took slow deep breaths, treasuring the sights, sounds and scents of home, storing them safely in her heart. Who knew when she would have a home of her own again? When her vision blurred, she knew it was time to get moving.

Her mobile buzzed in her pocket, making her jump, and she pulled it out to check the screen, expecting a message from the removal company. When she saw Kyle's name, her heart lifted.

Hey Mum,

Hope you're OK. I know today will be difficult, but you can do it! When one house door closes another one opens and all that. Let me know when you're safely at Nanna's.

Love you millions! X

Clare hugged her mobile to her chest for a moment, thanking the universe for the gift of her precious boy. Whatever happened, she had a wonderful son and she would always be grateful for that. After firing off a quick reply, she slid her phone back in her pocket then opened the door and stepped outside, put the key in an envelope and posted it through the letter box, preparing to start the next chapter of her life.

❄

Clare was ten minutes away from the village where she had grown up, but it would probably take her twenty to get there because she was stuck behind a tractor. Her Mini ambled along through the narrow country lanes and her feet ached from braking and pressing the clutch as she had to stop/start the car. Behind her, a row of cars was building and she knew it wouldn't be long before some of the drivers started beeping at her, pressurising her to overtake. But Clare knew better; these lanes could be deadly and visibility was poor. There was always the risk of crashing into some idiot taking the bends at sixty miles per hour.

The whole journey from Reading to Little Bramble in Surrey only took about forty minutes, but she had to admit that she hadn't made it very often, particularly over recent years. There had always been an excuse, whether it was a dinner with Jason's colleagues from the prestigious law firm in Reading where he had been a partner, or an author event at the library where she had worked for twelve years as a library assistant (a job she had adored until they'd had to make some staff redundant six months ago due to cutbacks), or generally just feeling too tired to make the effort. A lump formed in her throat from the guilt. Her mum was seventy-five, fit and healthy, a busy member of her local community, but she wouldn't be around forever and in some ways she'd taken her for granted. They hadn't ever been that close but, even so, she was aware that she could have made more of an effort to visit.

She turned the radio on and listened to the DJ chatting to a celebrity author called Cora Quincy about her latest self-help book. Cora was all of twenty-five but spoke as if she'd lived a long and difficult life. Admittedly, Clare had read about Cora (a fashion model turned actress turned author who'd married someone from a boyband Clare could never remember the name of) online, and knew that she had endured a challenging childhood, but even so, her tone was slightly patronising. Clare had been married for almost as long as the woman had been alive – surely she had more life experience to draw on, more wisdom in the bank? And yet here she was: homeless, jobless, clueless about what came next.

The traffic came to a standstill as the tractor stopped to make way for an approaching car. Clare pulled up the hand-brake and turned, gazing at the hedgerow to her left, almost bare of leaves now in October's colder days. Dark twigs poked out of the hedge, threatening to scratch any vehicles that got too close, and others stretched up to the sky like gnarled brown fingers. Beyond the hedges were fields where farmers grew corn and vegetables, where livestock roamed and nurtured their young.

As a child, Clare had thought she'd grow up to be a vet or own her own stables. She'd loved the wildlife around the village, had been a keen horse rider who had spent Saturday mornings at the stables then worked on Sundays at the local farm shop just outside Little Bramble, where she got to feed the chickens and ducks in her breaks, care for the motherless lambs in spring and play with the fluffy collie pups. Yes, she'd had a good childhood, even if she hadn't been as close to her mum as she'd have liked. At university, she'd studied English Literature (after deciding at sixteen that taking A-levels in the sciences was not for her), met Jason, and her ambitions had slipped away like smoke on the breeze. She'd been so infatuated with him, so taken by his apparent maturity and intelligence that she'd have followed him to the end of the earth if he'd asked her, so when he proposed, she'd accepted without hesitation.

The tractor started moving again and Clare released the handbrake and set off again at a snail's pace.

'Oh, absolutely!' Cora's decisive tone burst from the car speakers and broke into Clare's thoughts. 'I'd spent far too long worrying about what everyone expected of me, trying to be that perfect creature that pleased the world, and then one day . . . BOOM! I had an epiphany! I was like, alleluia!

Eureka! And all that jazz.' She giggled, clearly very pleased with herself.

'And so . . . do you have a message for our listeners?' Darryl Donovan, the long-time Radio 2 DJ asked.

'I do, Darryl, I really do. Whoever you are and whatever you've been through, put yourself first. Decide what *YOU* really want and go for it! I realised, and your listeners can too, that I had to live my life for *me* before I could be with anyone. If you don't love yourself, how can you possibly love anyone else?'

Clare rolled her eyes. It was all very well saying that at twenty-five. It was a message Clare had heard many times in the past, but not one she'd ever managed to take on board. She'd been a daughter, a wife, a mum, a library assistant (although that had been something for her because she'd enjoyed it so much) so her roles had been centred around others and she'd been content with that. The idea of shaking off those responsibilities and doing things solely for herself seemed unimaginable.

Now, for the first time in her life, Clare realised that she felt very much alone.

Clare had always been a daddy's girl and tried to make her father proud whenever she could. When he'd died ten years ago, he'd left a gaping hole which she'd struggled to fill. She didn't have a close relationship with her mum. Elaine Hughes had always been busy with her own life – for many years with her job as a drama teacher, then later on with her work as a chief examiner and as chairwoman of the village amateur dramatics society. With Jason bringing his and Clare's marriage to an end, she was no longer committed to making him happy, but this in itself was another difficult loss to deal with. And then there was Kyle: her darling son, her reason for everything, her joy. But Kyle was grown up and had gone off to university, leaving Clare feeling redundant in that aspect of her life as well, especially after losing her job. Her whole life had changed when she'd least expected it. She'd been prepared for Kyle leaving home, but losing her job and her marriage at the same time was too much.

Would it be possible for Clare to start again and live her life for herself? Could she turn things around and discover what it was that she really wanted?

The left indicator on the tractor started flickering and it pulled into a layby, so Clare put her foot down on the accelerator and drove past it, singing along to the uplifting track from the eighties that the celebrity had chosen as her theme tune.

Perhaps the young woman wasn't so naïve after all.

❄

Sam Wilson unclipped the soft leather lead from his yellow Labrador's collar then watched as she ran ahead, her long tail wagging, nose pressed to the ground. He looked forward to his twice-daily walks with Scout. It was his time out, his time to breathe deeply and enjoy the peace and quiet. He'd have walked anyway, but having Scout for company made the walks around the countryside surrounding Little Bramble even better. The two-year-old Labrador was good company: she enjoyed being outside as much as Sam did and she didn't feel the need to fill their time together with random chatter or demands. As long as she was fed and walked, could snuggle on the sofa and was praised for good behaviour, Scout was happy, and that made Sam happy too.

Moving to the village over three years ago had been a fresh start for him and for his younger sister, Alyssa. After years of living in London, renting flats and saving hard, Sam had wanted to put down roots and settle somewhere quiet, friendly and beautiful. Little Bramble was perfect, and when a colleague in London told him that a former university friend of hers was looking for a partner to invest in her village veterinary practice, Sam had felt a flicker of hope that he hadn't experienced in a long time. He'd travelled to the village to meet Miranda Fitzalan and had liked her blunt, no-nonsense approach, her devotion to the animals in her care – and the very reasonable asking price for a share of the practice. Miranda's former business partner had decided to retire to Spain and she was looking for someone keen to enjoy being a part of village life. Sam's years of saving and investing his money wisely had finally reaped a reward.

Scout came running back to him, a chunky stick in her mouth. She dropped it at his feet and looked up at him, wagging her tail, her mouth open in what looked like a wide smile.

'You want to play, do you?' He reached out and rubbed her soft head and she barked in reply. 'OK then, girl. Ready?'

He picked up the stick then swung his arm back and threw it as far ahead as he could, laughing as Scout scampered after it, knowing that this process would be repeated many times before they reached home again. Repetition and routine were the things that kept his life moving forwards and he didn't think to want for more.

Chapter 2

Clare pulled up in front of the secluded cottage at the edge of the village and cut the engine. She pushed her shoulders back, trying to ease the knots that had formed during the drive. Actually, who was she trying to kid? The knots had been there for months, possibly years, and most of the time she managed to forget about them, but certain seating positions – like driving – made them more acute.

Home.

The word made her start as if someone else in the car had whispered it.

Her mum's cottage hadn't been home for years, not since she'd left for university aged eighteen. Although she had returned to the village over the years, once she'd met Jason she'd made her home wherever he was. It had been a happy home when she was a child, a busy placed filled with music and laughter, where there always seemed to be people coming and going, where the aromas of coffee and freshly baked bread and scones filled the air and where Clare had felt safe.

But, of course, there was another reason why she'd avoided returning too often, especially for the last ten years. A reason that made her chest tight, her heart ache, a cloud of sadness hover above her . . .

Dad.

She closed her eyes and pressed her lips together hard, waiting for the pain to fade. If she just thought about something else, like the weather or the scuffs on the toes of her plimsolls, then she could forget.

For a while at least.

Clare could be remarkably good at pushing things away, at forgetting – something she suspected she'd inherited from her mother – but it also added to that feeling of sleepwalking through life. For years she'd managed to push away the fact that her marriage was struggling, to forget that, once upon a time, she and Jason had been friends, had been in something that she'd believed to be love, had been lovers. At some point it had lessened, weakened, but Clare had shut her eyes tight and ignored it, because the alternative had been devastating.

The failure of her marriage had left a sour taste in her mouth, left her questioning everything she'd thought she had, thought she'd wanted.

She opened her eyes and took a few slow deep breaths.

Too much to think about.

So she wouldn't.

For now.

She got out of the car, went to the boot and opened it, lifted out her two suitcases. Along with the three boxes on the back seat, the carrier bags for life stuffed behind the seats and the plastic crate on the passenger seat, this was all she had to show for the twenty-six years of their relationship, twenty-two of them married. A mutual friend at university in Reading had introduced them when Clare was nineteen and Jason twenty-two, both so young, she thought now. Clare was studying English Literature, Jason was three years into a law degree and they'd become inseparable immediately. When Jason graduated, he moved out of student accommodation and rented a flat and Clare had moved in while she finished her final year. They had married soon after her graduation. Of course, there was the furniture in storage and the things Kyle had asked her to keep for him for when he finished his degree and Jason's belongings (his half of everything), but she had brought what she could in her small car. She just hoped she'd chosen wisely because she'd hate to want something – a book, a DVD, a pair of shoes – that was in storage in Reading because there was no turning back now.

Jason was travelling lightly too. She tutted, something she'd found herself doing whenever she thought about how his eyes had lit up when their divorce was finalised. They had lived together, sleeping in separate rooms, until the divorce had been sorted, but once he'd realised it was done, that he was, at last, free to jet off and find himself, he'd not been able to hide his pleasure. That was what he'd called it: *finding myself.* As if he'd been lost since he was twenty-two and had met Clare, and now he was able to find the person he'd wanted to be all along. According to Jason, Clare had placed pressure on him, albeit unknowingly, to be the husband, father and provider that *she* wanted him to be and Jason had felt suffocated, trapped, stifled by the roles. Clare had been gobsmacked at first, numb with shock, but as the days had progressed into weeks and then months, as they'd talked over dinners and bottles of wine, as they'd weeded the back-garden side-by-side, the numbness had morphed into acceptance. At times, that acceptance had been tinged by anger (perfectly natural according to the counsellor Clare had seen for six weeks), and Clare had come to agree with Jason that they were not living their best lives at all. They were simply existing, having lost whatever it was that had brought them together in the first place. Clare had been replaced, not by another woman, but by her husband's realisation that he wanted more from life before it was too late, and she too had come to see that she also wanted something, but she had no idea how on earth she was going to work out what it was.

Time . . . the counsellor said. *Time would help her to find her way.*

She was still waiting and, while she did, her mum had suggested (to her great surprise) that she could come home and use that time to think.

Tick tock . . .

She wheeled one suitcase to the front door then went back for the other and locked the car. The stone cottage was chocolate-box pretty with small latticed windows set in thick walls and a heavy oak door with an antique brass knocker shaped like a lion's head. Over the years many festive wreaths had been tied to that knocker, often summery ones too when her parents had been entertaining, something they had loved to do. Her mum had enjoyed placing pumpkins of varying sizes outside on the path leading up to the door at Halloween and at Easter, she'd set out baskets of colourful painted eggs along with a few fibreglass rabbits. Props were important to Elaine and Clare was convinced it was the actress in her mother, the love of theatre of all kinds that led her to want to turn the ordinary, everyday setting into the extraordinary. Elaine was concerned with appearances, but Clare had often wished that her mum would lift up the rug and check what was going on beneath the surface.

Clare had a key to the cottage tucked away in her handbag but she didn't want to just walk in and startle her mum, so she used the doorknocker, hearing it echo through the hallway. A loud bark told her that she'd woken her mum's dog and she smiled, realising that she'd be living with that dog too for a while until she could pull herself together, find a new job and a place to live, which might mean returning to Reading or moving somewhere else. Clare had told her mum that she would be arriving that afternoon but had been unsure of timings because she hadn't wanted to rush leaving her old home, aware that it wouldn't be easy saying goodbye. The removal team had arrived at the crack of dawn to take her bed and sofa from the lounge – the only furniture still remaining at the house, what with the fridge and the cooker being integrated in the fitted kitchen – along with the final few boxes of Jason's things. All of it had gone to the storage facility on an industrial estate in Reading for now and Clare had no idea when she'd be in a position to collect her things, but she hoped it wouldn't be long.

As she waited for her mum to answer the door, she looked up at the darkening sky and smiled, because a plume of grey smoke was curling up from the fat chimney, which meant that the fire was lit and the lounge would be cosy and homely. Clare loved sitting in front of an open fire and the aroma of woodsmoke in the cold air was so familiar, so comforting, that her eyes stung. When the door swung open, she had to blink hard.

'Clare, darling! There you are.'

Her mum stood on the doorstep, her arms folded across her purple cashmere jumper, blue eyes sharp behind the thick black frames of her glasses, her sleek white bob pushed behind her ears. At her mum's side, gazing up at her with his big, brown eyes was Goliath, an enormous fawn Great Dane, the arcs from his swinging tail as powerful as an electric fan.

'Hi, Mum.' Clare felt her bottom lip wobble and she dug her nails into her palms, not wanting to crumble now after being brave for so long, but there was something about coming back here, about seeing her mum, that made her vulnerability rush to the surface. It was as if the little girl she'd once been had woken up and she needed to know that someone cared. 'Hi, Goliath.' She eyed the dog cautiously, hoping that he wouldn't rush at her and plonk those enormous paws on her legs because she already felt unsteady.

'Come here, darling.'

She stepped into her mum's hug, leaning forwards slightly because Elaine was two inches shorter than she was, and breathed in the familiar floral scent. They might not have been as close as some mothers and daughters were, and they might struggle living together again, but right now, Clare was glad to be home.

❄

Sam dropped his keys on the table by the front door then bent over to rub Scout's head.

'Hello, girl. Surprised to see me home so early?'

She wagged her tail then licked his hand and he laughed. There was nothing like a doggy welcome.

He walked through to the lounge and stuck his head around the door but the room was empty so he went back out to the hallway then into the open-plan kitchen-diner.

'There you are, Alyssa.'

His sister smiled at him.

'What're you doing home at this time? I thought you'd be at least another hour or two.'

'My last appointment cancelled so Miranda told me to head off early. She must think I look tired or something.' He laughed, but Alyssa shook her head, causing her shiny dark curls to bounce.

'You do look tired, Samuel. Perhaps you need to take a holiday.'

His sister was the only person who sometimes used his full name, to everyone else he was Sam.

'How did the interview go?'

'Really well.' She grinned, and for a moment his breath caught because she looked exactly like their mother. Alyssa was twelve years younger than him and sometimes he forgot that she was an adult, that she was thirty-four years old with a very strong will of her own.

'Really well as in you got it?' He was nervous asking because Alyssa really wanted the job at a tattoo parlour in Woking but he wasn't sure that it was right for her.

'I certainly did!'

'That's wonderful. Congratulations! When do you start?'

'Next Monday.'

'Great!' He tried to inject more enthusiasm into his tone than he felt. Alyssa was a talented artist and he'd always thought she'd end up designing clothes or selling her art at galleries or doing something incredible with her life that their parents would have approved of. After leaving school at sixteen, she'd studied Art and Design at college then decided not to go to university, even though Sam was prepared to support her through a degree. She'd refused, telling him she didn't want to be a financial burden. They'd been living in London at the time and Alyssa had decided to look for a job instead of pursuing her education. Sam had been disappointed but knew that trying to get her to do something she'd set her mind against would end in failure. Alyssa had got a job in a pub and then, through that, some seasonal work at music festivals across the country. At one of the festivals, aged only eighteen, she'd met a man the same age as Sam and moved in with him. The relationship had lasted six years, in spite of Sam's reservations, and only ended when things had taken an unexpected turn. The man Alyssa believed loved her turned his back on her and walked away when she needed him most, right after she was badly injured in a motorcycle crash.

Sam's shoulders tightened as he thought about Jerry and what he'd done to Alyssa. He couldn't help the rage he felt about how he had abandoned Alyssa, even holding up his hands and stating that he couldn't face being tied to someone in Alyssa's condition. If Sam hadn't been so cut up himself about it all, so overwhelmed with guilt and grief for his little sister, he might have gone after Jerry and done something he'd have later regretted. As it was, Alyssa had needed him too much so he'd swallowed his own feelings and focused instead on doing the best he could for her. She deserved the very best he could give her and that was what he'd always tried to do.

'What do you think?' Alyssa asked, breaking into his thoughts. He tried to let go of the tension that had gripped him as he thought about the past.

'Sorry?'

'I asked what you think about the job?' Her brown eyes sparkled with mischief; she knew he didn't think it was the perfect job for her but that he would keep quiet because it wasn't his decision to make.

'I'm happy for you. Really happy. In fact, we could go out tonight to celebrate if you like? I'll buy you dinner.'

Alyssa's eyes widened slightly.

'Thanks. I appreciate the offer but perhaps we could go out tomorrow instead?'

'Oh . . . OK.' Sam shrugged. He was tired and a bath and an early night was more appealing than eating out, but he'd have made the effort for Alyssa's sake.

'Sam, don't go mad . . . but I have a date.'

'A date?' Sam frowned. 'Since when?'

'Since my interview. The owner of the tattoo parlour introduced me to her younger brother, Sebastian, and he asked me out.'

'You're going out with your new boss's brother?'

'Yes. He lives in Woking and –'

'Alyssa . . .' Sam rubbed his eyes with the heels of his hands, trying to buy some time so as to work out what he wanted to say. 'Are you sure that's a good idea?'

He met her gaze and she glared at him, her nostrils flaring slightly, her lips set in a determined line. He knew at that moment that he had no hope of convincing her otherwise. The dynamic of their relationship was such that if Sam thought something wasn't a good idea, Alyssa would do it anyway and be damned with the consequences.

She sighed dramatically and Sam braced himself, prepared for her to tell him why he was wrong, but she merely shook her head, making him feel like a child being reprimanded.

'And before you ask, yes, he is a tattoo artist too and yes, he has lots of tattoos and piercings, some that I suspect I couldn't see because he was fully clothed.'

'But what if it doesn't work out? It could make things awkward between you and your new boss and –'

'Sam, you really have to stop being so negative about everything and so bloody overprotective! Go get a life of your own! Every time I meet someone I like I either have to keep it from you completely or downplay it so you don't get all stressed out.'

He opened his mouth to reply but couldn't find the words. Instead of standing there like a goldfish, he nodded, then left the kitchen, not wanting to make things worse or make Alyssa think he was even more pathetic than she already did. He was only trying to look out for her, but she clearly did not want him worrying as much as he did.

As for getting a life of his own – how exactly was he supposed to do that?

20

'There you are, Clare,' her mum said as she handed her a mug of tea. 'Are you sure you won't take a slice of lemon drizzle?'

'I'm sure, thanks. Tea is lovely for now.'

Clare sat back on the fat purple sofa and cradled the mug between her palms, savouring the heat. The lounge was just as she remembered it being when she was growing up: cosy, homely and scented with woodsmoke and vanilla and lavender candles, her mum's favourites. The open fireplace was the focal point of the dual aspect room, with a solid wooden mantelpiece and the gold-framed mirror above it. Amber and red flames flickered in the grate, casting dancing shadows across the room, and Goliath lay on the hearthrug, his chin resting on his large paws, his eyebrows raising in turn as he peered at Clare and Elaine. It was almost as if he could read their thoughts and feelings and wanted to watch over them; Clare found his presence comforting.

On the mantelpiece were family photographs of Clare, her parents, and her paternal grandparents, Alice and Terry, who had passed away over twenty years ago. Clare had never known her maternal grandparents and although her mum had briefly mentioned them being disinterested in their daughter, she had never elaborated on the subject, always found ways to avoid doing so. Even from a young age, Clare had sensed that it was a topic that upset her mother, so best avoided.

Elaine sat on the sofa opposite Clare, an emerald velvet affair with plump duck down cushions and a faded patchwork throw over the back.

'Goliath is keeping an eye on you,' she said, smiling at the dog.

'I know. I hope he doesn't mind me being here.'

'Oh, he'll love having more company. He gets a bit fed up with it being just the two of us, I think. He's a sociable dog, considering his age.'

'How old is he now?' Clare asked, then took a sip of her tea. It was hot and strong with just a splash of semi-skimmed milk, exactly how Clare liked it.

'About eight and a half, a good age for a Great Dane. I'll never know his exact age as I didn't get him as a puppy but I can't imagine not having him around. He's filled the space left by your father . . . well, not entirely, but he's helped.'

'Really?' Clare had heard her mum say this before but much as she liked animals, she found it strange to think that a dog could come anywhere close to replacing a human being. Her mum had adopted Goliath from an animal charity eight years ago. His first owner had abandoned him after he started growing bigger than expected and had an appetite to match, but when Elaine had seen him, she'd fallen for him instantly. During his first year at the cottage he had eaten everything Elaine fed him and more, including a piano chair, a bookshelf, a variety of valuable first edition hardback books, a table leg and two picture frames. Whenever Clare's mum had told her about the latest item to meet its demise, Clare had wondered how her usually no-nonsense mum didn't feel tempted to take the dog right back to the shelter. After each incident, Clare had tried to offer some cheery comment about Goliath growing out of it, and he had grown out of his puppy antics – all except one.

'Yes, Clare. Goliath keeps me company, warms my feet and is there to greet me every morning. A dog is a faithful companion. You should get one.'

'Perhaps.' Clare shrugged. It wasn't that she didn't like Goliath, or other dogs, because she really did, but she couldn't imagine the extra responsibility on top of everything else. Of course, Kyle had begged for a dog growing up but she'd found ways to avoid getting one, knowing Jason would have been indifferent to a dog and she'd have been the one cleaning up the poo, feeding and walking it and she'd had enough to do without being responsible for another living creature. Now that she was single and her son was grown, she *could* get a dog but then she would be tied to it and to its care. She wasn't sure how to help herself at the moment, let alone a dog.

'Maybe when I'm settled.' She raised her mug and finished her tea, hoping for a change of subject. When her mum had rescued Goliath, Clare had been surprised because they'd never had a dog when she was growing up. Her parents had both worked and said it wouldn't be fair to leave a dog at home alone all day, and Clare had been able to enjoy caring for the animals at the farm and the horses at the stables, so she'd never felt that she was missing out.

'Don't wait too long, Clare. Getting out for daily walks wouldn't be a bad thing for you, you know.'

And there it was!

Clare had known it would come. Elaine Hughes spared no one's feelings, especially not her daughter's. Clare knew that she'd gained a few pounds since Jason had told her he wanted to separate. She had comforted herself with wine and chocolate, as well as those big blocks of crumbly, golden mature Cheddar, but then why shouldn't she? After years of trying to keep an eye on her weight, of Zumba, boxercise and more, she'd thought, *What the hell?* She'd done all those things to stay in shape, to age gracefully, to be the best version of herself she could be – and it hadn't made a jot of a difference to her husband. He had barely noticed her towards the end of their time together. She'd told herself that all the exercise and healthy eating was for herself, and to a large extent it was, but she had also wanted to feel appreciated, to feel loved, to feel that even though she was past forty, she still had it. Whatever *it* was. So when she'd realised that all the effort she'd made hadn't stopped her husband from walking away from her, she'd stopped and found comfort in tasty food and nice wines, especially the wines that Jason had stocked his wine fridge with over the years. When he'd commented on it, she'd shrugged and told him he couldn't take them away with him, so she might as well enjoy them. Besides which, after years of supporting his penchant for purchasing wines with eye-watering price tags, she'd found great enjoyment in downing them as she slouched on the sofa in her pjs or in the bath with a paperback.

And yes, seeing her mum had been nice initially; she'd felt a surge of emotion as they'd hugged, but now she was back to reality with a bump. Clare's dad had somehow tempered the harsh edge that Elaine could show, had made her laugh and take herself and the world around her less seriously. Since he'd gone, she had been tougher, harder, colder. It was as if losing him had extinguished the tiny spark of warmth that she was able to demonstrate.

Clare had come back to stay with her mum because she felt her choices were limited. With no job and nothing appealing on offer in Reading, along with a sense of inadequacy about what she was skilled to do other than cook, clean, garden and sort books, she had floundered in uncertainty. She had a degree but she hadn't done anything with it. She'd loved working at the library surrounded by books, recommending them to customers who were as excited as she was about new titles and favourite authors, and had been able to work the ancient computer system there, but her IT skills weren't up to date and the idea of going for an interview was terrifying. She had money from the house sale, as well as some savings, but they wouldn't last indefinitely, especially if she ended up paying some extortionate rent, and she couldn't exactly land on Kyle's doorstep at his student digs and ask for shelter. All of her friends in Reading were either married or cohabiting and who wanted a newly divorced friend on their sofa or in their spare room? Besides which, Clare hated the thought of being a burden. But she needed some time, some breathing space, a chance to lick her wounds and heal. When her mum suggested that she return to Little Bramble, it had seemed like the only option. Yes, she knew it could end in disaster, that living with Elaine could be challenging, but she'd had to do it.

She stared into her empty mug as if she could find a smidgen of hope there at the bottom, but all she saw was a few leaves from the loose-leaf tea her mum used that had escaped the strainer.

How on earth Clare was going to get through the next few weeks, she had no idea, but she was here now, and she had to make the best of it.

What else could she do?

Chapter 3

Clare sat up in bed and winced at the bright light that hit her straight in the face like a laser beam. That wasn't right; her bedroom curtains were lined with a heavyweight blackout material that prevented even a gentle glow penetrating her bedroom. She'd bought the curtains because Jason struggled to sleep if the room wasn't in complete darkness. How he was going to manage when he was travelling the world, sleeping in tents and hostels, where mosquitos buzzed around and strangers snored next to him, she had no idea.

She rubbed her eyes as it dawned on her that she was not in her own home. She was at her mum's cottage in Little Bramble, in her old bedroom, in a single bed, with bright pink bedding that she'd bought in her teens with her pocket money. The bed was comfortable enough, but the pillows were – like every other pillow and cushion in her mum's home – duck down and not her usual bamboo hypoallergenic pillows. The pillows were soft and could be plumped up easily enough, but they always had a slight odour to them that she associated with her childhood and that elicited mixed feelings. She had slept well on them in her youth, but also cried into them after a disagreement with her mum.

She lay back down, which removed her from the ray of sunlight and provided immediate relief for her tired eyes. The ceiling was low with thick dark beams, some speckled with tiny holes where she'd hung things from drawing pins over the years and a few of which featured knots in the wood that were as familiar to her as the backs of her own hands because she'd gazed up at them so many times.

Being here, lying in her old bed like this, made her feel as if the years had fallen away, as if she hadn't actually grown up and moved out, married and had a child. Of course, she'd been back here from time to time, visited for lunches, dinners, birthdays, anniversaries, but never for long and usually she made the journey there and back in a day, not wanting to stay overnight, particularly since her dad had passed away.

Coming here had been due to a lack of options, and, perhaps, although she hated to admit this one, because a tiny part of her hoped that it would be different now. There had always been a part of her that had longed to connect with her mum, to find the woman that her dad had loved and cherished. However, her mum's reaction to Clare's weight gain yesterday afternoon, the comment about how having a dog to walk would do Clare good, had reminded her that she had always to be on her guard against Elaine's sharp tongue. Clare wasn't sure how much of that 'frankness', as Elaine called it, she'd be able to stomach now that her dad wouldn't be there to counter it. At times, he had been almost like a translator for her mum, smoothing things over and tempering her harsh comments.

Closing her eyes, she started to drift, allowing the sweet-sharp scent of the sheets (her mum folded her bedding away with home-made lavender sachets) to soothe her, to carry her on a wave of relaxation . . .

'What the hell?'

Heart pounding, she sat up again, her breaths coming thick and fast. Something had dragged her rudely awake and it was still going on.

She jumped out of bed and ran to the window that overlooked the small front garden with its privet hedge and driveway. Pushing open the sash window, she leant out so she could peer at the front door.

'Mr David?' she called to the man in full postal uniform. He froze, still gripping the large envelope that was halfway through the front door, his left foot pressed against the wall next to the door, then peered up at her window.

'Well, if it isn't our very own little Clare.' Even after over thirty years of serving as a postman in an English village, his Caribbean accent was warm, his manner familiarly avuncular. 'How're you doing, little lady?'

'I'm OK, thank you, although I'm not so little anymore.'

He laughed. 'No, of course not. Sorry, I haven't seen you in a while and I always think of you as being little Clare Hughes. I'll have to get out of the habit of calling you little.' He tipped his navy cap.

'It's fine.' Clare smiled. 'Uh . . . What are you doing?'

'I'm very well, thank you.'

He'd misheard.

'Good, uh . . . Can I ask *what* you're doing?'

His eyes widened and he gave a small laugh. 'Ohhhh, you know . . . I go through this every day.' Suddenly he was pulled towards the front door, so his right cheek pressed against the wood. 'See, Clare . . . that big old Goliath . . . he likes to play with the post.'

Clare snorted as she realised what was happening. Marcellus David was engaged in a bizarre tug of war with Goliath.

'Oh my goodness!' She gasped. 'Hold on a moment and I'll be right down.'

He nodded but didn't let go of the envelope even though he was pressed right up against the door and clearly in significant discomfort.

Clare grabbed her dressing gown, pulled it over her pyjamas then hurried downstairs and into the hallway. There was no sign of her mum but Goliath was blocking the front door emitting a low growl, his nose pressed against the open letter box, half an envelope between his jaws.

'Goliath!' she scolded. 'No!'

She might as well have tried to disperse a swarm of wasps by waving her arms and screeching. Something she had tried once and it definitely hadn't worked.

Taking hold of Goliath's collar, apprehensively, even though her mum insisted the dog was a gentle giant, she tried pulling him backwards. He didn't move a millimetre, just stood there as if he was made of stone, growling at the door as the envelope in his mouth got soggier.

'I'm so sorry, Mr David!' Clare shouted at the door. 'He just won't let go.'

'It's all right, Clare, I still have the letter this end.'

Suddenly there was a ripping sound and Goliath lurched backwards, his paws skittering on the slate floor. Realising he had half the envelope in his mouth, he darted from the hallway and through to the kitchen.

Clare shook her head, rushed to close the door to the kitchen, then opened the front door. The postman stood there, swaying slightly, beads of perspiration above his top lip, grinning.

'Goliath won this time!' He removed his cap and ran the back of his hand over his brow. 'But tomorrow is a new opportunity.'

'I'm so sorry, Mr David. Does this happen every day?'

'Most days, if Goliath can get to the front door. Sometimes your mum closes the kitchen door so he can't, but if she forgets then Goliath, he takes advantage.'

He reached into his bright red crossbody bag and pulled out three more envelopes, then handed them to Clare.

'I do them one at a time because once Goliath has one he usually runs off and the rest have a chance of making it to your mum.'

'Have you ... I mean, you shouldn't have to do this because I'm sure the experience is highly stressful, but have you considered using a dummy letter first? Just to let Goliath think he's won. Then you could deliver the actual post?'

Mr David nodded. 'I tried, but that dog knows a real letter from a fake one.' He tapped the side of his head then put his cap back on. 'He's wily, you see.'

'I'll speak to my mum about getting an external post box fitted,' Clare said. 'That might work.'

'Very kind of you indeed.' Marcellus smiled then turned and walked down the path before turning back to her. 'I'll see you tomorrow?'

'You will.'

'Are you staying long, Clare?'

She shrugged. 'I'm not sure yet, but possibly for a few weeks.'

'That's good. Be nice for your mum and you to have some quality time together.'

As he walked away, Clare closed the front door and leant against it for a few moments, then opened the kitchen door. Goliath was lying on his giant bed in the corner, a mess of chewed-up paper on the floor in front of him.

'You should be ashamed of yourself!' Clare shook a finger and he wagged his long tail in response, clearly quite happy with his morning's work.

Clare tutted as she filled the kettle then dropped a teabag into a mug. While the kettle boiled, she went to the sink and peered out at the back garden, frowning as she spotted her mum in the middle of the lawn.

Why her mum hadn't dealt with the post situation she had no idea. But then, there was a lot about her mum that Clare didn't understand, like why she was outside at seven thirty on a cold Friday October morning in her dressing gown. The garden was private with its high hedges and no neighbouring properties overlooking it, but even so it was a funny time for weeding.

She made a cup of tea then headed back up to bed. All that excitement first thing was more than she cared to deal with on her first full day in Little Bramble. She'd be kind to herself

31

and get some more sleep. What else did she have to do this morning, anyway?

✽

Sam downed his coffee while staring out of the kitchen window. The morning was grey and drizzly and the back garden looked almost sorry for itself as autumn colours faded, making way for winter. The trees had shed most of their leaves, the lavender bushes were bare and spindly and there were a few yellow patches dotted around the lawn from Scout. But none of that was bothering him.

What was troubling him was Alyssa and whether she'd come home last night.

He finished his coffee and swilled the mug, then traipsed through to the lounge. The house was so quiet this morning that he felt completely alone, as if he could be the last person alive. Alyssa used the cottage kitchen and sometimes the lounge when they watched TV together, but the garage conversion provided her with a private space of her own. It had a bedroom, a lounge area and a bathroom all created to allow her to move around freely in her wheelchair. Along with her specially adapted car, she lived an independent life. It worked for them both because it meant Sam could be there if she needed him but she could also be as independent as she liked, as an adult in their thirties should be. The only problem with it was that, in spite of straining to hear her coming home last night, Sam hadn't. He'd eventually fallen asleep then woken with a start at five thirty, his heart pounding as he worried that she might have stayed out.

But if she had stayed out all night, it really was none of his business and he had to accept that. If only he could let go and stop worrying about her, but since the accident, he'd felt more responsible for her than ever. What brother wouldn't, especially as both their parents had passed away?

He checked the clock above the TV and saw that it was six thirty. He'd wait until seven then text Alyssa to find out if she was home or if she had stayed out. If the latter, then he would just have to bite his tongue. Whatever had happened, he had to get ready for work.

Chapter 4

'Morning, Goliath,' Clare said as she trudged down the stairs. He was waiting at the bottom, tail wagging in wide arcs, his mouth open in what looked like a big grin.

Clare had been making an effort to get up earlier to try to reach the door before Goliath and save Mr David from the dog. So far this week, she'd managed Monday and Tuesday, even though she'd been so tired since arriving in the village that she could easily have slept through until eleven. She suspected that her exhaustion was due to the fact that everything was catching up with her, that the stress of Jason's confession, their divorce then selling the house, that she had bottled up for so long, had finally landed on her shoulders and now she was paying for it.

Each morning, she'd take the post from Mr David's hand and exchange polite chatter about the weather, her well-being and his, make a cup of tea then head back to bed. It was working so far, this being back at her mum's home. Well, kind of.

In the kitchen, she made sure to shut the door to stop Goliath from getting to the front door, then made tea. Through the window she could see her mum, standing on the grass, in the misty October morning, wearing just her underwear this time. She was lost in the slow, languid movements of Tai Chi, as she was every morning, not weeding as Clare had previously thought. Clare wondered how she could stand the chill on her flesh, how she found the motivation to get up so early every day to head outside to work through the low-impact exercise routine. Clare had to admit that it was a very graceful activity and she could see the relaxation on her mum's face as she moved. If only she could find the same relaxed state for herself.

As the routine came to an end, Clare heard the front gate and so did Goliath. He jumped up from his bed and Clare put up a hand. 'Sit!'

He stared at her, tongue dangling from his mouth, then he bounded to the kitchen door. Clare lurched at the handle, pushed it down and tried to squeeze through the gap as it opened without letting Goliath out. When she managed to get through and pull the door behind her, she was breathing heavily and sweating.

'Bloody dog!' She blew out her cheeks as she hurried to the front door, opening it just in time to take two letters from Mr David's hand.

'Morning.'

'Good morning, little . . . Sorry, *Clare*. And how are you today?'

'I'm well, thanks. How are you?'

'Can't complain.' He nodded. 'Although the weather is not our friend again this morning. It's so damp and grey.'

'It is.' She peered at the sky and shivered. 'A day for staying indoors, I think.'

He pushed his cap back on his head. 'You know, every time I see you, I remember how you were as a girl. You were a funny little thing and there was one time that sticks in my mind, when you were about four or five, and you answered the door all dressed up, wearing a big blonde wig and a tiara, along with a gold dress that was far too big for you. I asked where you'd got the clothes and you said they were for the Christmas show. Then you said the sweetest thing. You said, "I'm dressed up as my mummy. She's going to be the Queen of the Stage."' He placed a hand over his heart. 'It was clear as day how much you loved Elaine and wanted to be like her.'

Clare blinked. She had wanted to be like her mum? But wasn't that something that all children aspired to at some point, to be like their parents? After all, Kyle had dressed up in her clothes many times – and in some of Jason's. One time she'd laughed until she'd cried when she'd found him in front of her bedroom mirror in just a nappy, bright green frog print wellies and wearing one of her summery smock tops. He'd been just a toddler and she'd swept him up and held him close. She'd pressed her nose against the soft curls at his nape, inhaling his baby scent that lingered because she still had to use gentle shampoo, as anything else getting in his eyes made bath time far too traumatic.

'Have you been out and about in the village yet?'

Mr David's question took her by surprise.

'Uh . . . no. Not yet.'

He raised his eyebrows. 'Perhaps today.'

'Perhaps.'

'Have a good one, little Clare.'

'You too!'

She closed the door then made her way back through the hall. She pushed at the kitchen door but it only opened a crack then bounced back and smacked her on the forehead.

'Ouch!' She rubbed at her head. 'Goliath, are you behind the door?'

She pushed the door again, but it wouldn't move so she knocked on it instead.

'Yoo-hoo! Post is here!' She slipped one of the letters, a circular, through the opening and waved it about. There was a low growl then the envelope was snatched from her hand and she heard paws scurrying away as the door swung inwards.

Goliath was, as she had suspected, on his bed, making short work of the circular she'd given him.

Just then the back door opened and Clare's mum came in. Clare averted her eyes, not wanting to stare at her mum when she was wearing just her underwear.

'Oh, Clare dear, are you being a prude?'

'What?' She met her mum's laughing gaze.

'Are you afraid to look at an elderly woman in her lingerie?' She chuckled. 'Nothing too terrible to see, is there? Seventy-five doesn't look so bad, does it?'

Clare turned the kettle on and got two mugs out of the cupboard.

'No, Mum, you look great. Just great. But aren't you cold?' She pulled her dressing gown tighter around herself.

'Cold?' Elaine asked the question as if it hadn't occurred to her. 'Why would I care about that? Don't you know that it's just fabulous for my physique?'

'What do you mean?' Clare poured water on the tea leaves in the pot, then went to the fridge for milk.

'Well, I've always wondered why people bother having breast lifts and tummy tucks and all that malarkey when all they need to do to have a natural body lift is to step outside on a cold morning. It's just fabulous for tightening everything up.'

'Seriously?'

'Of course, dear. Your father and I used to have such a laugh sometimes, especially as we got a bit older, about how things tend to hang lower than they used to.'

'Mum!' Clare's cheeks burned. 'I really don't want to hear this. It's . . .' She sighed. 'Kind of inappropriate.'

And not the way I want to think of my dad.

'You *are* being a prude, Clare. As I was saying . . .' She leant against the worktop, her elbows resting on the edge and Clare set her focus determinedly on making the tea. She would *never* put Kyle through a scene like this. 'When you get older and things start to droop, just crack open a window and PING!' She clicked her fingers and chuckled.

'Ping?' Clare asked, dreading the answer.

Her mum reached for a garment draped over one of the kitchen chairs then pulled it over her head and it billowed over her body. It was a paisley-swirled kaftan in brown, red and gold, so light it must have been made of silk. 'Yes, you know, everything is back where it should be!'

Clare handed her mum a mug of tea, trying not to laugh. In spite of her reservations at where the conversation was going, she couldn't deny that it was quite a relief to hear her mum talking like that because since Clare's return to Little Bramble, something about her mum hadn't seemed quite the same. The formerly vivacious, exhibitionist, gin-drinking, show-tune singing woman that she had known had vanished and in her place was a quieter, far more solemn woman who Clare felt uncertain around. At least with the mum she'd known, she'd been prepared for the frank remarks, been ready to accept the somewhat stilted love – and known when to walk away. Now, something was very different, and she had yet to pinpoint why.

'What are your plans today, Clare?' her mum asked as they sat at the table.

'Oh, well . . . I thought I'd go back to bed for a bit then take a bath—'

'Clare!' Her mum cut her. 'That's enough of the wallowing. You've been here for six days now and not ventured into the village once. It's time for you to get out and about.'

'Oh . . . uh . . . I'm not quite sure I'm ready for that yet.'

'Nonsense! Do you think Jason is sitting around in a hotel room in Thailand or Dubai or Paris or wherever it is he's gone first? Do you think *he's* dwelling on what he's lost? I bet he's bloody well not.'

'Mum, that's not important. I don't care what Jason's doing.'

Although I would like him to be just a bit sad, just a bit lost . . .

'That's rubbish and you know it.'

Clare met her mum's steely blue gaze and tried not to wince.

'OK, I do care a *tiny* bit but yes, you are right, I doubt very much that he's mourning what we've lost. He was very keen to sell up and set out to find himself.'

'And so must you.'

'It sounds very . . . cheesy.'

Her mum shrugged. 'It's just words but the sentiment is right. Sadly, your marriage is over. It happens to lots of people. But, Clare, you're still young and you hopefully have as long ahead as you have behind you. It's time for you to re-evaluate and get back on the horse.'

Clare snorted. 'The horse?'

'Well, yes, why not? You used to love horse riding. When was the last time you went?'

Clare frowned. 'A very long time ago.'

'Then you need to go again, although it might have to wait until the spring – but you could at least visit the stables. You should make a list of things you stopped doing because you were married and get out there and do them.' Her mum's eyes were burning with something and Clare found herself hoping it was fervour and not fever; doing exercise in your undies at seventy-five in the chilly October air could well bring on the latter.

'I'll try, Mum.'

'Yes, you will, because Clare, much as I love you, I simply cannot have you hanging around here all the time, getting under my feet.'

A lump rose in Clare's throat. She'd been here under a week and she was already getting on her mum's nerves? She'd tried to be quiet, to do her bit around the cottage, to avoid saying or doing anything that would irritate her mum. She understood that having an adult child return home would be challenging for any parent, let alone for her mum. However, it seemed that she had inadvertently become annoying.

'Do you want me to leave?' Her voice emerged as little more than a whisper.

'Of course not, Clare, don't be such a drama queen! I merely want you to get out a bit more, not sit around moping.'

'I haven't been moping.'

Elaine raised her eyebrows and Clare realised there was no point trying to argue her case.

'OK, perhaps I have a little bit.'

Her mum nodded. 'Right, I'll make some breakfast then you can shower and take Goliath for a walk. That would be a good start.'

'Lovely, thanks.' Clare drained her tea then stood up, trying to conjure some enthusiasm for the idea of a dog walk. 'Are you . . . are you going to join us?'

Her mum turned around from the fridge. 'No, I don't think so. Not today.'

'Are you sure?' Some company might make going outside easier.

'Quite sure, Clare. I'm actually rather tired. Now, let me focus on making breakfast.'

Clare nodded, but her mum had always been an advocate of exercise in all its forms, so the fact that she wasn't keen on getting out for a walk was surprising, especially seeing as how she'd commented on how good it would be for Clare. There was definitely something different about her.

When they were seated again with plates of scrambled eggs and toast and another pot of tea between them, Clare decided to broach a topic that had puzzled her over the last week.

'Mum, why haven't you been to your drama society meetings while I've been here?'

Her mum's fork froze halfway from the plate to her mouth and her eyes widened but she seemed to recover herself and lowered her fork again. 'I . . . uh . . . don't go anymore.'

'What? But why not?'

'Well, since the old village hall was . . .' Her mum took a deep breath, her head shaking slightly as she did so. 'Since it burnt down, there hasn't been an amateur dramatics society.'

'What? Not for . . . how long ago did it burn down?'

She saw her mum swallow hard. 'It will be two years on 20th December. It burnt down the night of the Christmas show.'

'And you haven't been involved in any acting since then?'

'No.'

'But the drama society was such a big part of your life.'

Her mum shrugged. 'Things change.'

'They do, but aren't you sad? Why haven't you reassembled the village amateur dramatics society? Especially with Christmas just over two months away. You always did a village play and carol service and—'

'Please stop!' Her mum glared at her and Clare's confusion deepened. Elaine had loved to talk about the latest successes of the local drama society, the latest star they'd found who'd gone on to find success at RADA or some other prestigious performing arts college. Clare had enjoyed being a part of the shows as a child, but as she got older and reached her teens, her mum's bossiness, combined with her perfectionism, had started to grate on her. According to her mum, Clare never got the lines quite right or held the tune properly, and when she reached fifteen, she decided enough was enough and refused to take part in the shows anymore. She still helped out backstage and with the refreshments, but she stayed out of the limelight. Elaine had tried to get Clare involved right up until she'd gone off to university, and her dad had tried too, but Clare had been resolute, even though she'd hated to disappoint her dad. She'd still got to watch her parents as they performed, to enjoy how they perfectly complemented each other, and then felt a sense of regret at not being on stage with them. But she had known that it was how it needed to be for her own peace of mind. But now, thinking about her mum without the am dram society seemed so wrong. Her childhood had been centred around her parents' love of theatre – her mum had shone as director and actor; it was who she was. Every phone call they'd had after Clare had left for university and then married Jason had included at least one reference to a village event sponsored by the society or about the main annual event: the village Christmas show. If her mum had lost that, as well as Clare's dad, then what did she have left?

And now, almost two years after the village hall had burnt down, that part of her life was all over and her mum hadn't told her. Even worse, Clare hadn't noticed or asked during their phone calls. Had she been that caught up in her own problems that she hadn't had the time or compassion to care what was going on in her mum's life? Was she that terrible a daughter? What if she'd done the same with Kyle and failed to notice that he'd lost something as important to him as the society was to her mum? Guilt burned like bile in her throat and her heart ached. This was truly awful, and she wished there was something she could do to put it right.

'I don't think I ever asked you how the old hall burnt down.'

'I don't think you did.'

'Well?'

Her mum looked at her, then averted her gaze, her eyes darting around the room as if she was looking for inspiration. 'It wasn't determined.'

'The firefighters couldn't work out what happened?'

Her mum shook her head then set her fork down and folded her arms across her chest. 'Clare, could we drop this subject now, please? It's really difficult to talk about, what with the loss of the old hall that your dear father helped build – and the fact that the new hall just isn't the same.'

'The old hall was the centre of the community, wasn't it?'

'It was.' Her mum's eyes glistened and Clare wanted to hug her, but knew that displays of affection were limited to hello and goodbye. 'It was the heart of Little Bramble. The new hall was finished in August and while it's very pleasant on the eye, all clean lines and fresh paint, it's just not the same. Something was lost in that fire and I don't think we'll ever get it back . . .'

'Mum, I'm so sorry.'

Her mum lifted her chin and sniffed. 'Well, it's certainly not your fault, Clare.'

'I wish there was something I could do.'

'Don't get all sentimental on me now, dear. It is what it is and life goes on.' Her mum stood up and took her plate to the sink. 'I'm actually rather tired still, so I think I'll go back to bed for a bit. You really don't mind taking Goliath out, do you? He'll be very grateful. But make sure you clip his lead on and hold him tight! If he sees a squirrel, he'll drag you for miles chasing it, so wear sensible footwear.'

Clare nodded, although the thought of the walk now filled her with apprehension.

'He hasn't had a long walk in a-a while . . . I feel terrible, but I just haven't felt up to it. Of course, I have taken him out on short daily walks but he needs a good stretch of his legs. Now you're home, you can help out by taking him every day.'

'Of course.' Clare would have agreed to anything right then just to ease her mum's worries. At least now, though, she had some idea of why her mum seemed different. She'd lost the centre of her world in losing the society. Goliath and amateur dramatics had filled Elaine's life after she'd lost her husband and losing that too would have been a massive blow.

After Elaine had left the kitchen, Clare got up and took her own plate to the sink then scraped the food remains into the green waste bag and tied the top. As she took the bag outside, Goliath came and sat on the doorstep, his eyes fixed on her, his tail swishing along the kitchen tiles.

'Would you like me to take you for a walk?'

He jumped up and bounded over to her. Before she could blink, his large paws landed on her shoulders and his wet tongue covered her face in slobber. She staggered back under his weight until she was against the wall of the shed, struggling to stay upright as laughter made her knees weak.

'Goliath!' She giggled. 'Stop! Stop, please, so I can go and get dressed.'

He finally seemed to get the message and Clare ran the sleeve of her dressing gown over her wet face.

It might take a lot to make her mum smile again, but at least she could make Goliath happy. Dogs were easy to please, it seemed, and that was definitely a bonus. Clare needed some friendly unassuming company right now and apparently Goliath was delighted to provide it.

Chapter 5

Clare checked out her appearance in the hallway mirror. She'd brushed her shoulder-length brown hair until it shone, pulled it into a low ponytail and moisturised her face and neck. Wearing a pair of stretchy skinny jeans that were actually quite comfortable, along with a thigh-length grey wool jumper and her old green wax jacket that she'd found in the cupboard under the stairs, which actually fitted her better now she'd gained a few pounds, she was ready for a walk. Her dad had bought the jacket for her years ago, and she'd been a bit uncertain about it because while it was practical, it wasn't exactly high fashion, but now she really liked how it made her seem as though she belonged in the countryside and walked the dog every day, especially with her dark green wellies (also found in the cupboard). This look was something that she'd lost, as if a part of her had remained behind in the village, and it felt comfortable to come back to, as though she'd found her own skin again.

Gazing at her reflection was not something she really enjoyed doing. She'd never been beautiful or striking, but had thought that she was all right, that when she made an effort with her appearance she could pass for just about attractive. Jason had called her beautiful back in the early days of their relationship, but over time she'd been content to accept that he probably thought she was OK, and that it didn't matter all that much because they had a stable, solid relationship. Now she really thought about it, Jason had lost interest in her a long time ago and she couldn't remember the last time they'd been intimate. When had they lost that side of their relationship? She'd assumed it was just part of being in a long-term relationship, that sex was for special occasions and on those occasions, if you'd eaten too much birthday cake or drunk too much prosecco, then the last thing either of you wanted to do was to get naked and do *the deed*. So sex had fallen by the wayside. She hadn't missed it that much, had tried not to think about it, avoiding answering her friends back in Reading whenever they'd had a few drinks and asked each other how often they still 'did it'. The answers often surprised her. There was her neighbour Lucy, a fifty-something businesswoman who was married to a man eleven years younger than her. Lucy worked long hours and was completely dedicated to her career, but she confessed that she had sex three or four times a week. Clare had wondered if she and Jason had *ever* done it that often. Then there was Denise, a senior librarian, who was just thirty-nine and said sex happened once or twice a month, but then she had three boys under ten and worked five days a week, so she was understandably exhausted most of the time. Her husband was a paramedic who worked shifts, so Clare was filled with admiration that they managed to have sex at all.

No, sex was something other people did and enjoyed and Clare had come to accept that it wasn't for her.

A low groan from her side reminded her that Goliath was waiting for his walk. She grabbed the rope lead she'd found under the stairs and clipped it to his collar. She didn't know whether it was the lack of space in the hallway or the fact that the lead looked somewhat inadequate, but Goliath appeared to be a very big dog this morning. *HUGE*, in fact. Like a small horse. Which made her feel a bit apprehensive about taking him out. However, she had promised him and her mum must be struggling with something if she had felt unable to take him far. Concern nibbled at Clare again that her mum wasn't telling her something important.

'Let's get some air, shall we?'

She slid the looped end of the lead over her wrist then opened the front door and stepped outside. Just as she closed the door behind her, her mobile buzzed. She slid it from her pocket and checked the screen, hoping it would be Kyle.

Hey Mum,

Hope your week is going well. How's Nanna? How's Goliath?

Let me know how it's going when you get a chance. I'm still laughing after you told me about the postman and Goliath fighting over the letters.

Love you millions! X

Clare smiled and slid her mobile back into her pocket. She'd reply later as she didn't want to keep Goliath waiting any longer but there was something so comforting about knowing Kyle was thinking about her, that he cared how things were going. He was so different from his father and she hoped that was because of the part she'd played in his upbringing. Jason had never been particularly considerate, but Kyle was always thoughtful and caring.

The mist had gone and now the pale-yellow sun sat low in the sky. The air was cold and fresh, laced with woodsmoke from the fires and log burners of the villagers, and there was a hint of bacon from someone's breakfast. The smells were familiar and comforting and she marvelled at how they brought back so many feelings. It was a strange sensation to feel happy and sad at the same time and yet not be able to pinpoint why, but she had blocked lots of things out during her absence from Little Bramble and suspected that she would struggle to do so now that she was here.

Clare walked Goliath along the pavement until they reached the end of the street, then crossed the road and headed along the narrow track that would take them through the woods that bordered the village. Birds sang in the trees, nature's debris crunched under foot, and somewhere beyond the trees water gurgled. The grass at the sides of the path was long and damp with dew and it squeaked as her wellies brushed against it. Her footsteps disturbed the earth of the path, sending up a deep rich scent overlaid by the smell of rotting leaves and wood that seemed to hover in pockets of air that they passed through.

Every so often she stopped walking so Goliath could sniff the ground and she breathed deeply, filling her lungs. This wasn't so bad after all. There had been some lovely walks near her home in Reading but the countryside surrounding Little Bramble was glorious, even at this time of the year and now that she was back and had time on her hands, she could take lots of long walks with Goliath and get fitter, healthier. She hadn't put on that much weight, an extra ten pounds or so, but surely she'd soon lose that if she started walking the dog twice a day? She could even invest in one of those trackers and make sure she did her ten thousand steps a day.

Why not twenty?

She was lost in a reverie about how slim and toned she'd be, about how people she hadn't seen in years would comment on how she didn't look forty-five at all, how she could easily pass for thirty, and how Kyle would tell his father when they Skyped that Mum was looking better than ever, when the lead went slack and she realised that Goliath wasn't at the end of it anymore.

'Shit!' She pulled the lead towards her and stared in shock at the clip. How had it come off his collar? Hadn't she fastened it properly? 'Goliath?' she called faintly as she scanned her surroundings, hoping to spot him nearby.

She started to walk along the path, her head darting from side to side, hoping that she'd see him, hoping that he was in the long grass sniffing something he'd found or weeing on a tree or –

'*Goliath!*'

He was. Up ahead in a small clearing where the path branched out in four directions, each one marked by a sign-post, hunched over in a strange position. Horrified, Clare realised that he was doing a poo. A steaming smelly pile that she was going to have to pick up!

She dug her hands in her pockets, praying she'd find something to use, but apart from a small plastic bag holding two spare buttons, there was nothing. She glanced around and there was no one about, no one to ask for a poo bag and no one to see that she hadn't picked up what was, without a doubt, the biggest poo she had ever seen.

She approached the dog slowly, a hand extended, hoping to catch him before he finished so she could reattach the lead to his collar, but at that moment he jumped up and jogged away.

Clare stared at the revolting pile then after Goliath, knowing that she had to make a decision – and fast. It was guard the poo or catch the dog. Right, she could grab Goliath first then decide how to deal with the poo, so she headed in his direction.

'What on earth are you doing?' She whirled around to see a very tall man glaring at her. At the end of the lead he was holding was a yellow Labrador, its long tail swishing.

'Uh . . . I'm having a bit of a . . . a difficulty.'

'A difficulty? Is that what you call it?' His thick dark brows met above his nose. 'What are you going to do about that poo? Were you going to leave it there for some poor walker to step in or for another dog to walk through then tread into the carpets at home?'

Clare tensed. This man seemed furious with her and shame crawled over her skin like red ants.

'No, I wasn't, I swear! I was just . . . see, I was walking –'

'Is that Elaine Hughes' dog?' He peered over Clare's shoulder and she turned and followed his gaze. Goliath was trotting back towards them as casually as if he'd just popped to the corner shop for milk.

'Yes.' Clare nodded. 'Come here, Goliath!' Her voice wavered and she cursed herself for sounding weak.

The dog jogged straight past her and towards the angry man.

'Hello, Goliath. What have you been up to, boy?'

As the man smoothed his long fingers over Goliath's head, the dog leant against him as if they were old friends.

'I know this looks bad . . .' Clare felt the need to explain because this man was clearly a local who knew Goliath and presumably her mum, so she didn't want him getting the wrong impression of her. 'But this is the first time I've taken him out and I completely forgot to bring any poo bags. I was horrified when he managed to get off his lead then he did a poo, and . . .' She held out her hands. 'I'm not very experienced at this dog-walking lark.'

He raised his eyes to meet hers and she had to swallow a gasp because they were so furious. Why was she so warm? She unzipped her jacket and opened it a bit to let the air get to her throat. Oh God, was this one of those hot flushes that came with the menopause? Was that going to happen now as well?

'Firstly, I can see that; secondly, it's not a *lark*. You should always ensure that you've fastened his lead properly and you must always have poo bags with you. Did you know that you can get fined for leaving poo on the ground? Not to mention what happens to the person or animal that has the misfortune to step in it. Utterly irresponsible behaviour like that really winds me up!'

He shook his head and Clare felt something else rising inside her. It spread from her core and made her press her lips together hard in case she said something she would later regret. She had to remember that she wanted to get on with the locals, not fling insults at them because they clearly had their own issues, like this very bad-mannered man. She had tried to explain what had happened and he clearly did not want to know. He was probably a complete chauvinist who enjoyed catching out unsuspecting female dog walkers who forgot to bring poo bags. It probably gave him a superiority complex. Yes, that was it. He made a habit of this and –

'Here.' He held out a hand and she stared at it. Did he want to shake hands? 'Give me his lead.'

'Oh . . .' She passed it to him and he clipped it to Goliath's collar then checked it. 'It's fastened properly now but this lead is old so it would be worth investing in a new one soon.'

'OK, I'll do that.'

She took the lead when he offered it, then turned to go.

'Wait!'

She froze, wondering what else he was going to berate her for.

'You need to pick up that poo.'

Dammit! She'd forgotten for a moment.

'What with?' She could hear the shock in her tone, and he must have too because he started to laugh. It was a low deep rumble and, as he laughed, his whole face lit up. He was enjoying this interaction.

What a git!

When he'd finally stopped laughing, then wiped at his eyes with his thumbs, he pulled a handful of poo bags from his jacket pocket.

'Take these.' She looked at them as if suspicious of an ulterior motive. 'They're biodegradable ones. I have plenty.' He pressed the bags into her hand.

'Thank you.'

'You're welcome. And can I offer a helpful tip?' Clare nodded. 'Next time, make sure you've got plenty. A dog that size could take two or three bags per poo.'

'What do I do with it once I've picked it up? I haven't seen any bins.'

'There are bins around the walks, specifically for dog waste. They're easy to spot, so once you've picked the poo up in a bag, carry it until you find a bin.'

'Right.' She nodded, then she crouched down to pick up the poo, grimacing and not just at the smell. She tried to grab it with the bag without looking at it but kept missing bits, so instead she peered at it through half-closed eyes. When she stood up again, the heavy poo bag dangling from between her finger and thumb, she remembered that she hadn't introduced herself. 'I'm –'

But he was already walking away, clearly not interested in making her acquaintance, and every bit as rude as she had thought him to be initially. She watched him go, his broad shoulders encased in a dark grey wax jacket, his long legs in faded denim and his worn boots suggesting he walked a lot. He looked as if he fitted in around here. Clare had a sinking feeling that though she was dressed up to look the part, she'd failed at the first hurdle.

She shook her head and shrugged. What did it matter? She wasn't staying long anyway.

Goliath whined, then pulled on his lead as if he wanted to go with the man.

'No, boy, you're staying right here with me. I can't believe you gave me the slip and let me forget poo bags!'

She smiled as she rubbed his head. Yes, she knew that she was to blame but it was easier, and better for her self-esteem, to blame the dog.

'Let's find a bin and head home. I, for one, have had enough *excitement* for one day.'

❄

Sam strode along the path, keen to get home. Scout ran on ahead now that he'd unclipped her lead, pausing every so often to turn and check that he was still behind her. Her training meant that she'd never run off or too far ahead. She wasn't judging him for how he'd just behaved, but he was certainly judging himself.

If only he could take back the past thirty minutes, rewind and start again. But his mind just kept replaying what had happened when he'd encountered that woman in the woods and how he'd reacted. Or overreacted. He'd accused her of planning on abandoning Goliath's poo when he could see now that she had needed to grab the dog first. But if he was being completely honest with himself, it hadn't even been that. He'd been thinking about Alyssa, worrying about her, and he'd taken his tension out on that poor woman. There had been a time when he hadn't felt so weighed down by everything, when the responsibility for Alyssa and her well-being hadn't rested entirely on his shoulders and he knew he would never have attacked a stranger like that, never have inflicted his own irritation and stress on someone else.

The strangest thing about this afternoon was how he had then laughed in the presence of that woman, who he was now thinking might well be Elaine Hughes' daughter, as if his body had needed to release his tension through anger or laughter.

He'd better clear his head before heading home, or Alyssa would spot that there was something different about him and likely try to tease it out of him as she always did and he didn't feel like discussing his shameful behaviour right now. His sister always knew if Sam had had a bad day, a strange day or a good day and could tell by the way he opened the front door which it was. His mother had been the same. She could read Sam and his father like books. His father had often joked that he couldn't do a thing without his wife knowing about it, but he'd always said it with a smile and Sam had known that his parents were still very much in love. They had been lucky: they had found each other and fallen hard. Sam wasn't convinced that many people found that type of enduring love. Not that he was looking for it. He didn't have time for love or a relationship, he had the practice and Alyssa to consider, and no woman could ever come before those two things so there was little chance of him finding someone willing to come third on his list of priorities, fourth if you included Scout.

He called Scout back and clipped her lead on, then something occurred to him: Goliath was overdue for his OAP health check, something that they offered all the dogs on their books once they reached a certain age. He should have come in for his check about six months ago, but Elaine had been remiss in making the appointment. Come to think of it, Sam couldn't recall the last time he'd seen her at the surgery, unless she'd come in when Miranda had been working and he'd been off.

He decided to check when he went back to work later. If he didn't, it would play on his mind. So, if he was right and Goliath's check-up was overdue, he would phone Elaine. He hoped it had just slipped her mind and that it was nothing more, but now he was worried about her too. Perhaps Elaine wasn't feeling well and had enlisted someone to help her with the large dog.

Besides which, if that really was Elaine's daughter and she had returned to the village to stay, then she might just answer the phone and he could apologise, something he knew he was going to need to do.

Chapter 6

'Clare? Is that really you?'

Clare looked up, peering through her swollen eyelids. She had been limping home to her mum's, trying hard to keep hold of Goliath's lead while not putting too much weight on her right ankle, which she suspected was sprained.

She'd found one of the poo bins that the rude man had mentioned and deposited Goliath's waste in it, trying hard to do so with just one hand as she held onto the lead, when something had caught Goliath's attention and the next thing she knew the lead had been tugged hard and they'd been off. At first, she'd managed to run behind him, but as he sped up, her running had turned into a form of skiing through mud as he left the path, then she'd lost her balance and been dragged along like a sledge. Goliath was so strong that he hadn't seemed to notice her weight at the end of the lead and it was only the fact that what he'd been chasing – a squirrel – had shot up a tree and the dog had been unable to follow that had stopped him. Clare's ankle had twisted during the initial run and then she'd been dragged through something in the undergrowth that had caused her eyelids to swell. She'd also bruised a rib on a rock. What a mess she must look!

'Hello?' she croaked, her voice strained from screaming at Goliath to stop running.

'What happened to you?' The woman came closer and placed a hand on Clare's arm.

'Oh . . . long story and all to do with my mum's dog.'

'You poor thing.' The woman tilted her head then smiled. 'Do you know who I am?'

Clare blinked hard then looked at the woman again. Her long blonde hair fell in shiny waves to her shoulders, looking as if it had just been blow-dried. Her eyes were as blue as a summer sky and her skin glowed with health. In a white faux-fur coat over a black polo neck and a short black skirt with thick tights and knee-high brown boots, she was incredibly glamorous and pin-thin.

'Jenny?' Clare shook her head. 'Is it really you? You look incredible!'

'Yes, it's me!' Jenny opened her arms then seemed to think better of it. 'I would hug you, darling, but you're a bit . . .'

She gestured at Clare's clothing, which was covered in mud, leaves and, she suspected, fox poo.

'Muddy? Dirty? Stinky?'

'Yes, sweetheart. But . . . Oh, it's so good to see you. Are you here for long or is it a flying visit?'

Clare pushed her tongue into her cheek, testing how tender it felt. 'Umm . . . I'm not sure really. Not long, I hope, just until I get back on my feet.'

Jenny grimaced.

'I know, I don't look as if I'm getting back on my feet, do I? But well . . . this was just today.'

'Is everything all right?' Jenny asked. 'Apart from your current physical state, I mean.'

'Not really, but it's a long story. How about you?'

'We're all good, thanks: me, Martin and the girls.'

'How old are Tilda and Lizzy now?'

'Eighteen.'

'Wow! I can't believe it.'

'How are Kyle and Jason?'

'Oh, Kyle's great. Twenty-one now.' She shook her head. 'It's flown. But Jason . . . we've divorced.'

'I'm so sorry, Clare.'

'It's OK. One of those things.' She shrugged then gasped as pain pierced her side.

'Do you need to go to A & E?'

'No, no, I'll be fine. It's just a few bruises and scratches . . .'

'You're bleeding.' Jenny gestured at Clare's knees, so Clare looked down and gasped. The knees of her jeans were torn, her skin grazed and bloody.

'Oh no! I loved those jeans.'

'They might sew?' Jenny suggested, but Clare knew they were beyond repair.

'Ah well.' Clare tried to affect a nonchalant air, but she felt like crying. 'It's trendy now to have big holes in your jeans, isn't it?'

'My twins definitely think so.' Jenny nodded. 'What happened?'

'Goliath saw a squirrel and took me on a sprint. Unfortunately, I lost my balance and got dragged along behind him. It was like a form of medieval torture – but at least I wasn't hung and quartered. Although . . .' She rubbed at her tender stomach. 'I think he gave it his best shot.'

'He's a big dog. I have no idea how your mum walks him, but saying that, I haven't seen her out with him for a while.' Jenny frowned. 'Anyway, seeing as how you're here, do you fancy getting a coffee and having a proper catch-up? We could meet later or tomorrow.'

'I would love that, Jenny.' Clare nodded, secretly delighted to have run into this woman who used to be her closest friend. 'Tomorrow would be great. Shall we swap numbers?'

When Clare had tucked her phone back into the inside pocket of her coat, she smiled at Jenny.

'So, text me later and let me know what time suits you. I'm pretty much free anytime at the moment, although I think I might have to get my ankle checked after all.' The thought of having to go to the GP or spending hours in A & E did not appeal at all.

'Hopefully some ice or a bag of frozen peas will sort it out. Do you want a hand getting home?'

'No, I'll be fine thanks, Jenny. It was lovely to see you and I look forward to catching up properly over coffee and cake.'

'Wonderful! Ta-ta for now!' Jenny gingerly kissed the air either side of Clare's cheeks, then headed in the opposite direction, leaving behind a trace of expensive perfume and hairspray. Perhaps she had just come from getting her hair done at the village salon. Or did she still work there? Clare couldn't remember.

She crossed the road and limped towards her mum's driveway, glad that she was almost home. Every part of her seemed to ache more the closer she got and she was looking forward to a hot bath more than she could ever remember doing her whole life.

❄

'What on earth happened?' Clare's mum stared at her as she entered the kitchen. 'You look like you've been dragged through a hedge by your hair.'

'Something like that.' Clare nodded, wincing at the discomfort it caused just to move. 'Goliath spotted a squirrel and took off after it.'

'He didn't drag you after him, did he?'

'Yes.' Clare unclipped his collar from the lead then slid the lead off her wrist and rubbed at the tender flesh.

'Oh, Clare, look at your poor skin.' Her mum took her hand and examined where the lead had dug in. 'Let's get you cleaned up and get something on those eyes.'

'To be honest, Mum, I'd like to get straight in the bath if you don't mind. My jeans are ruined and my coat needs a wash.'

'Goliath, you are a naughty boy.' Elaine shook a finger at the dog and he whined.

'It's not his fault, really. I just didn't have control of him.'

'He's very strong.' Her mum nodded severely at the dog. 'On your bed, Goliath!'

He sloped off to his bed and lay down, peering up at them as if he'd the weight of the world on his back.

'I don't know how you can ever be angry with him,' Clare said, rubbing her eyes because the itching was driving her crazy.

'Well, I can't stay cross at him and that's the problem. It's why he's terrorised poor Mr David for years. I guess I've been too soft.'

Clare swallowed the comment that sprang to her lips. *Too soft?* Her mother had never been soft with Clare, but it seemed the dog was a different story.

'It looks like you've had a reaction to some weed you went through. It looks like it was probably hogweed or stinging nettles.'

'Whatever it was it's horrid.'

'I've some drops here so let's put those in and run the bath so you can go and have a soak.'

Clare shrugged out of her coat, then sat down while her mum gently took her chin and held it still, then applied the soothing drops to her tender eyes. She hadn't had anyone look after her for such a long time and it felt strange. Not bad strange, just unusual.

'There you go, Clare. Now go and enjoy a bath and when you come down, I'll make you some eggy bread. How does that sound?'

'That sounds wonderful.'

Clare got up and went to the door to the hallway.

'And Clare?'

'Yes?'

'Thank you for walking him. I really do appreciate it.'

Clare smiled then padded up the stairs, taking care with her sore ankle, no longer sure if the water in her eyes was the saline solution or her own tears.

Sam washed his hands thoroughly, then dried them before turning the computer in the consultation room off. It had been a busy afternoon and he'd seen three dogs with varying issues, a cat with gum disease who was going to have to have several teeth extracted and a guinea pig that was unexpectedly pregnant.

Working in a village practice he knew the majority of the people that came in. When he'd worked in London, he might not have seen anyone he'd met before for weeks, sometimes months, unless their pet was a regular with an ongoing condition, and even then, because there were so many vets working at the practice, chances were that they'd see a different vet each time. What he really liked about working in Little Bramble was being able to develop relationships with the locals, getting to know their pets and being able to see improvements in the animals' health as time went on. Of course, it meant that he also saw them decline as they aged or developed illnesses that were incurable, but even then, he was able to provide the personal caring touch that knowing the clients facilitated.

Then there was his business partner, Miranda. He really enjoyed working alongside her and had learnt so much in the three years of their partnership. She was wise and experienced, with a calm manner that Sam found soothing. Initially, she could come across as reserved and stern, but as he'd got to know her, he'd found her funny, friendly and incredibly helpful. Whenever he had a question about an animal's condition, he could go to her. Chances were that she'd encountered it before or had read about it in a journal, so her knowledge was incredibly useful, but if she hadn't heard of it or seen it, she'd go and find out about it. Sam aimed to be as useful to her as she was to him and often they'd leave work of an evening and return the next morning with a wealth of information that they'd read about overnight. He had so much respect for Miranda and her love of animals. She wasn't always as keen on humans and if she suspected that someone wasn't caring for their pet as well as they should be, she didn't spare their blushes, but she always got her message across and had improved the lives of many animals because of it.

He went through to the small staffroom and found Miranda there, swilling out a mug.

'You done for the day?' she asked as she set the mug on the draining board, then picked up a tea towel.

'Yes, all done.' He ran a hand over his dark hair. He'd let it get a bit longer than usual, wanting to see how it looked, and he was embracing his natural springy curls. He liked how they felt beneath his palm. 'But I've a feeling that I forgot to do something.'

Miranda laughed. 'I get that all the time and when I arrive home, as soon as the front door closes behind me, I remember.'

'But you only live next door.' Miranda had the cottage adjoining the practice building, which was very handy when she was on call for overnight emergencies.

'I know, but there's something about your own home that relaxes the mind and helps you remember.' Her hazel eyes twinkled. 'So, what could it be that you forgot? To request some tests? To phone a client?'

Sam's eyes widened. 'Yes! That was it. I saw Goliath out walking earlier, Elaine Hughes' dog, and he hasn't come in for his OAP check-up yet.'

'He was out walking alone?' She cocked an eyebrow.

'No, he was with a woman. I'm not sure who she was, but she was younger than Elaine.'

'Could be her daughter, Clare.'

'I thought she might be her daughter.' He chewed his bottom lip. So that could be her name? 'Although I haven't seen her round here before.'

'Clare moved away years ago and doesn't visit that often.' Miranda frowned, drawing her bushy grey eyebrows together above her long, straight nose. 'I think Elaine told me that she was living in Reading with her husband and son.'

Sam's stomach lurched. She was married and a mother? He shook himself. Why would it matter to him either way? He had no interest in the woman other than wanting Goliath to come in for a check-up and wanting to apologise, of course.

'Why are you looking at me like that?' Sam asked, realising that Miranda was staring hard at him.

'Is there something you'd like to share about your encounter with Clare? If it *was* Clare, that is.'

'Nothing to tell, no.' Sam rubbed the back of his neck and looked across at the small window that opened out to the car park at the rear of the surgery. The view was obscured by the patterned glass, but Sam needed somewhere to look other than at Miranda. She knew him well and would be able to tell that he was hiding something. The main problem was that he wasn't sure what he was hiding from her. Was it the fact that he felt bad because of how harsh he'd been towards the woman walking Goliath, or was it because he'd felt something in her presence that had unsettled him?

'From what I can recall of Clare, she was always an attractive woman.'

Miranda's words snapped him from his thoughts.

'What?'

Miranda smiled and inclined her head as if acknowledging that she'd hit the nail on the head.

'Don't worry, Sam, your secret's safe with me.'

He shook his head. She was way off the mark, but he didn't fancy explaining how he'd behaved in the woods. He'd hoped he might actually forget how ashamed he was as the day wore on but every time he remembered it, his mortification grew.

'I have no secrets, Miranda.' His voice wavered so he coughed. 'I just need to phone Elaine regarding that OAP check, but I'll do it tomorrow.'

'No problem, Sam. Have a good evening,' she said, as he reached for his coat and went to the door.

'You too.' He smiled, then went back through to the main reception and out of the front door, locking it behind him. The rest of the staff would leave via the back door to the car park to get in their cars or walk the short distance home. It wasn't far from here to Elaine's cottage so he could take a stroll and let her know about the OAP check-up, make sure everything was all right in person.

But as he stood outside in the darkness of the October evening, he knew that he wasn't going to go to Elaine's. He was heading straight home because he just wasn't ready to face the feelings he'd allowed to control him in the woods earlier that day, and he didn't feel ready to face his embarrassment either, so trying to apologise now might come across as insincere because his delivery would probably be too blunt. It would be better to sleep on it all and face it another day.

Chapter 7

Clare pushed open the door to the café, being careful to keep her weight off her sore ankle, and looked around. Jenny had sent a text the previous evening, asking how she was feeling and inviting her for coffee the next day during her break from work at the salon. Clare had been delighted – and a bit anxious; after all, they hadn't had a good chat in years.

The warm air smelt of toasted teacakes and coffee, freshly baked bread and mixed spice. She'd tried to peer through the window to see if Jenny had arrived, but the glass had been steamed up, so she'd swallowed her rising anxiety and gone inside.

She pulled off her hat and gloves almost immediately, not wanting to start sweating before she'd even sat down.

'Clare!'

Turning, she spotted Jenny sitting at a corner table at the rear of the café. She was smiling, her pretty blonde hair gently waved around her face, and for a moment it took Clare back to the times they'd come here as teenagers. Jenny had been her best friend from the first day at primary school when Clare had arrived at the school gates clinging to her dad's hand. Her mum had been unable to be there because it was the first day back at work after the summer holidays for her, whereas her dad had taken the morning off from his job as an accountant. Clare had been reluctant to let go of her dad until a small girl with blonde bunches had approached her and asked her name. Their bond had been instant and, as Jenny had taken Clare's hand, her dad had smiled and nodded and then the girls had walked into school together, chatting away as if they'd been friends for years. They'd been close throughout secondary school and had seen each other virtually every day, speaking every evening on the phone and driving their parents mad by tying up the phone lines in the days when they didn't have mobile phones and all calls were limited to the house landline.

Clare weaved through the other tables, taking care not to knock the elbows of elderly ladies having their buttery teacakes and cups of tea and avoiding the pushchairs weighed down with changing bags, toys and shopping.

'Hi, Jenny.' Clare bent and kissed Jenny's cheek then sat opposite her.

'How's your ankle?' Jenny's features were etched with concern.

'Not too bad, thanks. It's a bit sore but thankfully not sprained and my rib seems to be bruised but not broken. I must have looked a dreadful mess yesterday.'

'You just looked like you'd been dragged through the woods by a dog.'

They grinned at each other, the old warmth of friendship resurfacing.

'It's busy in here, isn't it?' Clare said.

'Thursday morning always is, following OAP sessions at the GP surgery and playgroup at the village hall.' Jenny nodded. 'Remember those days?'

'OAP sessions?' Clare giggled.

'No!' Jenny laughed. 'Although we're not far off.'

'I know – how did we become forty-somethings?'

'Time flies! But no, I meant remember having little ones? I could *not* do that again, let me tell you.'

'Well, I only had the one child.' Clare smiled sadly. She'd have liked more but it wasn't meant to be. 'But you had double trouble.'

'Didn't I just! The twins were so challenging as little ones and it was exhausting running around after them both. Thank goodness for wine and chocolate, that's all I can say.'

'I did enjoy the whole playgroup and school-run thing, though,' Clare said, thinking how lucky she'd been to do that with Kyle. 'Did you?'

Clare had moved away from the village long before she had Kyle, so she had not been around to see how Jenny had managed with twins, just like Jenny had not been there to see Clare become a mum to Kyle.

'I did. Wonderful times. I can't say that the teen years have been easy though.'

'What, with two girls?' Clare shook her head. 'I'm full of admiration for you. It was enough having just Kyle's mood swings to deal with, although he was never as bad as some of his school friends, so I think I got off lightly.'

'How is he?'

'Good, thanks. Enjoying university as far as I know.' Clare felt that familiar jolt of emotion that she always did when she thought of how much she missed her son. 'He texts me most days to keep in touch and I know I'm lucky with that as I suspect a lot of young men don't text their mums that often. How are the girls?'

'They're good. Eighteen going on thirty . . .'

'Taking care of themselves, are they?'

'You'd think, right?' Jenny rolled her eyes. 'I'm sure we were far more independent at their age.'

They held each other's gaze as the sounds of the café floated around them: the murmuring of customers, a grizzling baby, clinking of cutlery and a radio station on low, playing pop songs in the background.

'We wanted to grow up so quickly, didn't we?'

'And to escape from Little Bramble.'

'Which I did – but now I'm back, tail between my legs.' Clare gave a small shrug, expecting to feel worse than she did.

'Why'd you say it like that?'

'Oh,' Clare waved a hand, 'it's a long story but basically, as I said yesterday, I'm newly single. I'm OK – it's just a bit strange sometimes.'

'I am sorry.' Jenny reached for her hand and squeezed it. 'At least . . . should I be sorry?'

'It wasn't horrid or terribly drawn-out or acrimonious, Jen. We just – just realised we didn't love each other enough anymore. Or at least Jason did and I followed suit.'

'I guess that can happen, but lots of people probably ignore it and stay put. So where is Jason?'

'Gone to find himself.'

Jenny's eyes widened and she pressed her lips together. Clare watched her face carefully, wondering if she could still read her oldest friend's body language like she used to. And she could, because when Jenny suddenly snorted then covered her mouth with a hand, Clare started to laugh too. They laughed until Clare could barely breathe, until her hairline was damp and her ribs ached, especially the bruised one. Every time she tried to stop, all she had to do was look at Jenny again and she'd be off. It took a waitress arriving at the table to make them pull themselves together.

'I'll have a medium latte and a slice of chocolate fudge cake, please,' Clare said, trying to avoid making eye contact with Jenny.

'I'll have the same, thanks.' Jenny tucked her menu back behind the salt-and-pepper stand then shuffled in her seat. 'So, Clare, I guess we can still laugh like the old days, eh?'

'That was sooooo good.' Clare pushed her hair back from her face and fanned it with her hands. 'I can't remember the last time I laughed like that.'

'It was the bit about finding himself, Clare. It's just such a cliché. I really am sorry, though. Divorce, however amicable, is never easy.'

The warm air around them was thick with aromas of food: sweet frosted buns, toasted sandwiches and the tang of something acrid, as if an onion had burnt under the grill.

'I know – and thanks. I didn't expect it to happen and was actually quite surprised when Jason initially told me he wanted out of our marriage, but as time went on and we talked about it properly, I could see what he meant. Our relationship was over a long time ago and I guess if we'd wanted to work at it we could have done, but he had this thing in his head about quitting his job and heading off into the sunset, so I had to let go.'

'Well, his loss is my gain now that you're back.' Jenny knitted her brows. 'I mean . . . not that I'm taking anything for granted here, because I know you said yesterday that you're only here until you get back on your feet . . .'

'I'm not sure if I'll stay more than a few weeks, Jen, but everything is so up in the air for me at the moment. I need somewhere to live, but I'm nervous about the prospect of renting, let alone buying, in case it's the wrong decision. And I need to think about looking for work but don't know where I'll be. I'm also terrified at the thought . . . and I seem unable to think about any of it for long without my head aching.'

Jenny nodded sympathetically. 'It will all be scary because you thought your life was mapped out and then it suddenly changed. But from the sound of things you're taking steps in the right direction and, now that you're here, I'll help however I can. For what it's worth, I think you're being very brave and coping far better than I would. And however long you stay, I'm glad you're here now.'

'Thank you. I really appreciate your kind words.'

'There are plenty more where they came from because you truly are amazing and more capable of getting through this than you know. Getting a job and finding somewhere to live are things you'll manage easily, but I do understand that you need some time to think about where you want to settle and about what you want to do. Oh, Clare . . . I've missed you so much. The village hasn't been the same since you left.'

'But that was twenty-seven years ago!'

'Yeah, I know, but people have come and people have gone, but you were always my favourite.'

'Oh, Jen . . .' Clare's vision blurred. 'I-I don't know what to say. I've missed you too. I feel terrible for not staying in touch.'

There had been reasons why they'd let their friendship dwindle but nothing dreadful, nothing bitter, just a difference of opinion and the pursuit of their separate lives.

'Hey, that was me too, but with husbands, kids, jobs and so on, it's difficult. Don't beat yourself up, Clare. Remember that I swore I'd follow you to Reading when you first bought your house with Jason. I believed I would too, but Martin had his rugby and the family business here and it would have been such an upheaval. If you'd asked me when I was twenty if I'd still be living in Little Bramble at forty-five, I'd have laughed in your face. In fact, I think I did! But life doesn't always go the way we plan.'

'It certainly doesn't. And I don't think you'd have liked living close to Jason anyway.'

'True.' A grimace marred Jenny's pretty face. 'I did say some awful things about him, didn't I?'

'Sadly, though, you were right.'

'I thought it would have happened soon after you married him, not twenty-odd years later. I don't want to offend you by saying this, but he always came across as so . . . flaky. He didn't seem to have any substance and I never thought he was good enough for you.'

Clare smiled, grateful for the moral support, but also keen not to get into a character assassination of her son's father. Jason had flaws, but so did she, and she felt pretty certain that slagging him off wouldn't make her feel better about anything.

The waitress returned with their lattes and plates of dark, sticky chocolate cake. As Jenny accepted a plate of cake, Clare took the opportunity to look at her properly. And while Jenny was as beautiful as she'd always been, she was also changed. Her hair was still blonde and shiny, but there were fine lines around her eyes, slightly raised veins on the backs of her hands and her chin was no longer as sharp or defined as it had once been. She didn't look forty-five, but neither did she look twenty anymore. While Clare had seen Jenny in passing over the years, they'd never met up for a proper talk, never been close enough to get a good look at each other or to exchange more than fleeting pleasantries, and it was wonderful to finally have the opportunity to do so. They'd been Facebook friends – wishing each other and their families happy birthday and merry Christmas, liking posts from time to time. Clare had seen some photos of Jenny and her family that way, but people usually only posted their good photos, not the ones of the slight loosening of the skin on their necks, the annoying hairs that sprouted on their chins or the age spots that marred their complexions.

For years though, Clare and Jenny had not shared their deepest feelings with each other, had not pondered the meaning of life or shared their losses and their triumphs. Clare had missed it – a lot. If she hadn't got divorced and come home, then this meeting might never have happened and how sad would that have been? Sometimes, life did take you on unexpected paths, but that didn't have to be a bad thing. Look at this positive that had already come about . . .

'This cake is so good,' Jenny said through a mouthful of chocolate. She'd always had a sweet tooth and swore in her teens that it was only all the netball she played that kept her slim. Clare hadn't been sporty growing up so some people had been surprised at their friendship, especially with Jenny dating the captain of the school rugby team too, but Clare had gone to every netball match that Jenny played and cheered her on from the sidelines. Likewise, Jenny had supported Clare with her dreams of being a vet, helping her to prepare for biology tests and science practicals. Back then, Clare had been convinced she would work with animals – but she'd also believed she'd marry Corey Haim, Will Smith or Jon Bon Jovi. Jenny, however, had never wanted to marry anyone famous, only having eyes for Martin, even at fourteen.

'How's Martin?' Clare asked before trying the cake. 'Oh, this is delicious.' She nodded as the rich fudgy icing stuck to the roof of her mouth, the cake itself light and spongey, the combination perfection.

'He's good, thanks. Business is great, what with the new housing estate being built just outside the village – he's had a lot of work from that – plus the usual amount he gets from locals. He's coaching the under-fourteens rugby at weekends and generally being a good husband and dad.'

'I'm glad to hear it.' Clare smiled. 'Also, very happy to see that you two are so content together after all this time.'

Jenny sipped her latte. 'It's not that we don't have disagreements, because we do, but once we've cleared the air, we always make an effort to make up.'

'I can't imagine either of you being with anyone else.'

'Nor me.' Jenny shrugged. 'It would be weird.' She winced. 'I'm so sorry, that was thoughtless of me. What about you, Clare? Has there been anyone since Jason?'

'Gosh, no! It hasn't been long and I can't imagine being with anyone else right now either. I mean, I'm hoping that might change. At least, I *think* I am, but I'm happy just being alone for now. I do know that I need some time for me, to make myself happy before I even think about going on a date. I had a job as an assistant librarian for twelve years and I loved it, but then a lack of funding meant that they had to make some of us redundant and I was so disappointed. I'd love to find another job like that. I've also been thinking about how much I used to love horse riding and I'd like to go again, although it's been years since I even stroked a horse, let alone rode one.'

Jenny set her fork down and it clattered on the plate, causing the three women with toddlers at the next table to stare at them. She waved an apology. 'Sorry! Chocolate high.' They nodded their understanding. 'I completely understand all that and yes, you must do things to make yourself happy. However, you can't spend the rest of your life alone, Clare. You're a gorgeous woman with far too much to offer. We'll get you back in the game, don't you worry.'

Clare's heart sank. One of the things she now remembered about Jenny was her friend's dogged determination, and when she had an idea she liked, she tended to go for it without hesitation, eyes blinkered, until she reached the finish line. It was what had made her such a good sportswoman. If Jenny set her sights on getting Clare dating, then it would happen, whether Clare wanted it or not.

'Jen, I'm not really sure about that. Can we at least let the dust settle, please?'

Jenny reached for Clare's hand again and entwined her fingers with Clare's. 'Of course we can. Besides which, I've only just got you back, so I'm not ready to share you with any man for the foreseeable.'

Clare smiled and relaxed in her seat. It was as if the years had fallen away and she was back where she belonged, with her best friend, feeling that the world wasn't such a bad place after all. Then the café door opened and the fuzzy warm feeling disappeared.

Sam held the door so Alyssa could enter the café before him, then he closed it behind him, shutting the icy-cold air of the morning out. The café was Thursday-morning busy and he'd only come to grab a takeaway for him and Miranda and Alyssa was meeting a friend.

'Get me a hot chocolate and one of those giant choc-chip cookies, would you?' Alyssa asked and he nodded. She always did this, went to find a table so he had to pay. Not that he minded at all though; Alyssa could have had his last penny.

At the counter, he ordered two takeaway coffees that he provided reusable mugs for – he and Miranda each had their own with their initials on – and a hot chocolate and a cookie for his sister. When they were ready, he paid, then looked around for Alyssa. She'd taken a table near the window and was typing away on her smartphone. His stomach clenched as he wondered if it was Alyssa's new boss's brother, someone she'd seen twice since her interview, and someone he had yet to meet, then he shook himself. It was none of his business, she was a grown woman . . .

He headed across to his sister, avoiding pushchairs and elbows, wondering how Alyssa had navigated the space in her wheelchair, then remembered that people always made way for her – and if they didn't, she soon had a sharp word with them. She didn't take any nonsense, which was why he had to back off and let her live her life the way she wanted to. He couldn't protect her for ever and she didn't want him to.

'There you go.' He set Alyssa's drink and cookie down.

'Thanks, Sam. You heading back to work now?'

'Yes, I only popped out for coffee and to grab some fresh air. I think I might be coming down with something, to be honest; my throat's a bit tickly.'

'Poor thing!' Alyssa tilted her head. 'I'll get you some honey and lemons and make you a hot toddy after work.'

He smiled. 'Great. See you later.'

Alyssa nodded, her curls bobbing around the wide red and purple paisley headband she was wearing, her skin bright and fresh. He suspected some of this was down to clever highlighting and blusher, but there was something else about her today. She looked so happy that it was as if she was lit from within.

Oh God, was she falling in love?

He turned away before he could say anything and cause an argument, but an elderly lady was standing in his path, chatting to a friend, so he turned in the other direction and hurried along, keen to get out of the café before he got trapped again. Then he froze. There, right in front of him, staring at him as if he had just grown horns, was the woman from yesterday.

Her cheeks were flushed and her eyes bright, her dark hair hanging down around her face. His heart thumped hard and everything else in the café seemed to fade away. He opened his mouth, knowing that he had something to say to her, but he couldn't remember for the life of him what it was. She shook her head and turned to walk away.

'Uh . . .' He held out his hand and tried to remember her name. 'Excuse me?'

She turned and glared at him.

'I . . . uh . . . I wanted to apologise to you.'

Her green eyes were cold, her lips a thin line. He really had offended her yesterday.

'I was quite rude about the dog poo and I shouldn't have been. I should have waited and found out –'

'It's fine,' she said, then she turned and walked away in the direction of the toilets and left him standing there, his cheeks burning, his heart pounding.

What had just happened? He had been about to say something else as well as to apologise, about Goliath he felt sure, but it was gone. He had lost the words. In fact, he had lost all words and he was staring at the back of a woman he didn't know in the middle of a very busy café. Alyssa was probably wondering what he was doing.

He swallowed, squeezed through the tables, making for the door, desperate to escape the café than he had ever been – more desperate even than he'd been that day not long after his arrival in Little Bramble, when he'd agreed to be the professional guest at the annual Women's Institute coffee morning. After some polite preamble, it had become quite clear that they'd all wanted to find out if he was married, single or gay. It had, he'd thought at the time, been like something out of a Jane Austen novel and he'd felt the women assessing his prospects, evaluating his worth as a member of the community. They'd given him such a grilling that he'd gone home traumatised and had to take a nap.

Outside, he gulped down some fresh air. That had been strange, very strange. Perhaps he *was* coming down with something and had a fever. It would explain his irrational state, his inability to say something, anything, when face to face with a woman he didn't know. His reaction was confusing, so he'd put it down to a fever and make sure to drink lots of water and eat a healthy dinner, get a good night's sleep. Admittedly he hadn't slept well last night; he'd been plagued by dreams about losing Scout in the woods then, when he found her, she'd been three times her usual size and she'd dragged him along the ground as he'd called desperately to her to stop, to sit, to behave.

Loss of control . . .

He'd feared it all his adult life, mostly since that night when he *had* lost control and Alyssa had been hurt. He blamed himself for that – how could he not? Losing control and upsetting others was unforgiveable . . . and Sam knew that it was one of his triggers. He'd lost his temper yesterday when that woman, possibly named Clare, had been standing there without a poo bag and with Goliath charging around the woods.

Of course! The words returned. He had wanted to apologise properly, to explain that he didn't usually behave like that and to tell her about Goliath's OAP check-up. That was what he'd wanted to say, but instead he'd stood there, opening and closing his mouth like a fish out of water. She probably thought he was a complete idiot – and if Alyssa had witnessed it too, he'd be in for a grilling later, for sure.

82

He'd phone Elaine when he got to the surgery and tell her about Goliath's check-up, then all would be well and he could go on with his life . . .

Sam was a scientist, a sensible and practical man. He needed to focus on his job, to avoid any distractions and be a good brother, and that was what he aimed to do.

Chapter 8

Clare pushed her feet into her trainers, taking care with the ankle that was still tender, and slid her arms into her green wax jacket. She'd walked Goliath early that morning, enjoying the Saturday morning quiet of the village, aware as she passed cottages, houses and shops that most people would still be in bed or enjoying breakfast as they read the papers, their feet warmed by their Agas and wood burners, their dogs and cats stretched out in front of their hearths, just as Goliath was now.

She stuck her head around the lounge door.

'Are you sure you won't come, Mum?'

Elaine looked up from her knitting. 'No thanks, Clare. I'd like to finish the sleeve this morning, then I have a pile of ironing to do.'

'Don't worry about the ironing,' Clare shook her head. 'It really doesn't matter.'

'To you perhaps . . .' Her mum shrugged. 'But I know it's there and it will make me anxious.'

'What? Two T-shirts and a pair of jeans?' She laughed but her mum just stared at Clare as if she'd grown two heads.

'Clare, we're all different and I have today planned out and will go ahead with my plans.' She offered a small smile. 'Also, there's a documentary on TV tonight about the Tudors and I'd like to be able to sit down and relax when it's on. Therefore, I need to get my chores done.'

'OK, Mum. Well, I won't be long. I just want to have a wander and make the most of the dry morning.' Clare had found that since she first walked Goliath nine days ago, leaving the cottage was getting easier each time and she was enjoying going out again; indeed, she found herself craving the walks with Goliath to stretch her legs and the prospect of fresh air something to look forward to. Being in Little Bramble was having a positive effect and she hoped it would continue.

'See you later.'

'Bye, Goliath.' Clare waved at the dog. He was stretched out on the hearthrug, and he raised his large head in acknowledgement then lay back down, clearly content to stay where he was.

Clare put her leather gloves on then pulled a woollen hat over her hair. She paused on the doorstep, allowing her thoughts to settle. She'd worn Goliath out on their walk earlier, or rather, he'd worn them both out, so he wouldn't be any trouble for her mum, but she wondered if it could be that Goliath was becoming a bit troubled by his owner's behaviour? Clare's mum seemed so out of sorts. The Elaine she had known growing up would never have put knitting and ironing before a walk or an evening out. Her mum had been vivacious, sociable and almost scornful of people who stayed home to do chores when there was a life to be lived. She would never have chosen a TV documentary over an evening of amateur dramatics and Clare was becoming more and more concerned. It could, of course, be down to Elaine's age. Perhaps she was slowing down a bit, but Clare suspected that it was something more. That her mum might actually be a bit low.

A gust of cold air swirled around her, so she pulled up her collar then marched down the drive and out along the pavement. She walked quickly, head down against the chill, enjoying the stretching in her legs and the way the cold air felt as if it was cleansing her with every breath she took.

She passed other cottages, some owned by people she'd known since she was a child and others now owned by people she'd never met. They must have paid large sums for the properties because Little Bramble was a pretty village with the desirable English charm that was so in fashion and close to London, so it was a perfect location for commuting. A few years ago it had been named the third prettiest village in England, coming only after Snowshill in Gloucestershire and Ombersley in Worcestershire. Clare's parents had bought their property before she was born and paid a ridiculously low sum for it, so their mortgage had long been paid off and the cottage was now a significant investment. Elaine had been approached several times by holidaymakers, keen on securing a property in the village, but there was no way her mum wanted to move and she couldn't blame her. It was hard enough selling up your family home in your forties and having to deal with the thought of starting over, let alone in your seventies.

Clare slowed as she approached the low stone wall that enclosed the village church and grounds. The small church apparently dated back to the twelfth century and had been altered and added to over the years. Its shingle-clad spire pointed up to the sky and had always reminded Clare of a hat sitting upon the church roof. The stone wall was separated halfway along by a Victorian lychgate and many of the graves in the churchyard were so well tended that the dates could be read, some several centuries old.

Clare's favourite thing about the churchyard was the ancient yew tree that grew in the far corner. The tree was hollow and believed to be over 3000 years old. Some people visited the churchyard to have photos taken with it, especially those seeking help for fertility issues. Clare recalled asking her dad why people wanted to visit the tree and he had told her that yew trees were symbolic of rebirth and regeneration after a difficult time, of immortality and the cycle of life. She had asked him if it was true that the tree had such qualities and he'd shrugged, then told her that if it didn't, then what did it hurt for people to find hope by having a photo taken with it, and if it did, then all the better. Her dad had always been kind and keen to see the good in people, happy to let them believe whatever made life easier for them. She had liked that answer because it seemed to suggest that, whatever the truth, those who visited the churchyard could be winners. In fact, just to give herself the best chance of having a happy future, she'd go and take a selfie with the tree. What did she have to lose?

She let herself in through the lychgate which was covered with holly and ivy, then closed it behind her. A few times over the years, when it hadn't been closed properly, stray sheep and even a goat had got inside and eaten the flowers left on gravestones. The goat had gone into the church and eaten the altar cloth, something that had caused some of the elderly villagers much consternation but had made the vicar, Iolo Ifans – a rather eccentric Welshman – chuckle for hours. Her dad had liked the vicar and enjoyed a pint with him many times, debating every-thing from politics to existentialism to football and more. No topic was too big or too small for them to chew over and Clare had loved to see the sparkle in her dad's eye when he'd had a few beers and a good debate with Iolo.

When Clare reached the yew tree, she peered up at it, in awe of its size, just as she had been as a girl. It was a living giant, had witnessed goodness knows what while it had stood there, its roots plunging deep into the ground and holding it fast. Sometimes, Clare had imagined herself as being like a tree, having roots that held her in place. Even now, when she became anxious or insecure, as had happened more often since Jason had told her that he wanted out of their marriage, she had tried to picture her own roots holding her fast to the earth, keeping her in place and preventing her from drifting away. Sometimes it worked; sometimes it didn't. And when it didn't, having a good cry and letting it all out seemed to work, for a while at least.

Clare pulled her phone from her jacket pocket and located the camera app, then she flipped the camera so she could see her own face. She hated seeing herself up close, all her flaws exposed, from the crows' feet around her eyes to the stray brow hairs that had escaped her tweezers, to the freckles that had always covered her nose and cheeks, refusing to be covered by foundation or concealer – when she could be bothered to apply them, that was. She met her eyes in the camera and gazed into them. What did others see when they looked at her? To Jason, she had become almost invisible, part of the wallpaper until he'd wanted to redecorate. To Kyle, she was Mum, who washed and ironed his clothes, cooked his meals, phoned him regularly to check if he needed anything and sometimes got on his nerves when she worried too much about him. To Elaine, she was . . . a disappointment? She'd always felt that she was, but they'd never really had the conversation because Clare hadn't had the courage to broach the subject. What would have been the point when she would have hated to hear the answer?

She sighed and tried to smile for the photo, her gaze shifting from her face to the tree behind her. Its strength and resilience was something she wanted to emulate. Her thoughts snapped back to the celebrity, Cora Quincy, who she'd listened to during her journey to Little Bramble, to what the young woman had said about living life for herself and no one else. Clare didn't think she could ever be that selfish, that self-concerned, because the roles she had undertaken during her life as daughter, wife and mum were a part of her, but she could, perhaps, dig deep and find herself, find what she wanted from life without having to compromise in how she cared about others. There had to be a way to be herself and be fulfilled without hurting anyone else.

A loud clicking noise alerted her to the fact that she'd taken a photo, or rather, a series of photos. She scanned through them, seeing the flush on her cheeks and the shimmer in her eyes, the tree behind her like some sort of gnarled, ancient guardian. Coming home had been a good idea; it was giving her the opportunity to think, to reflect, to take a step back from all the things that had consumed her for what felt like a lifetime. There were landmarks like the yew tree that had been there since before she so much as existed, that she had seen almost every day growing up. It made her feel more grounded, somehow, less insubstantial, as if she had roots that connected her to this place. Then there were the people like her mum, Jenny, Marcellus David and others, who had known her all her life. That counted for something and made her feel less alone, more a part of something, more real. In just over a week, Clare was already starting to feel more like herself, like the person she'd been before she met and married Jason – and she liked it. She had been a person in her own right before she devoted herself to him, had lived and loved and had hopes and dreams – and she'd given them all up when she'd lost herself in him and their marriage. She didn't have any regrets because they were things she had chosen to do, but she had a second chance at life now and she wanted to seize it with both hands.

She put her phone back in her pocket and crossed the spongy grass to the church. If the doors were unlocked, she'd take a look inside while she was here. A few minutes out of the cold would be good for her circulation as well, as even with leather gloves on, her fingers were going numb.

❄

Clare turned the heavy iron handle then pushed the door to the church porch open, wincing as the sound echoed through the building. She pulled the door behind her, keen to keep as much warmth in the old building as possible.

The porch was small and shadowy, the stained-glass windows set high in the walls, the dark purples and blues of the glass blocking most of the daylight and giving the porch an underwater hue. A wooden bench took up most of the wall opposite the doors, a long thin embroidered cushion on the seat showing signs of wear and tear, an umbrella stand in the corner holding a solitary black umbrella coated in dust, forgotten or abandoned by its owner. To her left, the doors to the church stood open and dust motes swirled in the entrance to the brighter space, slowly, like glitter in oil.

Clare walked through, holding her breath for a moment as she listened, prepared to ask for permission to sit inside. But there was no one there, so she walked along the aisle, her trainers quiet on the strip of worn brown carpet that ran the length of the church to the altar. The stone walls were thick, keeping out the warmth on hot days and the chills of winter – whatever the season, the church was cool and airless inside. Whenever Clare had attended a sermon, wedding or christening, she'd remembered to bring a cardigan or coat, even on a hot August day.

She stopped two pews from the front and took a seat on a bench. It was hard, the polished wood unforgiving, and she wriggled a bit to try to get more comfortable. A memory enveloped her of sitting here with Jenny when they were around seven or eight, their short legs swinging because their feet didn't reach the floor, their breath appearing like white clouds in the chilly air. It had been Christmas, a carol concert, and the majority of the village had gathered to sing together. There had always been a Christmas show at the village hall and a carol service at the church, as well as carols around the tree on the green when the lights were turned on.

Jenny had held Clare's hand tight and they'd exchanged excited glances, aware that Father Christmas would soon visit their homes and hopefully deliver the gifts from the lists they'd written at school. Clare's mum and dad had sat together on her other side and her dad had winked at her in between carols. Then he'd got up to read a poem he'd written and she had beamed with pride. She'd almost forgotten that her dad loved to write poems. This one had been about Little Bramble at Christmas, about snow and robins and love and laughter, and it had made the congregation laugh, then applaud. He had been a very talented man and Clare had loved him deeply. As had her mum. She recalled glancing sideways at her mum and seeing the gleam in her eyes as she gazed at her husband, seeing the blush steal into her cheeks when he had held her gaze across the church. Her parents had been very much in love and it must have made losing him all the harder for Elaine to bear and, in that moment, Clare's heart ached, not just for herself and for how much she missed her dad, but also for her mum and for the pain she had endured.

Blinking hard, Clare looked around. Even though it was brighter in here than in the porch, the coloured glass panes depicting scenes from the Bible blocked a lot of the natural light. The air was stale and waxy, permeated with mint, incense and the chocolate-coffee aroma of old paper.

Fastened to each windowsill was a brass candleholder, each one holding a candle that had yet to be lit. Were they kept for special occasions as the vicar tried to make the budget stretch? There was a time when the church would have been the centre of village life but that was long ago, and she knew from things her dad had said that money was tight for the vicar, his budget shrinking each year as his congregation dwindled, as the world changed. And it had been over ten years since her dad had spent time with the vicar, so she suspected that the situation might be even worse now.

She could picture her dad outside the church, chatting to the vicar on sunny Sunday mornings after the service and on those days when he'd been persuaded to read at a wedding or funeral. A tear rolled down Clare's cheek and she let it go until it slipped off her chin and plopped onto her coat where it sat, a clear crystal orb on the dark material. She took off a glove and wiped it away, feeling the wet on her palm, remembering the tears she had cried on the day of her dad's funeral, the tears she had tried to hold in until she'd felt as if she would burst. Her mum had been an ice maiden that day, cold as marble, and Clare hadn't seen one tear fall from her eyes. Kyle, just gone ten, had commented on it afterwards in the car on the journey home. Why hadn't Nanny cried? Wasn't she sad about Grandad? Jason had reassured their son, told him that Nanny had shed her tears in private and that she wanted to be strong for her family. Elaine did not do emotion in front of others, would prefer to grieve in private, but Clare knew that seeing her mum break down would have been more comforting. Just a tear or two glistening in her mum's eyes would have made Clare feel better about her own overwhelming emotions, but no, her mum had been strong, and Clare had been . . . weak? A loving daughter? Human?

Human . . . yes. That was it.

And that was why – she could admit it now, in this sanctum of tranquillity, where memories could safely surface and emotions could flow, this quiet place where humanity was exposed in all its glory, where births were celebrated, love was bound and goodbyes were said – she could accept that she had not returned to Little Bramble as often as she could have done because she had been afraid of those emotions overpowering her. This village had still been home, a refuge she believed she could come back to, until her dad died and returning was too painful. The church, the village, the cottage – all were intrinsically tied to her dad and with him gone, they were changed beyond recognition. It had taken the breakdown of her marriage, the loss of another of the three men in her life to bring her back to this place. Clare was changed, but now she recognised that didn't need to be a bad thing, and this time, perhaps, she could help her mum too. After her dad died, Elaine had been cold, but perhaps that had been her way of holding herself together. Everyone dealt with things differently and, having lost her own husband and needing to be strong for Kyle, Clare now had a better understanding of why her mum had acted in the way that she had.

Suffused with a new sense of calm, she stood up and shuffled out of the pew, then turned and headed back along the aisle to the rear of the church. Next to the open doors stood an iron rack where a few votive candles burned, flickering in their red holders. That meant that others had been here too on this cold October day, possibly praying, possibly seeking a few peaceful moments for reflection. Clare pulled a few coins from her purse and dropped them into the locked box underneath the rack, then picked a candle and lit it from one of the others. As the flame flickered, she smiled.

'I love you, Dad,' she whispered. 'I'm sorry I didn't come back sooner but I'm here now and I'm ready to make some changes.'

Chapter 9

Sam waited for the kettle to boil. The weekend had passed quietly with him working Saturday at the surgery and spending Sunday walking Scout, reading the latest thriller he'd downloaded to his e-reader, and he had made a roast dinner for him and Alyssa. He liked to cook but as always he'd made far too much food for just the two of them, so they'd have to have cold meat and bubble and squeak a few times in the week, and he'd curry some of the leftover chicken. Alyssa took it for granted that her big brother enjoyed being in the kitchen and although she made a great spaghetti Bolognese and baked a light and delicious lemon drizzle cake, she left most of the culinary jobs to Sam. He didn't mind; it gave him something to do in the evenings, although he did occasionally think it might be nice to get home from work to find someone else had made dinner. But he guessed that was one of the things about being in a relationship that he had missed out on; there would presumably be more give and take and someone else to take on some of the domestic duties. To make the first cup of tea of the day and to load the dishwasher, to clean out the oven (although this was such an arduous job that he'd probably have done it anyway to save anyone else from having to do it) and someone to just . . . be with and to cuddle.

What?

Cuddle?

When had Sam ever worried about having someone to cuddle? Not that he didn't like a cuddle, because he did as much as the next warm-blooded human being, but it wasn't something he thought about. He was forty-six, six foot one, weighed around sixteen stone (he'd worried he was getting a bit overweight but Alyssa always said it was mainly muscle and that he had a rugby player's build) and he'd never had a serious long-term relationship. He just hadn't found the time or hadn't (perhaps) allowed himself to be open to anything serious. Why would he? He had a job that involved long hours and dedication, and he had Alyssa to think of. He had a truck load of guilt that prevented him from even thinking of falling in love . . .

'Penny for them?'

Sam turned to find Magnus Petterson, their senior veterinary nurse, smiling at him as he rubbed a large hand over his thick blond beard.

'Ha! Sadly, nothing very interesting, Magnus.' Sam shook his head.

'It looked interesting. Anything to do with a woman?' Sam would never tire of listening to Magnus's lilting staccato English.

'Only if that woman is my sister.' Sam raised his eyebrows.

'Ahhh . . .' Magnus nodded as Sam raised a mug to offer him a coffee. 'The lovely Alyssa is still causing problems for her big brother.'

'Always.' Sam gave a low laugh, although it didn't feel very funny, particularly today, when Alyssa was starting her new job.

'Isn't she starting at the tattoo parlour today?' Magnus asked, as if reading Sam's thoughts.

'Yes.'

'Well, that is a good thing, surely? If it will make Alyssa happy.'

'I know and I want that for her.' Sam handed Magnus a mug of coffee. 'It's just that I'm worried about the fact that she's . . .' He paused. He didn't like discussing Alyssa with anyone, but over the two years that Magnus had worked at the surgery, he'd become a friend and he'd proved to be reliable and discrete. 'She's started seeing the owner's brother.'

'I see.' Magnus sipped his coffee. 'And how old is Alyssa now?'

'I know, I know, I get your point.'

'But you'll always be the overprotective big brother?'

'It's a habit I'm trying to break.'

'Well, come to the pub quiz at The Red on Friday and help me win. It'll help distract you.'

The Red Squirrel – The Red as it was fondly referred to by locals – was one of the two village pubs, and they held a Friday quiz there every week. Sam had been a few times but wasn't a regular, blaming being on call and early weekend shifts – like Saturday morning surgery and the pro bono work he did at the local animal sanctuary – for his lack of socialising, but Magnus tried to persuade him to go every week.

'I'll think about it.' Sam raised his mug. 'Not promising anything, though.'

'Great!' Magnus tapped his mug against Sam's. 'Oh, and I got through to Elaine Hughes first thing this morning. I saw the note on her file that you'd been trying to ring her and having no luck. She said it had completely slipped her mind and booked to come in later this morning.'

'Brilliant. It's been a while since we saw Goliath. I don't like to pester anyone to come in but the big boy's getting on a bit and it certainly won't hurt him to get checked over. Besides which, they're covered by the monthly plan Elaine pays, so she's wasting her money if she doesn't bring him.'

'Exactly.' Magnus nodded then drained his coffee and swilled his mug in the sink. 'Best get on with morning surgery then.'

'Indeed.'

Sam swilled his own mug and set it on the draining board then followed Magnus through to the consultation room, preparing for another busy Monday, wondering if Elaine would bring the dog or if it would be a certain some-one else . . .

✴

Walking into the surgery reception, Clare felt her stomach clench. Her mum had made the appointment for Goliath's OAP check-up and then asked Clare to take him. Initially, she'd been happy to do it, but as she'd got ready to go, she'd remembered that the horrid man from the woods was one of the veterinary practice owners. When she'd met Jenny for coffee last week, Horrid Man had walked into the coffee shop and Jenny had told her that his name was Sam Wilson and that he was one of the village vets. He had been with a pretty woman in a wheelchair, who Jenny said was his younger sister. He had tried to speak to Clare, giving her what she thought was a reluctant apology, but she'd been compelled to escape him, finding it all a bit much in the warmth of the café, aware that her heart was beating quickly.

Clare, wanting to be as supportive to her mum as she could, didn't like to change her mind about going to the vets'. It would have raised questions and how could she explain to her that she'd bumped into the vet in the woods and he'd been mean? She was a grown woman with a grown-up son, so admitting that she'd found the vet intimidating would be extremely embarrassing. Besides which, she didn't want to worry her mum and add extra pressure to whatever it was that she was going through.

So here Clare was, standing in front of the reception desk and waiting for the receptionist – a woman of around Clare's age with a shiny red bob and green-rimmed glasses that matched her bright green eyes – to finish her phone conversation. Clare tried not to listen as the receptionist made an appointment for an animal named Donaldo (was it a footballing duck?) before putting the phone down.

Once Goliath was booked in and had been given a treat by the receptionist – something he clearly expected – Clare led him over to the dog waiting area. The reception was divided into three areas: one for dogs, one for cats and the third for small animals, which Clare thought was very sensible.

The front door opened and a man came in carrying a tiny Yorkshire terrier in his arms, Goliath stood up and Clare braced herself, planting her trainers firmly on the lino and wrapping the lead more tightly around her hand, hoping she wasn't going to be dragged across the floor. Goliath took a step forwards and the lead tightened, the rope crushing her fingers together.

'Goliath, sit!' she said, injecting her voice with far more confidence than she felt.

He whined, licked his lips, then, to her surprise, he sat down. Relief coursed through Clare, accompanied by confusion. Why Goliath had listened to her when he never usually did, she had no idea, but she hoped it was because he was getting used to her and because they'd had a few more walks, during which she'd taken some treats in her pocket. He might be a giant of a dog, but he'd do just about anything for a dried fish crunchie. At that moment, Goliath turned and his eyes met hers, so she dug in her coat pocket for a treat, which he took gently from her fingers.

The reception was spotlessly clean, but even so, there was a heavy animal odour in the air, balancing on a cloud of disinfectant and pet food, a hint of bleach stinging her nostrils. There were four doors leading off the reception: consultation rooms 1 and 2, one that opened from behind the reception desk and one labelled WC. Which one would open for Goliath, she wondered. How would he feel about being poked and prodded, examined and more? She had no idea exactly what an OAP health check would involve. What if they found something ominous? Clare would have to go home and deliver the news to her mum and that was not something she would relish doing. The bearer of bad news always became tainted with it. Why hadn't she thought about this before she agreed? If Goliath had anything wrong with him at all, Clare would have to tell her mum and her mum would probably, subconsciously at least, blame her.

'Goliath Hughes?'

A voice broke through Clare's thoughts. She looked up and there he was.

Tall, broad and handsome with his dark brown eyes fixed on her. How long had he been standing there like that? Minutes? Seconds?

Was he angry again?

Get yourself together, Clare! Now is not the time to lose it. This man already thinks you're an idiot.

She forced herself to her feet and walked on stiff legs across the reception area. Somewhere, deep within the surgery, a cat yowled, and Goliath tugged at his lead, causing Clare to lurch forwards in the direction of the waiting vet. She screamed and flung out her hands, grabbing whatever she could to prevent herself from faceplanting on the floor.

A hush fell over the reception: the cat (wherever it was) fell silent and the receptionist stopped speaking to the man holding the Yorkshire terrier. Clare raised her eyes slowly, knowing she wasn't going to like what she saw.

And she didn't. Because as she'd fallen, she had grabbed hold of the front of the vet's navy chinos, and she was still holding them as she slowly slid down to the floor. Meanwhile, he was hanging on to the waistband, trying to stop his trousers from falling down to his ankles.

Heat flooded Clare's cheeks and she peeled her fingers from the material just as Goliath leant down and licked her cheek. She lay there for a moment, then she slowly moved to a sitting position and sent out a silent prayer for the floor to open and swallow her whole.

'Are you all right?' a deep voice rumbled from somewhere above her and she reluctantly looked up again, meeting his eyes.

'I-I think so and I-I'm dreadfully sorry,' she said, as he held out a hand and helped her to her feet.

When she was standing in front of the vet, Goliath at her side like some sort of canine guardian, he asked her again.

'Are you sure? Can I get you a glass of water, or do you need to sit down?'

Clare was painfully aware of the other people watching them, so she shook her head and gestured at the open doorway behind the vet.

'I'm fine. Could we just, uh, get this done, please?'

'Of course.'

He released her hand and led the way into the consultation room. Clare squashed her urge to run in and slam the door behind them so that no one could see what embarrassing stunt she'd pull next. When they were away from everyone else, the heat in her cheeks faded a little and she tried to shake off the humiliation of what had just happened.

'It's a good job I was wearing a belt,' the vet said as he knelt down next to Goliath and ran his hands over the dog's fur. 'These chinos are a bit big – on a different day that could have been even more mortifying.'

'Oh God!' Clare covered her face with her hands, the burning in her cheeks intensifying again. 'I'm so sorry. Goliath lurched and I lost my balance and I just grabbed the nearest thing.'

A funny sound filled the room: low, deep and warm, and she peered between her fingers, wondering what it was.

The vet was laughing. At her? At himself? At the situation?

'I'm sorry,' he said finally. 'That was just one of those awkward moments that could have been a lot worse. No one was hurt and that's the main thing.'

Clare lowered her hands and let herself relax, then smile and then some laughter slipped out as well. He was right. It was awkward, but no one was hurt.

'I'm Sam, by the way,' he said.

'Clare.' She shook his hand firmly.

'I take it that you're Elaine's daughter?'

She nodded.

'Nice to meet you,' he said, trying to hold her gaze, but her eyes flickered away. 'For the second – I mean *third* time. But our first meeting wasn't exactly ideal, was it? I'm sorry about that. I didn't mean to come across as rude but sometimes I can be a bit blunt. My sister keeps telling me I need to work on my social skills. I did try to apologise in the café but I don't blame you for rushing away. You must think I'm an awful person and I've no excuse other than the fact that I had a lot on my mind when I bumped into you.'

'In the café?'

'No, in the woods. I was inexcusably rude and . . .' He rubbed at the back of his neck. 'I . . . I'm just really, terribly sorry.'

'It's OK.' She shrugged and he winced inwardly, recalling exactly how blunt he had been towards her and also cringing at himself babbling away while she was observing him quietly, probably hating him more by the minute. And here she was, petite and blushing and . . . How had he not realised *exactly* how lovely she was? Shame crawled over him and he shook himself. He needed to heed Alyssa's advice and think before speaking, before acting on his impulses, because he didn't want to give the wrong impression, go around offending people when distracted by his own worries.

'Do you think you can accept my apology?'

She smiled then – a small smile but a smile nonetheless. 'I guess so.'

'Phew!' He laughed loudly, then felt even more awkward than before. What was he, Hugh Grant in a romcom? Something about Clare made him feel wrongfooted, keen to please. 'Right then, let's have a look at Goliath, shall we?' It was time to focus on doing his job, something he could feel confident about.

Half an hour later the dog had been weighed, his teeth and gums checked, his heart and lungs listened to, his abdomen, skin and coat examined, his ears and eyes checked and his microchip scanned to ensure it was still functioning.

'Everything seems to be working well at this point,' he said, as he rubbed Goliath's ears. 'But because of his age it's important to keep an eye on him and to let us know about any changes or concerns immediately.'

'Of course.' Clare nodded. 'But obviously, I don't usually live with him so I wouldn't know if he was behaving differently.'

'Does he still go after the post whenever Marcellus delivers it?'

'Yes.'

'Does he still water your mother's plants?'

'Water?' She frowned.

'Yes, you know, raise his leg and . . .'

'Oh!' She nodded. 'Yes. Sometimes. At others he's quite lazy and he just squats.'

'And when you've walked him, have you noticed anything about the way he walks? For instance, is he struggling at all? Does he seem to tire easily? That sort of thing.'

'This dog does not tire easily. I swear that in the week and a half since I arrived in Little Bramble, he has exercised me rather than the other way around.'

Sam smiled. 'He's still enjoying his walks, so that's good.' Then something occurred to him. 'Is your mother still walking him at all?'

Something passed over Clare's face, but he barely knew her and it was gone so quickly that he couldn't be certain what it was.

'She uh . . . since I got back, I've noticed some changes in Mum, and one of them is that she barely leaves the cottage anymore. She was walking him, but she said they weren't going as far as they used to.'

Sam nodded, his professional head taking over. Even though he was essentially an animal doctor, he had a lot of contact with people and, although he could be rather abrupt, he could also be very sympathetic. He was, although Alyssa might argue otherwise, a good listener, especially when someone needed to offload.

'Are you worried about her?' he asked gently.

Clare's expression changed then, as if she'd slammed an emotional door shut and she sighed. 'No, I'm sure she's fine.' Clearly this was not a woman who was about to discuss family with a stranger, and who could blame her? Not only was Sam a stranger, but he had also given her no reasons to want to entrust him with information about her mother. He had been the epitome of rudeness when they'd first met and for all she knew, he was like that most of the time.

Or perhaps she wasn't used to trusting people.

Just like him.

'Look . . .' He held out his hands. 'I don't know your mother very well, nor do I know you, but I have been in the village for over three years and I care about the animals here and being supportive of their human beings is part of that care. If there is anything you'd like to talk about, or if you have any concerns, then I'd be happy to talk them through.'

'You mean if I think Mum isn't up to looking after Goliath?' Her eyebrows rose slightly as if in challenge, her lips becoming a thin line of determination. She was strong, someone who wouldn't take any nonsense. No wonder she had given him the cold shoulder at the café.

'No! Not that at all!' He shook his head. 'I meant more from the perspective of . . . if you just wanted to have a chat to someone. I can come across as a bit of an idiot, but I do have a caring side.'

She eyed him, as if evaluating him carefully, then she inclined her head. 'Thanks. I appreciate the offer.'

But you won't take me up on it.

'Are you staying in the village long?' He winced as his voice rose on the final word.

She toyed with her bottom lip, then shrugged, a gesture he had noticed her use several times, as if she was lost for answers on more than one matter.

'I'm not sure yet. I came back because . . . well, for reasons I'd prefer not to discuss right now, but I could be here for a few weeks. I have some things I need to sort out.'

'OK. Good to know.'

Why did his heart just lift? What was it to him whether this woman stayed local or not?

'Good to know, why?' Suspicion filled her eyes and he felt his throat tighten with embarrassment.

'Because of Goliath, of course! Yes . . . Goliath will surely enjoy having you around.'

'I'm not really a dog person,' she said, then she seemed to realise she was talking to a vet. 'I mean, I like Goliath, don't get me wrong, it's just that I've never had a dog before and it's taking some getting used to.'

'It does, but I promise you that it's worth it. Dogs are the best friends we can have.'

'More loyal than humans?'

'Definitely.'

'Goliath *is* kind of growing on me.' Colour filled her cheeks as she peered at him from behind dark lashes. 'He seems to be tuning into my moods.' She rubbed the dog's head and he turned to her and sniffed her palm.

'He cares about you.' Sam nodded.

'Really?'

'He wouldn't be looking at you like that if he didn't.'

They stood there for a moment in silence, gazing at Goliath, who was gazing up at Clare, then she seemed to gather herself.

'I guess I'd better go and pay then?'

'I'll show you out.'

'There's no need.'

'Oh . . .' He opened the door and held it for her. 'I forgot to say that there's no charge for today because Elaine pays into a plan for Goliath.'

'That's great, thanks.'

She smiled at him, then walked Goliath out of the reception area and onto the street. Sam went over to the reception desk to check who his next client was, but he couldn't help turning to look out of the front window to watch Clare walking away.

She was staying in Little Bramble for a few weeks, and for some reason that made him feel a little bit better about everything.

※

Clare strolled away from Goliath's appointment feeling more than a little bit strange. In fact, she felt kind of mixed up, unsure about exactly what she was feeling and whether or not she liked it.

Sam Wilson had turned out to be quite pleasant. His apology had seemed genuine and she respected him for it. Admitting to being wrong about something took courage and Sam had seemed keen to let her know that he was sorry for being so rude in the woods. He was also wonderful with Goliath and actually rather kind towards her, which she hadn't been expecting at all, especially when she'd nearly pulled his trousers down. That could have annoyed him, but instead he seemed to find it amusing. Her cheeks warmed at the thought of how it must have looked. Bloody Goliath pulling on his lead just because he heard a cat yowl.

She wrapped the lead around her wrist and held it tight, trying to stay alert in case he spotted something and decided to run again. There might not be a pair of chinos attached to a tall, handsome man around to break her fall next time.

Handsome?

Now she thought about it, when Sam wasn't angry, he was quite attractive. Not that she was in a place to be noticing if men were good-looking or not, of course.

The site of the old village hall came into view and she decided to go and take a look. She could walk the long way around the village with Goliath and take in some of the sites she hadn't seen since her return. The land where the hall had stood for over sixty years had been levelled and cordoned off with a small picket fence, almost as if it was a site of a great tragedy. Surely it was premium land and would fetch a good price? Ah, it was owned by a local family and would have to be sold by them, preferably with the approval of the locals. Perhaps they were waiting for a while for things to settle. After all, the old village hall had burnt down almost two years ago and it had taken a while to clear the land and to get the insurance money to build the new one, which sat on the opposite side of the road.

Clare looked both ways then crossed over, Goliath trotting at her side as if he was a show dog at Crufts (he obviously knew she had more treats in her pocket) and not the lumbering, overexcited oaf he had shown he could be. She passed the new hall, admiring its pale-blue exterior, the large windows complete with roller blinds – some currently pulled down – and the Velux roof windows that would let in a lot of natural light. It reminded her of a Scandinavian building, all clean lines and so very different from the old hall. That had been built over sixty years ago then extended, had small circular windows in the upper rooms and sash windows that jammed on hot days. That hall had been old, had been in need of repairs and decorating, but it had been a warm place, the centre of the village for a very long time.

Clare's mum had loved that hall and so had her dad. It had been the place where many people had held wedding receptions, birthday parties and wakes, where there had been jumble sales and book clubs and exercise classes and, of course, the annual Christmas show. Those shows had sold out every year and Clare knew that they had been the highlight of her mum's year, the time when she got to forget that she was a hardworking teacher, driven into the ground by paperwork and deadlines, and had been able to let her own theatrical talents shine, both on and off stage.

This new hall looked very pleasant and no doubt had potential, but Clare knew that it wouldn't have the plaques on the walls that were dedicated to locals such as her father. It wouldn't have walls covered in photographs of local celebrations and village shows, of her mum and dad in the early days of their marriage when they had been big-haired and starry-eyed, when they had been devoted to each other and excited about their future together. Her parents had starred in the shows together, had sung and danced and performed, both of them confident, larger than life, happy to be a part of the community. And now that was all gone. No wonder her mum was struggling.

The old village hall had meant so much to so many people, not just Clare's mum, and she could understand how hard the community must have felt its loss. Being back for just over a week and a half, Clare could feel that the village was different. The locals were still warm and friendly, but it was as if the heart, the hub, of this pretty little village had gone.

And with it, Elaine had lost her joie de vivre.

How many others had too? But at least they might still have husbands and wives, lovers and family member nearby. Elaine was, apart from Goliath, alone, and she had clearly been sinking with each week, each month that passed. It broke Clare's heart to think of her mum suffering. She wanted her to be happy, wanted to know that when she did leave Little Bramble again, that Elaine would have a full and enjoyable life. In fact, until Clare was certain that Elaine was OK, she realised she would be unable to leave.

She would think about the hall situation and see if she could come up with a plan. There must be a way to restore the sense of energy her mum had always had, a way to give her something back that would make her happy once again.

Clare left the hall then and headed for home, Goliath at her side, the weak October sunshine warming her in spite of the chill in the air. Little Bramble was getting under her skin in more ways than one and she was starting to think that she might stay for more than just a few weeks.

Chapter 10

'I am so relieved that everything's OK with Goliath,' Elaine said as she handed Clare a mug of hot chocolate, then placed her own on a side table.

'Me too.' Clare pulled the soft blanket she'd found in the airing cupboard over her legs, then sipped her hot chocolate. The lounge was warm and smelt of rosemary and pine from the twigs and pine cones that her mum had put on the fire. They crackled in the grate and tiny sparks flew up the chimney, pinpricks of red and gold that flashed and popped. Goliath was stretched out on the hearthrug, his favourite spot, snoring gently, mouth vibrating with each exhalation. There was something hypnotic and incredibly soothing about the regular sound and it was making Clare feel very relaxed.

After returning from the vets' she had decided to take a nap as she had no other commitments that day – or any day soon – and was feeling quite emotionally drained. An afternoon nap was a luxury and one she really appreciated being able to enjoy. As she had slipped from consciousness, her thoughts had hopped from her concerns about her mum, to the village hall, to Goliath and then to the handsome vet, Sam, who had turned out to be not such a horrid person after all.

When she'd woken, she'd come downstairs and found her mum knitting, so Clare had made them dinner – simple baked potatoes with cheese and beans, the ultimate comfort food for her. After she'd filled the dishwasher, she'd taken a shower, then put her pyjamas straight on and come through to the lounge, where the fire had been lit and the lamps cast a warm golden glow in the corners of the room. The TV was on, some soap opera flickering across the screen, the volume down low, so that the clicking of her mum's knitting needles, the crackling of the fire and Goliath's snoring were the main sounds. When her mum had offered her a hot chocolate, Clare's mouth had watered. What else could make such a lovely evening more perfect?

Clare's mind was busy, occupied with plans and ideas, and she knew that it would help if she let her subconscious work it all through. As she sipped the delicious drink, she thought about the village halls – old and new – and about the differences between them, about her mum and dad and how they had enjoyed treading the wooden boards of the stage together and how happy they had been.

'Mum, where are the photo albums?'

Elaine looked up from her knitting. 'Oh, I haven't looked at them in ages, but they should still be in the chest behind you. Unless they've grown legs and walked away, that is.'

Elaine gave a small laugh at her own joke and Clare smiled in response, then she nodded. She'd hoped they would still be there, just as they always had been.

She slid her legs out from under the blanket and walked around the sofa, then moved the tray of small china containers that her mum had collected over the years and the tiger doorstop (that for some reason sat there instead of holding a door open) from the lid, then pushed it open. The aromas of lavender, chamomile and spice floated into the air, reminding her of soap, curry and her childhood all at once. The chest had belonged to her paternal grandmother and when her parents had married, she'd given it to them as a housewarming gift. Apparently, it was very old, a valuable antique, and as a child, Clare had loved to look inside it, often included it in her games, pretending she was on a medieval ship and that the chest contained many treasures. And it did contain treasure, but of the sentimental kind.

Family photographs, birth, death and marriage certificates, school reports, love letters (her parents to each other, not that she'd read them, but they were there, tied with red ribbons), her Christening gown and shawl, her grandmother's silk wedding gloves and more. Memories overwhelmed Clare as she gazed at the contents, the years of life and love swimming before her eyes, the physical evidence that people she'd loved and lost had existed, that she hadn't imagined them.

She blinked hard and sniffed. What was it with the senses and nostalgia? She'd been catapulted back to her childhood by the familiar aromas and experienced myriad emotions as she looked at things she'd seen many times before. What would happen to these things in the future? She shuddered. That was not something she even wanted to consider, but one day, she might have to.

But not now . . .

'There they are.' She reached for the top photo album and pulled it out, then sat back and rested it on her lap. It was filled with pictures of Kyle, from not long after his birth to more recently when he'd turned eighteen. For some of the photographs, her mum had been present, but others had been sent by Clare or Kyle himself, enclosed in birthday or Mother's Day cards. Clare flicked through the album, enjoying seeing her beautiful boy's condensed journey from babyhood to adulthood, although it was missing more recent photographs, so perhaps she had been remiss and forgotten to send them, bound up as she was in her own problems, or perhaps her mum had been too distracted to place them inside.

She put the album down and reached for the next one. It was older, the plastic cover wrinkled as if someone had rested a hot mug on its surface, the red paisley print underneath hinting at its seventies origins. On the cover, her mum had, long ago, cut the letters for *Our Family* out of silver foil then glued them to the cover. As Clare carefully opened the front cover, the sweet musky smell of old paper, a bit like stale coffee and cocoa, rose to greet her nostrils and she was again hit by waves of emotion.

As a child she had looked through this album practically every day, fascinated by the images of her parents with their old-fashioned haircuts and clothes, her mum's beehive and green polyester mini dress and her dad's brown bell-bottom trousers, paired with a rusty orange waistcoat over a blue and white striped shirt with an enormous collar. Her dad's face was almost swallowed up by his thick sideburns and handlebar moustache and she ran a finger over his face, wishing she could hold him again, hug him tight and smell his woody cologne just one more time.

'Clare? Bring them here and we can look together.'

'OK.'

She grabbed two more albums and carried them to her mum and sat next to her. It had been many years since they'd looked at photos together and Elaine had rarely displayed any kind of sentimentality, but even so it would be nice to share these memories, to reminisce and, hopefully, make her mum smile again.

An hour passed with them looking at photographs, pausing after each one so Elaine could tell Clare who it was of, if she didn't remember, and when it was taken. There were photographs in the garden, in the cottage and on holidays in locations like West Wales, Scotland and Cornwall. Clare's face changed from chubby toddler to plump ten-year-old to awkward teen, but always there was a smile and a sense of belonging to a family unit. Even though her mum could sometimes border on cold, Clare had known she was loved, and whenever her mum's attitude had upset her, her dad had been there to smooth it over and provide her with the security she needed. It was as if Elaine had felt she needed to be tough on her daughter . . . Perhaps that was her way of trying to get Clare to avoid making mistakes. Although Clare didn't believe her mum was ever knowingly unkind, she could be quite unnecessarily blunt.

As well as photographs of Clare, there were ones of the village, of her parents' friends and the shows at the village hall. It was in these photographs that she saw a difference in the mum Elaine had been in family life. Gone was the reserved teacher smile, the guarded look in her eyes, and instead there was a glow to her cheeks and a shine to her gaze. She came alive when she was acting, singing and directing. Clare knew that feeling from being a mum to Kyle; he had been her world, her

116

focus, her joy since the day he was born, but she also knew that the sense of loss she had experienced since he'd flown the nest was down to the fact that she didn't have much else in her life to focus on. She had enjoyed her time at the library, had looked forward to each day there and found arranging events such as author appearances and book clubs exciting, but she wasn't sure that she'd ever had the same enthusiasm for those things that her mum had had for her shows. And now that Clare had lost her job, was a divorcee, and her son was grown and someone else was living in her home, what did she have left? She was lost, adrift, bordering on bereft. Did her mum feel like that too since she'd lost the village hall and her drama society? In life, people have different anchors, and if they lose them, they drift as if on open seas.

There were so many ways in which Clare and her mum were not alike and yet, here, today, they shared a common condition. They both needed something else in their lives to feel fulfilled, to bring them out of the ruts they had fallen into. Was there a way of combining their needs to reach a common goal?

'And look at this one.' Elaine pointed at a photograph and Clare peered at it, taking in the festively decorated stage, the casts' costumes in red and green, and the tinsel draped around their necks, pinned to their hats, wrapped around their ankles. They beamed at the camera, arms around one another's shoulders, cheeks rosy, eyes filled with joy. And at the centre of it all was Elaine, wearing a damson dress made of crushed velvet, her hair pulled back from her face with a gold headband, her face the most beautiful Clare had ever seen it.

'A Christmas show?' Clare asked.

'Yes. From two years ago.'

'So quite a while after Dad –'

'Yes.' Her mum nodded, her lips curving upwards. 'But that evening, as with every show, I felt happy. I lost myself in preparation for the show for weeks, rehearsing with the cast, decorating the hall, selling tickets, making costumes. I got involved in every way I could and it was bliss.'

'And since the old hall was lost you haven't had that sense of fulfilment from anything else?'

Her mum closed the photo album softly and sighed. 'I miss it . . .'

'I'm sorry, Mum.'

Her mum reached out and covered Clare's hand with hers. 'It's certainly not your fault, Clare, and you've your own issues to deal with.'

'Life can be tough, can't it?'

'Very.' Her mum nodded. 'But it can also be wonderful. Good times come and good times go. People come and people go. At the end of the day, we have to rely on ourselves to keep going through the good and bad. But sometimes . . . sometimes it's just harder than others.'

Clare turned her hand and squeezed her mum's fingers.

'It'll get better, Mum.'

Elaine smiled at her then, but it was a sad smile and it didn't reach her eyes. Oh, there had to be a way to give Elaine back what she'd lost, a way to make the new village hall become what the old one had meant for her mum and for the community.

Christmas was just around the corner, but far enough away to put a plan into action. It was worth a shot. Anything was worth a shot if it brought the joy Clare had seen in that photo back to her mum's eyes.

❋

Sam placed the oblong dish on the kitchen table, then removed the oven gloves and went to the fridge to get the salad he'd prepared while the fish pie was cooking. Scout was sniffing around the kitchen, clearly drawn in by the delicious aroma. Sam smiled at her. He'd been lucky with Scout because she'd always been well behaved, had never given him any grief, except perhaps for when she was a pup and had a few accidents indoors. He'd heard plenty of stories over the years about dogs that had jumped onto tables and stolen whole roasted chickens, or freshly baked loaves of bread, that had torn apart their new beds or dug giant holes in the lawn. There were no good or bad dogs, just dogs, and each one was as unique as its experiences and its start in the world; just like humans.

The back door opened and Alyssa came in with a gust of cold air and a waft of perfume. She sniffed loudly.

'Mmm . . . What's for dinner?'

'Fish pie.'

'Did you put cheese on top?'

'And breadcrumbs, then grilled it to perfection.' He gestured at the table. 'If Mademoiselle would like to take her place, I'll get the wine.'

'Wonderful.'

Alyssa wheeled her chair across to the table, then tucked in neatly. Sam watched her for a moment, admiring her easy smile and hearty appetite. There had been a time when he'd thought she'd never smile again, when she'd barely been able to swallow a bite of toast, when he'd thought he'd lost her forever. But ten years on, after several surgeries and rounds of physio, sleepless nights and many tears, she was more like the happy young woman she'd been before that terrible day. And yet she was different: stronger, more resilient than he remembered her being before the accident. She was incredible.

He opened the fridge and reached for the bottle of sauvignon blanc. Back at the table he poured some into two glasses.

'Do you want anything else with it?' he asked.

'No, this is fab. Now sit down.' She tapped the table. 'Let's eat!'

He sat down, sipping his wine while Alyssa scooped up steaming portions of pie and set them on their plates. Sam helped himself to salad, then handed the bowl to Alyssa.

'So, how was your first day?'

Alyssa nodded while pointing at her mouth, her way of letting him know she'd tell him when she'd finished chewing.

'Just brilliant! I had so much fun,' she eventually said.

'Glad to hear it. What did you do?'

'I learnt all about safety practices and how to clean and sterilise the equipment and how to take bookings and payments.'

'Right.' He took a drink from his glass.

'And I watched some of the tattooists inking people and –'

'Inking?'

'Tattooing.'

'OK.'

'And it was all really impressive.'

'Good.' He nodded. 'When do *you* start inking people?'

'Oh, not for ages. I'm there to learn through observation. And I got this.' She shrugged out of the loose black cardigan she was wearing and his stomach sank as he saw the cling film wrapped around her left wrist. She peeled away the medical tape holding it in place and held out her arm.

Sam took a deep breath, then peered at it.

'It's a dragonfly.'

'Yes! Isn't it beautiful?'

He bit the inside of his cheek to stop himself jumping to respond.

'It's . . . certainly a dragonfly.'

'Sam!' She rolled her eyeballs. 'Get over it, please. I'm thirty-four, I have a new job, I'm entitled to get some ink if I want to.'

'I just don't see why you'd put yourself through that after everything else you've been through.'

She slammed her fork down on the table. 'Will you just not do this today? Please, Sam, for once can we not talk about everything I've been through and see who I am *now*?'

Sam winced. 'I'm sorry. I just hate the thought of you having more needles in you, hate the thought of you being hurt in any way. I mean, didn't it hurt?'

She shrugged. 'A bit, but not anything I couldn't handle. And let's be honest, it was nothing compared to what I've experienced in my life.'

'I know. But surely that didn't exactly tickle?'

'In a way it did. It was like a stinging tickle and some areas were worse than others, but you know what? I love it. I love that I *chose* to have it done and this time having a needle pierce my skin was my choice and not because I *needed* to have it done.'

Sam did understand what she meant. She'd spent so long with her life on hold, having blood taken, steroid injections, surgery to try to make her more comfortable, and this time it had been her choice to have something done to her body.

'I get what you're saying, Alyssa, and I'm sorry if I seemed disapproving in any way but I care about you so much and would have saved you every single thing you went through if I'd had the chance.'

'I know, Sam, I really do. But that's all behind us now. I have a new job that I think I'm going to love. I have a new tattoo that is just so pretty and for me it symbolises transformation, independence, wisdom and growth. Sam, life lies ahead of us, not behind.' She raised her glass. 'Here's to living without fear and hesitation and not just existing.'

He tapped his glass against hers then drank.

'To living.'

It sounded like a wonderful idea; he just wasn't sure how it would work in reality.

❄

Clare rolled over in bed and opened her eyes. The room was dark apart from a weak grey light that seeped through the gap in the curtains so she guessed it was early morning. So why had she woken?

Then she realised: somewhere there was banging. Someone or something was banging. She pushed the duvet back and went to the window, then opened the curtains. The shadowy garden appeared eerie, as if she was living inside a negative from an old-fashioned camera.

More knocking! Frantic now.

Opening her window, she leaned out.

Someone was hammering on the front door.

'Who are you and what do you want?' she called out, and the person stepped backwards and peered upwards.

'Mum?' He pushed the hood from his head and in the pale light, his face was white, his eyes black holes.

'Kyle?'

'Let me in, please, Mum. I *need* you!'

Her heart fractured at the desperation in his tone. It was her baby boy and he'd come to her. At a very strange time and he sounded upset, but he needed her.

'I'll be right down.'

'Hurry up, Mum, *please*, because the VERY worst thing has happened!'

Chapter 11

Clare grabbed her dressing gown and threw it on as she hurried down the stairs towards the front door, trying not to trip over her own feet in her haste.

What on earth had happened to Kyle? What could *the VERY worst thing* be? Her heart raced as she ran to him, her maternal instincts screaming at her to be at his side already.

The kitchen door was open and she wondered where Goliath was and why he hadn't rushed to greet their visitor, but as she passed the lounge, she heard him snoring. Elaine must have left him there overnight so he could sleep by the fire. Perhaps he sensed that Kyle didn't have any post with him, so it wasn't worth rushing into the hallway.

Clare opened the front door, then flung her arms wide and her son dashed into her embrace.

'Mum! Oh, Mum!'

She held him tight while he cried, his tears trickling down her neck and onto her dressing gown as she stroked his hair. Kyle was a good bit taller than she was, but she could reach his head as he was bending forwards to hug her.

'Why don't you come in, darling, and let me make you a drink?' she asked and felt him nod against her shoulder. 'It's very cold and you must be in need of something warm.'

'M-my things are in my c-car.'

Things? Had he come to stay?

'Where is your car?'

'Out on the road.'

'It'll be fine as long as it's locked. It's very quiet around here. We can get them later.'

'O-OK.' He sniffed, trying to be brave, reminding her of the little boy he had once been. Love for him welled in her chest, overwhelming, all-encompassing. Even though he was officially, legally, an adult, she would do anything for her baby.

She closed the door and led him into the lounge, her heart skipping with his every sniff.

'You sit down while I build up the fire then I'll make some tea.'

He nodded and slumped onto the sofa, kicked off his trainers and dragged the throw over himself. Clare turned to the fire and stepped over Goliath, who opened one eye and then closed it again. Once she'd thrown some logs on the fire and stirred the embers into flames, she set the fireguard in place and returned to Kyle's side.

'I'll make some tea then we can talk. Are you hungry?'

He shook his head, his lower lip trembling. 'I c-couldn't eat a thing.'

'Not even a runny boiled egg with soldiers?' She couldn't help herself. When he'd been a little boy this meal had always been her way of tempting him to eat.

'Oh . . . OK then.' He nodded, his eyes downcast, his dark hair ruffled as if he'd been dragging his fingers through it all night. 'But just two eggs and three pieces of toast with plenty of butter and a pinch of salt on the side.'

'Of course.' She squeezed Kyle's shoulder, then went through to the kitchen, working quickly so she could get back to him and find out what had happened. She knew that a warm drink would help, and that food was a good idea if she wanted to get any sense out of him. Kyle with low blood sugar could be as incoherent as a toddler having a tantrum.

When she'd put the food and two mugs of tea on a tray, she carried them through to the lounge and found Kyle on the sofa, his legs now tucked under him, Goliath next to him with his head on Kyle's shoulder. It was the sweetest sight.

'He remembers you, darling,' she said, trying to work out how long it had been since Kyle last visited Little Bramble. She handed him the tray then took her own mug of tea from it and placed it on the side table before sitting on the sofa her mum usually occupied. It felt strange, like sitting in the head teacher's chair.

'I haven't seen him in about two years,' Kyle said, meeting her gaze. 'That's awful isn't it, Mum? I haven't seen Nanna in that long, apart from that day when she met me in Bath just before the summer.'

'She met you in Bath?'

'She was on one of those OAP trips, a coach thing, and because she was in Bath, she rang me and asked to meet for a cuppa.'

'I didn't know that.' Clare felt a bit hurt that she hadn't known, but then why would she? They didn't have to tell her everything. What was a positive here was that her mum had been out and about, even if it was a few months ago. 'But look at how Goliath's gazing at you.'

Kyle turned his head slightly and laughed. 'He's a lovely dog. I think he knows I'm upset.'

'Yes, love, and about that . . .' She let the not-quite-a-question hang in the air, hoping that Kyle would feel ready to explain why he was so distressed.

He sipped his tea, then dipped his soldiers into the eggs, exploding the runny yoke so it ran over the edge of the shells like lava from a volcano, as Clare tried to stay patient and drink her tea. Even when Kyle shared his breakfast with Goliath, she bit her tongue and took deep breaths. Kyle could never be rushed into anything and she knew well enough that he needed to eat before talking. When he finally wiped his mouth and hands on the piece of kitchen roll she'd put on the tray, then drained his tea, she almost cheered.

'OK, Mum, firstly I'm sorry for turning up unannounced like this and for dragging you out of bed.'

'Don't worry about that, Kyle, and you are always welcome wherever I am. I know this is Nanna's home but for now it's mine too. Besides which, Nanna will be delighted to see you. So . . .' She put her empty mug on the side table and waited.

'You know how well Rick and I were getting on?'

Clare nodded. Rick Brody was Kyle's boyfriend of eleven months. He was the same age as Kyle and they'd met in Bath, where they were studying performing arts and working part-time as baristas. Rick was blond, blue-eyed, thin as a lath and, from what Clare could remember of him (she'd only met him a handful of times because he found parents tedious) very stylish. He shopped for vintage items in charity shops and loved combining colours, so whenever he entered a room, he was sure to be noticed, often like a scarlet macaw. She'd found him pleasant enough, in spite of his aversion to parents, and Kyle had been besotted with him, so she'd done her best to accept him as part of the family and to encourage Jason to do the same.

'I thought you two were quite serious?'

She ran her gaze over Kyle's dark hair, his shadow of stubble that still hadn't really spread from his upper lip or chin, leaving gaps whenever he had tried to grow a beard. His eyes were the same shade of green as hers but in the lounge, lit only by the fire and one lamp, they seemed much darker.

'We were, at least until I caught him shagging that bloody area manager.'

'Oh . . .' She shook her head. 'I'm so sorry, Kyle.'

'That's OK, Mum. It was weeks ago.'

Weeks?

'But you didn't tell me?'

He looked up. 'Didn't I? Gosh, Mum, I really thought I had.'

'It's OK as long as you're OK. But you still seem upset. That's understandable, love, a relationship breaking up is a big deal –'

'No, no, Mum. See, after I caught them in the stockroom, I told him it was over. *SO* over!' He shuddered. 'No way was I putting up with cheating.'

'OK, then, so why are you so sad?'

He rubbed Goliath's head and the dog grunted in appreciation.

'See, I fell in love with Lydia.'

'Lydia?' Clare tried to keep the surprise from her tone and her face, but last thing she'd known, Kyle and Rick had been discussing their life together after university and now there was someone else. For both of them.

'Oh, she's gorgeous, Mum, and she fixed my broken heart after that bloody cheating Rick. In fact, Mum, you'd just love her. Well, you would have loved her. But the . . . the utter bitch has . . .' His eyes filled with tears and he fanned his face with his free hand, the other one still caressing Goliath.

'Has she cheated too?'

He shook his head. 'She said she thinks I'm too young.'

'How old is Lydia?'

'Twenty-six.'

'And you two dated?'

He nodded. 'For a few weeks but now she doesn't want me . . . but I *LOVE* her!'

'Her?' Elaine appeared in the doorway, her face scrunched up in confusion, her hair doing its best impression of an upturned brush. 'I thought you were gay, Kyle.'

'Nanna!' He held out his arms and she hurried towards him. While they hugged, Clare picked up her mug and Kyle's tray.

'I'll make some more tea while you explain to Nanna why you're here.'

Clare left the lounge, wanting to give herself a chance to think about what Kyle had said. She knew he was a gentle young man and that he wore his heart on his sleeve, but to fall in and out of love so easily? Well, it worried her. He really had seemed to be deeply in love with Rick and now there was a woman instead? Or there had been a woman but she had decided he was too young, after sleeping with him, it seemed. The phrase *young people of today* flashed through her mind and she shook it away. Was she really at that stage of life where she found the younger generation's behaviour confusing? Not really, she realised, she was just confused by Kyle's ability to transfer his affection from one person to another within such short spaces of time.

The thought that it could be because he was from a broken home made her heart sink, but then her common sense remonstrated that Kyle had been an adult when her marriage had ended, so for most of his life he'd had parents who lived together. It was habit for her to blame herself, but in this case she suspected it had more to do with Kyle's libido and choice of partners than anything she or Jason had done.

When she'd made three mugs of tea, she went back through to the lounge. Kyle was flanked now by Goliath and Elaine, the blanket covering the three of them, and it was a heart-warming sight. Her mum had never been this affectionate with her, but when it came to Kyle she was far more tactile. Perhaps it was a grandmother-grandson thing; or maybe it was because something had affected Elaine's ability to love Clare in that way. Whatever it was, she was glad right now that her mum could love Kyle as she did. She popped another log on the fire then sat back and sipped her tea.

'Tell me again, Kyle, why you were in love with a woman. I've always told people that my grandson is gay and I'm quite confused. Does that mean you're a bisexual?' Elaine tilted her head as she waited for an answer.

Kyle sighed and pulled a face at Clare.

'I'm not *gay*, Nanna, or even bisexual – I'm pansexual.'

'Pansexual?' Elaine asked, her lips pursing together. 'That's a new one for me.'

'I thought I was gay initially, then I thought I must be bisexual, but then I realised it's got nothing to do with gender at all. I just find myself attracted to the person.'

'Right.' Elaine was nodding and smiling, clearly pleased with learning something new.

They sipped their tea in silence for a bit then Clare asked, 'So is it definitely over between you and Lydia?'

Kyle's lower lip jutted out and he looked as if he was five years old again.

'Yes. She said she needs a mature man, not a . . . a boy!'

He started sobbing and Elaine pulled him into her arms, whispering platitudes and stroking his messy hair. Clare watched them, filled with admiration for her mum for being so understanding about this new revelation and for her son, a young man who loved openly, loved people for who they were without any form of prejudice, and who wasn't afraid to love. To be able to make yourself vulnerable enough to care about someone was incredible and Clare doubted that she'd ever be able to do it again. She had committed herself to Jason, had worked hard over the years to stay true to him and their relationship and look what had happened. She couldn't imagine feeling that way again, ever wanting to open herself up to the possibility of hurt. It was a big ask and she felt she was at the stage of her life now where it was too much, where the risk was too high. She hoped her son wouldn't feel the same, that he would pick himself up, dust himself off and find love again.

'Can I stay here for a while, Nanna?' Kyle took the tissue Elaine offered him and blew his nose loudly. 'I don't want to go back to Bath.'

'What?' Clare jumped to her feet. 'You can't quit now, Kyle. You're almost there.'

'Mum, I have practically a full year left and I just can't face it. I want to defer for a year.'

'Oh, Kyle, but it'll be harder to go back.'

'Mum, I know what I want.' He met her eyes and she saw in his, despite the tears, a steely determination that was all too familiar. Her son might be gentle, he might fall in love easily, he might be the sweetest man she'd ever met, but he was no pushover and when he made up his mind about something, that was how it was going to be.

'Of course,' she said, offering him what she hoped was a reassuring smile. 'You know best. Just please promise me that you'll take a few days to think about it. Let the dust settle.'

'That sounds like a good idea, Kyle,' Elaine said, 'Your mum's right.'

Clare swallowed her surprise. Her mum was backing her up?

'I'll think about it.' Kyle nodded.

'But you are welcome to stay for as long as you like,' Elaine said. 'We can make up one of the spare rooms for you, make it all comfy and cosy.'

Kyle's eyes lit up and Clare's heart swelled. He wanted to be here with them and that was fine with her. Better than fine, actually. For a few days, weeks or possibly longer, she would have the chance to spend time with her mum and her son.

'We could even have an old-fashioned family Christmas,' she said, enthusiasm taking hold of her and sparking an unfamiliar feeling in her belly.

Was that excitement? She hadn't felt excited about anything in what felt like a very long time.

'That would be lovely!' Her mum grinned. 'We can get a real tree and get Goliath one of those little hats and . . . Oh!'

Clare smiled at Kyle as Elaine covered her face, clearly embarrassed that she'd actually become a bit emotional. It was as if Kyle's arrival had brought something they had been missing and clearly, it seemed, needed.

'That sounds wonderful, Nanna.' Kyle clapped his hands. 'I'm already excited.'

Sinking back onto the sofa, Clare watched the flames in the hearth, sipped her tea and listened to her son and her mum as they chatted about what they'd like to eat for Christmas breakfast, then dinner, about their favourite brands of champagne, and about whether bread sauce was actually any good.

A feeling washed over her, soothing the excitement and the worries about Kyle, gently reminding her that she was sleepy and that she could drift off if she just closed her eyes.

It was, she realised, contentment. She was experiencing a moment of true contentment and really, really enjoying it.

Chapter 12

'What'll you have?' Jenny asked.

'Um, I'm not sure really. What are you having?' The aromas of beer and chips met Clare's nose, along with something garlicky. The Red Squirrel offered basic pub meals and had a restaurant at the rear with a Michelin-starred chef.

'A gin and tonic.'

'I'll have the same then, thanks.' Clare nodded.

'Why don't you go and find us a table?'

Clare looked around the bar of the village pub. It was Friday evening and quite busy, so there weren't many spare seats, but she spotted a table for two in the corner near the fire. She weaved through the tables until she reached it, then she removed her coat and scarf, draped them over the back of the chair and sat down.

When Jenny had sent her a text the day before asking if she fancied going for a drink, Clare had paused before replying. It wasn't that she didn't want to see Jenny again, but she felt a bit nervous about the thought of going out in public for a drink. It had been quite some time since she'd been to The Red and the last time she'd been there she'd been married with a young son. Her life and circumstances were very different now and something had fluttered in her belly as she'd got ready to come. It was a mixture of anxiety and anticipation. Why, she wasn't sure, because it wasn't as if she and Jenny were going out 'on the pull' as they'd called it when they were younger. (Not that Jenny had ever been looking for herself because she'd been devoted to Martin even as a teenager.) But even so, she was a single woman now and she wasn't sure how she felt about that. There was a certain vulnerability to it that hadn't been there before she married Jason, as if, now that she was single, she no longer had that security.

When Jenny turned around at the bar, Clare waved at her. Jenny smiled, then made her way over. When she reached the table, she set down two glasses filled with clear liquid, ice and slices of lemon.

'I figured you'd want ice and a slice. I also got something for us to nibble.' She pulled two packets of crisps and a bag of roasted nuts from her bag.

'Great, thanks.'

'I don't know what's wrong with me but I'm constantly starving at the moment.' Jenny ran her hands through her hair. 'I'm thinking that it could be the big M.' She grimaced.

'The big M?' Clare frowned.

'Yes, you know . . .' Jenny lowered her voice '. . . the menopause.'

'Oh!' Clare laughed. 'That bloody thing.'

'Exactly.'

'Does it increase your appetite then?' Clare had been trying to forget about the fact that she had been experiencing some changes in her own body. Yes, there had been some weight gain, but she'd put that down to comfort eating. Anyway, walking Goliath was having a positive effect on her waistline and she hoped it would continue to do so.

'It can do.' Jenny raised her eyebrows. 'Well, it can make you put on weight, anyway, and I'm certainly experiencing that.' She opened her black waterfall cardigan to reveal a black T-shirt and skinny jeans.

'Jenny, you're like a stick.' Clare shook her head.

'Look at this.' Jenny glanced around them, then raised the bottom of her T-shirt to reveal a small belly. 'I've not had a pot like this since after the twins were born. It's appeared all of a sudden and I am not amused. Martin thinks it's really funny.'

'Your belly is tiny and actually quite cute, Jenny. I wish mine was that small.' Clare ran a hand self-consciously over her own stomach, feeling the curve beneath the high-waisted leggings she'd put on under her thigh-length grey wool tunic. With the grey knee-high boots she'd purchased in the January sales last year, she'd felt that she looked casual but smart enough for an evening at the local pub.

'You look amazing, Clare. Divorce really agrees with you.' Jenny winced but Clare smiled. Trust Jenny to put a positive spin on the end of her marriage, but then, as a hairstylist who worked with people all day and heard their problems, she was used to counselling them and trying to make them feel better about their lives. 'Sorry, honey, I didn't mean to say that. Anyway, you do look fab.'

'It's fine.' Clare smiled, then took a gulp of her drink. Delicious!

Jenny tore open one of the bags of crisps and started munching. She gestured at the open bag, but Clare shook her head. 'I'm all right at the moment, thanks.'

'Have you had any menopausal symptoms?' Jenny asked in between crisps.

'I put on some weight but think it was down to comfort eating. I do get a bit warm sometimes, especially at night, but it only really happens a few times a month.'

'Horrid, isn't it?' Jenny cocked an eyebrow. 'We go through all those years of periods, then we get lumbered with the big M. Not bloody fair.'

'Not at all.'

Clare took another sip of her gin and tonic and sat back in her chair smiling. This was nice. They might be talking about things she'd always thought only happened when women got older, but it was just lovely to spend time with Jenny. She had missed this type of friendship. She'd had female friends over the years, of course, but none of them as close as she and Jenny had been and although it had been years since they'd spent any time together, they seemed to be as close as ever. The thought warmed her right through and she sent out a silent thank you to Jason for bringing this friendship back to her. He might have caused it inadvertently, but if he hadn't decided to make some changes then Clare wouldn't have come back to Little Bramble and she wouldn't have bumped into Jenny.

'Jenny, do you remember what we were like as teenagers?'

'Do I ever?' Jenny giggled. 'We used to have so much fun, didn't we?'

'I'm sure that getting ready to go out was as much fun as actually being out.'

They smiled at each other, remembering how things used to be.

'We used to swap outfits, do each other's hair and makeup, down as much MD20/20 or alcoholic lemonade as we could get our hands on.' Clare shivered.

'Never as much fun coming back up though, was it?'

Clare shook her head. 'Like that time when we went out and drank too many of those blue shots, then you threw up all over your mum's cream sheepskin rug?'

Jenny rolled her eyes. 'She went mad! The stains would not come out. I blamed the dog, said it had got an ice pop out of the freezer and chewed it up.'

'She didn't really buy that, though, did she?'

'Who knows?' Jenny chuckled. 'It seems like a hundred years ago now.'

'Time flies.'

Jenny raised her glass and held it out. 'Cheers.'

'Cheers.'

'Ew!' Jenny stuck out her tongue. 'Does your drink taste funny?'

Clare shook her head. 'It's really nice actually.'

'There's something wrong with mine. I think I'll go and get a lemonade instead. I really fancy some citrus right now, you know, I could actually bury my head in a basket of lemons and just sniff . . .' Jenny's jaw dropped, and she covered her face with her hands. 'Oh noooo . . . noooo, it can't be that.'

Concern filled Clare. 'What's wrong, Jen?'

'Nothing.' Jenny pressed her lips together and pulled her purse from her bag. 'I'll just go and get a lemonade. Same again?'

'It's my round.' Clare stood up. She wanted to ask Jenny what was wrong but could see that her friend wasn't ready to share just yet. 'I'll get it. Do you want ice and lemon?'

'Just lemon, thanks. Lots of lemon.'

Clare nodded, then grabbed her purse and went to the bar. The gentle hum of conversation in the pub was interspersed with the clinking of glasses and the pinging of the till. When the barmaid had finished serving a very tall man with a mane of wavy blond hair and a big beard, Clare asked for a lemonade with extra slices of lemon and a gin and tonic.

After she'd been served, she turned to head back to the tables and her breath caught in her throat, because sitting at the table where the tall blond man was now was the vet. And he was smiling at her, his brown eyes warm with recognition.

'I thought it was you,' he said as he stood up, holding her gaze with an intensity that made her lightheaded.

'Oh . . . hi.' As heat flooded Clare's cheeks like boiling hot water, she tried to will it away. Why was she blushing like a teenager around this man? Her eyes ran over him, as if she'd lost control over them, taking in the white T-shirt stretched across broad shoulders, his flat stomach, his faded jeans and brown boots. God, he was gorgeous! How hadn't she noticed before? 'What're you doing here?' she squeaked.

'We've come for the quiz.' *That voice . . .* it was so deep and low it seemed to rumble through her, making her feel things she hadn't felt in a very long time. 'Have you?'

'No. No, I'm here with Jenny. My friend. We're catching up. She wanted lemons.' Clare raised the glass of lemonade and as she did, the lemons bobbed, making the lemonade fizz and some of it burst over the edge of the glass and landed on Sam's shoe. 'Oh no! I'm so sorry.'

She leant forwards to try to wipe his shoe, sending more of the drink spilling over his other foot as well as his crotch and making him jump backwards.

'Careful!' he shouted, shaking his foot and staring in horror at the damp patch on his groin.

'I am *so* sorry.' She looked at the glass, now more lemons than lemonade.

'It's OK. No harm done, I guess.' He looked down. 'Well, my foot's a bit wet and I look like I've wet myself, but it'll dry.'

'I don't know what happened then.' She shook her head vigorously. 'I just splashed you and wanted to try to dry your shoe and I forgot I was holding the drinks and –'

Just shut up, Clare. Stop talking right now.

'It's fine, honestly.' He smiled, flashing beautiful straight teeth while tugging his T-shirt from his waistband and flattening it over his groin. 'It's a bit creased from being tucked in, but it'll have to do. You want me to get you another?' He nodded at the glass.

He was being incredibly understanding about this, especially in light of how he'd reacted when he'd thought she was leaving a dog poo on the path. But then, she reasoned, he had apologised for that and perhaps he really was a decent person after all.

'No, it's fine. I'll get it. It was just lemonade.'

'I don't think that's a good idea, do you?' He cocked an eyebrow in a way that she found incredibly sexy. 'I only have so many pairs of trousers and when you're around, they seem to be in danger.' He chuckled, then ran a hand over the back of his neck. 'I'll get it and bring it to you. Where are you sitting?'

She pointed at Jenny, now unable to speak for pure embarrassment. She found that she wanted to apologise again but knew that it wouldn't change what had happened, just make her look even more of an idiot. Jenny was grinning back at her and the flush on her cheeks spread to the roots of her hair and sweat prickled under her armpits. She nodded, then forced her feet to move, begging her legs not to give way.

'What happened?' Jenny asked, as soon as Clare sat down. 'It looked like he said something that embarrassed you and then you threw your drink – rather, *my* drink, all over him and now he's getting you another.'

Clare sighed. 'I'm mortified. I don't know why that happened but the poor man! I can't believe I just soaked his groin. And I almost ripped his trousers *off* the other day.'

'What? Tell me more.' Jenny cackled.

When Clare had filled Jenny in on *chinogate*, Sam appeared with the fresh glass of lemonade.

'Here you go.' He placed it in front of Clare.

'Oh, it's for Jenny, but thank you.'

'No problem.' He was still smiling. Why was he smiling when she'd just almost ruined his jeans? 'Here you go, Jenny.'

'Thanks, Sam.'

'Uh, look, if you fancy taking part in the quiz we'd be grateful for two more on our team.'

'I'm rubbish at quizzes,' Clare said, frowning.

'I'm not brilliant but that's the point of a team. Everyone has something to offer.'

'We *could* go and join them,' Jenny said.

'Perhaps in a bit.' Clare flashed Jenny a glance that said *Hold on, stop pushing things.*

'It starts in about twenty minutes. Be great if you could join us. Besides which, no pressure, but I think you kind of owe me this evening.' He gestured at his creased T-shirt with a smile on his face and Clare nodded, then buried her head in her hands.

As he walked away, Jenny nudged Clare.

'He's lovely, isn't he?'

'What?'

'Samuel Wilson. Our gorgeous village vet.'

Clare shrugged. 'He seems nice enough now, but he was very rude the first time I bumped into him, although I guess that was partly my fault.'

'Well, it seems like you've certainly made an impression on him. You know, I haven't seen that man with anyone since he moved to the village.'

'Perhaps he likes to keep his private life very private.'

'Perhaps . . .' Jenny picked a slice of lemon out of her glass, then sucked on it. 'This is just what I needed to get rid of that funny taste.'

'About that . . .' Clare met her friend's eyes. 'You don't have to tell me what's bothering you, but I'm here if you want a sounding board.'

'Thank you. I'm all right at the moment but I'll keep you posted. I'm not even sure that what I'm worrying about is rational and I don't want to say it out loud in case I curse myself.'

'Well, you wait until you're ready and I'll be here.'

Clare said the words then it dawned on her that she'd initially only expected to stay for a few weeks, but the more time passed, the more experiences she had being back in Little Bramble, the more she could imagine herself staying a bit longer.

※

'What was all that about?' Magnus asked Sam.

'What?' Sam sipped his beer.

'You and that woman. She threw a drink over you, then *you* bought *her* another.' His Norwegian accent made his teasing tone seem stronger and Sam knew that his friend could see right through him.

Sam smiled and shrugged. 'She just has a thing about ruining my trousers.'

Magnus leant his elbows on the table then rested his chin in his hands. 'I'm listening.'

Sam shook his head. 'Nothing to tell. Clare is Elaine Hughes' daughter. Earlier this week she slipped in the surgery when she brought Goliath in and grabbed at my chinos to save herself from faceplanting on the floor. Then just now, as you witnessed, she accidentally spilt some lemonade over my shoes and my crotch. I bought her a replacement drink because, well, I'm that kind of guy.'

'I see.' Magnus nodded slowly. 'I also saw something between you two, one of those sparks they talk about in romance novels.'

'What do you know about romance novels?' Sam chuckled.

'I have a very broad taste in books, I'll have you know. And there was definitely a spark of something between you and Clare. The air crackled when your eyes met.' He laughed.

'She's an attractive woman, I won't deny that, but that's all there is to it.'

'How long have I known you, Sam?' Marcus squinted. 'Over two years now and I have never seen you with so much as a date.'

'And I doubt you ever will.' Sam cleared his throat.

'Never say never, Sam. I really don't see what's stopping you. One life is all you get and finding love is a glorious thing.'

Sam swallowed his dismissive reply and finished his beer instead. 'Another?'

'Better get a full round in.'

'What?' Sam followed Magnus's gaze and spotted Clare and Jenny walking towards them. His pulse sped up. Were they going to join their quiz team?

'Hi,' Clare said as she smiled at Sam. She had two spots of colour high on her cheeks and her eyes seemed wary.

'Are you going to join us?' Magnus asked, confident as ever. Sam had never seen Magnus even slightly awkward around women. He had charm that came as easily as his smile and Sam sometimes envied him that. It would be refreshing to coast through life with that much confidence instead of the awkwardness that had plagued Sam all his life. Although, of course, Magnus wasn't yet thirty and still had the confidence of youth.

'If that's OK?' Clare looked from Magnus to Sam, then back again, clearly finding Magnus easier to interact with. And why wouldn't she? The handsome Norwegian was easier on the eye than Sam and his ability to make people relax around him made him a natural first choice. But as Clare sat down, she took the seat closest to Sam's and he had to bite the inside of his cheeks to stop himself grinning.

Then another thought occurred to him and his eyes flashed to her left hand. Miranda had mentioned a husband and son but there was no wedding ring or engagement ring there. It didn't mean she wasn't with someone, of course, and it could be that she didn't wear her rings. The thought made his spirits sink and he reprimanded himself silently for even thinking about her relationship status. It didn't matter at all, because Sam was not looking for love.

Half an hour later and the quiz had begun. Clare had agreed to write the answers down and there were six rounds: recent news, nature, sport, music, history and general knowledge. Despite what she'd said, Clare was actually very knowledgeable, especially about nature. It seemed that she knew a wealth of facts about animals and the natural world, could name the largest shark ever caught following an attack and the most toxic plants to humans. Along with Magnus's music knowledge and Jenny's ability to name key sports personalities from the past five decades, they were doing well. When the landlord, Jimmy Burton, called half-time, Sam was certain they might be in with a chance of winning.

'That was fun,' Jenny said. 'I'm in need of another lemonade though.'

'I'll give you a hand.' Clare pushed her chair back.

'It's OK,' Magnus said. 'I'll help you, Jenny.'

When they'd gone to the bar, Sam turned to Clare.

'You're really good, you know.'

'Pardon?' She met his gaze, and he looked at her, taking in her small nose and the way it turned up slightly at the end, the smattering of freckles across her cheeks and the intense green of her eyes. Her skin was so pale it was almost translucent and he was hit by an urge to stroke her cheek to see if her skin was as soft as it looked. He couldn't tell how old she was; she could have been thirty-something or forty-something, and while she'd sometimes had an air of being world-weary about her on the few occasions they'd met, as if she'd been through some difficult times, she also had an air of innocence, as if she had been sheltered from certain harsh realities. It made him want to ask her about her life, her experiences, her hopes and dreams and, simultaneously, to take her hand and pull her close to him, to hold her and bury his face in her silky hair and –

Whoa! What was going on?

This wasn't who Sam was at all. His mother had always told him that when he met that special someone, he'd know and that it would be different to any other relationship he'd ever had, but he'd dismissed it as her being sentimental and soppy. Sam was neither of those things and he was heading towards fifty, for goodness' sake sake. He wasn't about to become a romantic, to fall head over heels with a woman he barely knew.

'Sam?' She frowned at him. 'You said I'm really good?'

'Oh, yes – at the quiz. You said you weren't any good at them but you're proving yourself wrong.'

She looked down at the table and ran a finger through a puddle of condensation, then reached for a napkin from the container in the centre of the table and soaked the water up.

'It's been years since I had a go at a pub quiz, to be honest, and I'm actually surprising myself.'

'It's nice when that happens, isn't it?'

She smiled and her eyes crinkled at the corners. 'It is. I'm learning more about myself all the time.'

'I think we all do.'

'Your knowledge is pretty impressive.' She peered at him from behind her long dark lashes.

'I read a lot. Plus, Magnus makes me swot up during breaks at the surgery. He was my Secret Santa last year and he bought me one of those thick quiz books to develop my knowledge.'

She giggled. 'He seems very nice.'

'He is, and he's been a good friend.'

'Do you come to the quiz every week?'

'Not every week because of work and my sis—. Uh, other commitments. But I come when I can.'

'It's a lot of fun.'

'We should try to make it a regular thing . . .' He swallowed, realising what he'd just said. 'I mean, if you fancy it, that is. No pressure.'

'Thank you. If I'm here for a while, I'll consider it.'

'Are you not staying in the village for long then, or don't you know?' he asked, his mouth suddenly very dry.

'I'm not sure yet. I came here thinking it would only be for a few weeks, but my son arrived earlier in the week and he's already talking about Christmas.'

'Christmas, eh?'

'Yes, he wants to quit his course – well, to defer his final year at uni and, as he put it, sort his head out.'

'You don't look old enough to have a son at university.'

She laughed out loud then and shook her head. 'Really?'

'Really.'

'Well, thanks for that, but I certainly feel it.'

She sighed then, seeming sad, as if there was something on her mind. Someone as lovely as she was should never be unhappy, stressed or worried, Sam thought.

147

'Is your partner joining you for Christmas too?' He had to ask; the more time he spent with her, the more he wanted to know.

She frowned and folded her arms over her chest.

'I-I don't have a partner. I'm recently divorced.' She grimaced as if the word was distasteful to her.

'I'm really sorry to hear that.' He swallowed hard.

'It's just life, right? Lots of marriages end in divorce these days.'

She hung her head and closed her eyes, and Sam's skin prickled. Had he upset her?

'They do and it's very sad. I'm sorry if I've upset you. I have a tendency to be a bit tactless sometimes.'

She opened her eyes and looked at him again. There was no anger or bitterness in her gaze and relief coursed through him.

'You didn't upset me, Sam. My marriage was over a long time ago but I'm just still coming to terms with it, I think. However, I'm very glad to be here in the village. Being back is nicer than I thought it would be.'

'You weren't looking forward to coming back?'

'Well, you know, middle-aged divorcee returning to her childhood home, son off at uni and no job to speak of. It's not exactly a fairy tale, is it?'

She smiled and he smiled in return. 'It could be better, I guess, but it could also be a lot worse.'

'I know. You're right. I'm actually glad to be back – and I'm also glad to be here this evening.'

He opened his mouth to reply, but Magnus and Jenny arrived with their drinks, so instead he nodded at Clare then raised his pint of beer. 'To winning the quiz.'

'To friendships,' she said, 'old and new.'

Then she clinked her glass against his bottle and Sam felt something inside him loosen. He hadn't even realised he'd been so tense, but like a spring uncoiling, something started to give.

Chapter 13

'What's up with Nanna?'

Clare closed the fridge door and turned to her son.

'What do you mean?'

He was juggling with three apples just outside the back door, wearing only a pair of cartoon-character pyjama bottoms and a black vest top.

'Kyle, come inside, you must be frozen.'

He flashed her a cheeky grin. 'I'm fine, it's good for the circulation.'

'You sound just like Nanna.' She shook her head. 'But please come inside because I'm cold even if you're not.'

He caught the apples, then came through the door, closely followed by Goliath, who had a trickle of drool hanging from his mouth.

'Want one, boy?' Kyle asked the dog, then he rolled the apple across the kitchen floor.

'Kyle, don't give him that! He'll make an awful mess.'

'Chill out, Mum, he'll be fine. It's one of his five-a-day.'

Clare rolled her eyes and watched as Goliath grabbed the apple, then ran through to the lounge.

'If he buries it in the sofa and it goes mouldy you can clean it up.'

'Yes, Mum.' Kyle gave a small salute and she shook her head at him. 'Anyway, I asked what's up with Nanna.'

'She's not herself, is she?'

'Not at all.' Kyle put the two remaining apples back in the fruit bowl, then went to the fridge and got out a pint of milk. 'She seems really sad.'

'She's been better in the two weeks since you turned up.'

And she had seemed brighter. The three of them had fallen into a routine of sorts, with Clare and Kyle walking Goliath twice a day, Elaine doing her morning Tai Chi in the garden and them all doing their own thing before having an evening meal together. Clare had met up with Jenny a few times, and each time her concern about how pale her friend looked and how tired she seemed grew, but then she tried to reason that Jenny did work long days at the hair salon. Jenny had also confided in Clare that her twin daughters were being particularly difficult because one of them had a boyfriend that the other one liked, so they were arguing a lot.

Clare hadn't seen much of Sam, not having been able to pluck up the courage to invite herself along to the quiz again, but then she was trying to be sensible about him anyway. Yes, they had said they were friends, but she still wasn't quite sure how that worked. She'd never really had a male friend and wasn't sure how she could be his friend when she was quite attracted to him. And being attracted to him was causing her some anxiety, because it wasn't a feeling she'd had to deal with in a long time and it was, she was quite certain, something she could do without.

Anyway, her main concerns were right here under this roof and she wanted to give them her time and attention.

'Is there something we could do to make her happier?' Kyle asked.

Clare couldn't help herself, she grabbed hold of him and hugged him. He was a lot taller than her so his chin rested on top of her head and he smelt of his deodorant, a peppery, woody aroma, of her mum's fabric softener and also of himself. She felt sure she could pick him out of a crowd by his scent alone.

'I've been trying to think of something that I could do since I got here,' she mumbled into his chest. He was so slim, his chest almost concave, and she vowed to try to feed him up a bit while they were under the same roof.

He gently released her and stepped back to look at her. 'Like?'

'Well, you know Nanna and her love of theatre?'

'She used to love the village drama society, didn't she?' He frowned. 'But she told me the other day that since the old hall burnt down, they haven't met up.'

'It's really got her down. Between us, I think there's something a bit fishy about the accident at the village hall, but she won't talk about it. Perhaps someone she knows was responsible and she finds it too upsetting.'

'It's possible.' He rubbed his chin between his thumb and forefinger. 'What about if we tried to get something organised for Christmas at the new hall?'

Clare nodded. 'I was wondering if that might be a good idea. But there are only seven weeks until Christmas. Would it even be doable?'

Kyle took a deep breath and looked out of the kitchen window. Clare followed his gaze and saw a tiny robin hopping about on the lawn. It was so small that she could barely believe it was strong enough to survive, but there it was, its tiny head turning quickly from side to side, its eyes wide and watchful as it went about its business.

'Hey, I bet that's Grandpa come to tell us to do something nice for Nanna.'

'What?'

'Don't you remember?' He slung an arm around her shoulders. 'Dad always used to say that robins were loved ones come back from the dead.'

Clare shivered.

'Not in a bad way.' He laughed. 'He meant that they're just popping back to let us know they're all right and that they'll always be with us.'

'I don't think your dad ever said that to me.'

Kyle squeezed her shoulders. 'He's a bit of an odd one, my dad, isn't he? I love the old man but even I can see that he's a bit eccentric, especially for a lawyer.'

Clare snorted. 'Eccentric?'

'Yeah, and not that great a husband either.'

Clare pressed her lips together. She had never been negative about Jason in front of their son and she never would be. Kyle loved his dad and he had every right to make up his own mind about him. She would never try to influence how he saw his father, unless it was to try to put a more positive slant on things.

'It's OK, Mum, I know you won't say a bad word about him, and I love you for that. Rick used to hate how his parents

153

were always arguing and putting him in the middle and it tore him apart at times. I feel lucky that you never did that to me.'

She patted his arm, glad that he had been spared any suffering as a result of her divorce. She'd hate to be *that* parent.

'Anyway, Mum, I think that if we give Nanna a hand to get things up and running, it's perfectly doable. I spoke to my senior lecturer yesterday about deferring for a year and she thinks it's a good idea if it's what I want. I need to send a few emails, but I'll sort it out this week. I'd like to stay around while you're here too. This might make me sound like a bit of a baby, but since you and Dad sold the house, I've felt like I lost my base.'

'Oh Kyle, I'm so sorry. I know how you feel. I've been a bit lost too.'

'So if we have a family project, it could be good for the three of us.'

'That's true.'

'Right, let's get our heads together and come up with a plan. We need to decide what type of production it could be, work out who to ask for help, speak to all the former members of the society, and when we have an idea of what's achievable, speak to Nanna about it.'

'Kyle, I do love you!'

'I love you too, Mum.'

He filled the kettle and switched it on. 'Now, let's have a cup of tea and make some notes while Nanna's out. Good thing I wanted some coconut macaroons, isn't it?'

'You asked for those?'

'It occurred to me this morning that she needs a boost and Tai Chi alone isn't enough, so I came up with a craving for something she'd have to go searching for as a way to get her to leave the house.'

'You clever boy.' Clare giggled. 'And oh so crafty because you're the only one with Nanna wrapped around your little finger.'

'I have my talents . . .' He winked. 'Right, let's get to work.'

He made tea and took it to the table while Clare searched for a pen and paper. Then they sat down together and started to plan.

❆

The next morning Clare came downstairs wearing a pair of old jogging bottoms and a sweatshirt. Kyle was waiting for her in the kitchen, also in jogging bottoms and a hoodie.

'Are we ready to do this?' she asked.

Kyle yawned and stretched his arms above his head. 'I guess so. Seeing as how our plan is to spend more time bonding with Nanna, and this idea made our list last night, it seems like a good place to start.'

'No time like the present!' Clare took a deep breath and opened the back door.

Outside, on the lawn in her flesh-coloured undies, Elaine, her eyes closed, palms and heels together, readied herself to start her Tai Chi routine.

Clare approached her and stood on her one side and Kyle went to the other.

'Good morning, Mum.' Clare adopted the same pose as Elaine but kept her eyes open. Her mum opened her eyes and peered at Clare, then at Kyle.

'What's going on?'

'Well, see, Nanna, we thought we'd join you and find out what all the fuss is about.' Kyle winked at Clare.

'Are you sure?' Elaine asked.

'Absolutely.' Clare smiled. 'So you start and we'll follow. Neither of us has done this before, though, so please bear that in mind. We'll try to keep up.'

Elaine looked from Clare to Kyle and back again, a smile playing on her lips. 'I don't know what to say.'

'Then hurry up and start teaching us.' Clare nudged her mum's arm. 'Come on, I'm keen to feel the benefits.'

Her mum nodded. 'All right then. Follow me . . .'

Clare kept her eyes on her mum, imitating her movements and her breathing. At first, she felt clumsy and self-conscious, but as their session progressed, she forgot about what she looked like and the noises she might be making and found beauty and elegance in the flow of the movement that was at once graceful, gentle and strong.

When her mum finally stood still, Clare did too, and she was overwhelmed by the sense of inner peace that had settled over her. While she'd been following the flow of movement that had reminded her of water, her mind had slowed down and emptied, her focus on breathing and accuracy of poses. She felt as cleansed, relaxed and renewed as she would following a good night's sleep.

'How did you find that?' Elaine asked, placing a hand on Clare's shoulder.

Clare met her mum's eyes and was surprised to see them glistening, which made tears spring to her own. Then Kyle was between them, his arms encircling them both and the three of them stood there in the fresh morning air, in a kind of group hug. Clare didn't even mind the tears that trickled down her cheeks because she didn't feel sad, just as though something good was beginning.

'Where are you going, Clare?' Elaine asked later that morning as Clare put her coat on.

'To get my hair done.'

'Oh?' Her mum knitted her eyebrows. 'Where?'

'Turning Heads. Where Jenny works.' Clare rinsed her mug in the sink.

'Yes, I know it.' Elaine nodded. 'What are you having done?'

'Just a trim, I think.'

Elaine ran her eyes over Clare's head and Clare fought the urge to cover it with her hands. She knew that her roots were showing, had seen the glint of silver when she'd looked at herself in the mirror. But at forty-five, how many people wouldn't have some grey hairs? She'd thought about giving in to the grey like the women she'd seen on those hashtags #silversisters and #greyhairdontcare, but she wasn't sure that she was quite ready to fully embrace them just yet.

'You could do with a colour too,' Elaine said, and Clare nodded, not having the energy for a debate right then, especially as she knew that her mum was right. Over the years she'd found it was often easier to just agree with her mum than get into a discussion. She didn't have time this morning – and following their Tai Chi session, she was too relaxed to worry about Elaine's frankness anyway.

'Right.' Clare picked up her bag and coat from the back of one of the kitchen chairs. 'I don't suppose you fancy coming too? They might be able to squeeze you in?'

'No, thank you, Clare. I still have my hair cut by Felicity.' Elaine ran a hand over her grey bob, then tucked a stray strand behind her ear.

'Felicity Flick's Mobile Hair Studio is still going?'

'Clare, she's only sixty-two and she knows how I like my hair. Plus, we get to have coffee and cake and all within the comfort of my own home.'

'Of course.' Clare smiled. 'It's nice that she still does your hair.'

'I think so. Where's Kyle?' Elaine asked.

'Back in bed.' Clare pointed at the ceiling. 'I think he was on a late video call, and I think he wanted to grab a few more hours after being up early for Tai Chi.'

'I thought I heard voices late last night.'

'He was probably speaking to his dad. Right, Mum, I'll see you later.'

The morning was bright and crisp and the ground and cars sparkled with frost. As Clare walked, her breath puffed out in front of her in great clouds and her boots crunched on the pavement. It was only a short walk to the salon, but she made the most of it, filling her lungs with cold, cleansing air and absorbing the beauty of the village. From cottages that were hundreds of years old, with fat chimneys and small-paned windows, to the old drystone walls, to the village green with its solid wooden benches commemorating those who had passed over the years and the huge Norwegian spruce at the centre, cordoned off with a small hexagonal fence to keep dogs from destroying the lower branches, it was a lovely location. The tree had stood at the centre of the village green for as long as Clare could remember and as she passed it, a tiny shiver ran down her spine as she recalled standing there with her parents every Christmas throughout her childhood, clapping and cheering as the lights were turned on.

This year, she would be able to see the lights turned on again, with her mum and son. *But not Dad.* She rubbed her chest as if she could soothe the ache of grief that was always there, no longer completely overwhelming but ever-present. And, of course, this would be her first Christmas as a single woman. No Jason to buy for, to try to surprise then to hide her disappointment from when she saw his disinterest in whatever she'd bought him. No Jason to grimace if she hadn't got the gravy just right or to decline the champagne breakfast she'd prepared because he didn't like to drink before noon or had decided he didn't like smoked salmon or, one year, scrambled eggs.

Goodness, had she really put up with all of that?

Yes, she had, because she had believed that marriage was about give and take, about accepting that it wasn't all passion and romance, all fun and laughter. And yet, none of it had been about any of those things for years. Her marriage had, for a long time, been lacking in anything good.

Except for Kyle. Kyle had come from her relationship with Jason and he was such a gift.

When she reached the end of the green, she crossed the road and headed towards the row of buildings with their large glass windows and colourful signs which included a sweet shop, a bakery, a charity shop and the salon. Her belly clenched as she got closer and saw the glint of scissors and the large mirrors, the stylists in their black tunics and trousers. She'd always felt a bit like this whenever she'd gone to have her hair done, as if she was out of place, a bit of a mess. But then she also knew that when she'd had her hair washed and styled, when she walked out of the salon, she'd feel a lot better about her appearance too. There was something so luxurious about having her hair washed and conditioned, then cut and blow-dried by someone else. And this time, just as when she was younger, it would be her dear friend Jenny styling her hair. Jenny had always known how Clare liked her hair done, how it had suited her.

Yes, this was a good thing.

She caught sight of her reflection in the mirrors as she passed the window to get to the door and she sighed. She definitely needed something drastic.

Jenny spotted her and rushed to open the door.

'Hello, darling, I'm so excited about this.' Jenny gave her a quick hug in the doorway then Clare entered the warmth of the salon, where the scents of fruity shampoo and conditioner, of perming solution and hair dye all hung in the air, heavy yet pleasant because they offered the promise of transformation, of pampering and luxury, of self-care.

'Me too.' Clare smiled, hoping her lips wouldn't quiver and show how nervous she felt.

'This is my friend, Clare,' Jenny said, as she ushered Clare towards the rear of the salon, past mirrors where women sat with their hair plastered to their heads with dye, with segments wrapped in silver foil or as a stylist brushed and snipped, curled and dried their freshly washed crowning glory. Clare raised a hand as she passed them, taking in how young all of the stylists looked and how sophisticated they seemed. 'I'll introduce you properly later but let's hang your coat up and start your consultation.'

'OK,' Clare squeaked.

Jenny pulled out a chair in front of a mirror surrounded by bright lights and gestured for Clare to sit.

'Right, what are we doing for you today?' Jenny asked as she placed her hands on Clare's shoulders.

Clare met Jenny's gaze in the mirror and had to swallow a gasp because her friend was so pale and there were purple shadows under her eyes. It had only been a week and a half since the pub quiz, but Jenny looked much worse than she had then.

'Are you all right, Jen?' Clare asked, searching her friend's face for clues about why she looked so poorly.

'Yes, yes. I'm fine, just still a bit off colour.'

'Shouldn't you be at home resting?'

'The twins have an INSET day and I'll get no peace there, so I'd just as well be at work. Anyway, if this is just the big M, I can't be taking days off for that, can I?'

'You look like you should be in bed.'

'Gee, thanks.' Jenny gave a weak laugh. 'I'll get over it, I'm sure, or learn to live with it. Anyway, forget about me and let's think about you.'

Jenny ran her hands through Clare's hair, parting it this way and that, rubbing the ends between finger and thumb, then she nodded. 'I think you could definitely do with a good trim, perhaps a bit of feathering around your pretty face – and how about . . . if we add some colour? Lighten it a bit.'

Clare looked from her own brown tresses to Jenny's blonde ones. 'Ooh. I'm not sure, Jen. I mean, it looks fabulous on you, but I've never seen myself as a blonde.'

Jenny laughed. 'Not blonde, Clare, but you have such lovely chestnut brown hair that some highlights would really show it off. I could add some caramel and some gold and that will lift it.'

Clare looked at her hair in the mirror, at the colour that she was used to (although she did usually make an effort to tone in the greys with a home-dye job, using a colour as close to her own as possible) and then nodded. 'Why not? Perhaps it's time for a change.'

'Yay!' Jenny clapped. 'Let's do it.'

Two hours later, Clare was so relaxed, she was almost comatose. She'd had her hair combed, parted, painted with three different colours – a base colour the same as her natural one then two others running through in thinner strips and sections of it wrapped in foil. Then she'd been told to relax as a timer was set and Jenny had handed her three glossy magazines and a caramel latte.

Clare had sipped the delicious drink and watched the goings-on in the salon. Women and men of all ages came in and had haircuts, colours, booked appointments and some visited just to say hello to the stylists, who were all warm, friendly and welcoming. There was a gentle ambience to the salon; it was so relaxing, comfortable and safe, womblike in its ability to cocoon the customers from the outside world for a few hours. The chairs were padded, the footrests the right height. The white noise of hairdryers, the hum of conversations, the melodies from the radio and the snipping of scissors all flowed around her, soothing, mellow, comforting. Added to that the aromas of coffee, hairspray, perfumes and colognes and the vast array of styling products that came from the cupboards next to the chairs were uplifting, familiar, cheering. Clare could see herself returning to the salon time after time because it was just wonderful. There was no sense of feeling threatened as she had expected, no feeling of being undermined or scorned; it was all incredibly positive and she felt that she was important, a part of something there. Of course, it helped that her friend was the senior stylist, but even so, she knew that she'd have missed out by not visiting Turning Heads.

When the timer had buzzed, Jenny had slid a few strands of Clare's hair from the foil and checked them, then smiled. 'Come to the basin, my dear.'

She had washed Clare's hair twice, running her long capable fingers through it then over Clare's scalp, making Clare so relaxed she almost dribbled. The conditioner Jenny had massaged into Clare's ends had smelt like a mouth-watering combination of mango and coconut and Jenny had then worked it through with a wide-toothed comb and Clare had been transported to the edge of consciousness.

After it had been rinsed away, Jenny had wrapped a soft fluffy towel around Clare's head and led her back to her chair in the front of the salon. The woman who looked back at Clare in the mirror looked sleepy, practically seduced by the experience, and Clare had chuckled.

'You could charge way more for that, you know.'

'You don't know how expensive it's going to be yet.' Jenny winked.

'I don't care. I'd give you all my money just to have that delightful sensory experience again.'

'Good.' Jenny gently squeezed Clare's shoulders. 'You deserve to be pampered. Now we need to get you cut and blow-dried.'

When Jenny had finished working on her hair, Clare gasped at her reflection.

'Oh my God, Jenny! Is that really me?'

'I told you.' Jenny fluffed Clare's hair gently, sweeping it from side to side so Clare could see how the colours caught the light and how they added depth and volume.

'It's wonderful! Thank you so much.'

'My pleasure. I'm so pleased with how good it looks. I knew it would suit you.'

Jenny frowned suddenly and Clare turned in the chair and reached for her hand.

'What is it, Jen?'

'Low blood sugar probably. I just feel a bit nauseous.'

'Well, let me treat you to a drink at the café.'

'Mmm. I could take my break now.' Jenny nodded.

'I'll go and pay, and you grab your things.' Clare picked up her bag from beside the chair.

'I've told the girls to give you my discount.' Jenny smiled. 'I'll grab your coat from the back.'

'You don't need to give me a discount. That's far too generous of you.'

'It's fine.' Jenny shook her head. 'Just go pay and I'll be back in a moment.'

Clare went to the counter, flushing at the positive comments she received from the stylists and other customers.

She kept stealing glances at her reflection and feeling waves of delight as she took in how good her hair looked. But when Jenny appeared at her side, holding out her coat, Clare's delight faded away and concern for her friend took over.

There was something wrong with Jenny and she had a feeling she was about to find out exactly what it was.

Chapter 14

Sam strolled around Tesco, pushing the trolley in front of him and browsing the shelves. He'd got the usual groceries and needed to pick up some toiletries, paracetamol and eye drops. Working long hours and using the computer often left him with gritty eyeballs, so saline drops were incredibly soothing and he liked to have some in the cabinet at home.

He gazed at the Christmas candles on display. There was a three-for-two offer on them and he paused and picked one up. Alyssa liked candles, especially festive ones, so he could get some now and put them away for Christmas. Being the only family she had left meant that he had become very organised with things like Christmas shopping; and, of course, he had no one else to buy for – except for work colleagues and they ran a Secret Santa for that. He always ended up with a cupboard full of gifts for Alyssa and loved seeing her face on Christmas morning when they drank Buck's Fizz and she sat on the floor in front of the sofa and opened her stocking, then her larger gifts. She was like a little girl and always got so excited about it, which made it all better for Sam too.

After he'd selected three candles, he placed them in the trolley and continued on his way. The next aisle had an array of random festive gifts, deliberately positioned to catch shoppers as they went from fruit and veg to toiletries. He picked up a box of Belgian truffles and a hot chocolate mug set with a tiny whisk, knowing that Alyssa would appreciate both. As he passed a section of cuddly toys, he glanced at them and smiled. He'd occasionally felt a bit sad that neither he nor his sister had become parents. Deep down, he guessed he'd always sort of wanted kids, but the time had never been right; he'd never met the right woman and there had, perhaps most importantly, been medical issues to worry about. He sometimes felt that they'd missed out on something, because he'd always enjoyed preparing Christmas for Alyssa, so doing the same for his own children would surely have been wonderful. He was under no illusions that it wouldn't be tiring and sometimes stressful being a dad, but felt sure that the rewards would outweigh those things.

Familiar laughter made his ears tingle and he peered around the end of the aisle. Was it? If not, she had a laugh doppelganger who shopped at Tesco. What would she be doing here at this time on a Wednesday? He was shopping in his lunch break, but surely she should be at work right now?

But no, there she was, holding up a packet of pasta and grinning broadly, looking for all the world like the sweet, carefree young woman she'd once been. And apparently still was when she was with her new beau.

Sam stared at the tall, broad man standing next to his sister, one large tattooed hand resting casually on the back of her wheelchair as he leant forwards and whispered in her ear. Her grin was broad, her eyes bright and she looked . . .

Delighted. Happy. In love!

Looking both ways, Sam went to reverse his trolley, but an elderly couple had paused right behind him and were poring over the tins of festive biscuits, so he tried to turn the trolley in the opposite direction but an employee was wheeling a large cart of vegetables towards him. The only way he could go was forwards . . .

'Sam!' He met his sister's eyes. 'What're you doing here?'

'Shopping, of course.' He glanced into his trolley and realised her gifts were on display, so he quickly dropped one of his large shopping bags over the top of them.

'Ha ha! Of course, I can see that. I meant at this time of day.' Alyssa smiled at him, seemingly unaware that he was feeling quite agitated. 'Never mind, anyway – this is Seb.'

'Seb?'

'Yes, Sebastian Monmouth. Seb, this is my big brother, Sam.'

'Pleased to meet you.' Sebastian held out a hand and Sam looked at it, picturing a garden spade being thrust at him, before shaking it. 'Alyssa's told me lots about you.'

Sam cringed inwardly at the cliché but told himself Sebastian was just being polite. He suddenly felt very small standing in front of the other man, although there could only have been about two inches height difference, but Sebastian was built like a professional wrestler. His bulging biceps were displayed in a faded black rock band T-shirt that had had the short sleeves hacked off (with a knife or his spades, it seemed) and his black combat trousers were stretched tight over meaty thighs. He wore scuffed black lace-up boots and his long black hair was pulled into a ponytail at the back of his head, exposing the shaved and tattooed sides. Everything in Sam screamed at him not to judge this man on his appearance, not to assume that he would hurt Alyssa or take advantage of her, but the big brother in him, the one who had looked out for Alyssa all her life – and especially since the accident – wanted to grab the handles of her chair, push her out to his car and take her straight home.

Shame crawled over him as he realised that he was being prejudiced. He'd met prejudice himself over the years and had never wanted to be that person. This was, he knew, a gut reaction because he wanted to ensure that Alyssa never got hurt again, and whatever Sebastian had looked like, Sam would have had a hard time coming to terms with the fact that this man was in a relationship with his sister. No man would ever be good enough for Alyssa, but that didn't mean that no other man was good. He gripped the handle of the trolley and took some slow deep breaths, hoping that his gut reaction had gone unnoticed.

Luckily, it had, because Alyssa and Sebastian were waving at someone at the end of the aisle. He followed their gaze and his mouth dried up as a young girl in jeans and a fluffy cerise jumper skipped towards them.

'Sam . . . I'd like you to meet Betty.' Alyssa held out a hand to the girl.

'Betty?' he asked, trying to smile at the pretty child, whose shiny black hair was pulled into bunches and whose pale skin contrasted with the pink of her jumper.

'My daughter.' Sebastian nodded, his face drawn into a proud smile.

'Hello, Betty,' Sam said, and the girl who looked about nine or ten smiled back. 'It's very nice to meet you.'

But in his mind, a voice whispered . . . *I haven't heard lots about you.*

And he could see from Alyssa's expression that she'd been saving this news for another day.

※

'Do you need to get anything?' Jenny asked as they entered Tesco.

The vents poured the mouth-watering aroma of freshly baked bread and buttery pastries over them and Clare's tummy rumbled.

'I could pick up some bread for later, I guess,' Clare said. 'And perhaps something for dinner. Possibly some almond croissants.'

'Thank goodness for that.' Jenny hooked her arm through Clare's. 'I didn't want it to be the only thing in the basket.'

'Are you going to tell me what we're buying now?' Clare glanced at Jenny as they walked past fruit and vegetables, then milk, yogurts and cheese.

'Hold on . . .' Jenny led Clare straight to the medicine aisle. 'I'm not sure exactly where they'll be as it's been so long since I bought any but . . . here they are!' Jenny glanced furtively around them, then grabbed a white and blue box off the shelf and flung it into the basket that Clare was carrying.

'What?' Clare stared at the photo on the box of a small, white plastic stick. '*Really?*'

'I'm hoping not, and if not then I need to book an appointment with the GP because it has to be the menopause, but I've been so nauseous this week and I passed out in the bathroom this morning with my head down the toilet.'

'Ewww.' Clare shuddered.

'I know. Gross, right? But it was my en-suite toilet, so it was clean. I thought I was going to be sick, so I knelt down and next thing I knew, I came round with my head on the seat.'

'Do you think you should get two? Just in case one's . . . inconclusive?'

'Good idea.'

Jenny dropped another pregnancy test into the basket, then wiped her hands on her coat as if worried they were contaminated.

'Shit!' She stiffened and turned her back to Clare. 'Quick, put something else in the basket.'

'What?'

'Quickly! Before he sees!'

Clare reached out and grabbed a box from the shelf in front of her then scuttled a bit further along and grabbed a packet from the shelf, tucking them over the tests.

'Hello there.'

It was Sam, standing behind a trolley, looking a bit out of sorts.

'Hi, Sam.' Clare smiled but her heart was pounding, and she felt the familiar heat he seemed to invoke crawl across her chest and into her cheeks. 'What're you doing here?'

He knitted his eyebrows, then gave a small smile. 'That's the second time I've been asked that, but I thought it would be obvious.'

Clare laughed nervously, the sound weak and bordering, she thought, on hysterical.

'Shopping!' she said.

'What are you doing here?' Sam asked, cocking an eyebrow as if in challenge, then he peered into her basket and she spluttered as she followed his gaze.

Horror turned her blood cold as she saw what she'd thrown on top of the pregnancy tests: a bumper pack of rainbow-coloured condoms, ribbed for her pleasure, and a packet of disposable elastic-waisted knickers for bladder leaks.

'It's uh . . . they're for uh . . . my mum.' She nodded. 'Yes, for my mum.'

When she met his eyes again, he was smiling, and she willed her body to spontaneously combust. In that moment, if the only thing left of her had been her shoes and a plume of smoke, she wouldn't have cared because she didn't think she had ever felt so mortified.

'I see.'

'Anyway, we'd best get going.' Jenny had reached Clare's side and she took hold of her friend's elbow. 'Nice to see you, Sam.'

'You too, Jenny.' He looked at Clare again. 'Nice hair, by the way. It really suits you.'

Clare raised her free hand and touched her hair. She'd forgotten that she'd had it done. 'Uh . . . thanks. Jenny did it this morning.'

'It's lovely.' Something in his eyes made her belly flutter and she had to look away to break the spell.

'Yes, she looks gorgeous, doesn't she?' Jenny nudged Clare. 'Right, let's go!'

As they marched away, Clare turned to Jenny. 'Do you think he's OK?'

'Why?'

'Well, he seemed a bit . . .' A bit what? She barely knew Sam, but in spite of the nice things he'd said, and in spite of the humiliation she'd felt as he'd looked at her incontinence knickers and giant pack of condoms, she'd picked up on something else about him. He seemed sad, a bit lost, and as if he could do with someone to talk to.

Jenny guided her quickly around the rest of the supermarket, throwing bread and buns and a few ready meals on top of everything else, and Clare commented on each item, but her mind kept straying back to Sam.

She wondered if she could be that someone for him to talk to.

❄

Sam loaded his shopping bags into the boot of his car, closed it, then returned the trolley to the store. When he got back to the car, he sat in the driver's seat with his hands resting on the steering wheel and closed his eyes.

That had been the most eventful trip to Tesco he'd ever had. Not only had he found out that his sister's new lover had a daughter, he'd also found out that Clare was apparently an incontinent nymphomaniac. The latter made him smile. Perhaps the pants *were* for her mum and perhaps the condoms weren't for her; either way, it was none of his business, but seeing her had brought the feeling of vulnerability rushing back. He felt raw and bruised after bumping into Alyssa and Sebastian, as if he'd been left out of a secret, and that in itself bothered him. Alyssa was perfectly capable of choosing who she dated, who she became involved with, but Sam was hurt that she hadn't told him the full story. Although he had to admit that, if she had, it would have given him something else to worry about. And now he knew. His sister was involved with a man who had a child – and that was going to be a complicated situation if ever there was one.

As for Clare . . . He had wished she'd been alone and not flanked by Jenny, who hadn't actually looked very well. She'd been pale with deep dark shadows under her eyes and she'd been quite curt with him, as if in a hurry to get away.

He opened his eyes and gazed out of the windscreen across the car park to the grey brick wall with its coating of dark green moss. Someone had tried to scrape the moss away but given up after the first metre of bricks, leaving a jagged line. He understood that feeling; he tried to do the right thing by Alyssa, tried to adopt new ways of thinking and to be more open to new ways of acting, but he kept circling back to the same thoughts and feelings. And he knew why. He still hadn't properly faced up to what had happened that night when Alyssa fled the house, hadn't accepted that, even though he blamed himself, he couldn't change a thing.

And in the here and now, Alyssa had a whole new life and he was all alone.

❉

The hot chocolate was rich and sweet, the teacake dripping with butter, the air in the café laced with aromas of toast, roasted coffee beans and cake. Clare sat opposite Jenny at a table by the window, watching her friend carefully while trying not to seem as if she was.

Jenny only nibbled at her toast, but she gulped down the hot chocolate and Clare was relieved to see that it brought some colour to her cheeks.

'Eat your toast if you can, Jen. You've got a full afternoon of work ahead of you.'

Jenny nodded and picked up her toast but instead of taking a bite, she started pulling it apart then dropping small pieces onto her plate.

'What if it's positive?'

Clare tried to think of how to reassure Jenny.

'What if it's not?'

'I hope that's the case. But then, if it's not menopause it could be something else ... like ... *cancer* ...' She whispered the last word, clearly finding the idea too horrific to say it out loud.

Clare shook her head. 'It's nothing bad, I'm convinced of it. You *are* probably just menopausal.'

Jenny crossed the fingers of both hands and tapped them against the sides of her head.

'I'm going to do it now.'

'Now?'

'Now.' Jenny's jaw set. 'I have to go back to work soon and I just need to know. I could wait and do it later at home with Martin, but I'm not even sure how *I'm* going to react, so I'd prefer to do it now, with your support. If that's OK?'

'Of course it is! I'm just glad I can be here for you.'

Jenny reached across the table and took Clare's hand. 'So am I, Clare, so am I.'

'You want me to come through with you?' Clare asked.

'No, love, I'll do this bit by myself, but when I come out, can we go for a walk away from people so we can find out in peace?'

'Of course.'

Jenny stood up and unhooked her bag from the back of the chair, then trudged away, hunched over as if she'd aged twenty years in the past hour.

When she had gone through the door to the toilets, Clare drained her mug, then stood up and put her coat on. She went to the counter, paid the bill, left a tip, then picked up Jenny's coat and waited by the door.

Five minutes later, Jenny emerged, her bag clamped to her side, her lips pale. She hurried to Clare's side and they left the café, heading out into the now bitter wind.

The bench they chose was at the end of the village green, the furthest away from Turning Heads and the village café. As they sat down the breeze swirled crumpled leaves around their feet and whipped their hair, so they kept having to tuck it behind their ears.

Clare shivered, wishing she had a hat and gloves as well as her coat, but she suspected that Jenny was shivering for another reason. She put an arm around her friend's shoulders and squeezed.

'Are you ready?' she asked.

Jenny nodded, but her face was ashen again.

'Whatever the result, Jen, I'm here for you.'

'Thanks,' Jenny whispered, then she opened her bag and pulled out a wad of tissues. She unfolded them on her lap and Clare held her breath.

'What does it say?' She peered at the stick.

'I don't know. I can't look.' Jenny had closed her eyes and was holding the test away from her as if it was toxic.

'Shall I?'

'Please.'

The ends of the tissue waved in the breeze and covered the result window, so Clare reached out with a finger and pushed them out of the way. She grimaced and her surroundings seemed to lurch.

'Do you want to know, Jen?'

Jenny opened her eyes and turned to Clare, who took her friend's hands in hers, ignoring the test that was now enclosed in Jenny's palm.

'No, but I need to.'

Clare licked her lips.

'You're going to have another baby, Jen.'

She held Jenny tight, waiting for her reaction.

Jenny's face changed from white to grey to puce, then the colour drained away altogether. She snatched her hands from Clare's grasp, stood up, letting the test and wad of tissues fall to the ground, then she vomited into the bin behind the bench.

Chapter 15

'What time do they start the fireworks, Nanna?' Kyle sashayed into the kitchen and Clare started to laugh.

'Oh my goodness, you look amazing!'

'Why thank you, Mum!'

He gave her a twirl so she could fully appreciate his outfit. He was wearing red jeans with an orange shirt, a red puffa jacket and red lace-up boots.

'But why are you dressed up?' Elaine asked.

'To celebrate it being bonfire night, Nanna, of course. It was something we did when I was growing up, wasn't it, Mum?'

Clare nodded. It was a tradition that she'd started as a bit of fun when Kyle was a toddler, where they'd dress up in all the red and orange clothing they had on 5th November . Jason had gone along with it for a while but even after he'd stopped joining in, Kyle and Clare had continued. Although over more recent years, with Kyle preferring to go out with friends then away at university, Clare hadn't been to see any fireworks, so she was really looking forward to the display.

'Where are your special clothes, Mum?' Kyle eyed her outfit of black jeans, boots and black jumper.

'I haven't got everything with me,' she explained. 'A lot of it's in storage.'

He nodded. 'Well, I brought all my red and orange things because I had a feeling I'd be here for bonfire night. I have a red scarf and hat that you can borrow.'

Elaine looked at him and pursed her lips. 'Hold on a moment.' She left the kitchen and was back five minutes later wearing a red knitted dress with red boots and she handed Clare a red faux fur coat.

'There you are, Clare. If you borrow Kyle's hat and scarf and wear this coat, we can all coordinate.'

Clare smiled, enjoying the sense of unity, and accepted the coat while Kyle got his scarf and hat for her.

When they were ready to leave, Kyle made them stand together for a group selfie with him between them. 'Aren't we a family of firecrackers?'

They all had to agree.

As they walked to the village green, Clare asked for the fiftieth time, 'Are you sure Goliath will be OK?'

Her mum nodded. 'I've put that soothing plug-in on that Sam recommended and left the radio up high, but to be honest with you, fireworks have never bothered him. Most dogs hate them, I know, but Goliath isn't fazed by them. If he's in the garden when they're going off, he runs up and down and barks at them but it's an excited bark. I know that Sam said we could leave Goliath with him if we wanted to because he does a kind of "dogs' night-in" at his, so that anyone with nervous dogs can drop them off then pick them up after the fireworks, but I didn't think we needed to.'

'Sam won't be there?' Clare's heart sank; she'd assumed that as one of the villagers, he'd attend the fireworks.

'When he arrived in the village he encouraged everyone to be considerate of the local pets with regard to fireworks and requested that they only run for a few hours at most. So the display only lasts about an hour and a half and everyone else is respectful enough to either attend the village green or to only light their own fireworks during that time.'

'That's a really good thing to agree on as a community,' Clare said, thinking about how, over the years, she'd heard fireworks going off at all times of the day and night and set the local dogs howling for hours.

'Little Bramble is a lovely community,' her mum said and nodded as if just remembering that fact.

They reached the green and saw the local firefighters in full kit standing in a square area at the opposite end from the large tree that they'd cordoned off with yellow tape. Some stood around the outside of the square to stop anyone from getting too close to the fireworks.

'Safety first, eh?' Kyle said.

'Definitely.' Clare looked around at the gathering crowds, wondering if Jenny would turn up. She'd texted earlier to say she wasn't sure if she'd come because she still felt rough, so Clare told her to stay warm and get lots of rest.

'Ah look, there's the vicar.' Her mum waved at Iolo Ifans, and he waved back then made his way over to them.

'Good evening, Elaine.' He smiled broadly. 'And who have we here?' He winked at Clare to let her know that he recognised her.

'You know Clare, Iolo, you joker, and this is my grandson, Kyle.'

'Lovely to see you both again.' Iolo shook their hands in a warm greeting. He was so well-wrapped up in a thick coat, boots, scarf, hat and gloves that only his mouth, nose and eyes were visible. 'The last time I saw you, Kyle, you were about so high.' He gestured at his knees and Kyle laughed.

'I don't think he was ever that small.' Clare peered up at her son.

'How are you, Elaine?' Iolo said, and Clare followed his gaze to her mum, who flushed. It was dark, but under the street lamps, Clare could definitely make out some colour in Elaine's cheeks.

'I'm all right, thanks, Iolo.'

'I've brought a flask of hot chocolate with me,' he said, sliding his arms out of a backpack and opening it. 'And I have extra cups. Isn't that lucky?'

Clare laughed. For as long as she'd known Iolo, he'd carried a backpack and always had something useful in it, whether it was bottled water on a hot day, a flask of something hot on a cold one or tissues when someone had a cold or was emotional.

He handed a large flask to Elaine, then pulled out a packet of thick paper cups. Clare and Kyle watched as her mum and the vicar shared the hot chocolate between the cups, then handed them out. She accepted hers gratefully, glad to hold the warm cup between her gloved hands.

A cheering spread through the crowd as one of the female firefighters tapped on a microphone. 'Good evening, Little Bramble!'

'Good evening!' the crowd replied.

'I'm Helen Boden, the Fire Station Manager here in the village, in case you don't know me. I'm just going to run through some safety regulations, then we can get started.'

While the station manager spoke to the crowd, Clare gazed around her, absorbing the contrast of the lamps that lit up the green and the seemingly velvety black of the sky. It was a clear evening and, high above, the stars twinkled, silver pinpricks in an endless ebony canvas. The air was icy, fragranced with woodsmoke, black powder and frying onions and meat from a burger stall at the far end of the green. Clare thought she could see some familiar faces, but with hats pulled down over eyebrows and scarves up to noses, it was difficult to tell. And it had been so long since she'd been a part of the village community that she wasn't sure how many people she would actually recognise.

Next to Clare, Kyle sipped his hot chocolate and slid his arm through hers, pulling her closer. Her mum and the vicar chatted quietly and she felt her lips curving upwards. It had been a long time since she'd felt a part of something, that she belonged, but here, in a familiar setting, with a warm drink and her son and mum close, something inside her was flickering. Like a candle flame, it was fragile and could easily be extinguished, but it was there, it was lit, and she could feel its delicate warmth spreading out through her belly and lifting her mood.

When the first fireworks shot into the sky, spiralling upwards like shooting stars then exploding and catapulting shimmering orbs of red and green in all directions, the crowd gasped and clapped. The air was filled with crackling, whistling, booming and humming and plumes of grey smoke drifted off on the breeze. More fireworks were sent whirling upwards, splattering the sky with silver glitter and golden waterfalls. Clare felt like a child, filled with joy and excitement as all of her troubles and cares melted away.

When the last rocket had been fired into the sky and the air was heavy with smoke, Clare turned to Kyle to find him grinning at her.

'That was brilliant, wasn't it?' she said, as she hugged his arm tight.

'I was half watching the fireworks and half watching your face.'

'Why?'

'You look so happy, Mum. It's wonderful to see.'

Clare kissed his cheek, then gazed back up at the sky, blinking away the tears that his words had conjured. He was right; she knew it. She hadn't been truly happy for a long time; being back in Little Bramble was having a very positive effect upon her. She had no illusions the being back home was the answer to her problems, but spending time with her family was lifting her, giving her a sense of belonging and of not being as alone as she had felt even before her marriage had officially ended.

It was as if she was finding her way again in the place where she had grown up – and there was a lot of comfort to be found in that.

Chapter 16

'Where did you learn to cook like that?'

Clare leant against the kitchen unit and admired her son's efforts. They'd agreed to make dinner for Elaine that Saturday evening and had told her not to make any other plans, which she'd scoffed at because clearly she had no intention of going out. Clare and Kyle had gone to the local farm shop to buy some supplies and Clare had expected to be the one cooking while Kyle observed and drank some of the chilled Chablis they'd purchased. Growing up, he had always liked to help out in the kitchen but usually followed Clare's lead, mainly because she'd done the shopping and had the week's meals planned. However, it seemed that Kyle's time away had led to him becoming a very accomplished cook and Clare's mouth was watering at the delicious aromas filling the kitchen.

'Oh, here and there, Mother.' He winked at her. He only called her 'mother' when he was being facetious, and his reaction made her suspect that he'd learnt his rather polished culinary skills from some of his romantic acquaintances.

'Well, you certainly didn't get it from your father,' Clare said, then she winced. 'Sorry . . . after everything I said about not wanting to be *that* parent. I really didn't mean it like that, Kyle, it was just a joke.'

He laughed, then scooped more seasoned juice over the chicken he was frying. 'No problem, Mum, I know that. And you're right, Dad is a shit cook. In fact, I can't recall him actually trying in the kitchen at all. Now you can see that the advantage of having a pansexual son is that I'll try anything.' He giggled and Clare shook her head at him; sometimes his jokes ran a bit risqué.

'So we're going to tell Nanna tonight. I mean, ask her what she thinks.' Clare blinked hard. They intended raising the Christmas Show idea she and Kyle had come up with over dinner and she had no idea how Elaine would react. Their idea was a good one, Clare thought, but whether Elaine would think so had yet to be determined.

Clare hadn't seen Jenny since Wednesday when they'd discovered that she was pregnant, but they'd been in touch via text at least three times every day and she felt sure that Jenny knew she was there for her. She'd asked Jenny if she'd like to join them that evening, but her friend had declined, saying that Martin and the girls had plans: he was meeting an old rugby mate for a beer and the twins were going on dates, so she was looking forward to a bubble bath and an early night. She hadn't told her family about the pregnancy yet, only she and Clare knew, so the secret was safe until Jenny felt ready to share the news.

Goliath got up off his bed and went to the back door, standing with his nose almost touching it, his body tense.

'He wants to go out,' Clare said, as she wandered over to the door and opened it. Goliath jogged outside, activating the sensor on the security light, and started sniffing around.

Clare stepped back into the warm kitchen, leaving the door ajar.

'I swear the temperature has dropped dramatically this week.'

'It's freezing, isn't it?' Kyle said as he transferred the chicken to a Le Creuset pot, then poured the juices from the pan over it. He topped it with the lid, then slid it into the Aga. 'I was quite surprised that Halloween passed so uneventfully here, with it being such a big event in some places now. Apart from a few trick or treaters out on the village green and the spooky decorations in the shops and hair salon, I didn't see anything at all.'

Clare thought of the fuss some of the parents in Reading made of Halloween, with decorations, costume parties and traipsing the streets to knock on doors. 'No, there wasn't much of a fuss, was there? I know that we used to have a party here because Mum and Dad loved hosting parties and they used to decorate the cottage, but that hasn't happened since Dad . . .' She trailed off, not wanting to feel the sadness that accompanied the words.

'It's a shame for the children, though. They can have a lot of fun dressing up and playing games.'

'I expect that if the village hall had more use, then something could be done there – perhaps a disco or something.'

'That's a fab idea, Mum.'

'And at least we still have the bonfire night celebrations in the village.' Clare was still riding the high of the night before last when they'd gone to watch the fireworks, enjoyed the vicar's hot chocolate and Kyle had commented on how happy she seemed.

'Yes, it was a good night.'

Clare peered through the glass pane in the door at the dog. 'Goliath would nose around outside all day and night if we let him.'

'He doesn't feel the cold like us humans.'

'Although he does love stretching out in front of the fire.' Clare took another sip of wine. 'What's next?'

'Now we prep the vegetables, then we can whip up the chocolate mousse, sit back and relax.'

Half an hour later they sat in the lounge together on one sofa. Elaine had been taking a long soak in the bath and when she came downstairs, she drifted into the lounge in a pair of silky pink pyjamas and a navy kimono. Her hair was damp and her cheeks were rosy. She looked relaxed.

'Would you like a glass of wine, Nanna?' Kyle asked as he stood up.

'That would be lovely, darling.'

Kyle took Clare's empty glass with him.

'He's a good boy,' Clare's mum said and smiled.

'He is. I'm very lucky to have him as my son.'

'You are – but then he's lucky to have you as a mum. Not all mothers are as kind as you.'

Clare swallowed hard. Compliments? From her mum?

'Uh, thank you.'

Her mum waved a hand. 'I'm only telling the truth. You *are* a good mum, Clare, far better than I ever was.'

Clare opened her mouth to protest, but Elaine held up a hand and shook her head. 'I know I'm hard, Clare, and I always have been. It was never fair on you and for that I am truly sorry, but I always felt your dad made up for it, that he compensated for the areas where I was . . . somewhat lacking.'

'Mum –'

'He did though, didn't he? And his parents, weren't they just lovely? So refreshingly sweet and kind after what I'd grown up with.'

Clare's ears pricked up. It wasn't often that she was given an insight into why her mum behaved as she did, but it seemed something was about to be shared. Then, 'Here we are.' Kyle entered the room and she saw her mum stiffen, withdraw, then drag a smile to her lips.

'Thank you, darling.' Elaine accepted the glass from Kyle, then he handed one to Clare. 'Mmm . . . This is very good wine.'

'Isn't it? Mum chose it.' Kyle beamed at them both, then sat on the sofa next to Clare, making her bounce slightly so she had to hold her wine carefully to avoid spilling any.

'Your mum has excellent taste.' Elaine smiled at them both, then took another sip of wine.

Clare didn't know if she was relieved or disappointed that her mum had been stopped in her tracks just as she was about to tell Clare more about her childhood, but either way, if it was meant to come out, it would. When the time was right.

Elaine leant forwards on her sofa and placed her glass on the coffee table. 'Now, Kyle, tell your old nanna . . . What are you making for our dinner because it smells divine?'

❋

Kyle set the fresh bottle of wine on the kitchen table, then sat down.

'This looks incredible,' Clare said, as she eyed the feast her son had prepared. There was a dish of herby chicken, roasted garlic potatoes, buttered carrots, steamed asparagus and freshly baked pumpkin and sunflower-seed soda bread.

'Well done, Kyle!' Elaine held up her glass. 'You truly are a wonder in the kitchen.'

Kyle grinned at them, clearly enjoying the praise, and so he should. Clare was so proud of her son and her heart squeezed as she looked at him. He was a man now, but she could still see the little boy with thick brown hair that could never be combed down neatly and big green eyes that revealed his open and caring nature.

'Tuck in!' Kyle said as he gestured at the food. 'If we don't, I think Goliath might get in there first.'

The dog was standing next to the table eyeing up the chicken. His eyebrows moved in turn as he hoped someone would take pity on him and spare him a morsel. Clare cut a piece of her chicken, then held it out for him and he took it gently from her fingers, licking his lips. Dogs were certainly good at emotional manipulation and Clare was finding that she fell for Goliath's charms more often than not. It was funny how it had happened, because when she'd arrived in Little Bramble just over four weeks ago, she'd had no idea she'd come to like dogs so much. She was learning more about herself every day of her new life – and it was a good feeling.

When they'd finished eating, Clare got up to clear the table, but Kyle held up a hand.

'No, no, Mum. You stay there. I'll do it.'

'It's no problem, Kyle.'

'You've done enough for me over the years so now it's my chance to repay some of that.'

'Don't be silly.' She made to get up again, but he shook his head and placed a hand on her shoulder.

'Seriously, Mum, stay there and pour some more wine.'

Clare refilled their glasses and took a sip. The wine was cold, zesty and floral and had matched the food perfectly.

'Are we having dessert?' Elaine asked.

'We are, Nanna, as I promised.' And Kyle set the ramekins of dark chocolate mousse down on the table. 'I have to warn you though, this is highly calorific.'

Clare's mum chuckled. 'Oh, I don't mind that. And it looks simply luxurious.'

When Kyle had joined them at the table again, Clare spooned some mousse into her mouth. It was as good as it looked and they ate in silence, thoughts of speaking to Elaine about their ideas temporarily forgotten by the sensual pleasure of eating. When the ramekins had been cleared – Clare had even used a finger to clear the bottom of hers of mousse – she sat back and sighed with contentment.

'That was perfect, Kyle.'

'Almost as good as an orgasm,' Elaine said, causing Clare and Kyle to look up in shock. 'Ha! Look at you two,' Elaine said and laughed. 'The horror on your faces! I *am* a human being too, you know. I did once have a sex life.'

'Mum, please!' This was the last thing Clare wanted to hear about over dinner.

'Nanna, you are funny.' Kyle sipped his wine. 'Of course you did – and I'm sure it was very adventurous.'

'Kyle!' Clare stood up and carried the ramekins to the sink, hoping that the topic of conversation would change. She tried to picture the three of them outside on the lawn doing Tai Chi as they had done the past four mornings, Clare and Kyle dragging themselves out of bed to join Elaine because they believed it was a good way for the three of them to bond. Elaine was also a very good instructor, probably due to her years of experience as a teacher, and Clare was finding that she really enjoyed the early morning exercise.

Clare filled the kettle and put it on to boil and returned to the table, where she drained her glass, then toyed with the stem, wondering if now was the right time to broach their plans.

'Anyway, Nanna . . .' Kyle took charge and Clare was glad. She hadn't known how she was going to begin. 'Mum and I have an idea.'

'Oh, do you?' Clare's mum nodded. 'I take it from the way you're both looking at me that it has something to do with me.'

'You'd have made a great detective, Nanna.'

'Don't be cheeky.' She smiled. 'Tell me.'

'Mum?' Kyle handed the baton over to Clare and she swallowed hard, glad of the wine she'd drunk as it would give her the courage she needed.

'Right . . .'

What was she so worried about? What was the worst that could happen? She knew, of course; she was never certain how her mum would react to things, especially if she wasn't keen or didn't approve. Like that time when Clare was sixteen and she had announced that she wanted to run the

London Marathon. Her mum had laughed, then explained exactly why it was highly unlikely that Clare would ever run that race. In retrospect, Clare could see that her mum had been right as she had never been particularly athletic, but she had found her response difficult at the time. And then there had been another time when Clare had spoken about her dream to work at Camp America the summer between college and university. Elaine had pressed her lips together in a thin line, then shook her head. Clare had asked what her mum thought about it, but she'd refused to comment, and Clare had assumed that she didn't think it would be a good idea. As it happened, she hadn't applied, but it had been more to do with the fact that Jenny hadn't been going and Clare didn't want to leave her best friend behind. But there had been other times when her hopes and dreams had been approved of and supported, like when she'd yearned to ride a horse. Elaine had taken her to lessons every Saturday morning for years, even when it had been rainy and cold. She had also encouraged Clare, aged seven, when she'd wanted to learn to play the violin, arranging lessons and buying her an instrument. But then, when Clare had wanted to quit seven months later because she was bored with it, her mum had sighed, nodded and something in her eyes had flickered as if resigning herself to the fact that Clare would never be a great musician after all. It was that uncertainty for Clare that was so hard, sensing that she had been a disappointment for her mum, that she had never been enough. She shook herself inwardly; time to get this done, no point in dwelling on the past anymore.

'Mum, Kyle and I are a bit worried about you. Since you lost the old village hall, and along with that, the village drama society, you seem somewhat . . . depleted. As if you've lost your focus.'

'My focus?' Elaine's eyes widened, and Clare reached for her glass, realised it was empty, and tucked her hands together on her lap, pressing her short nails into her palms.

'Yes. We know how important the village hall was to you –'

'And to others in the village,' Kyle cut in.

'Yes.' Clare nodded vigorously. 'To many, many others.' *Make Mum feel like it's not just her, that others need this too. Because they probably do.* 'But there's a new village hall and although it's not quite the warm, weathered hub that the old hall was . . .' Clare paused, trying to find the right words.

'It has potential.' Kyle rescued her. 'Doesn't it, Mum?'

'Oh yes, it does.' Clare tried to inject enthusiasm into her voice. They'd had a look inside and the new hall was so clean and sparse, not at all warm or welcoming, but that could change. 'It has so much potential. And . . . well . . . wouldn't it be nice to get the am dram society back together?'

'Am dram?' Her mum snorted.

'Well, that's what you called them sometimes, Mum.'

'It just sounds funny coming from you.' Elaine cocked an eyebrow at Clare and she felt like stomping from the room. Her teenage self was not at all happy, but she had to remember that she was a grown woman now and she was trying to do a good thing here. This wasn't about a long-standing war with her mum, but about helping her to help herself. And perhaps

Elaine's reaction came more from her own nerves than from a desire to be unkind to Clare.

'But wouldn't it be nice, Nanna?' Kyle winked at Clare and she felt instantly reassured. He knew this wasn't easy for her, even though she'd never really gone into detail about how her mum made her feel.

Elaine pouted as she mulled the idea over, so Clare decided to strike while the iron was hot.

'And . . .' She raised a hand, pointing a finger in the air as if to illustrate her point, 'Wouldn't a Christmas show be a great way to kick things off?'

She pressed her hands together again and dropped her gaze to the table. There. She'd sent the idea into the room, and it would either explode, roll away like tumbleweed or find acceptance.

'A Christmas show?' Her mum tapped her fingers on the table and Clare waited, hardly daring to raise her eyes. If this idea wasn't accepted, then she wasn't sure what else they could do to help. Her mum's whole life had been about her job as a drama teacher and her drama society. What else could possibly drag her from the depths of despair and help her to live a full life again? 'With a variety of acts?'

'Yes!' Clare and Kyle replied in unison.

'I'm not sure . . .' There it was, the hesitation. Would it be followed by rejection? 'I mean, it's already the first week of November and there would be so much to do. I couldn't possibly manage it all by myself.'

Clare looked up, raising her gaze slowly to meet her mum's eyes. They twinkled, as if there was mischief there, the shoots growing from the seed that they had planted.

'We were thinking of it being more of a talent show than a play or a pantomime, Nanna. So all the acts could organise themselves. You could be the director, overseeing the running of it and the auditions and so on.'

'And we could help you.' Clare put it out there and the air seemed to crackle, as if electrified with anticipation.

'Help me?' Her mum licked her lips. 'You two?'

'Of course, Nanna.' Kyle nodded. 'I have drama experience, as you know, and Mum's a pretty useful creature. Don't underestimate her.'

Clare glowed under her son's praise and her heart shifted. Even if her mum would never see her as she would like, her son did, and it was wonderful. He loved her and appreciated her more than she had realised, and his kind words made her feel like she was walking on air.

'All right, then,' Elaine rested her elbows on the table, then steepled her fingers beneath her chin. 'If you're both prepared to help out, I'll give it some serious thought.'

❄

The next morning, Clare took Goliath on a long walk. She got up early for Tai Chi, fed him, then had some breakfast, and was ready to leave before the post was due. They were just heading down the drive when Marcellus arrived, his black lace-up boots practically screeching to a halt when he spotted the dog.

'Good morning, Clare.' His warm tone brought a smile to her lips.

'Good morning, Marcellus. How are you?'

He nodded. 'Not bad, not bad at all, although it is getting colder and darker by the day, which makes my morning rounds a bit less enjoyable.'

'Winter has truly arrived,' she said, enjoying the easy sharing of banalities.

'Indeed it has, and it will soon be Christmas.'

'Talking of Christmas . . .' Clare tilted her head. 'Didn't you used to be in the village drama society?'

He gave a booming laugh. 'I did, yes, but that was a long, long time ago, back when your dad was still with us and when we had the old village hall. It used to be a lot of fun in the old days, Clare, let me tell you. We used to put on plays, pantomimes, talent shows . . . you name it. Every single one was an absolute blast! Then,' he looked around as if not wanting to be overheard, 'it all got a bit too serious for me.'

'Serious?'

'Yeah.' He nodded. 'New people coming to live in the village, all thinking they were Anthony Hopkins, Whitney Houston and the like, giving it their shiny Shakespeare and their best Brecht.' He dropped into a low bow, making a sweeping gesture with his arm, and Clare laughed. 'They didn't have room for the likes of me with my sense of humour, you know. Some of the lines – like Shakespeare's puns and things – were so funny and I'd often end up in hoots of laughter.'

'I can imagine.'

'Anyway, according to some of them, I wasn't taking it all seriously enough – but Clare, life is too short to be serious all the time.'

'You're right there but I'm sorry the drama society didn't work out for you.'

'Not your fault, little Clare. *Sorry!* There I go again, still calling you little! Old habits are indeed hard to break. But it's not for you to be sorry. I went and found a different hobby. All's well that ends well.'

Clare smiled. 'I see what you did there.'

He winked at her and chuckled.

'The drama society hasn't been together for a while though, has it?'

He shook his head. 'Not since the old hall burnt down. It was a terrible tragedy.'

'Such a shame,' she agreed. 'But we were thinking that it might be nice to get things going again.'

Goliath tugged at the lead, trying to get closer to Marcellus so he could sniff his Royal Mail messenger bag. Marcellus stepped back. 'Just in case he's after the letters.'

Goliath licked his lips and Marcellus stepped back again, widening the distance between him and the dog.

'Would you be interested in auditioning for a Christmas show?'

Marcellus stared off into the distance and Clare watched his face carefully. His silence went on for seconds, but it felt like much longer, and Clare stepped from foot to foot to try to keep warm.

'Auditioning, you say?'

'Yes.'

'What type of show?'

'A combination of music, recitals, dance and more. A kind of showcase of talents.'

'I'll be honest, Clare, I'm not that keen on the idea of auditioning.'

'Oh . . . OK.' She felt herself deflate. What if everyone they asked reacted in the same way?

'However . . .' He grinned. 'I'll be happy to help out backstage with lighting, electricals, props and scenery. Or I'll sit on the door and take the tickets.'

She couldn't help herself, she skipped forwards and hugged him. 'Thank you so much, Marcellus!'

He gave a low chuckle as she disengaged herself and Goliath whined.

'I'll be in touch when we have more information.'

'OK, Clare, you do that,' he said.

Clare gave him a nod, then set off along the street, Goliath trotting at her side, the cold forgotten as the positivity of knowing she'd recruited at least one member of the village to help with the show kept her warm.

Chapter 11

The next week flew by as Clare and Kyle got to work planning for the show. They created leaflets and posters, including a digital one to send via email, and went to see the vicar, who was also head of the committee who ran the village hall, to check that a Christmas show would be allowed. Iolo Ifans was overjoyed at the prospect and didn't seem at all surprised, which made Clare think that perhaps her mum had already mentioned it to him – and they booked the hall for the last week of November for auditions and for the night of 19th December for the show itself. Elaine even got involved by digging out her old notebook and finding email addresses and phone numbers for the previous members of the drama society. Some of the older members had sadly passed away and one had retired to Tenerife, but there were still enough around who could be approached to audition for, or to at least support, the show.

On the Friday of the second week of November, Clare and Kyle set off around the village to deliver leaflets and to ask local shops to put posters up in their windows. The reaction surprised Clare, as she hadn't known if the villagers would be keen to resurrect the village Christmas show, but the majority were very happy about the idea. It was almost as if they had been waiting for something like this, for someone to set the ball rolling, and call them to action.

As she passed the vets' surgery on the way to the café, she realised that she could ask if they would put a poster in their window. She stopped to go in, changed her mind, then stopped again and backtracked, before changing her mind again. Something about the thought of going into the surgery made her stomach flutter, but she didn't want to think too hard about why that was.

Obviously, nothing to do with a handsome vet . . .

She was just walking away, reluctant to return to the scene of *chinogate* when she heard someone calling her name. Turning, she saw him, standing in the doorway of the surgery, his handsome face every bit as gorgeous as she remembered.

'Oh. Hello, Sam.' She smiled, she hoped nonchalantly, and Goliath tugged on his lead, evidently keen to greet Sam.

'Were you coming in?' he asked, gesturing at the door.

'No.' She shook her head. 'Well, yes, but then I wasn't sure.'

He knitted his brows.

'What I mean is . . . I'm delivering these leaflets and posters and asking local businesses if we can put them on their noticeboards and in their windows, and I was going to see if you and Miranda would mind putting one up.'

He peered at the folder she was holding. 'What's it for?'

Clare tapped her forehead. 'Sorry. I'm not making much sense, am I? It's for a Christmas show.'

'A Christmas show? There hasn't been a show in the village since the old hall burnt down.' He gazed into the distance. 'In fact, there's been nothing special at the new village hall – not a concert, not a play, not a game of bingo, not a bake sale. Such a shame.'

'Well, we're hoping to bring the Christmas cheer back to the village with a talent show this year.'

'And you're organising it, are you?'

His gaze was so intense that every tiny hair on her arms and neck stood to attention as something else stirred at her core, something she hadn't felt in a very long time.

'Clare?' He smiled, flashing his lovely teeth.

'What?'

'I asked if you're organising the show?'

'Oh. Oh, yes. Yes. Along with my son and my mum.'

'Fantastic. It'll be such a great thing for the village.'

'I hope so.'

'It will be.'

'So do you think you could . . .' She waved the folder.

'Of course. I'd be happy to. Give me some leaflets as well and I'll put them on the reception desk in case anyone wants more information.'

Opening the folder, she got a poster and some leaflets out.

'Do you have any talents you'd like to showcase?' she asked, meeting his chocolate brown eyes again.

The smile that played across his lips told her that she'd just said something he found funny. She ran the question through her mind and cringed inwardly. It sounded so suggestive, more so as she replayed it.

'Goodness! I didn't mean that how it sounded.'

'How it sounded?' He was grinning now, and she wanted to turn and run. But at the same time she wanted to step closer and see if he smelt as good as he looked.

Something funny was definitely happening to her. Perhaps it was the regular exercise of walking and Tai Chi improving her fitness levels and sense of well-being, the burgeoning excitement about the show, or finally being free of the shadow of her marriage. Perhaps it was just down to this man and the effect that he had upon her; it could be that their pheromones were a perfect match and her body was letting her know.

Whatever it was, despite the embarrassment, she liked it. For the first time in a very long time, she felt alive, filled with anticipation about what could happen; she felt as though she might be learning to live her life for herself and not for others. She had needs, desires and wants and she was finding herself very attracted to this man. Each time she saw him, the attraction seemed to deepen, just like her blushes.

'Well, I thought it sounded a bit suggestive, but perhaps I'm wrong.' She took a moment to rub Goliath's head, willing her colour to fade, hoping that Sam didn't think she was a complete idiot.

'It sounded good to me.' He cleared his throat. 'However, I'm not sure about *my* hidden talents, but my sister has a very impressive voice and could possibly be persuaded to take part.'

'What does she sing?'

'Lots of different types of music but she's particularly good with Adele songs. She has that throaty, husky thing going on and she's been known to bring tears to my eyes on occasion.'

'That would be wonderful!' Clare said. 'Exactly the type of act we're looking for. Do you think she'd audition? Could you ask her?'

Sam's expression changed, the smile fading away and something filled his eyes. It looked like uncertainty and he seemed to hunch over as his mood changed.

'If I see her.' He nodded slowly. 'I'll definitely tell her about it if I see her.'

The temptation to ask why he might not bubbled in Clare. She thought Sam lived with his sister – she couldn't recall if he'd told her that or if it was someone else – so surely he'd see her later. Unless, of course, she wouldn't be home.

'Thank you.'

'No problem at all.' He ran his long fingers over Goliath's head. 'How's this boy doing?'

'He's good.'

'He's been looking a lot better since you arrived.'

'Really?'

'He's more streamlined because he's lost some weight. He needed to shed a bit because it's not good for dogs to carry excess fat. It must be the longer walks.'

'It's not just him.' Clare bit her lip, wondering why she'd blurted that out.

'No?' Sam raised an eyebrow.

'All the walks have helped me to tone up too.' She lowered her gaze to her feet, suddenly shy at the confession.

'You always looked pretty good to me.' His voice was gruff now, and when she raised her eyes again to meet his, something crackled between them. She felt sure that if she reached out and touched his hand, sparks would fly.

'You're too kind.' The words emerged as a little more than a whisper and they stood in silence, swaying slightly as if to music only they could hear.

'Do you have plans tonight?' His question broke the spell, bringing them both back to reality.

'Uh, not really. I was going to have a quiet night in. I think.'

'You think?' That smile was back.

'Why?'

'I thought I might go to the quiz.' He scuffed the toe of his shoe against the kerb and she saw a glimpse of the boy he would have been: serious, shy, unassuming. Sweet. Kind. Also, cold, she realised, as he rubbed his arms and folded them across his chest. He was out here with her in just his shirt and chinos and it was freezing.

'With Magnus?'

'I think so. You're very welcome to join us.'

'I'll let you know.' She nodded.

'OK.' Reaching into his pocket he pulled out a mobile. 'Can we exchange numbers then?'

'Of course.' She told him hers and he typed it into his phone, then her mobile buzzed in her pocket, so she pulled it out and saved Sam's number.

'Text you later.'

'I'll put these up.' He waved the poster and leaflets.

'Fabulous. Now get inside and warm up.'

'I am warm.' He flashed her a cheeky smile and heat radiated through her chest. She didn't know about warm, he was hot!

Turning to walk away, Clare didn't feel the cold, in spite of the grey sky and biting wind. Not only had Sam agreed to display the poster about the show, he had asked her out that evening (she knew it wasn't a date, but that was fine) and she had learnt a bit more about him and about herself. It seemed that every interaction she had in her home village was teaching her something new – or was she simply relearning what she'd already known once upon a time, before she gave herself to her life with Jason, before she lost who she really was?

Chapter 18

Clare had stopped by the salon before heading home, to see if they'd put a poster up and to check how Jenny was getting along, and she'd been filled with concern when another stylist had told her that Jenny had phoned in sick that morning. Clare determined to go straight to Jenny's house to see how she was.

She stopped at the small village shop and purchased some tins of soup, ginger ale and ginger biscuits, then walked quickly to Jenny's house. When she got there, she realised she still had Goliath with her and took him back to her mum's first.

Outside Jenny's, she admired the stone façade with the climbing ivy, the roses around the door – currently bare but presumably beautiful in the summer months – and regret filled her. This was the house her friend had raised her children in, the home she'd made with her childhood sweetheart, a place Clare would have liked to visit more often over the years.

She peered up at the bedrooms, wondering if Jenny might be sleeping, but the curtains in the two front rooms were open, so she could well be downstairs. She knocked quietly on the front door, the reusable shopping bag swinging on her arm, the cans clinking together. She'd bought three different types of soup, not able to recall what Jenny's favourite was and knowing that morning sickness made even your favourite foods smell funny anyway, so it was better to have a variety for Jenny to choose from. Ginger biscuits and ginger ale had been helpful when she'd experienced morning sickness herself so she hoped they would help ease Jenny's as well, and soup was always soothing.

Presumably, hopefully, Jenny's girls would be at college at this time on a Friday and Martin would be at work. That would give Clare and Jenny a chance to talk freely. Clare wasn't sure that Jenny hadn't told her family about the pregnancy yet. She hadn't liked to ask again and Jenny hadn't volunteered the information.

A noise inside, like a door closing, made her step closer to the front door. She could see movement behind the stained-glass pattern that was like a rainbow at the top third of the door. When the sunlight caught it, Jenny probably had a rainbow across her hallway. Colour and light, two beautiful things to provide comfort and lift spirits.

There was a click, then the door opened slowly, and Jenny peered out. Her blonde hair hung lankly around her face and her skin was a horrid shade of grey.

'Clare?' Jenny said, frowning. 'Was I expecting you?'

'No, lovely, but I went to see you at work and they said you'd called in sick. I brought you some bits and bobs.' She held up the bag. 'Just some soup and biscuits to help with nausea.'

Jenny stepped back and opened the door and Clare followed her inside. The hallway smelt of cooking, and as she followed Jenny, she got a waft of unwashed hair. It wasn't like Jenny to slack on personal care, so her friend must be feeling seriously rough. Clare looked around as they passed through a hallway with a staircase that curved around to a galley-style landing that led off in two directions. There was a large gilt-edged mirror on the wall opposite the door and it added extra light to the space, created the illusion of the hallway being bigger than it was, though it wasn't small by any means. There were plants in large pots dotted around the hallway, a yucca and a few that she recognised as ferns and palms.

Walking into the kitchen-diner, Clare's mouth fell open. Apart from the fact that Martin was a lovely man, there were clearly other advantages to being married to a builder. It was huge and had clearly been extended into the garden. It had Velux windows in the ceiling of the extension that bathed the room with natural light and off to the left was the kitchen, complete with granite-topped goose grey units and a range cooker. There was a large island at the centre of the kitchen, with four high stools tucked underneath, and on that was a sink and one of those fancy taps that provided water in any form you wanted, from still to sparkling to boiling, that Clare had seen advertised. She tried to ignore the dirty dishes piled on the counter and the pile of washing dumped in the doorway to the utility room.

To her right was a large rectangular table with grey leather chairs, then off at the end of the extension was a large grey leather sofa with plump cream and yellow scatter cushions. In here, the food smell was, ironically, fainter, and there was an overriding aroma of lavender and coffee.

Jenny went straight to the sofa and slumped into the cushions. It wasn't lost on Clare that she cupped her stomach as she sank down or that she winced as if in discomfort.

'Are you going to tell me what's wrong?' Clare set the bag she'd brought on the floor, removed her coat and gloves, then perched on the sofa next to Jenny. 'I don't think it's just the morning sickness, is it?'

Jenny's eyes shone and she pressed her lips together until they turned white.

'I . . .' She blinked rapidly then rubbed her eyes with balled-up fists. 'I don't know what to do.'

'What do you mean?' Clare took Jenny's hand between both of hers.

'It's such a mess.'

'Why is it a mess?'

Jenny stared out of the bifold doors at the perfect square of garden with a neat green lawn and tall trees edging the rear fence. They must have lost a fair bit of the garden to the extension, but there was still enough for a table and chairs and a small shed.

'The girls have been arguing a lot lately and Martin is working really hard to get a build finished before Christmas and I just don't feel well. I have no energy and I want to sleep all the time to escape the nausea. It's as if, since doing the test, my body has decided to go full-on with pregnancy symptoms.'

'Have you told Martin?'

Jenny shook her head. 'He's been so tired lately, and I started to try to tell him a few times, but then I look at him and see him for the forty-five-year-old man that he is, and my heart breaks a little. How can we possibly have a baby now? How can we go back to sleepless nights and nappies? I mean, when the baby is ten, I'll be fifty-five, almost fifty-six. He or she will have sisters who are nineteen years older. Then there are all the things that could go wrong. The risks are so much higher for me as an older mother and for the baby. It's just not a good thing.'

Clare held Jenny's hand, knowing that her friend needed to get everything off her chest.

'Shall I make us a cup of tea?' Clare asked after a bit.

'Please.' Jenny nodded, so Clare got the packet of ginger nuts out of the shopping bag and placed it on the coffee table in front of them. She hadn't registered the table when she'd sat down, because she'd been so concerned about Jenny, but now she looked, she saw it was gorgeous. Clare couldn't help running a finger over its surface to see if it was as smooth as it looked. 'It's black walnut with a blue resin river. It cost a fortune, but Martin bought it for my fortieth.'

'It's incredible.' Clare said, knowing that whatever Jenny felt right now, she would be OK.

When she'd made tea, she took a tray over to the table and set it down carefully then opened the biscuits and placed two on Jenny's knee. 'Try to nibble them if you can.'

Helping herself to a biscuit, Clare dunked it in her tea, then bit into it, enjoying the familiar flavour and heat of the ginger. She would have reached for another just weeks ago, but now she didn't feel the need. One was enough, and she liked the way that her jeans were looser on her hips and thighs, the way that her belly had stopped folding over itself concertina-style when she sat down.

'I'm so glad you're home, Clare.' Jenny had a bit more colour now. 'I don't know how I'd get through this without you.'

'I haven't done anything, Jen.'

'But you have. You were there with me when I did the test and now you've come here when I really, really needed to speak to someone.' A tear rolled down Jenny's cheek and plopped onto her stained pyjama top.

'I'm always here, Jen.' Clare squeezed her hand gently. 'Look, I'm free this afternoon and evening . . .' She swallowed her thoughts of meeting Sam later. 'So how about if I stay for a few hours and help you out a bit? I can tidy up while you have a shower or a soak in the bath, then I'll make you something to eat.'

'Oh, Clare, are you sure? It's just that Martin's working late and the girls are going straight to the cinema from college and normally I'd be delighted at the thought of having the TV to myself and a few glasses of wine, but today I'm just so tired and I didn't even have the energy to tidy up after breakfast.'

'Of course I'm sure.'

'I know that I need to tell Martin, I really do, but it hasn't been the right time.'

'Perhaps you could tell him tomorrow. Does he take Saturdays off?'

'He's trying to finish a job, so he's been working some hours on weekends, but if I tell him it's important, I'm sure he'll make time. We need to decide what to do as a family, anyway. I can't make these decisions alone. They're just too big.'

'Do you mean you've considered . . . ?'

Jenny's bottom lip wobbled. 'It's not what I want to do. I'm a firm believer in a woman's right to choose, but whenever I've tried to imagine not going ahead with the pregnancy, I've been hit by the reality that this baby is part of me and Martin and a sibling to Tilda and Lizzy. Then I go through the whole, *it'll work out* pep talk, and it seems fine until I wake in the morning and the fears start choking me all over again.'

'You really do need to speak to Martin. At least you could work this through together then, because at the moment you're carrying everything on your shoulders. He'll be able to help you, I'm sure.'

'How would you feel though, Clare? If you got pregnant now?'

Clare sipped her tea. How would she feel? 'Honestly?' She shook her head. 'I don't know. My marriage wasn't . . . physical for a long time. It wasn't that I didn't want to . . . but Jason wasn't interested. He hadn't looked at me in that way for ages.'

Her cheeks burned at the confession. Knowing that her husband hadn't wanted her, even when she had tried to reason it away as being down to the fact that they'd been together for so long, had been humiliating. She'd felt undesirable, frumpy, unwanted.

'I'm sorry, Clare, that's not fair.'

Clare shrugged. 'It stopped worrying me after a while, I think I just assumed that most marriages were the same. It wasn't that I didn't think about how nice it would be to have a man gaze at me with interest, or kiss me passionately . . .' Her mind strayed to Sam and how it would feel to have his lips against her own, his strong arms embracing her, and adrenaline coursed through her, making her momentarily lightheaded. She put her hands self-consciously to her cheeks and took a few slow deep breaths. 'I'm only human, I guess, and I do have desires.' She giggled then and met Jenny's eyes. Her friend was nodding.

'Of course you do – and you're a beautiful woman, Clare. Any man would be lucky to have you and you deserve to be happy.'

'Hardly.' Clare huffed. Then she considered her reaction. She wasn't in bad shape, she was warm and loving, and she *did* deserve to be happy. 'No, you're right. I do deserve happiness. I'm not sure that it needs to come in the form of a man, but a hug and the odd night of hot sex wouldn't go amiss.'

They both laughed and it felt good for Clare to have someone to talk to about these things again. Someone who wouldn't judge her for having these feelings, for wanting to be held by a man again, at least once in her life. What was so wrong with that? But, of course, there were other things she wanted too; she just needed to figure out exactly what they were.

'Look, Clare, life doesn't end once you hit forty. I've read enough articles in magazines at work and spoken to enough clients in the salon in their forties, fifties, sixties and beyond and sex doesn't stop just because you're no longer twenty-five. Where there's a will – or a willy, in some cases . . .' Jenny winked, 'there's a way. And why shouldn't there be? Life is for living.'

'You're so right, Jen.'

'Unfortunately, though, my desire for my husband and his for me led to this little accident.' Jenny patted her belly, slightly rounded beneath her top.

'Do you know how far along you are?'

Jenny pursed her lips. 'I haven't been to the GP yet, but I had a look back through my dates on the app on my phone and I could be around four months.'

'Bloody hell.'

'I know. I didn't know I should still be using protection. Bloody fertile body having its last hurrah, I bet.'

Clare nodded. 'But if you're that far along, Jen, then the pregnancy must be pretty strong.'

Jenny pulled up her top and Clare gasped. Jenny's belly was round and tight, the skin shiny where it was being stretched. 'It seems to have popped out overnight.'

'Well, at least the morning sickness should pass soon then.'

'I don't know – it's like my body is getting revenge for feeling fine and leaving me in blissful oblivion for the first few months.'

'Will you go to the GP soon?'

Jenny nodded. 'I've made up my mind – I'll speak to Martin tonight. I won't wait until tomorrow.'

'Are you sure?'

'He'll be tired, but I'll make him dinner, then I'll tell him.'

'You don't think he has any idea?'

'He just thinks I've been eating too many treats at work and that I've had stomach flu these past couple of weeks. You know what men can be like. They don't want to believe that there's anything to worry about unless you actually spell it out for them. Martin works so hard and he just wants a quiet life.'

'He's not going to get much quiet for the next few years.'

Clare winced, wishing she could take the comment back because Jenny hadn't made any decisions yet, but Jenny sniggered nervously. 'He's going to go mad.'

'Well, you didn't do this on your own, so he has to take responsibility too.'

'Two to tango and all that?'

'Exactly. As you said, where there's a willy . . .' Clare smiled again, enjoying that they could be silly together too. 'Right, Mrs Rolands, you go and have a bath and put some clean clothes on and I'll tidy up a bit. Not that I'm suggesting that your home is a mess or anything, but . . .'

'It's fine, don't worry. You could never offend me, Clare.'

'Well, there was that one time . . .' she said, thinking about when they'd argued about Jason.

Jenny waved a hand dismissively. 'We were young and hot-headed. We just needed to clear the air and if you hadn't left the next day, we'd have made up again. Just like always.'

They stood up and Jenny hugged Clare, causing a host of emotions to flood through her. Seeing her oldest friend in her home, knowing how vulnerable she was right now and realising exactly how much they'd missed out on over the years was proving to be very emotional. She loved Jenny and had done for as long as she could remember. At least now they could be there for each other again.

Jenny released her, then padded across the room and Clare rolled up her sleeves. It was time to get to work.

❄

'What's up?' Magnus asked as he set two pints of beer down on the table at The Red. 'Your face looks like you're chewing a wasp.'

'What?' Sam frowned at Magnus. 'I look like I'm chewing a wasp?'

'Yes!' He chuckled. 'Especially now.'

'Oh . . .' Sam pulled his mobile from his pocket and checked the screen again. No text messages or missed calls. It was just gone seven. Should he text Clare to find out if she was coming or would that be too pushy? What were the rules of engagement these days anyway? It had been so long since he'd dated, since he'd pursued a woman or had so much as expressed an interest in anyone. Liking Clare was probably a really bad idea and not going to get him anywhere. They weren't dating, were barely even friends, and perhaps she'd been keen to get away from him today and had no interest in seeing him socially again. And yet, when he was around her he felt certain that there was something between them, a spark, something that fizzed like champagne, things yet to be said, yet to be done.

'Why do you keep checking your phone?' Magnus asked. Sam looked at him, his eyes drawn to the foam that was clinging to his blond moustache like an extra layer of hair. 'Are you waiting for a message from her?'

'It depends who you mean by her.' Sam sipped his drink, wishing he'd ordered a spirit instead, something to numb the rising anxiety.

'I mean *Clare*. Are you expecting to hear from her?'

Sam shifted on his seat. How did Magnus know?

'You're wondering why I said Clare?'

'Yes. Why would you think it was her?'

'I'm part psychic.' Magnus closed his eyes and placed his forefingers either side of his brow, then exhaled loudly. 'You were expecting Clare to come this evening. Yes?'

Sam nodded. *Great.* Now Magnus could read him like a book. He'd never been very good at hiding his emotions, but he had been quite good at pushing them away. Clare coming to the village, Alyssa getting into a relationship, the past threatening to catch up with him . . . it was all building like a tornado that would, sooner or later, whip him off his feet and carry him away. Sam was always, always in control, but he had a feeling that the tight grip he'd exerted on his life was slipping and some days he thought it might actually be nice to let go and feel that release. Surely no one could control everything in their life? Surely, at some point, something had to give . . .

'I'm teasing you, Sam. The reason I thought it was Clare was because, firstly, you have chemistry with her. I've never seen you act like that around another woman before. With Clare, it's like you come alive.'

'Come alive?'

'Yes. You become animated, you relax a bit and let go of the . . .' Magnus tapped his chest with his fists. 'The tension that you always hold there. That slightly awkward way you carry yourself.'

'Right.' Magnus wasn't doing a lot for Sam's self-confidence. Sam pushed his shoulders back, suddenly painfully aware of how tight they were, of the tension across his chest and the way it made his head ache. 'I'm awkward.'

Magnus laughed. 'And secondly, because I saw you earlier from the surgery window, you and Clare, gazing intently into each other's eyes like the whole world had come to a stop and nothing else mattered.'

'Ha! I think you're getting carried away now, Magnus.' Sam coughed, trying to clear away his embarrassment.

'I don't think so. You exchanged numbers, right?'

'Uh . . . yes.'

'And you asked her to come tonight?'

'We're friends.'

'Good.' Magnus nodded. 'That is a good basis for a romance. Friends first, love comes next with all the passion and fun.'

Sam couldn't help himself then, he smiled. 'You're an old romantic, Magnus.'

'I know. It's my Viking blood. It runs hot and red like a river of fire.'

'Is that the line you use on dates?'

'Sometimes.' Magnus winked to show he was teasing.

Just then, Sam's mobile buzzed on the table where he'd put it face down after checking it for the hundredth time that hour. Magnus stared at it. Sam stared at it.

It buzzed again.

'Go on then, take a look.' Magnus smiled.

Sam shrugged. 'Maybe later.'

'I'll check it for you, shall I? To be honest, Sam, I can't stand the suspense.'

Sam laughed, then picked up the phone and, sure enough, he had a message from Clare. Reading it twice, disappointment swirled inside him.

'She can't make it.' He put the phone down on the table again and picked up his glass. 'She's with a friend and won't be here in time for the quiz.'

'Sorry, man.' Magnus patted Sam's shoulder. 'Another time maybe?'

'Maybe.'

'It's a genuine reason, Sam, and at least she did text you. She could have left you wondering all evening.'

'That's true.' Sam sighed. Magnus was right. Clare could have left him wondering all night, but she had taken the time to send him a text. He was disappointed, wanted to see her and to talk to her again, watch as the light shone on her silky brown hair and observe the endearing way she worried her bottom lip whenever the blush bloomed in her cheeks. The blush that rose so readily when he teased her and sometimes when he didn't. Would that same blush fill her cheeks in a moment of passion? Would she bite her lip then as she was carried away with desire and delicious sensation?

He took a long drink from his glass. Thinking like this wasn't helping matters. The text could be Clare's way of letting him down gently, of informing him that she did have better things to do on a Friday evening than spend it in the pub with him. It wasn't a nice thought but sometimes it was better to face the truth, however much he'd prefer to reassure himself with other possibilities.

With hope.

'That feels better.' Jenny entered the kitchen-diner wearing fresh pyjamas, her hair damp and her face shiny.

'You look better too.' Clare smiled, glad to see some colour in Jenny's cheeks.

'Thanks. It's amazing the difference a bath can make to how you feel. Just washing my hair helped.' She pushed her sweeping side fringe back from her forehead and tucked it behind a small ear. 'Wow, Clare! You've cleaned up in here. Thank you so much.'

Clare shrugged. 'It's no problem – and it wasn't that bad.'

The dirty dishes had been loaded into the dishwasher, the surfaces cleared and disinfected, and the washing sorted into lights and darks, then the first load put on. Clare had also run a duster around the furniture in the diner and lit a scented candle that she'd found under the sink, so the room smelt of ginger and vanilla.

The light was fading outside so she'd turned on the lamps in the corners and the room had a cosy feel. She could imagine summer days spent here with the bifold doors open, letting in the aroma of roses and honeysuckle as the birds sang into the twilight. Would she be here in the summer to spend time with Jenny and her family? She wouldn't have thought so just weeks ago, but she was starting to consider staying here as a definite possibility. Jenny might well have her new baby by then and Clare could come and help her, possibly even do some childminding for her when she returned to work after her maternity leave. Anything was possible now that there were no other commitments holding Clare back. She had her half of the money from the sale of the house, after all, so she could put a deposit down on somewhere local and create a new home of her own. Of course, she did need to consider looking for a job and would do so if she decided to stay in the village. Otherwise, she could go anywhere that she found work. Having been back now for over five weeks, the idea of leaving was difficult, but if she couldn't find a job, she'd probably have to leave at some point. Kyle had spoken about having Christmas together and she really wanted that, plus there was the show to think of, so if she did leave, it would be in the New Year. That gave her time to think more and to check out the local job market.

Whatever happened, she would be fully independent, in control of her own life, and no man would be able to tell her that she couldn't buy what she wanted for dinner, that she needed to pluck the hair that had sprouted on her chin (a recent and unwelcome addition, but one that she found quite amusing at times) or that she should try to exercise more. Clare would exercise if she wanted to, take care of herself *for herself*, and no man would ever make her feel as low as Jason had done again. Even though she tried not to blame him, he had been responsible for his own behaviour, and he hadn't always been as kind or considerate as he could have been.

'Are you all right?' Jenny asked, placing a warm hand on Clare's arm.

'Oh . . . yes.'

'You looked miles away then and a bit sad.'

'I'm not sad. Just thinking about all the good things to come.'

'I hope so.' Jenny sighed. 'I hope it's all good.'

'It will be.' Clare gave her a hug. 'What time will Martin be home?'

'Any minute now.'

'Good, because dinner is ready.'

'You cooked as well?'

Jenny peered at the range cooker, but it wasn't on.

'Well, I hard boiled some eggs and made a salad from what was in the fridge. There was some cooked salmon in there too, so I thought you could have that or I could heat some soup for you.'

'Salmon will be fine. I can stomach that and, again, thank you.' Jenny's eyes glistened. 'I'm not used to this.'

'To what?'

'Having a friend around to take care of me.'

'Jen.' Clare pulled her into another hug. 'I'm so sorry.'

'What for?' She sniffed.

'Not being here.'

'I wasn't there for you either. Who took care of you when you needed a friend? Did you have friends in Reading?'

'Some. But they weren't like you. They were people at work and other mums with children Kyle's age, and I don't know . . . I never let them get close, was always on my guard. I think that after I left here and we drifted apart, I was afraid to trust in friendship again.'

'Now I feel even worse.' Jenny's nose started to run as she cried.

'No! Don't! That wasn't what I wanted. I was just trying to explain why I didn't get close to anyone. I was just as much to blame as you were. I could have tried to heal the rift between us, made more of an effort to come and see you.'

'It doesn't matter anymore, Clare. You're back now when I need you most.'

Clare started to cry and they held each other tight, rocking gently from side to side.

'What's going on?' Martin's deep voice made them start and Clare gently released Jenny and wiped her tears away with her fingers.

'We were just being sentimental,' Jenny said, as she pulled a tissue from the pocket of her pyjama bottoms.

'And reminiscing.' Clare smiled wanly and Jenny took her hand and squeezed it.

'Looks and smells lovely in here, Jen,' Martin said as he went to the fridge and brought out a bottle of beer. 'Either of you want one?'

'No, thanks.' Clare shook her head.

'Jen? No?' Martin looked at Clare. 'My wine-loving wife has turned teetotal recently. Saved us a small fortune on dry white.' He laughed but Jenny caught Clare's eye and raised her eyebrows.

'Nothing wrong with giving your liver and your bank balance a break.' Clare tucked her hands into her pockets.

'How was your day, Martin?' Jenny gave him a kiss and he gazed at her adoringly, his big arm around her waist. They still made such a handsome couple, him with his height and broad shoulders, his bald head shadowed with stubble where the hair he had left was growing through. He'd always kept it short, even when they were teens, telling Clare once that he hated how wavy it was, but now it seemed that it had receded and thinned out enough for him to decide to shave it off altogether. He had a well-shaped head and a handsome face with a strong square jaw, so he could get away with it. If Jason had ever gone completely bald, Clare suspected he'd have looked a bit like a fence post, especially as he'd got older, because his chin had seemed to become one with his neck.

'It was busy, tiring, but I'm nearly done, so it's all good. How was work?'

'Oh . . .' Jenny stepped out of his embrace and got a glass from a cupboard then filled it with water. 'I came home. I wasn't feeling well.'

'Again?' His brows furrowed and Clare saw worry cross his face, his knuckles whiten as his fingers tightened around the beer bottle.

'It's fine. Nothing to worry about.' Jenny sipped her water.

'Perhaps you'd better make a GP appointment. What do you think, Clare? Jen hasn't been feeling great lately and she doesn't know why, can't pinpoint anything, so a trip to the doc might be best.'

'Probably a good idea.' Clare's gaze slid from Martin to Jenny. 'Right, I should be going. I need to get back for Mum and Kyle.'

'You're welcome to stay for dinner,' Martin said. 'Be great to catch up, Clare. I know you've been back for a few weeks, but this is the first time I've seen you properly. We've missed you over the years.'

'I missed you both too.'

'And I was sorry to hear about you and Jason. His loss, I say.'

'Thanks, but it really was for the best.'

'We could order a takeaway?' he suggested. 'Chinese or Indian.'

Clare saw Jenny's face blanche. 'Another time, perhaps? I really do have to get going.'

Martin nodded. 'No problem. I need to shower and wash the day away, then I think I just spotted a tasty salad in the fridge.'

'You did. Clare made it for us.'

'Thanks, Clare.' He smiled, looking slightly bemused. 'You meals on wheels now?'

'No, Jen went to have a bath, so I just threw a salad together. It was nothing, really. There's also salmon you can have with it.'

'Great.' Clare suddenly felt sorry for Martin. He looked like he wanted a takeaway or something stodgy after a day's work, not a healthy salmon salad, but he was perfectly capable of looking after himself. She just hoped Jenny wouldn't feel the need to make something else for him because she clearly needed to rest.

'We'll see you soon then, Clare?' Martin asked.

'You will.'

He left the room, beer in hand, and soon she heard his heavy tread on the stairs.

'I'm going to tell him after we've eaten.' Jenny placed her hands on her hips as if steeling herself. 'It needs to be shared now. Thanks so much for today.'

'Let me know how it goes and ring if you need me. I haven't got anything planned.'

Clare thought of Sam who would be at the pub right now, the quiz well underway, the chair he might have saved for her empty at his side. She felt bad for letting him down, but he'd be fine, Magnus would be with him.

'I will.'

Jenny walked her to the door and Clare pushed her arms into her coat and zipped it up.

'Try to eat, won't you?'

Jenny nodded. 'I promise.'

Clare let herself out into the evening air. As she walked away, she sent out a wish to the universe to let Jenny and Martin work things through. They would face challenges as a result of this, but it was nothing they couldn't handle. And Clare would be there for Jenny now, just as she had always, secretly, longed to be.

Chapter 19

The next morning, Clare took Goliath along their usual woodland walk, reaching the crossroads where she'd first bumped into Sam. She stood there for a moment, gazing around her at the trees, the small sign that read Little Bramble and then the one that led to her left, towards a place she used to visit often: Old Oak Stables.

She'd wanted to go there since her return, but something had held her back. Of course, she'd been quite busy, but as well as that there had been a sense of anxiety about returning to a place she had loved so much growing up. She had initially gone to the stables to learn to ride when she was ten, and had spent practically every Saturday morning there until she'd gone off to university. She'd visited a few times during the holidays, but when she'd got together with Jason, she'd stopped going altogether. Jason hadn't been keen on horses, so Clare had put that part of herself away, sacrificed it for her marriage, and been content to do so because she believed that everybody made compromises when they fell in love. But it had been a big sacrifice for her because she loved horses: riding them, caring for them . . . and it had been twenty-six years since she'd gone to Old Oak Stables. Could she go back?

'Come on, Goliath,' she said, deciding. 'Let's go this way for a change.'

They turned left and made their way along the narrow lane that led beneath a canopy of tree branches. In the summer months, this canopy would be thick with leaves, creating a cool dark tunnel, but in the winter the bare tree branches that grew up from each side and met above the path kept most of the light from reaching the ground. Her feet slid on the mud and she did her best to guide Goliath away from the worst patches, knowing that he'd have to have his feet washed when they went home.

When they emerged at the end of the tunnel, Clare followed the path as it veered to the left. The stables could be accessed via a road, but she had always walked there this way, so it was as instinctive as finding her way home. She reached a gate at the bottom of the lane and let herself and Goliath through it, then crossed the field towards the stables. She could see them now, two long narrow buildings that housed the horses and a larger building that was used for lessons when the weather was too bad to ride outdoors.

Beyond the stables was a large farmhouse where the owner, Georgia Baker, had lived with her husband and three daughters. The eldest, Verity, had been nine years younger than Clare and she'd followed Clare around the stables whenever she went there, asking her endless questions about herself and about the world in general. She'd been a sweet girl with a mass of ginger curls, lots of cute freckles and the most enchanting eyes – one blue and one green. Verity's sisters had been much younger. Bonnie was five years younger than Verity and the other, Fran, was seven years. As Clare neared the stable block, she realised that Verity would be thirty-six now and her sisters in their late twenties and early thirties. That thought made her mouth dry up. A lot of time had passed since she'd last been here and she wasn't sure if they still owned the place, let alone if they would recognise her.

The smell of horses hit her then, a combination of manure, leather, hay and wood chippings that was so familiar it brought a lump to her throat. The hours she had spent here, the days mucking out the stables, grooming the horses, riding across the fields had been a special part of her youth. She had never wanted to ride competitively, never longed to be a part of the show jumping world, but had enjoyed spending time with the horses and trekking around the countryside, whether alone or with Jenny.

A whinny from the stables made Goliath's ears prick up and Clare tightened her grip on his lead. She wasn't sure if he would be all right around horses but she decided to see how he went.

Taking a deep breath, she opened the gate and she and Goliath walked through it, then closed it behind them. Goliath's nose was wriggling madly and she knew that the smells would be even stronger for him. She decided to head towards the house to see if she could find anyone, but just then one of the stable doors opened and a woman emerged with a saddle over her arm. Wearing beige jodhpurs, black knee-high riding boots and a checked shirt with a padded gilet, she looked as if she probably worked there. Her hair was covered by a navy scarf.

'Hello, can I help you?' the woman asked when she spotted Clare.

'Yes, actually. I was wondering if the Bakers still own this place.' Clare felt Goliath moving forwards as the lead tightened around her hand.

'We do indeed.' The woman frowned. 'Do I know you?'

'I think you might.' As Clare approached her, she saw the different coloured eyes. 'Verity?'

'Yes.' Verity's eyes widened. 'You're not Clare Hughes, are you?'

They both burst into laughter.

'Oh my goodness, how'd you recognise me?' Clare placed a hand to her chest. 'I must look so different now. The last time I came here was the summer after my first year at university, when I was just nineteen.'

'You've barely changed at all,' Verity said, smiling 'and your hair is lighter but you're exactly how I remember you. How are you, Clare?'

'I'm good, thanks. What about you?'

Verity shrugged. 'Not too bad considering the fact that I'm divorced with three kids under eleven. We live at the house now,' she gestured over her shoulder at the farmhouse, 'because I've taken over with Mum being poorly.'

'Oh, I'm sorry.' Clare shook her head.

'She's better than she was this time last year.' Verity shook her head. 'Cancer. Bloody disease. I blame the stress of Dad dying two years ago, though. I think it weakened her.'

'You lost your dad, Verity? I am so sorry.'

Verity waved a hand. 'Dad was a heavy smoker, as you might remember? We told him and told him to quit smoking, but he wouldn't listen and in the end, he had a massive stroke. He was fifteen years older than mum, but they doted on each other and she's been lost without him.'

'I can imagine.' Clare found her hand moving over Goliath's back, seeking comfort from his warmth and soft fur.

'Mum's in remission, thank goodness, and it hasn't all been bad news, I promise.' Verity tucked a few strands of red hair back under her headscarf. 'You look wonderful, though, Clare. How's life treating you? Are you just visiting or back living in the village?'

'Well, like you, I'm divorced, and I've come back to stay with Mum for a while. It was only meant to be a few weeks initially, but it looks as though I'm staying until the New Year and then . . . well, I'm not sure. I need to look for work –'

Verity held up a hand. 'Really? You need a job?'

Clare nodded slowly.

'I'm in desperate need of someone reliable to come and help out here. One of my stable hands is finishing for maternity leave in February and I've advertised the vacancy, but had no takers. I was hoping to get someone local who'd be happy with three days a week, but it seems the local youth all want to move away or work on their computers being . . . what do they call it? . . . social influencers?'

'Right. Yes.'

'If you do stay, how would *you* feel about doing three days a week here?'

Clare swallowed her surprise. Working at a stables? With horses? Staying in Little Bramble indefinitely . . .

'No pressure at all!' Verity shook her head. 'I mean, I haven't even asked if you still ride. Do you?'

'I haven't ridden in years but I've missed it. Really missed it.'

'I'm pretty sure it's like riding a bike.' Verity shifted the saddle to her other arm. 'You're very welcome to come out with me any time you like. We're still running lessons and treks through the winter months, but we're a lot quieter at the moment. It usually picks up in the spring when the weather improves. We get requests for a lot of those company team bonding days when they bring their employees from London for pub treks and outdoor mindfulness days. It's great for business.'

'It sounds amazing,' Clare said, imagining how busy it could be here.

'How long has it been since you've actually been near a horse?'

'Twenty-six years!'

'Come with me.'

Verity set the saddle on a bench in the centre of the yard, then returned to the stable she'd just emerged from and beckoned to Clare.

'Oh, what about Goliath?'

'Doreen is fine with dogs. Is he OK with horses?'

'I'm not sure.' Clare looked at Goliath, but he seemed calm, so she followed Verity to the stable door. There was a hook on the wall near the door so she looped Goliath's lead around it, then stroked his head. 'I won't be long.'

Inside the stable she blinked as her eyes adjusted to the dim light. Verity was standing next to a mare, which was munching hay from a trough attached to the wall. The stable smelt of clean hay and warm animal and Clare inhaled the aroma, holding it to her like a treasured memory.

'This is Doreen. She's one of our older, calmer mares and she's a special one.' Verity ran a hand over Doreen's head and Clare did the same, feeling the smooth black hair beneath her palm, the movement of Doreen's head as she munched at her food and then the thicker, coarser hair of her mane, which was flecked with white.

Clare stepped closer to the horse, smoothing her hands over her back, her flanks, admiring the muscles beneath her skin, the smooth curves of her back and belly. She rested her forehead against Doreen's neck and closed her eyes as tears started to fall, just as she used to do when she was younger, and a sense of calm swept over her. Horses were beautiful, powerful creatures, but they could also be incredibly gentle, friendly and soothing to be around.

'You want some time here?' Verity asked, and Clare opened her eyes and stepped back. 'I've got some chores to do but you're welcome to stay around for as long as you like. You can decide if you'd like to come join the team. We're all very friendly and it would be great to have someone like you who loves horses and knows the layout here.'

'I've missed this.' Clare wiped at her eyes with the back of a hand. 'Now that I'm back here, I can't believe that I haven't been around horses for so long. How could I have let that happen?'

'We all change to suit other people.' Verity wrinkled her nose. 'Hell, I did to suit my ex. He did to suit me. It's relationships, isn't it? You have to compromise a certain amount or it would never work. Luckily, I didn't give up too much of myself and I had this place to come back to. The kids love it here and they're a tonic for Mum to have around, especially seeing as how Bonnie and Fran live so far away.'

'They left?'

'Yeah. Bonnie's in Scotland and Fran's in Canada. I was the only one who stayed local, but now I'm actually back under the same roof as my mum.'

Clare smiled. 'Like me.'

'It's good to have somewhere to run to, though, right? Plus, the difference now is that Mum needs me to help her out.'

'I know that feeling.'

'Your mum OK? I see her sometimes in the village, but we're so busy here that I don't get up there as often as I used to. With three kids who want feeding, lifts and the school run, along with general running of the business, I don't get time for much else.'

'Yes, she's all right, thank you. And I can imagine exactly how busy you are.'

'Anyway, do you want to hang around for a bit?'

Clare thought of how wonderful it would be to spend the day here, but then she remembered Goliath.

'I'd better get back because of the dog – but can I have a think about the job?'

'Of course you can.' Verity placed a hand on Clare's arm. 'Let's swap numbers, then you can let me know either way. It would be amazing to have you join us, but I understand if it's not the type of thing you want. I'll send the link to the job advert too, so you have more info about the hours, pay and so on, and you can think about it in your own time. But I can see that you've still got an affinity with horses.' Verity grinned and gestured behind Clare.

Turning around, she found Doreen's head up close to her and then nudging her arm.

'She likes you.'

'I like her too.'

Clare pressed a kiss to the white star on Doreen's head, then leant closer and whispered in her ear, 'I'll be back.'

Outside, she found Goliath sitting like a statue, watching as a group of riders entered the yard, the horses' hooves clip-clopping across the cobbles as they snorted and whinnied and shook their heads.

'You ready to go home, boy?' Clare asked him, and he stood up and wagged his tail. She swapped numbers with Verity, then her mobile buzzed as Verity sent her the link to the job advert.

'Thank you for this,' Clare said. 'I'll be in touch.'

'Great! Speak soon.' Verity picked up the saddle from the bench and headed towards the group of riders who'd just come in and Clare led Goliath out of the stable yard and back towards the gate they'd come through.

As she walked home, she smiled, thinking about how glad she was that she'd gone to the stables and seen Verity again. She'd told her she'd think about the job and she would – and Verity would surely need to give her some sort of interview – but she had a feeling she already knew what her answer would be.

And that thought was very exciting indeed.

❄

Alyssa hadn't been back all weekend. Sam had arrived home after the pub quiz on Friday and quickly checked to see if she'd eaten the lasagne he'd left in the fridge, but it had remained untouched. On the Saturday he'd got up early to walk Scout, then he'd gone to the supermarket to stock up on some essentials, and stopped at the farm shop, purchasing some of the little fairy cakes topped with buttercream that

Alyssa liked. But Saturday and Sunday had passed and there had been no sign of his sister. He'd sent a text on Saturday evening, just to make sure she was OK, because he'd started imagining her trapped in a supermarket toilet cubicle where the door had jammed, or on the floor of the garage conversion, unable to call for help. He hadn't wanted to go into the garage because it was her space and she was entitled to her privacy, and he hadn't phoned her in case she didn't want to speak to him. However, she had replied to his text, telling him she was fine, but not when she'd be back.

Sam felt like a parent whose child has flown the nest. It was, he knew, ridiculous for him to be so worried about her, but old habits were hard to break, and he just wanted to know that she was safe and happy. Sunday had involved some time in the garden as he tried to distract himself, pruning bushes and clearing leaves from the grass.

Winter had taken hold of the landscape now, and in the garden and on his walks, many of the trees had shed all their leaves and their dark branches reached into the gunmetal grey sky like gnarled old fingers. Time was passing, the seasons changing as they did every year. Sam was not getting any younger and yet his life was the same as it had been for years. He worked, he slept, he walked the dog, he read scholarly articles, he went to the pub quiz. But something was missing. He hated to admit it, but he was becoming more and more convinced that this wasn't really living, it was merely existing. It wasn't that he didn't have happy times, because he did. Scout's wet nose tickling his ear first thing in the morning when she wanted to go out made him laugh. Miranda and Magnus, along with his other work colleagues, were warm and caring people who loved animals and together they made a good team. He enjoyed his Friday evenings at the pub, and he'd watched some gripping TV series recently. He was actually happy that Alyssa seemed to be forging ahead with her life, that she had found someone and fallen in love, even if he was scared of seeing her hurt.

So what was it that he missed? That left him feeling as if something was absent from his life?

Was it love? Companionship? Knowing that another human being had his back, no matter what?

A noise from outside drew him to the kitchen window and his chest tightened: Alyssa was home. She came up the ramp from the back garden and he opened the door to her, smiling, glad to see her at last.

'Good morning.'

'Hello, Sam.'

'You just get back?' he asked, even though he knew she had.

'Yes. I needed some fresh clothes and I thought I'd better check on you.'

'On me?'

Scout scampered into the kitchen and over to Alyssa, then jumped up, her front legs on Alyssa's lap so she could lick her face. 'Get off, Scout.' Alyssa giggled as she hugged the dog. 'I'll have to shower now you've licked all of my face.'

Sam looked at his sister. Something was different. She was radiant, her dark skin glowing, her eyes bright and her hair . . . that was it. She'd brushed her hair out of its styled curls, setting her Afro free, and it was beautiful, natural, magnificent – and just like their mum's hair.

'Your hair looks great,' he said.

'Sebastian suggested I brush it out. He said I have great hair. So I thought, why not?'

Sam nodded. Sebastian clearly had influence over Alyssa. He hoped it would only ever be a positive thing.

'Stop it, Sam.'

'What?'

'I can see it in your eyes. Stop worrying. Seb's a good man, we're in love.'

Sam swallowed his doubt. Sebastian hadn't tried to get Alyssa to have a weave so that her natural hair was hidden, he hadn't tried to get her to have her hair relaxed to make it lie straight – he had encouraged her to be herself, to set her real hair free. That had to be a good thing, surely? Alyssa did have beautiful hair; she was a beautiful young woman. She'd also shed those artificial lashes that gave Sam the shivers. It wasn't that they didn't make her look pretty, because they did, but in a fake way, kind of like a doll.

'I'm happy for you, Alyssa. Truly I am.' He cleared his throat. 'Before I forget, though, Clare asked me to tell you that she's planning a village Christmas show. There are posters around the village and I have a leaflet for you with more information. I told her that you have a fabulous voice and I think she'd like you to audition.'

Alyssa frowned. 'A Christmas show?'

'Yes.'

'There's not much time before Christmas to prepare.'

'I think it's a bit of a last-minute thing, but there's time and you'd be great. You know you would.'

'I'll think about it.' She rubbed Scout's ears and the Lab wagged her long tail. 'If I'm around, that is.'

Sam inhaled sharply. 'What do you mean?'

'Well . . . Sebastian's invited me to spend Christmas with him and his family.'

Sam blinked hard.

'I won't if you don't want me to, Sam, but I'd really like to spend it with him.'

'It's fine.' Sam's voice wavered so he coughed, swallowed hard. 'Absolutely fine. You should spend the day with Sebastian.'

'Not just the day . . .'

'Oh. OK.' He nodded. This *was* fine; this was how it should be. It was moving quickly between Alyssa and Sebastian, but sometimes relationships did.

'Will you be all right?' she asked, her eyes filled with guilt and concern fixed on his face.

'Of course I will.' He bobbed his head and gave a small laugh. 'It's just Christmas.'

'I know how you love the build-up and all that.'

'Honestly, Alyssa, it's fine. I'll probably be on call anyway and I'm old enough and ugly enough to fend for myself. Besides which, it's you who loves Christmas and I go along with all the fuss for you.'

'Thank you.'

She held out a hand and he took it, hoping he hadn't made her feel bad.

'What date is the show?'

'I think Clare said it's the nineteenth of December.'

'I'm sure I can make that.' Alyssa smiled. She was offering him something in exchange for him having to be alone over Christmas. But then he was a grown man and the holidays had always been about Alyssa and her joy, hadn't they? The gift buying, the festive movies, the anticipation . . .

Or had she been doing it for Sam?

Times were changing and Alyssa was moving on.

It was high time that Sam did too.

❄

Kyle set a mug of coffee in front of Clare, then sat opposite her at the kitchen table.

'Come on then, Mum, let's hear what's been on your mind since Saturday.'

It was Tuesday already. She'd gone to Old Oak Stables on Saturday and since then she'd been thinking about Verity's offer, aware that she needed to text the stable owner with her answer. She'd gone to do it several times, but nerves had stopped her. Was she qualified enough to do it? What if she started there then Verity found her lacking? What if she'd forgotten how to ride?

'I'm OK.' She nodded.

'But there is something bothering you, right?' He raised his eyebrows.

'Not in a bad way. Not really. It's just that I'm a bit nervous about something.'

'Are you going to tell me, or do I have to tickle it out of you?'

She smiled. 'No, it's fine. On Saturday I went to Old Oak Stables.'

'Where you used to horse ride?'

'Yes.'

'And?'

'I met Verity Baker there. She was just a child when I last saw her but, obviously, she's a grown woman now. She's managing the stables and needs someone to work there from February.'

'That sounds interesting.' Kyle grinned over his mug.

'Uh-huh.' Clare sipped her coffee. 'She asked if I'd be interested. She advertised and didn't have any takers and said she knows me and how much I love horses and that I'd be ideal.'

'This is brilliant! I hope you said yes.'

'But it would mean that I'd be staying in Little Bramble indefinitely.'

'It's not a ball and chain around your leg, Mum, it's a job. If you don't like it, you can always quit. But from what you've told me over the years about how much you used to love spending time there, I'm sure it would be a good thing for you. Get you some of your sparkle back.'

'Really?'

'I always wondered why you didn't go horse riding anymore.'

'I was too busy for starters. Weekends were for you and . . . your father . . . and as time went on, it seemed like one of those things I'd left behind.'

'Well, now you have the opportunity to get it back.'

'You think I should accept?'

'Absolutely. I mean, what else are you going to do? We've a busy time up to Christmas, and January would be a rubbish time to look for work. Then if you decided to leave the village it would be hard to find somewhere to live. I think this is a chance for you to get *you* back.'

'Get *me* back?' She giggled.

'Yes. Text Verity now and say yes.'

Clare swallowed more coffee to try to push her anxiety down. Accepting the job would be a big deal and she wouldn't be able to go back on it because that would mean letting Verity down. Clare had looked at the job description that Verity had sent her and she knew it was hard graft for not much money, plus it was three days a week so wouldn't provide enough money to pay rent or a mortgage, but she had money in the bank from the house sale and some savings and could always find something else to do around the days at the stable. Best of all, she'd get to be around horses, to ride sometimes, and it would be a positive step towards putting her life back together.

'I'll do it!'

She composed a text to Verity, asking if the job was still available and expressing her interest, then sent it and placed her mobile back on the table.

'Well done,' Kyle said, squeezing her hand. 'I'm very proud of you.'

Clare beamed at his praise, then jumped as her mobile pinged. It was Verity. She swiped the screen, then read the message aloud to Kyle.

Great news! This is so exciting! We'll need to have a proper chat and you must come and spend some time here to check it's what you want. Let me know when is good for you. Much love, V. Xx

'There you go then.' Kyle clapped his hands. 'You have a job and will be staying in L.B. Now you just need to find somewhere to live.'

Clare coughed nervously. 'One thing at a time!'

'Then back to our other business.' Kyle gestured at the table where they'd laid out their show plans.

'I can't believe how many people responded.' Clare stared at the list on the table. There were twenty-five possible acts for the show and all would need to audition the following week.

'It's very exciting, isn't it?'

'Are those cookies you made cool enough to eat yet?' Clare sniffed the air appreciatively. Kyle had made a batch of peanut butter cookies and they smelt amazing.

'Almost ready, Mum, be patient. It's only two minutes since you last asked me.' He winked. 'They need to cool down first or they'll be too soft.'

'I guess I can wait.' She smiled at her son, love filling her heart.

'So, what acts do we have?'

Clare put her glasses back on and looked down at the file pad in front of her. 'We have a choir from the local primary school, a magician, a contortionist, several singers offering different cover versions, one of them operatic, a dance duo, a parkour group made up of local teenaged boys, a free-running group of local firefighters, a trampoline act and . . .' She scanned the list. 'A reading from any Shakespeare play that we choose.'

'Quite a mix then.'

Sitting across from her, wearing a checked shirt, his arms folded on the table, Kyle looked so grown-up. Some days Clare could hardly believe that he was her son, that she had carried him in her womb and delivered him into the world. When did he get so big, so handsome, so mature?

'Mum, stop looking at me like that.' His Adam's apple bobbed.

'Sorry, Kyle. I'm just . . . I love you so much.'

He peered at her from under his lashes. 'Don't get all soppy now, Mum.' He chuckled. 'But I love you too. You know that, right?'

She nodded, a lump of emotion making her throat ache.

'Thank you. I'm so proud of you.'

'I know your game!' He clapped his hands. 'You're just after a cookie.'

She covered her heart as if she'd been shot. 'You know me too well.'

He waggled his eyebrows at her. 'It's a trick I've used a few times myself.'

'Don't I know it! Ooh, did you have a chance to check if the hall will be ready for us to use next week?'

'I spoke to the vicar this morning and he said it's absolutely fine.'

'Brilliant. I just didn't want us to clash with the WI or a yoga class or something.'

'I'm not sure how much use the hall gets.' Kyle was shaking his head. 'I think it needs something, like this Christmas show, for instance, to bring the community together again.'

'I agree.'

'OK . . .' He glanced at the clock on the wall. 'Cookies should be ready now. Why don't we wrap up warm and have our coffee in the garden, Mum?'

'That sounds like a nice idea.'

They grabbed coats and hats then took their coffees and cookies outside, sitting on the wooden bench under the pergola. The air was icy and laced with woodsmoke. It nipped at her fingers and the tip of her nose, making her think of times gone by – as a child, as an adult – when she'd felt a rush of excitement that Christmas was on the way, bringing festivities and cosy family times. There were so many wonderful things to enjoy in life and Clare believed that she had appreciated the good times, had paid attention when it had mattered most; that she hadn't always been looking ahead, yearning for more, when she needed to appreciate what was right in front of her. She had loved her husband and her son, had done everything in her power to make them both happy and comfortable. She had sacrificed her own wants and needs many times, believing that was what good mums did. Her own mum, after all, had set a different kind of example and Clare had vowed that she wouldn't be as distant as Elaine had been, had tried to be more present for her child, more loving, more supportive. In doing so, though, she had lost herself, had forgotten to allow herself some time to consider what it was that she wanted and needed.

Something deep inside her wobbled and she took a few slow, deep breaths. Putting herself first did not come naturally and it irked her, made her uncomfortable, reminded her of something her mum had accused her of being on more than one occasion . . . memories she tried to push away and ignore.

You're being selfish, Clare, wanting me to stay home when other people need me and I've things I need to get done. You're perfectly capable of putting a sandwich together. I can't be home all the time, I have a show to organise, rehearsals to oversee, Christmas to prepare for . . .

And there it was. The sum of her fears. That her mum had always been right, and that Clare was, indeed, selfish. She had striven all her adult life to be selfless, not to become the person her mum had seemed to believe her to be.

Focusing on the present, on her surroundings, she returned to the moment and looked around her. Everything needed a lick of paint, some TLC, and Clare decided then and there that she would help her mum to spruce the place up after winter had passed. There was no point painting the pergola or outdoor furniture right now, but come spring, it would be something to do to help her mum. And seeing as Clare now had a job, she had committed to being here in the New Year.

'These are delicious,' Clare said in between chewing bites of cookie. 'You are such a good cook.'

'I learnt from the best.' He nudged her. 'You and a few of my . . . friends.'

It wasn't the first time he'd joked about his 'friends' and Clare swallowed her concerns. Kyle was a man now and she had to trust him to be careful, to look after his body, heart and mind. She couldn't wrap him up in cotton wool for the rest of his life, as much as she sometimes wished she could. The little boy who had swung high on the garden swing, who had ducked under the water in the swimming pool for so long that she'd dived in after him more than once to check he wasn't drowning, who'd made her legs weak when he'd fallen and cut his knees, broken his arm and chipped his front tooth, was still here, but he was capable of look-ing after himself now. Still, she knew that however old he got, she would always be his mum and always worry about him. It came with the job.

Again, she wondered at Jason's behaviour, heading off like that for goodness knew how long. How could he do it? What if Kyle had needed him, wanted to spend time with him, missed him? But then, Jason knew that Kyle always had Clare. Jason had that security, whereas Clare knew she'd be unable to trust in Jason to be there for their son. He was just too selfish, too full of his own self-importance, too egotistical. It wasn't that he was a bad father, he just wasn't the one she would have chosen for Kyle, had she the opportunity to do so all over again.

And yet she knew that she had made her choices for reasons that were right at the time. She didn't have many regrets, but her main one was falling out with Jenny and not seeing her for all that time and, perhaps, not looking out for her mum as much as she could have done. But when she'd got together with Jason she had loved him and they had, for a time, been happy. Kyle had been a baby born from love and that, surely, was the right way to go about having children?

'It's lovely here, isn't it, Mum?' Kyle shuffled closer to her on the bench and she was glad of his warmth. Their breath puffed out white in front of them like smoke, catching the light that shone through the kitchen window.

'It is. It always was.'

'After living in Reading and Bath, what I can't get over here is how quiet it is. There are animal sounds, obviously, but no traffic, no sirens, no drunks . . . It's like a different world.'

'I know.' Clare nodded. 'I've found that since I came back, I'm sleeping better. I feel more relaxed . . . It could be the clearer air and the exercise, I guess. It's probably all linked, actually. We should have visited more often when you were younger.'

She felt Kyle watching her.

'We could have, Mum, but we had a life in Reading.'

'I know, and I know we were busy. Then there was your dad . . .'

'And let's be honest, Dad wasn't keen on coming here, was he? In fact, he was a bit of a stuck-in-the-mud, really. Born and raised in Reading, went to university there then stayed there as an adult, even though he lost both his parents before he graduated. Probably why he felt the need to spread his wings before he reached fifty.'

Clare turned to meet Kyle's gaze. 'That could well be spot on about your dad. But thinking about not visiting Little Bramble often enough . . . I could have come and brought you.'

'It would have been nice, but I had a great childhood, Mum. Don't regret anything because you don't need to. You know, I used to feel sorry for some of my friends because their parents worked long hours and they had to make their own tea, or they'd get a burger on the way home. You were always there to listen to me talk about my day and to make me a decent meal. You did your best and I know that, Mum.'

'I can remember you getting a bit fed up when I wouldn't give you money for burgers, except on weekends.' Clare nudged him.

'Of course, as a kid I wanted junk food, but I did understand that eating them every day wasn't good for me. You saved my skin – and my waistline. I appreciate that now more than ever.'

'I'm glad you see it now. I did feel quite mean sometimes.' Clare swirled the dregs of coffee round in her cup. 'Do you . . . do you wish we'd visited Nanna more? Especially with her being your only grandparent?'

He shrugged. 'I knew how it worked. Besides which, Nanna could also have visited us.'

Clare finished her cookie and the last bite stuck in her throat, making her cough. Kyle patted her back firmly, dislodging it. She sipped her coffee to wash it down. Her son had been aware of far more than she'd known.

'It's getting colder. Shall we go inside?' she asked.

'Yeah, come on then. There's that baking show on TV at nine that I'd like to watch.'

'Fab.'

Clare opened the kitchen door and they went inside. She placed her mug in the sink, then turned as she heard Kyle's gasp.

'The cookies – they're all gone!'

'What? How?'

Clare stared at the cooling rack, then picked it up and looked underneath it as if the cookies might have fallen through.

They hurried through to the lounge and there, on the rug in front of the hearth, was Goliath, surrounded by crumbs, licking his lips,

'Did he eat them all, do you think?' Kyle asked.

'Looks like it. There wasn't anything bad in them, was there? For dogs, I mean.'

'No – no chocolate, so he should be all right.'

'Thank goodness for that. We'll just have to keep an eye on him.'

Goliath suddenly belched loudly, filling the room with the aroma of peanuts.

'That was naughty, Goliath.' Clare wagged a finger at him. 'You could have had one but not the whole damned lot.'

'I can make more.' Kyle was shrugging out of his coat.

'It's not that, it's just that he doesn't need the extra calories and his wind will be dreadful tonight.'

Kyle snorted and covered his mouth with his hand. 'Bloody dogs! I keep forgetting how big he is. He swiped my sandwich off the table yesterday just by walking past and grabbing it with his mouth. He did it so quickly that I only noticed when I looked up from my magazine and saw him chewing it by the back door!

'Right, come on then, Mum, let's get our pyjamas on and make some hot chocolate, then we can get comfy on the sofa. Nanna's been in the bathroom for over an hour, but she did say she wanted to watch the programme too, so I'll give her a shout when I go upstairs. She'll probably resemble a prune by now.'

Chapter 20

'I'm not sure about this now.' Clare's mum walked around the largest room of the empty village hall, where there was a stage, a piano and adequate seating for a decent-sized audience. 'It just doesn't feel right.'

Clare suppressed a sigh. Auditions week had arrived and she was feeling quite optimistic about it all, as was Kyle. Her mum, however, was a different matter.

'What's wrong with it?' Clare looked around, assessing the double doors that led out to a hallway and the front doors, the large windows with their heavy blackout curtains that were closed against the wintery afternoon darkness and the fire exit at the end of the room that led straight out onto the car park. The best bit, in her opinion, was the large stage to the right of the doors from the hallway, with its velvet damask curtains fringed with gold tassels, the sweeping pelmet draped along the top of the stage and the stage itself, as yet unused, the fresh wooden boards smooth and unmarked, ready for performers. In front of the stage was a large piano, its polished mahogany surface shining in the electric light.

'There's just no atmosphere. It's all too new, too . . . unused.'

'Then use it, Mum, and create some atmosphere. Breathe life into the boards, the walls and the curtains. Bring music and song and dance and words to its core. Make this village hall the thing that Little Bramble is missing. Get up on that stage and perform!'

Elaine did a circuit of the hall again, then stood in the centre of the room and closed her eyes. She started moving slowly, her arms outstretched, raising her legs, then lowering them in turn – the Tai Chi routine Clare had seen her perform in the garden in her underwear.

'Right now?' Kyle whispered.

'By the look of it.' Clare met her son's curious gaze.

'Why?' His brows met.

'Who knows? Clearly she thinks it will help.'

'Well, while she's altering the Zen of the room or shifting the aura or whatever it is, give me a hand getting things set up, will you?'

Clare nodded, but she was tempted to join in. She enjoyed their morning Tai Chi sessions and could understand why her mum was doing it now. It was relaxing, energising and cleansing all at once. But there were things to be done, so she helped Kyle carry two tables from under the stage and set them in front of it, along with three chairs. She hung her bag over the back of one chair, then got out her list of the afternoon's performers, three notebooks and some pens. She added three bottles of water and a tube of mints.

'It's like one of those reality TV shows, Mum.' Kyle pulled out a chair and sat down. 'Can I be the baddy?'

'The baddy?' Clare asked, as she sat next to him.

'Yes, you know, the judge who says all the acts are rubbish and gets booed by the audience.'

Clare giggled. 'I can't imagine you ever being a baddy, Kyle.'

'I could, you know.' He curled his lip and pointed at the stage. 'That, *young man*, was appalling! How can you call yourself an act? You should go home with your head down and never, ever perform in public again.' He turned to Clare. 'Well?'

'Scary.'

'Excellent.' He rubbed his hands together. 'That's my role sorted then.'

'The problem, though, is that we have lots of local people coming to audition and if you treat them like that . . .'

'It could make me a pariah?'

'Exactly.'

'Better tone it down then, hadn't I?'

'I think so. Especially if you're planning on staying around for a while.' She crossed her fingers under the table. Having Kyle around was lovely and she didn't want him to leave the village just yet.

'That's better.' Elaine pulled out the chair the other side of Kyle and sat down. 'I needed to realign my energy.'

'Fabulous, Nanna! I knew it was something like that.' Kyle nodded. 'Now that your energy is realigned, do you think that the hall will do for the show?'

'We'll see.' Elaine cocked a grey eyebrow, but a smile played across her lips and Clare suspected that her mum was warming to the idea.

'And are you going to be on stage yourself?' Clare asked.

'I have an idea, but I'll need Kyle to accompany me.'

'We'll see.' Kyle winked, echoing Elaine's words. 'Right, who's first?'

'The firefighters.'

'What?' Her mum peered around Kyle. 'And what are they doing?'

'There's five of them, two women and three men, and they're doing –'

'Free running!' There was a shout from the hallway, then five people raced in through the door and up the steps to the stage. In blue trousers and T-shirts with trainers and red sweatbands on their wrists, the team began their performance. The curtains swished open to reveal a range of props that the team had set up in the hall earlier that day. They moved quickly, running up and down what looked like a see-saw, jumping on and off a table and a freestanding ladder and bouncing into forward rolls and cartwheels, as well as lifting one another and somersaulting off shoulders and backs and landing in elegant poses.

Throughout their performance, they emitted a series of whoops and whistles, all completely in tune with one another, all at ease, as graceful and light-footed as professional gymnasts. A few times Clare gasped and covered her mouth, convinced that one of them would mistime their leap or bounce and fall off the stage, but nothing went wrong and by the end of their performance, she was breathless.

When the five firefighters held hands at the front of the stage and bowed, Clare stood up and clapped, as did Kyle and Elaine.

'Wow! Just wow!' Clare shook her head. 'That was amazing!'

'It really was.' Kyle nodded. 'We'll be in touch soon.'

The firefighters bowed again, then quickly set about moving their equipment to the back of the stage to make room for the other acts.

When they'd left the hall, Clare turned to her son and her mum.

'What do you think?'

'I'm not sure.' Elaine shook her head. 'That was not exactly what I'd call . . . appropriate.'

'I disagree,' Kyle said. 'That's exactly what we need to inject some life into this place.'

'It's hardly festive, is it?' Elaine wrinkled her nose.

'We'll ask them to wear Christmas jumpers, reindeer antlers and perform to a Christmas tune,' Clare said firmly. 'It's a yes from me. Kyle?'

'Yes!'

'Mum?'

'No.'

'Well, that's two to one, so it's a yes.'

Clare drew a large tick next to the act on her list. She could feel her mum's indignation brewing like strong coffee, and part of her felt really bad, but another part felt quite good. Standing up to her mum was something she'd rarely – if ever – done, and she wouldn't have done it over nothing, but the firefighters had been brilliant, and Clare believed that they would make a good addition to the show.

'What's next?' Elaine asked, thawing faster than Clare could have hoped.

'The vicar.'

'Isn't he performing a contortionist act?' Kyle waggled his eyebrows.

'He is indeed.' Clare smiled, wondering exactly what Iolo Ifans was going to do.

She didn't have to wonder for long because he entered the hall wearing a long taupe raincoat and wellington boots with a trilby pressed low on his head.

'Good afternoon,' he said from the stage.

Kyle sniggered. 'He looks like a flasher.'

'Shhh!' Clare nudged her son.

'Hello, Father Ifans.' Clare waved. 'We're looking forward to your performance.'

'Thank you!' He took off his hat, then placed it on the floor next to him before removing his coat and wellingtons.

Clare swallowed a giggle when she saw what he was wearing underneath.

'Really?' Kyle muttered, shuffling the notepad in front of him and shifting in his chair. 'That Lycra is practically indecent. You can see every lump and bump and saggy bit!'

'Hush, Kyle.' Elaine tapped his arm. 'It's fine.'

Kyle grimaced at Clare and laughter bubbled in her chest. The sixty-something vicar was wearing a lime-green Lycra bodysuit which clung to his frame, leaving very little to the imagination, exposing his pot belly, bony shoulders and more. She wished they had a red button that they could press to end the act before it began, but this was real life and not a TV show.

Five minutes later, Clare was standing up and clapping again. The vicar did not look like he'd be able to bend over backwards and wrap his legs over his shoulders, but he had done, and he had also folded himself into a variety of shapes that made her wince. But it had been highly entertaining and funny.

She looked at her son and her mum and they all nodded.

'It's a yes!' she announced and Iolo grinned broadly, a hand resting on his concave chest.

He picked up his coat and hat and slid his feet into his wellies. 'The Lord moves in mysterious ways.'

'And so does the vicar,' Kyle said behind his notepad, making Clare snigger again.

Most of the rest of the acts were good, including the school choir, made up of children aged from six to eleven. They were accompanied by their head teacher on the piano, and Clare found herself swallowing hard as emotion rose in her throat while they performed a medley of Christmas songs, their smiling faces and angelic voices just beautiful. There was also a large male bulldog called Mr Spike who sang (or rather howled) along to opera music while his owner, Amanda King, watched proudly from the wings, an elderly man, Greg Patrick, who crooned 'White Christmas' just like Frank Sinatra and a reading of Clement Clarke Moore's 'A Visit from St. Nicholas', performed by Miranda Fitzalan.

When the final act had left the hall, Clare looked at the list in front of her and all the ticks. There had been only two rejections, a twenty-something couple who'd done a ventriloquist act that had been abysmal and a young man who had claimed to be able to breakdance but who had simply rolled around on the stage and kicked his legs in the air.

'Will there be room for any more acts?' Kyle asked, voicing Clare's thoughts. 'I mean, we have more to see at the next auditions.'

'Lose the free runners next and you'll be fine,' Elaine muttered.

'No, Mum. Absolutely not. Anyway, this just means that the show will be a bit longer than we'd anticipated. To be honest, I hadn't expected to see such high-quality performances. It's as though the community's been waiting for something like this to showcase their talents.'

'Hmmm.' Elaine pushed her glasses back on her head, pursed her lips and folded her arms across her chest. 'Perhaps.'

'There's no perhaps about it, Nanna.' Kyle took a drink from his water bottle. 'Local people clearly want to get involved. This show could really bring the community back together.'

'I hope so.' Clare smiled, excitement trickling through her like warm spiced wine. 'It will be a wonderful way to start the festivities.'

As they put on their coats and tidied the tables and chairs away, Clare realised that she was looking forward to Christmas. Not just because she would be with her son and her mum, but because she would, for the first time in years, be part of a community, and she intended on doing everything in her power to make it a very special Christmas indeed.

❄

'Are you sure you didn't mind coming?' Jenny asked Clare for the fiftieth time as they sat in the waiting room of the clinic.

'Of course not.' Clare squeezed Jenny's hand. 'I'm happy to be here.'

'We're both grateful,' Martin said, smiling at Clare.

His face was pale and he kept chewing at his nails. He was clearly very nervous. Jenny had been to the GP the week before and had her pregnancy confirmed, then she'd been booked in for a scan so they could determine how far along she was and if there were any medical issues to contend with.

'I really need to pee.' Jenny wriggled on her seat, pulling her stretchy black top down over her belly. In the week and a half since Clare had seen her friend, Jenny had grown bigger and now had a lovely beach-ball sized bump under her clothing. 'I'd forgotten how uncomfortable having to have a full bladder for the scan is.'

'Jenny Rolands?' A woman in pale-blue scrubs stuck her head in the waiting room. 'We're ready for you now.'

'I guess this is it.' Jenny sighed.

'I'll wait here for you,' Clare said.

Jenny and Martin stood up and walked slowly towards the doorway of the sonographer's room.

'I can't do it.' Martin turned from the doorway. His face crumpled and he covered it with his hands.

'It's OK, Martin.' Jenny rubbed his back. 'It will be fine.'

'I can't.' He shook his head and when he lowered his hands, his cheeks were wet. 'I'm so worried that something will be . . .'

Jenny had told Clare on the phone that Martin had been shocked when she'd broken the news about the pregnancy, then elated, then terrified, and that he kept swinging between joy and fear. Clare could understand why.

'Do you want to sit out here, Martin?' Clare got up and asked. He was such a big man with the build of a rugby player, but when it came to his wife's health and well-being he was as soft and vulnerable as they came. 'I'll go in with Jenny, if you like.'

He met her eyes and she saw relief in his gaze.

'Do you mind?'

'Not at all. I'll hold her hand, I promise.'

'Thank you. Jenny . . . do you mind?'

'Of course not. I understand.'

Jenny hugged him and told him she'd be fine. It was one of those moments when Clare was struck by female strength and resilience. Martin loved Jenny, he was a good husband and a kind and caring man, but in this instance, he couldn't be by his wife's side because of his fears for her. Jenny, however, had no choice; she had to go in for the scan and while doing so, she was being strong for her husband, but also for herself and her baby. Clare was filled with admiration and love for her.

'Thank you so much.' Jenny took Clare's hand and they walked into the small, darkened room together. It reminded Clare of times at school when they'd had to go to the medical room for injections, or to the head teacher's office for misbehaving, which hadn't happened often as they were usually well behaved, but it had happened. Clare had supported Jenny and Jenny had supported Clare. And now, here they were, years later, holding hands again and about to go through a life-changing experience together. Clare had a feeling that, from this point on, there would be nothing capable of driving them apart. She certainly had no intention of letting go of their friendship again.

'OK, lovely, if you can just lie on the bed, then let me have access to your belly,' said the sonographer, a woman with dark hair in a ponytail.

Jenny pushed her elastic skirt down to her thighs and pulled the top up to her chest.

Clare sat in the chair next to the bed and Jenny reached out for her hand.

'This will be a bit cold,' the sonographer said as she squirted some gel over Jenny's belly. 'I'll take some measurements, then I'll be able to talk you through what I've found. Is that OK?'

'Yes,' Jenny whispered.

While the sonographer ran the probe over Jenny's belly, a series of clicks and beeps filled the room, and Jenny kept her eyes on the ceiling. Clare knew that Jenny's thoughts would be on the baby in her womb, hoping that all was well. She squeezed Jenny's hand gently, sending her love and strength.

'Ah!' Jenny gasped.

'Sorry, did I press a bit hard?' the sonographer asked.

'A little and I really need the toilet!' Jenny bit her lip as the probe was swept over her lower abdomen.

'I won't be long. I've almost got everything I need.'

'OK.' Jenny met Clare's eyes and Clare could see the fear, the anxiety, the hope and the love that was already there for this child. More than anything else, she hoped that the baby would be healthy.

'Right, there we are.' The sonographer turned the screen towards Jenny and Clare. 'Everything looks fine. You're about seventeen weeks along . . .'

'Oh my God!' Jenny pushed herself up on her elbows. 'It has four legs!'

'Not exactly.' The sonographer moved the probe slightly and it was Clare's turn to gasp.

'Twins!'

'Yes. You're having twins.'

'Oh. My. God.' Jenny sank back on the bed and closed her eyes. 'What will Martin say?'

'But everything else seems to be in order?' Clare asked, wanting to ensure that if Jenny had any questions they'd be answered now.

'It does.' The sonographer smiled. 'Do you want to know the sex of the babies?'

'Jen?' Clare asked and Jenny opened her eyes and nodded.

'OK, hold on one moment . . .'

Ten minutes later, they left the room and Jenny went straight to Martin. He stood up and opened his arms and she stepped into his embrace. Clare's vision blurred as she waited for them, seeing Martin's relief and pride as Jenny told him the news. Of course, it was still early days for a multiple pregnancy and Jenny had been described in medical terms as a geriatric mother, but she was fit and healthy and she'd have people looking after her, including Clare.

'Clare, thank you. I'm so embarrassed, but I just couldn't go in.' Martin held out an arm and Clare stepped closer so the three of them were hugging. 'I don't suppose you fancy helping us tell the girls now, do you?'

Clare smiled. 'Of course not. That's the easy bit.'

They left the waiting room together, three friends bound by a shared past, by the promise of what the future held and by love. There had, and always would be, love.

Chapter 21

November was almost over and Sam could hardly believe how quickly it had gone. The mornings were crisp and cold, dark and uninspiring, and he found getting out of bed more difficult, especially now that Alyssa was spending most nights at her boyfriend's, so breakfast would be eaten alone with just Scout for company. Dinner was a solitary affair, consumed most days in front of the TV. He'd always made an effort with Alyssa to eat at the table, believing that it gave them a chance to talk about their days and to connect, but there seemed little point in sitting there alone; he had more than enough time to connect with himself these days.

He'd taken to walking Scout quickly before and after work, but tried to get back around lunchtime to give her a proper walk while it was light. He'd managed to get away today and Scout had been delighted to see him. He put her coat on – it was that cold outside now – then clipped her lead to her collar, dug his own warm jacket out from the cupboard, then swapped his work shoes for his hiking boots with a pair of extra-thick socks. With gloves on and a hat over his short hair, he was ready to go.

In the hallway mirror he caught sight of his reflection. He'd received compliments over the years about his looks, but never been able to see it himself; he saw his own slightly weathered face, the visage of a man who'd worked hard to get where he was but who had let his sister down. Grief etched itself on someone's features, dug deep into the skin, leaving grooves and fine lines that deepened over time like excavations in the earth. His face was his and yet it was a melding of his mother and father, of the grandparents he had seen photographs of – wide eye shape here, square chin there, shadow of a chin dimple. At times, he saw flashes of Alyssa in his reflection, and yet he didn't. It was more to do with expressions that they shared, a widening of their eyes when they were exasperated, a curling of the upper lip when they felt distaste. It was now highly unlikely that he would pass his genes on to another generation and had thought that Alyssa wouldn't either, but now he wondered about that. It would be risky for her, but she was still young enough to become a mum. And she'd be a great mum, he had no doubt about that at all. But he couldn't shake the feeling that it would be very unwise for her to get pregnant, all things considered.

Scout tugged at her lead, reminding him that she was waiting, so he let them out of the cottage, then locked the door and marched along the pavement. He passed another row of cottages and The King's Arms, then turned left and onto the woodland walk. The trees rose above him, some completely bare now, and the smooth silvery-grey bark of young sycamores contrasted with the purplish brown of adolescent alders, the scaly steel shade of beech trees and the ridged and furrowed grey-green of mature English oaks. Holly broke up the greys and browns, bright red berries and prickly green leaves welcome dashes of colour on the landscape. The woods were a cornucopia of colours and shapes, of scents and textures.

Sam unclipped Scout's lead from her collar so she could run on ahead and sniff to her heart's content and a robin hopped from tree to tree, its red breast like a beacon of hope, keeping him company for a while.

When he reached the crossroads of the path that led in four directions, he slowed his pace and called to Scout. She raced back to him and followed him to the fence that bordered the gently sloping fields, which spread out behind the trees. He stood and gazed at the uninterrupted green and the trees beyond like small sentries watching over the land. Sam loved the openness of living in rural England, the sense that he wasn't far away from people and cities and events, but that he was far enough away to avoid them all if he wanted to. He had the luxury of choice and he knew that not many people did. Sam appreciated what he had but he also knew that he'd worked hard to get there. However, he was also aware of something missing. He had so much and yet there was no one to share it with, no one to turn to and say, *Aren't we lucky to have such natural beauty on our doorstep? Aren't we blessed to be able to walk for miles and to breathe fresh air? Aren't we lucky to have each other?*

'Sam?'

He turned. A petite figure was walking towards them, accompanied by a very large dog.

'Clare?'

His heart started to pound. It had been two weeks since he and Clare had exchanged texts when she couldn't make the pub quiz. He hadn't liked to invite her the following week in case she thought he was being pushy. Plus, he'd had other things on his mind with Alyssa, as well as work. Seeing her now, he wondered for a moment if she had been avoiding him or if she was just really busy as well.

He clipped Scout's lead to her collar, then waited for Clare to reach him. If it wasn't for Goliath, he probably wouldn't have recognised her because she had a pink bobble hat pulled down to her eyebrows, a purple scarf up to her chin and was lost in a long black wool coat and dark green wellies. She looked like a child wearing her older sister's clothes. The tip of her nose was red and her breaths emerged like puffs of steam in the chilly air.

'I thought it was you,' she said, smiling up at him. 'Couldn't be sure until I got closer, but then I saw Scout.'

'Recognisable by our canine companions.'

'Sorry?'

'I didn't recognise you either, but Goliath gave it away. Of course, you could have been your mother, but seeing as how you've been the one walking Goliath recently, I thought it must be you.'

I'm glad it's you . . .

And he was. Strangely. Inexplicably. Confusingly. Glad to see her.

Goliath and Scout sniffed at each other happily, and Clare stood next to Sam and gazed out at the fields. 'It's so beautiful here, Sam. Even in winter, the landscape is fabulous. I think it's the freedom, right on your doorstep. Do you know what I mean?'

She turned to him and his cheeks warmed because he knew she'd caught him staring at her. He could barely drag his eyes from her face to look at the scenery because she was, he knew now, the most beautiful thing he had ever seen. How could this be happening? What was wrong with him? He was heading towards fifty and yet here he was, falling for a pretty face and a kind smile, just like a teenager.

There was no rational explanation. No logic behind it. But there was something about Clare that reached into his soul and grabbed hold of his heart and just . . . squeezed. And if there was a chance that she was feeling the same way, then there could be the potential here for something very special to happen between them.

He gripped the top plank of the wooden fence and sighed. He'd never been what he'd thought of as a romantic, but something was happening here, and it was powerful.

Clare was special. It was as clear as the air they were breathing.

'Are you OK?' she asked.

He met her questioning gaze. 'I think so.'

'You seem troubled.'

'Do I?' He cleared his throat, buying some time to find the right words. But how could he tell this woman, someone he had yet to have an extended conversation with, that he felt drawn to her? She might think him mad – and perhaps he was . . .

'I'm a good listener.' She smiled, her pink lips curving upwards, her bright green eyes inviting as tropical lagoons, her nose cute as a small red button.

'Where to start?' He shook his head. 'I wish I knew where to start.'

'Wherever feels right,' Clare said as she reached out and squeezed his hand where it rested on top of the fence. They were both wearing gloves, so their skin didn't meet, but she still felt his warmth, the tension in his fingers. Something was wrong; he was clearly battling some internal conflict and she wanted to help if she could.

'Aren't the auditions for the show this week?' he asked, frowning.

'Yes. Tonight's the last night. We've seen some fabulous acts. The show should . . . *will* . . . be wonderful.'

He nodded. 'That's good. Did Miranda audition?'

'She did. She's in.'

'Really?'

'Yes. She's a perfect fit. We've had all sorts of different acts, which is perfect because it's exactly what I envisioned – an eclectic mix to showcase the talent of our community.'

'That's good news.' Sam smiled, but the smile slid from his lips quickly and he stared out at the fields again.

'I guess it has to be a woman.'

'A woman?'

'Whoever has messed with your head.' She removed her hand from his, not wanting to overstep the mark or unsettle him further.

'Oh . . . I see what you mean.' He rubbed his eyes with the heels of his hands. 'It is, kind of.'

Clare leant her arms on the fence and let the quiet flow between them. Perhaps he just needed to be near someone, or perhaps he didn't. Maybe she had read him wrongly and he would prefer to be alone right now.

'Would you . . .' He licked his lips. 'Would you like to come back to mine?'

'To your home?'

'Yes. For a coffee?'

'Oh . . . yes. Of course. A coffee!' She laughed, the sound sending a crow that had perched on a nearby tree squawking into the air.

'You're probably busy, aren't you?'

'No! Well, not for a few hours. I have more auditions to oversee later but I'm free now.'

'I have to get back for afternoon surgery but I need to eat and it's cold so we could warm up with some lunch and a drink.'

'That sounds lovely.'

'Great.' He smiled shyly at her, making her insides shift like sand under the tide. Something was tugging at her heart, reaching deep down to feelings she'd hidden for years, suppressed as she'd become convinced that they would only bring her heartbreak. 'Do you like soup?'

'I do!'

'Great. I have some home-made soup in the freezer that I can warm up and we could grab some bread from the bakery.'

'And some cakes?'

He smiled then, and his face lit up. He was definitely one of the most handsome men Clare had ever seen.

'Why not?' He hooked his arm and she slid hers through it, then they walked back to the village, dogs at their sides.

Clare wasn't quite sure what was happening, or even if anything was, but it felt right, and she was happy – and she was fairly certain that Sam was too.

At Sam's cottage, Clare followed him into the hallway and tried not to stare. It was strange going to a man's home alone, something she couldn't recall ever doing. She'd always been with Jason, had never had cause to go to another man's house, so this was a first. It was both exciting and terrifying, though why she felt afraid, she wasn't sure except that something about this felt a bit like a date . . .

She went to remove her wellies, but he shook his head. 'No need. I have wooden floors throughout the ground floor, except for the kitchen, which is tiled.'

'Are you sure? I'd hate to make a mess of your home.' She looked at the bottom of each boot, but they were clean from the walk back along the pavements.

'Absolutely. Don't worry.'

Clare, her heart racing, absorbed the unfamiliar scent of Sam's home. It was a combination of citrus and spice, as if he used herbs and spices in his cooking, and she could also smell clean washing, which she understood when they entered the kitchen and saw the pile of freshly laundered sheets neatly folded on the table.

Sam caught her looking at them. 'I did an early wash this morning, then put them through the tumble drier before work. Just need to pop them in the airing cupboard now.'

Clare smiled. Jason didn't know how to operate the washing machine, let alone wash and dry sheets then fold them and put them away. But then, Clare had always been there to take care of him, so he'd had no need to figure it out for himself.

The kitchen was clean and tidy, no paperwork spread on the table or the heavy oak worktops. The sink, taps and cupboard door handles were chrome, and everything shone, making it look a bit like a showroom kitchen. However, touches like the bonsai growing on the windowsill and the yucca in the corner near the large window made it feel homely.

What Clare noticed most about the kitchen was the space – there was plenty of it, and she realised that it must be so that Alyssa could move her chair around in there unhindered. The work surfaces were also lower than at Elaine's, again to accommodate Alyssa.

'There are two reception rooms on the ground floor and the kitchen, then there's a bathroom and two bedrooms upstairs.' Sam pointed at the ceiling.

She frowned. 'How does Alyssa manage?'

He gestured at the kitchen window and Clare went to it and peered out. There was a large garage conversion at the end of the driveway.

'She has her own space,' he explained. 'She has a bedroom, wet room and a small lounge. Not that she uses it much these days.' He shook his head.

'No?' Clare didn't want to pry but left the door open for him to talk if he wanted to.

'She's involved with someone and has been staying at his quite a bit.'

'Isn't that a good thing?' she asked, keeping her gaze on the garage.

'I'm trying to convince myself of that. Anyway . . .' He went to a large freestanding fridge freezer and opened the left door. 'I have vegetable or tomato and pepper soup. Which do you fancy?'

'Both sound good.'

'Please choose.' He turned and flashed her a smile. 'I hate having to decide for other people. Not that I get many other people here, mind you, but even deciding for Alyssa makes me twitchy.'

Clare laughed. 'Vegetable then, please.'

'Good choice.' He reached into the freezer and brought out two freezer bags then set them on the worktop. 'It won't take long to heat these up.'

Clare reached for the bag from the bakery and got the bread out, then looked around.

'Plates are in there.' He gestured at a cupboard next to the sink unit. 'And butter is in the dish next to the bread bin.'

Clare got out a large plate and two bowls and set them on the worktop, while Sam put the soup into a saucepan and set it on the hob of the range cooker. She found spoons and a breadknife, then cut large chunks of bread and slathered them with soft golden butter. She put the plate on the table.

'What are we drinking?' she asked.

'There's cranberry juice in the fridge and there's a water jug.'

When the table was set, she looked around.

'Where are the dogs?'

'Probably in the lounge in front of the log burner.' He pointed at the doorway. 'Take a look.'

She walked along the short hallway to the door they'd passed on their way in. It was ajar, so she stepped into the room and sighed, because on the hearth in front of the log burner were Scout and Goliath, side by side, completely re-laxed after their walk. Clare stood there for a moment gazing at Sam's furniture – two sofas in a deep green leather, an oak coffee table with a shelf underneath that seemed to be piled with paperwork, a large flat screen TV and four heavy book-cases along the back walls that were stuffed with books, with some of the shelves two-deep with extra books on top. Sam clearly liked to read and her stomach fluttered as she realised that was something they had in common. She would be able to talk to him about books, possibly start a book club now that it seemed that she was staying in the village and perhaps Sam would join.

There was a free-standing lamp behind one sofa with a shade that looked like a stained-glass window in a variety of red tones, and there was another one on a side table next to the other sofa. The room smelt of woodsmoke and vanilla with a hint of dog. It was a warm and comfortable room and Clare wondered what it would be like to sit here on a winter's evening, curled up on the sofa under the patchwork throw that was folded on one of the seats and to sip wine while watching a movie or reading. The dogs would lie on the rug, the fire would crackle, the wind would howl around outside and she could snuggle up to Sam, all six foot some-thing of him and . . .

Whoa!

What was she thinking? She was definitely getting carried away.

But as she turned and went back to the kitchen, she couldn't deny that the thought had left her smiling and made her warm right through.

Sam poured the soup into bowls, then carried them to the table. He set them down then paused, wondering if there was anything else he should get. Glancing at the clock on the wall, he suppressed a sigh. He only had about thirty-five minutes left of his break.

'They're so cute together.' Clare was back in the kitchen.

'Sorry?'

'The dogs. You were right, they are snuggled in front of the log burner.'

He nodded. 'Best place to be after a wintery walk.'

'Your home is lovely.'

'Thank you.'

'And I love your bookshelves.'

He laughed. 'Bit messy, aren't they? I keep meaning to tidy them up, but then I buy more books and it just adds to the chaos on the shelves.'

'I love reading too.'

'Do you?' He tilted his head. 'What genre?'

'Anything really. Romcoms. Thrillers. Historical fiction. I have a broad taste. Like you, by the look of your shelves.'

'Guilty!' He held up his hands and laughed.

'I used to work in a library.'

'Wow! That must have been fabulous. Did you have early access to all the new books?'

She nodded. 'There were definite advantages. I didn't want to leave but the funding was cut and they had to make some of the staff redundant.'

'That's a shame. Do you work now?'

'No, but I've got something in the pipeline . . .'

'That sounds exciting.'

'It is, but it's not public knowledge yet.'

He nodded, but he didn't want her to feel pushed into sharing the details with him.

'I was a keen horse rider growing up and used to go to Old Oak Stables. I was there the other day and Verity offered me a job.'

'That's incredible news. Verity has some beautiful horses there. Did you accept?'

'I did. Please keep it quiet for now as I need to go and have a proper talk with her about it, but it means I'll be staying in the village after Christmas.'

He grinned at her, unable to conceal his delight.

'I'm glad to hear that. Really glad.' He pulled out a chair at the table. 'Would you like to sit down?'

'Please.' She placed a hand over her belly. 'I'm quite hungry.' Then she frowned. 'I should text Kyle so he knows I won't be back for lunch. He can let Mum know too.'

'Of course. I should check in with work anyway.'

They sat opposite each other at the table, both typing on their phones, then when texts were sent, they set their phones down.

'This smells delicious,' Clare said as she picked up her spoon. 'Do you come home for lunch every day?'

'Most days. It means I can walk Scout at lunchtime in the winter months because it's usually too dark by the time I finish for the day.'

'That makes sense.'

They ate in silence for a bit, tearing chunks off the crusty bread, then dipping them in the soup, the only sounds the ticking of the clock and the clinking of spoons against bowls. Occasionally, Sam looked up to find Clare's gaze on him. It was good to have company, to have another human being close by, even when they weren't talking. He realised how much he'd missed having human company. Scout was wonderful and he knew he'd always want to have a dog around, but having Clare here was better than he'd imagined it could be.

'Thank you so much, Sam. That was delicious. I'm afraid I ate it a bit quickly.'

He shook his head. 'Not at all. I'm really glad you enjoyed it. And don't forget, we have cakes!'

Her face lit up and he was struck again by her beauty. Her high cheekbones were emphasised when she smiled, and he found the smattering of freckles across her nose very sweet. He could see how she would have looked when she was younger, knew that she would have been stunning in her twenties and thirties. He suspected that she was in her forties now, certainly younger than him, but her beauty was that of a woman who has lived and experienced life, has matured like a fine wine. He smiled inwardly at the cliché, but it was the best way of summing up his thoughts. Clare would certainly have been attractive when she was younger, but he felt sure that she was at her most beautiful right now. She had a calm aura that he found comforting. And that came with maturity, with having been through tough times; it was soothing, far more so than the erratic chaos of youth. Clare was becoming who she was always meant to be and Sam hoped that the same could be said of him. There would always be uncertainties; those shifting beliefs and doubts were what helped a person to grow, and he wanted to have room to grow through the rest of his life. But how incredible would it be to have a woman like Clare by his side to grow old with?

'I don't know if Alyssa has told you, but she's auditioning this evening for the show.'

'She hasn't, no, but I did tell her about it and hoped she would. She has a wonderful voice.'

Clare nodded. 'I'm looking forward to hearing it.'

'She was in all the school shows growing up.'

'Your parents must have been so proud.'

He put his spoon down and stared into his bowl at the remaining portion of soup.

'What is it?'

He met her gaze, saw the concern in her eyes.

'My . . . *our* . . . mum passed away not long after Alyssa was born.'

'I'm sorry. That's so sad.' Clare placed a hand on her chest.

'It's one of those things in life that I always feel is such a shame. Mum was a lovely woman. She was strict but fair – and always kind.'

'How old were you when she passed?'

'Twelve.'

'That must have been so hard. You really need your mum at that age. Your dad too.'

He nodded. 'It was a difficult time, but Alyssa was there, a tiny baby, needing me and my dad, so we had to get on with it for her.'

'That's what happens, isn't it?' Clare gazed out of the window. 'You keep going, even when it hurts.'

'I'm sad for Alyssa that she missed out on having Mum around. Mum would have been a great help after the accident. Dad too.'

'Alyssa was in an accident?'

He sighed. 'About ten years ago. It's how she ended up in a wheelchair. She came off her motorbike; she was overtaking a truck and the driver didn't see her . . .' He shifted in his seat. Rarely speaking about that day was one of the ways he coped with it; letting the memories in made him feel as if he was suffocating. And here, in his home, was this lovely woman and he didn't want to tell her the full truth about that day. She was gazing at him with sympathy, with compassion. If he told her the full story, it might change how she saw him and he would hate to see the shift in her eyes as she realised that he was to blame. It would mean seeing the same emotions he saw in his own eyes every day in the mirror: the blame, the doubt, the shame.

'I can only imagine.' Clare sipped her water. 'It must have been a difficult time.'

'Very. She went through so much surgery, then years of physio and follow-up appointments.'

'She certainly doesn't seem to let her disability get in the way of living.'

'No. Not now. But she struggled at first, as anyone would. She had to adjust to a different way of living.'

'Does she have no feeling at all?'

'Initially she didn't, but now she has some sensation in her right leg and her waist. It's what they call partial paraplegia.'

'She's lucky to have you.'

'I don't know about that.' He gave a wan smile. 'Mum and Dad would have been better, but we lost Dad too, sixteen years ago.'

He took a drink of water, wishing the conversation hadn't gone down this path. The last thing he wanted was to bring Clare down or for her to think he was after sympathy. But he did appreciate how open she was with her questions; she wasn't afraid to ask, wasn't tiptoeing around Alyssa's disability like some people did.

'What happened to your dad?'

'He had sickle cell anaemia. He always had it but lived with relatively few symptoms. However, after Mum died, he didn't look after himself very well and as Alyssa got older and more independent, it was as if he felt that he could let go. He drank a fair bit and didn't eat very well, and he developed an infection in his lungs and that just got progressively worse. It was a slow deterioration but one he didn't seem to want to battle. It was as if the fight had all left him.'

'I'm so sorry, Sam. You've had a hard life.'

'No, I haven't. It's been much better than for a lot of people. I mean, when I was a child, we lived in Hackney in a two-bedroom council flat in a tower block. Dad used to sleep on the sofa after Alyssa came along so she could have a room to herself. It was small and there was damp and I doubt that helped with his health issues. Alyssa was eighteen when Dad passed away and by then I'd moved out, so she came to live with me. She was still at college, studying art, and I didn't want her to quit.'

'Were you working as a vet then?'

'Yes. I didn't go to university until I was twenty-three because I worked to save money to pay for it all, but I'd been qualified for a year when Dad died. I had a flat not far from theirs and it was much better, so it made sense for Alyssa to move in with me.'

'Have you lived together ever since?'

'No. Alyssa moved out after six months because she was in a relationship. He was twelve years older than her and . . .' He gave a wry laugh. 'I didn't really approve, but she was legally an adult, so what could I do? They met at a music festival and she fell madly in love and . . . well, that was that. I carried on working, she got on with her life, then things changed when she turned twenty-four and she . . . was in the accident.'

'Did she move back in with you then?'

'Yes. I found a ground-floor flat in central London. It wasn't cheap but we needed to be close to the hospitals and physios.'

'Where was her partner?'

He shrugged. 'He wasn't as loyal as she thought he was.'

'Goodness, that's awful.'

'Sadly, it happens.'

'It seems to me that Alyssa has been very lucky to have you, Sam. You're a good man.'

'I'm not sure she sees it that way.'

'So how did you come to move to Little Bramble?'

'I saved and saved. Then a friend told me about the possibility of a partnership with Miranda and I went for it.'

'Such a brilliant move.'

'I think so. I bought the house and had the garage adapted and we've been here for just over three years. It was a good move to make because it's such a lovely place to be and it's been good for Alyssa. She suffered several bouts of depression over the years – to be expected, I guess – but since we've been here she's come through it. She has a job and a new boyfriend so . . . It's all good.'

'It sounds like it's all worked out.'

Sam met Clare's eyes, saw the warmth and kindness there and it was all he could do not to slide his hand over the table and take hers, to press his lips to her palm and confess everything to her. Letting go of all his concerns, his guilt and his fears would be liberating. He was almost certain that she wouldn't judge him; she seemed so compassionate and so caring. But it was too much of a risk to take and the thought of losing this new friendship, of overburdening their fledgling relationship with a confession of his darkest secret, would surely be foolish.

'I guess you could say that.' He smiled, then stood up and picked up their bowls. There was still some soup in his, but he'd lost his appetite for it. 'I'll make some tea, shall I, and we can have our cakes?'

'Good plan!'

❄

'Shall we take these through to the lounge?' Sam asked as he handed Clare a mug of tea.

'That would be lovely.' Sam's kitchen was bright and pleasant but the idea of sitting in that cosy lounge in front of the log burner and next to those exciting bookshelves was very appealing. She was surprised at how much she'd found out about Sam and Alyssa over lunch. It was clear that Sam found it hard to open up about his life and his past, but he also seemed glad to have the chance to talk. Jason had been a closed book for much of their marriage, so knowing that Sam felt he could trust her and talk to her felt good. She sensed that he was holding something back about Alyssa's accident, but if he wanted to share it, then she would listen. If not, that was fine too.

They sat on the same sofa in the lounge, their knees just a few inches apart. Clare cradled her mug between her palms, making the most of the warmth.

'Are you OK?' Sam asked, nodding at her hands.

'Yes, thanks, but I have found that my fingers get cold easily as I've got older. I saw something on TV recently about Raynaud's disease and wondered if I might have it.'

'What's that?'

'It's an issue with circulation in cold weather. When my hands get really cold, the tips of my fingers go white.'

He put his mug down on the side table.

'May I?' He held out a hand.

'Of course.' Clare placed her mug on the coffee table in front of the sofa, then gave him her hand.

When their skin touched, something shot through her and Sam met her gaze. Did he feel it too? He held her hand in his, where it looked small, then he ran his thumb over her palm slowly, gently, in a way that made her whole body tingle. He turned it over and ran his forefingers over the back of her hand, then raised it to examine her fingertips.

'Your fingers *are* quite pale and cold, so if we warm them up a bit, it should help. Give me the other one too.'

His hands were warm and strong as they enveloped hers, his thumbs smooth as they ran over her fingers in turn, massaging, warming, bringing heat to Clare's hands, but also to other parts that made her blush. How could holding hands be so sensual, so powerful?

When was the last time a man had held her hand? Jason certainly hadn't held her hand as they walked, when they lay in bed side by side, or even when she was upset. It was a simple act of physical contact and yet it was so powerful.

When Sam stopped massaging, then held her hands up as if to present them to her, she almost groaned. She didn't want him to stop; it was too good.

281

'You have lovely hands, Clare.'

He pressed his lips to each one and she almost swooned.

'I'm sorry.' His eyes widened and he seemed to tense up. 'I shouldn't have done that.'

'No . . . it's fine. It was lovely.'

'Are you sure?'

'The massage *and* the kisses.'

'Good. That's good to know.'

He picked up his tea and the moment was over. Clare swallowed her disappointment, but then perhaps Sam felt awkward; maybe he was shy and it had been a long time since he'd touched or been touched. He'd told her about Alyssa and his past and not once had he mentioned having a partner there supporting him, not once had he referred to a significant other and surely he would have done, had someone been there for him. For all his strength, there was a vulnerability about Sam that made Clare want to hug him tight.

'I should probably finish my tea then get back to work,' he said, making her heart sink, even though she knew he was only on a lunch break.

'Of course.' She drained her mug, not wanting this moment to end, the thought of not seeing him again for a while leaving her with a dull ache in her chest.

'Not that it wouldn't be nice to sit here all afternoon.' He smiled and she smiled back. He did like being with her.

'Sam . . .' Clare adjusted her position on the sofa. 'Do you have plans this evening?'

'I don't.'

'Would you . . . like to come and see the auditions?'

'Would that be all right?'

'I don't see why not. You can help us decide which acts go through.'

'I'd like that.'

'The first audition is at six, so if you can get there for about quarter to?'

'I'll be there.'

They stood up and Clare nudged Goliath gently with her foot. He also looked as though he'd have stayed in front of the log burner all afternoon if he'd been allowed, then she put on her coat, hat and gloves.

'See you later,' she said, as she let herself and Goliath out onto the street.

'You certainly will.'

And just like that, something between them had changed. They had arranged to meet again and Clare had to stop herself from cheering as she walked along the street, because she knew that he was watching her go.

Chapter 22

'What time did Nanna say she'd be here?' Clare asked Kyle as they set the hall up ready for the final auditions. It was five thirty and Clare was trying to ignore the fluttering in her belly every time she thought about seeing Sam again.

'She should be here already.' Kyle frowned.

'I'm here! Stop fussing, Clare,' Elaine said, rushing in at that moment.

'Where have you been?' Clare asked, then realised her hands were on her hips, making her appear quite confrontational.

'I met someone for lunch.'

'Lunch?' Clare glanced at Kyle, but he was lost in his mobile phone.

'Yes, Clare, you know that meal you eat between breakfast and dinner?'

'Mum!' She shook her head. 'I've been back in the village for seven weeks and you haven't been out for lunch once.'

Elaine shrugged, a smile dancing on her lips. She looked so much better than she had done since Clare had come back to Little Bramble. She'd even put some make-up on.

'Where did you go?'

'To the vicarage.'

284

'You had lunch with the vicar?'

Kyle lowered his phone. 'Was he wearing the lime-green Lycra, Nanna?'

'No, he wasn't, Kyle! And yes, Clare, at the vicarage.'

Clare stared at her mum, taking in the glow on her cheeks and the sparkle in her eyes. Was there more to this than just lunch?

'But he's a bit younger than you.'

Elaine rolled her eyes. 'I had lunch *with* him, Clare, not *on* him, and even if there was more to this than sandwiches, why should it matter?'

Clare searched for an answer that didn't sound condescending or petty. Her mum was seventy-five and perfectly entitled to have lunch with whomever she liked, but it was more the fact that it had come out of the blue. Or had it? She'd been worried about her mum seeming low, about how they still seemed to clash over the same things they had when Clare was younger. She'd been caught up with showing Elaine how well she managed things, with not letting her barbs hit home, with being a good mum to Kyle and trying to ensure that everything ran smoothly between the three of them, with preparing everything for the auditions and the show, that she hadn't noticed her mum making any extra calls or sending texts or leaving the cottage. Was this a new thing that had happened just this week or was it more long-term? Was it the magic effect of the show, bringing people together?

'Nanna has a toy boy.' Kyle laughed. 'Good for you, Nanna.'

'Thank you, darling. Although he's only eight years younger than me.'

'You're in good shape for your age, Nanna, don't you worry.'

'For my age?' Elaine raised her eyebrows at her grandson.

'I meant for *any* age, Nanna. You're a hottie.'

Elaine giggled then, raising a hand to cover her mouth. 'I shall have to tell Iolo that I'm a *hottie*.'

Clare shook her head. Her mum had gone from seeming incredibly low to being almost as vivacious and effervescent as she had been when Clare was growing up. That was the contradiction that was her mum; she was both bubbly and harsh, the life and soul of the party and yet the cool disciplinarian. Thinking about it now, Clare became aware that the version of her mum that she knew was different to the version that others knew. It wasn't that she expected her to be her best friend in the whole world, more that she wanted to understand why her mum had been the way she was to her only child.

She resolved to speak to her about it later on. Some things could be ignored, but for Clare, finding out why her mum was such a woman of contradictions was becoming paramount.

'Ooh! Who's that?' Kyle tapped Clare's shoulder and she turned to the door. Her stomach lurched and she inhaled sharply.

'That, Kyle, is Samuel Wilson. The local vet. He's come here to help judge the auditions.' Clare felt rather than saw her son's gaze burning into her face. Was she that transparent?

If so, at least Kyle would understand her. At least *she* wasn't a mass of confusing contradictions.

Walking into the hall was quite daunting for Sam, with Clare, Elaine and a man he thought must be Clare's son all staring at him. He hoped he wasn't about to trip or sneeze or do anything else that might affect his entrance. He felt as if he was auditioning – and perhaps he was, in a way. He was trying on the role of being Clare's friend, and being judged by her mother and son was a part of that. They had every right to assess his suitability, just as he had assessed Sebastian's. Although that matter was still not resolved and until he had the time to have a proper conversation with Alyssa, he wasn't sure how it could be.

'Evening.' Clare smiled at him and some of the tension in his shoulders drained away. 'I'm not sure you know my son, Kyle. Kyle, this is Sam.'

'Hi.' He smiled at them and Kyle gave a small wave, then looked him up and down. He pretended not to notice.

'So, you're here to help us with the auditions, are you?' Elaine nodded.

'Clare invited me.' He felt the need to explain, in case she hadn't told them, then he did a double take at Elaine. She looked different, healthier somehow. Perhaps having her family around her was having a positive impact.

'Wonderful!' Elaine took a seat at the table in front of the stage. 'The more the merrier.'

'How was your afternoon?' Clare asked Sam, as Kyle took a seat next to his grandmother.

'Not bad. I had to empty a bulldog's anal glands and X-ray a bearded dragon's broken tail, but apart from that, it was quiet.'

'Your job is so interesting.' Clare blinked up at him and he knew that she meant it. 'I always wanted to work with animals.'

'Why didn't you?'

'I fell for a man's charm, got married, had a child.' She sighed.

'All good things to do, but you could still have worked with animals.'

'Perhaps. Time just got away from me.'

'It's never too late, Clare, and with your job at the stables, you have that opportunity now.'

'I do.'

'Hey, I know – why don't you come and spend some time observing at the surgery? You could see what we do, learn about the different roles there, see if you'd fancy it. If you're too busy at the moment with the show, we could arrange it for after Christmas.'

'I'm too old to retrain.'

'That's nonsense.' He shook his head. 'You can do anything you put your mind to.'

Her eyes flickered from side to side and when she looked up again, he saw that they were glistening.

'Hey . . .' He lowered his voice, not wanting to draw Elaine and Kyle's attention to her. 'What's wrong?'

She shook her head, pressing her lips together until they turned white.

'Tell me. You can trust me.' He flashed her a smile. 'I trust you.'

'I-I'm not used to being told things like that. No one's ever said things like that to me before. Except my dad and Kyle.'

Sam squeezed her shoulder, then hugged her quickly behind her mother and son's backs. Before he knew what he was doing, he had pressed a kiss to her hair, inhaling her sweet scent. 'Believe in yourself, Clare. You're amazing.'

He gently released her and she looked up at him again, but the emotion in her eyes had changed to something that made his nerve endings tingle and he had to fight the impulse to pull her close again. It was probably a good thing that her family were there because Sam was finding his attraction to Clare and his emotions when he was close to her quite overwhelming. Telling her so much about his past earlier that day had created a bond between them and it was an unfamiliar feeling for him, but one that he liked.

He just hoped that they would be able to continue to nurture whatever it was that was growing between them.

❋

Sitting next to Sam, trying to concentrate on the acts as they performed, Clare found it difficult to keep still, even with her mum and Kyle on the other side of her. Sam had kissed her hair in the way a lover might. The strangest thing about it was that it felt so natural being with him, having his hands on her, his lips against her hair. It was, if she allowed herself to be extremely romantic, almost as though they were meant to be this way.

She was aware that it had been a long time since a man had held her, kissed her or caressed her and that she could be experiencing such a dramatic reaction to Sam because he was the first man to show her any attention in quite some time. She might be naïve about some things, but she could, at least, understand that. Even in the early days with Jason, he'd never been particularly affectionate or attentive. They'd been in love, she didn't doubt that, but it had been a different type of love. Clare had been so young, so keen to prove to her parents – especially her mum – how grown-up she was, how strong she was and how she could make her own life, create her own home. It was even possible that she had latched onto Jason as the first decent man to show her some attention other than her father; he had made it easy for her to fall for him. But their relationship had not been one of equals and she had not felt valued for a lot of their time together.

Sam made her feel valued, and it was refreshing. Finally, she knew what it was to see herself through someone else's eyes – not as a daughter, wife or mother, but as a person with value just for being herself – and she liked what she saw. Perhaps this was what she'd read about in novels and magazines, finding that special someone who made you the best version of yourself because they believed in you. She knew that she shouldn't ever need a man to feel confident, that she didn't need a man full stop, and that she was enough on her own, but it was still very enjoyable to see herself from his perspective . . .

The acts they'd seen so far had included a salsa dancing team of six ten-year-olds and a teenaged boy playing acoustic guitar while his girlfriend sang 'Rocking Around the Christmas Tree' and shook a tambourine. The final act was Alyssa Wilson.

She entered the hall in her wheelchair and went to the stage, then up the ramp on the far side. When she'd parked in the middle of the stage, she announced her name, which all the acts had been asked to do, even though the judges knew who everyone was.

Kyle leant over the desk. 'Is she your sister, Sam?'

He nodded.

'She's gorgeous.'

'And in a relationship, Kyle,' Clare added quickly, not wanting him to get any ideas.

'Shame.' He folded his arms and sat back in his chair.

'Thanks,' Sam whispered. 'I don't think I could cope with her being involved in a love triangle.'

Clare hid her smile behind her hand. Kyle was right, though, Alyssa was gorgeous. Her hair had been styled into a curly top-knot, exposing her beautiful face and long, elegant neck. She was wearing a red skater-style dress with tiny white moons on it and black knee-length biker-style boots. Next to Clare, Sam tensed, and her heart went out to him. There was something not quite right between the siblings and she suspected it was linked to the accident in some way. She hoped that Sam would tell her at some point, not because she was nosy, but because it was clearly bothering him, and it might help him to get it off his chest.

'Are you ready?' Kyle asked Alyssa.

'I didn't realise you'd be on the panel,' Alyssa said to Sam. 'Do you mind?' he asked.

'No. It's fine.' She shrugged and then, unaccompanied by an instrument, she started to sing . . .

❄

'That was incredible, Alyssa!' Elaine stood up and clapped loudly. 'You have the voice of an angel. You can be the star of the show.'

'I agree!' Kyle said as they all stood up, even Sam, who must have heard his sister sing many times before.

'I don't think we need to confer,' Clare said when she could speak again. 'We want you in the show.'

Alyssa beamed at them all. 'Thank you. I'm delighted.'

'We'll be in touch with the arrangements and rehearsal times.' Clare smiled.

'I'll look forward to it.' Alyssa pushed herself down the ramp and across the hallway.

'Alyssa!' Sam hurried after her. 'Can I have a word?'

They went out into the hallway and Clare turned to her mum and son. 'So we've seen all of the acts now.'

'Except for mine, but I'm polishing it at the moment and will reveal all soon. Thank you so much for organising this, you two.' Elaine grinned at Clare, then cupped Kyle's cheek before kissing it. 'I'm so excited about the show. It will make Christmas all the more festive this year!'

'It will.'

'Now, I have a date – I mean – oh hell, it's a date. Who am I trying to kid?' Elaine giggled as she put her coat on. 'Soooo, don't wait up for me.'

'Wait!' Clare held up a hand. 'A date with whom?'

'The vicar again?' Kyle asked, raising his eyebrows.

'Who else?' Clare's mum replied.

'But you had lunch with him.' Clare shook her head.

'And I'm having dinner with him too.' Elaine pulled a hat over her hair, then zipped up her coat. 'As I said, don't wait up.'

She marched out of the hall and Clare was left alone with Kyle.

'What on earth . . . ?' Clare let the question hang in the air and her son started to laugh.

'Well, it's good to see her in a better mood.'

'I can't disagree with that, but it's a bit strange.'

'Seeing your mother dating?'

'Yes.'

'But you're happy she's happier?'

'I am.'

'Then don't worry about it.'

'I'll try not to. Don't you think she's turned around quite quickly from being so low to being so . . . excited?'

He nodded slowly. 'Perhaps, but Nanna was never one to do things by halves, was she? And, Mum, I'm convinced that your presence in the village, along with the show, has had a wonderfully positive impact upon her.'

'I hope so, because I really wanted to help her. But I can't take all the credit. You've helped enormously.'

'We're a great team, Mum.'

They hugged and Clare's heart brimmed with love for her family, her mind whirling with thoughts of how things could continue to improve. Then she heard raised voices from outside the door and her thoughts returned to Sam.

What on earth was going on?

Chapter 23

'I'm moving out and that's the end of it!'

'But why?'

'I've already explained twice, Sam.'

Alyssa glared at him, her pretty face contorted with frustration.

'But you've only known him five minutes, Alyssa, and it's a hell of a responsibility to take on.'

'How dare you!' Her knuckles were white because she was gripping the wheels of her chair so tightly.

'What do you mean?'

'I'm not a responsibility.'

'I didn't mean *you* were the responsibility.' He slapped his hands against his head. 'I meant you taking on him *and* his child.'

'Oh . . . Well, that's my decision to make. Not yours!'

'I know it's your decision, Alyssa, I really do, but I'm worried about you. Don't you see that? I love you, I'm your brother and I feel that I should look out for you.'

'Looking out for me and trying to wrap me up in cotton wool for the rest of my life are two different things, Sam. Can't you see that?'

Sighing, he experienced the sensation of sinking, as if someone had wrapped a heavy chain around him then padlocked it and thrown him into the sea. He was drowning in the complexities of the situation. It was so hard to get it right, to say and do the right things. To show Alyssa that he loved and cared for her, that he did not want to control her or ruin her life.

'I can see that, Alyssa, but I just want what's best for you. Since Mum and then Dad passed away, I've felt that I have to look out for you.'

'Do not start down that route again, Sam. You can't use being there for me as an excuse to avoid living your own life. You've done it for years, shied away from relationships, avoided feeling anything for anyone because you're scared.'

'What? That's not true.'

'Isn't it?' Her eyes shone and her bottom lip was trembling. 'Sam, I do appreciate what you've done for me, but you can't spend the rest of your life trying to make up for something that wasn't your fault.'

He gasped as pain ricocheted through his chest. 'But it was –'

Alyssa was shaking her head furiously. 'No. It wasn't. *I* made the choices. You didn't force me to rush out that night or to get on my bike when I could barely see for tears.'

'I should have stopped you going.'

'You wouldn't have been able to, Sam.'

'But I'm so sorry.'

'I know. Me too. But now I have a chance to be happy, to have a family of my own.' She placed a hand over her belly. 'Also . . .'

'No!' His mouth fell open. 'Really? Alyssa, how could you? I mean, you know the risks. And after last time . . .'

A tear rolled down her cheek and plopped onto her chest.

'I had hoped that you'd be more understanding. It's very early days and it took me by surprise too. But this child, the possibilities it offers for me to live the life I've always wanted . . . Can't you be happy for me, Sam?'

He sucked in a breath and closed his eyes. He couldn't believe this was happening again. Alyssa had been so irresponsible. Not just once, but twice. And matters were even more complicated now.

When he opened his eyes, she had turned her chair and was heading for the front doors of the village hall. They opened automatically and she gave him a brief glance, her eyes filled with sadness and pain, then disappeared into the late November evening.

Bewildered and ashamed at his own emotional outburst, Sam leant against the wall, resting his head against the cool, painted surface. As the doors closed, his broken reflection stared back at him from the glass and he knew that something had to change. He couldn't keep going over the same ground, time after time.

Alyssa was his baby sister and he loved her, but she had to make her own choices in life, as did he.

❄

Peering out into the hallway, Clare spotted Sam leaning against the wall, his shoulders slumped, knees slightly bent, suggesting it was taking all of his strength to stay upright.

'Sam?' She approached him cautiously, as if he was a wounded animal that might start and run away. 'Are you all right?'

Reaching his side, she placed a hand on his arm, and he turned to her. He looked hollow-cheeked, as if the life had been sucked out of him, and his eyes were haunted.

'I . . . just keep getting it so wrong, Clare. How do I keep getting it wrong?'

'Getting what wrong, Sam?' she asked.

'Alyssa . . . I try to be what she needs me to be but my stupid, stubborn need to protect her surfaces and causes problems. I have to change, Clare, I have to do something. How do I change?'

He pressed his knuckles into his eyes and she faltered. What did he need right now? What could she do to help him?

Voices from the kitchen at the rear of the village hall filtered through and she realised that there were still other people around, including Kyle. She needed to get Sam out of there.

'Let me grab my bag and we can go and get a drink,' she said, and he nodded. 'I'll be quick.'

Hurrying back through the doors to Kyle, she grabbed her bag and paperwork.

'Kyle, something's come up. Would you be OK to finish up here, then take this paperwork back to Nanna's?'

He looked at her, one eyebrow raised. 'This is about the vet, right?'

'I need to take him for a drink. He argued with his sister and he's in a bit of a state. He needs a friend.'

Kyle rolled his eyes. 'You and Nanna both? Bloody hell! You're putting me to shame the way you two are carrying on.'

'I'm not carrying on, Kyle. I'm being a friend.'

'You keep telling yourself that, Mum, but I saw the way you two were looking at each other this evening. I've witnessed the sparkling attraction between you.'

'There's no attraction, Kyle.' Clare glanced behind her, fearing that she might get back out there and find Sam gone. And yet she didn't want to rush off and leave her son thinking she was *carrying on*. It made her feel as though she was doing something wrong.

'What is it? You think that just because you're a mum, a daughter and an ex-wife that you can't have your own wants and needs?'

She frowned. 'My own wants and needs don't matter, Kyle.'

'They bloody well do, Mum! You're only forty-five and you've spent the majority of your adult life tied to a man who didn't even notice you. You're free now, so have some fun, enjoy yourself a bit.'

'It's not like that.' A flush crept over her skin. She could barely believe this was her son speaking to her in this way.

'Mum,' he placed his hands on her shoulders, 'I'm an adult now. No one ever wants to think of their parents as sexual beings, but you *are*. You're warm, kind and beautiful.' He gave her a quick hug. 'Now go get your vet.'

She was about to deny it some more but then she realised she didn't have the energy and Sam was out there, needing a friend. Kyle could wait; she didn't know if Sam could.

'I'll see you at Nanna's later, OK?'

He nodded.

'And don't forget to let Goliath out.'

'I won't.' He kissed her cheek, then released her. 'Be careful.'

'Of course.'

In the hallway, Sam was still leaning against the wall, his eyes glazed over, as if he'd retreated into his mind.

'Sam? Shall we go?'

He met her eyes. 'OK.'

She took one of his large hands, laced her fingers through his and led him towards the doors, which swished open automatically, then they stepped outside into the icy air. After the brightness of the hall, the darkness of the village evening seemed impenetrable, the streetlights golden orbs set high above the ground, the spaces between their circles of light black and unfathomable.

They walked slowly at first; Clare didn't want to rush him while he seemed so dazed. The Red wasn't far from the village hall, but she wasn't sure if he would want to go there. On a Thursday evening it might be busy and she didn't know how he'd manage if he had to make polite conversation.

'Do you want to go to the pub?' She peered up at him.

'I'd prefer to go home, if that's OK with you? I just can't face people at the moment.'

'No problem.' Did he mean her as well? Was she people, or did he want her company? If she just managed to get him home, she could find out if he wanted her there or not, and then at least he'd be safe, whatever he decided.

They walked hand in hand, Clare conscious of their skin touching, his long fingers wrapped around hers. How big yet vulnerable he seemed . . . She felt that there was a connection between them that went deeper than friendship; they had both been through difficult times, both been strong and resilient, and they had that in common. But now there was a difference – they could be there to help and support each other. They went past the café and the veterinary surgery on one side, and the village green on the other. The wind rustled the trees and cast eerie shadows across the pavement and the road, carrying the aromas of woodsmoke, chips and garlic, picking scents up as it travelled through the village. Clare pulled her coat up around her neck, the chill creeping under the collar and sending shivers down her spine.

Sam's cottage came into sight and his grip on her hand relaxed a bit. He needed to go home, to hide away from the world for a bit to gather his strength. Clare knew that feeling, had experienced it after Jason had broken the news that he no longer wanted to be married to her. At that moment, in that raw period, it had left her bewildered, desperate to hide under the duvet and rest, regain her strength before facing the world again.

Outside his cottage Sam fumbled with the key, so Clare took it from him, opened the door, then stood back as Scout rushed at them. Sam murmured hello to the dog, stroking her head and her ears, then turned to Clare. She put her hands in her pockets, expecting him to say goodbye.

'Would you come in?'

'Oh . . . uh, now?'

'It's OK. I understand that you probably want to go home.'

'No! It's fine. I told Kyle we were going for a drink anyway, so he won't be expecting me home for a while.'

'You can have a drink here.' He gave her a small smile. 'I have spirits, wine, beers in the fridge.'

'That would be lovely.'

She stepped inside and closed the door behind her, then followed Sam through to the kitchen. He let Scout out into the garden, then went to the fridge.

'Yep, beer or lager or white wine. Then there's red in the wine rack . . .'

'Red would be great, thanks.'

He nodded and selected a bottle from the wine rack.

'Would it be OK if I use your bathroom?' she asked as she removed her coat.

'Top of the stairs, first door on the left.'

'Thanks.'

When she'd washed her hands, she stood for a moment in front of the mirror above the sink. The bathroom was very clean and smelt of bleach and Sam's cologne. It was deliciously masculine and made her feel a bit light-headed, as if his scent knocked her slightly off-kilter. In the mirror, her reflection stared back at her, skin pale and freckly, eyes seeming to be a darker green than usual, but that was probably due to the lighting, hair slightly messy from where the breeze had ruffled it. She ran her hands through it, smoothing it down, then tucked it behind her ears. It was like looking at herself through someone else's eyes; she was herself, but she was changing, going through a metamorphosis of sorts as she left the wife she'd been behind and morphed into the woman she was going to be. The woman, perhaps, she was always meant to be, but had somehow lost along the way.

Feelings rushed through her: she was nervous but excited, pensive yet happy as she stood on the line between one life and another. She could do anything, be anything, go anywhere; life was hers for the taking.

At last.

Downstairs, she paused by the lounge doorway and popped her head into the room.

'There you are,' Sam said as he smiled at her from the sofa. 'I've poured the wine, stoked the fire and Scout has been out and done what she needed to do.'

Clare crossed the room and the dog wagged her tail from where she was lying in front of the log burner, the regular thump as it hit the rug reminding Clare of a heartbeat. Of her heartbeat, as it sped up in her chest when she took a seat on the sofa next to Sam. It seemed wrong to sit on the other sofa, too far away, as if placing a physical distance between them would leave him feeling lost. She wanted him to feel safe, cared about, and that he could talk if he needed to or just sit quietly and sip wine while gazing into the fire.

On the sofa, she turned her body so she was facing him, and he handed her a glass of wine.

'Thank you.' Clare savoured the aromas of blackcurrant and vanilla, then the spicy, chocolate undertones as she rested the wine on her tongue. 'The wine is delicious.'

'Can't beat a good red.' Sam nodded, then sipped his wine. 'Thank you, Clare.'

'What for?'

'Getting me home.' He laughed. 'All six foot one of me. I'm so sorry.'

'Why are you sorry, Sam?'

He gazed into his glass, swirling the wine around. 'For losing it back there. I just . . .' He glanced sideways at her. 'I felt like I'd been catapulted back through the years to when Alyssa had her accident. It was like some delayed shock or something.'

'A kind of PTSD?'

'I guess it could be. I didn't see the accident, though, just Alyssa at the hospital and photographs of the scene in the newspapers.' He rubbed his forehead as if to try to erase the images.

'It must have been awful.'

'It was dreadful. To think what could have happened to her. I would have died if I'd lost her.' He grimaced. 'When Mum . . . when she was dying, Mum told me to take care of Alyssa. It was as if she thought it would be too great a task for Dad, as if she knew he wouldn't last long enough without her there. He did, though, he lived for eighteen years after her death, but it was like he wasn't there for most of it and I had to take it all on, you know. I helped him out as much as I could with money, food, being there as often as I could. It drove me to get my qualifications, I guess. I knew I'd need to help him and Alyssa as much as I could. I mean, that's what families do, right?'

'Some.' Clare sipped her wine. 'Not all, though. Some families aren't close at all.'

'Alyssa is furious with me, Clare. I'm afraid that I've pushed her too far this time.'

'I'm sure she'll come around.' Clare reached out a hand and he took it, wrapping his long fingers around hers. Touching was reassuring, grounding, and very nice, she thought as she gazed at their entwined hands. 'She's just angry at the moment.'

'Did you hear the argument?'

'Not much of it. Just raised voices mainly, and I caught a few things, but none of it made sense.' She smiled, holding his gaze, hoping she was offering him some relief from the embarrassment of having such a personal argument in public. 'No one else would have heard anything.'

His eyes widened. 'There were still other people around?'

'In the kitchen. They wouldn't have heard you.'

He sank back onto the cushions. 'Thank goodness for that. I feel like such an idiot. What if I've lost her for good?'

The pain in his eyes made Clare's heart ache and she shuffled closer to him on the sofa, so their arms were touching, their fingers remaining entwined.

'She'll come back to you. Just give her some time to cool down.'

'I haven't told you the full story, Clare.' He worried his bottom lip, biting it so hard she feared he'd break the skin.

'It's OK. You don't have to.'

She released his hand, leant forwards and put her glass on the table. When she sat back again, she smoothed the backs of her fingers gently down his face, hoping to ease his anxiety, to comfort him in the way he clearly needed.

'I need to tell someone, Clare . . .' He looked at her, then across to the log burner, where flames flickered, casting shadows around the room. Clare pressed a gentle kiss to his cheek, breathing him in, wishing she could take away his sorrow.

'Tell me then, Sam. I'm listening.'

'I'm worried you'll hate me when you know the truth.'

'That won't happen.' She kissed him again. 'I'm here and I'm not going to judge you. I promise.'

He nodded, drained his wine glass, then placed it on the table.

'OK, here goes . . .'

Sam could barely believe that he was sitting on his sofa with Clare, that she was gently stroking his face, showing him understanding and compassion. He had never thought he'd come close to telling anyone what had happened that day with Alyssa, that he would be able to share details of his childhood, his life before he moved to Little Bramble. But here he was, about to tell her the things he had kept under lock and key for years. It was terrifying, yet exhilarating.

'Growing up in a small flat wasn't easy. Don't get me wrong, I always knew I was loved and that Mum and Dad loved each other too. Then Alyssa came along when I was twelve and she filled our lives with so much joy but we lost Mum because of the difficult labour and complications. Dad adored Alyssa, he really did, but he also . . . well, in moments of despair, when he'd had a lot to drink, admitted that he resented her.'

'Oh Sam!' Clare took his hand and squeezed it, giving him the strength to go on.

'She was the reason we'd lost Mum. Obviously, it wasn't her fault, but if Mum hadn't got pregnant with her, then lost so much blood and developed an infection, she would have still been around. It's why Dad sank into such a deep depression. He couldn't unite the two parts of his life, his love for Alyssa and the resentment he felt towards her. It tore him apart.' Shame crawled through Sam now and he sucked in a deep breath, preparing to tell Clare the rest. 'And . . . I also felt it too.' He met her eyes, then looked quickly away, unable to witness the horror that he was certain would be there. 'I came to resent her because she'd taken my mum away from me. I'm so ashamed of that, Clare, and I hope I never let it show, but I was only a boy and some days I just wanted my mum.'

'Of course you did. Those feelings were perfectly natural and it was understandable that your dad would feel that way too.'

'I don't know. I can't forgive myself for feeling that way about Alyssa. I mean, I adore her. She's my baby sister and she never deserved resentment. She deserved love and understanding and support.'

'You've given her that, all her life. Don't be so unkind to yourself, Sam. You're a good man.'

He gave a wry laugh. 'Am I, though? A good man would never have felt that way towards an innocent baby.'

'You were a child, Sam. Would you blame a child from the village for feeling that way if they lost their mum in childbirth? You and your dad were grieving, but that didn't take away from your love of Alyssa.'

He met her eyes then and relief flooded through him at the understanding in her gaze.

'I guess not. I'd feel sorry for them, think they needed support, help . . .'

'Counselling?'

'Yes. Of course.' He nodded.

'Then you mustn't blame yourself. You were a child; you lost your mum and your dad was struggling. *You* needed love and nurturing too.'

She slid her arm around his shoulders and he sighed, feeling suddenly liberated at getting the confession out in the open. Clare didn't hate him. But . . . there was more.

'Then, when Alyssa was twenty-four, that day she was hurt in the accident? That was my fault.'

'How could the accident have been your fault? You weren't even there.'

'We argued. See, as you know, Dad lived with sickle cell all his life. He was mostly OK, but there was a chance that Alyssa and I would have inherited the gene.'

'But you're not ill? Or Alyssa?'

He shook his head. 'No, but we were tested, and we do carry the gene. It means that we could have children with the condition.'

'Sam, I'm sorry. That must be really hard to live with.'

'It was one of the reasons why I decided not to have children. I wouldn't want to pass it on.'

'But your dad wasn't ill all his life?'

'No. Some people live with it and manage it throughout their lives but I couldn't allow myself to pass it to another generation. That can only happen if both parents are carriers or if one of the parents has sickle cell themselves, but it's still a risk I don't want to take.'

'And Alyssa?'

'She was pregnant. She came to tell me on the day of the accident and we argued because I said she was being irresponsible. More than anything, though, I was worried about her. She's such a warm and loving person and I knew that if she had a child with the condition, she'd feel guilty and would suffer seeing her child suffer. It would hurt her, and I couldn't bear to see her hurting.'

'Goodness, Sam, you've carried so much all these years.'

'She left after we argued and jumped on her bike and sped off . . . She was upset, crying . . . I should have stopped her, but I didn't and she . . . then she was hurt. The accident was life-changing for her.'

Clare's gaze remained fixed on Sam's face; he could feel her warmth at his side. She hadn't removed her arm from his shoulders or stiffened when he'd confessed. Hope flickered inside him. Did she understand? Or did she think he was a terrible person? Surely she would have flinched by now, shown signs of shock or disapproval. He wanted to curl up and place his head on her lap, to find comfort in her arms, to lose himself in her.

'It was life-changing for you too.' Clare leant her head against his and he turned so his face was buried in her soft hair. She smelt so good and he wished he could stay that way forever. 'Did you . . . never get involved with anyone?' she asked after a while.

'No.' He raised his head. 'I had a few very brief encounters . . . flings, I guess you could call them. But I never let anyone get close. I had excuses, see. First of all, I told myself I had to ensure that Alyssa had a good life, that I needed to earn a good wage and get her out of that tiny flat. My guilt over resenting her because of our mum dying drove me forwards. Then, after she'd been hurt, I vowed to get her the best medical care I could and to always be there for her. I wanted to support her and be a good brother and, I suppose, thinking about it now, I was scared to fall in love.'

'Why?'

'My dad suffered so much after losing my mum that I never, ever wanted to feel that level of pain. Why risk being broken by loving someone then losing them? Plus, I felt so guilty about Alyssa's accident that I didn't feel I deserved to love or be loved.'

'Sam . . .'

He met her eyes and saw that they were filled with tears.

'Don't cry.' He stroked her cheek, as a tear escaped her eye and trickled down it, a liquid diamond on her beautiful skin. 'I don't want to make you cry.'

'I feel so bad for you. You never allowed yourself to fall in love. You've missed out on so much of life.'

He shook his head. 'I've had a good life in many ways. I was loved by my parents. I love my sister. I have a great dog. I love my job.'

Clare smiled. 'That's all very positive.'

'Yes, and I love living in the village. I could never have moved here if I hadn't been driven to work so hard and been earning enough to save like I did.'

'True.'

'And . . . I never would have got to meet you.'

Tears flowed from her eyes now, running in rivulets down her cheeks. He took her face in his hands, cupping her cheeks gently.

'You don't hate me?' he asked.

'I could never hate you, Sam. Everything you've told me, I understand.'

'Alyssa lost the baby in the accident.'

'I thought as much.'

'Now she's pregnant again.'

Clare smiled. 'That's wonderful news.'

'I don't know. I mean, all the risks . . . they're still there.'

'It is a risk, yes, and all pregnancies come with risks, but there's a good chance the baby won't inherit the condition. Plus, she has you and her partner and she's strong.'

'She's one of the strongest people I know.'

'You're strong too.' She covered his hands with hers and his heart contracted.

She understood. She hadn't judged him as he'd feared. He had told her his darkest secrets and she hadn't abandoned him.

'You're still here,' he said aloud, needing to hear the words. 'Yes.'

He held her gaze for a few seconds, then he shifted closer to her. When their lips met, she exhaled against him. Her breath was sweet from the wine, her lips soft and she tasted delicious. Like coming home.

He slid his arms around her and held her tight, finally feeling the tension that had gripped his heart, body and mind for so long begin to slip away, as he found comfort from another human being. They fitted together in ways he had never expected to find with anyone.

She was perfect and he knew that he wanted to be with her.

❄

Clare draped the chenille throw from the back of the sofa over Sam and gazed down at him. They had talked for hours, drunk more wine, and kissed – such beautiful gentle kisses that lit her up inside – then they had snuggled on the sofa as the fire glowed in the log burner and Scout snored on the rug. They had all drifted off to sleep and Clare had jumped awake when her phone pinged with a message. She'd checked it to see that Kyle was off to bed, telling her to be careful, and that Elaine was home safe and fast asleep, so Clare didn't need to rush back. It made her smile, her son's easy acceptance that his mum was with a man. The mum who had been married to his father until very recently. She was very lucky to have such a wonderful, non-judgemental son.

And now, it seemed, something new was happening in her life. She was . . . what exactly? Dating? No, it wasn't that; too early. Involved? They were definitely involved in something. Involved in each other.

She could stay, could snuggle back down with Sam and spend the night there, but it wouldn't be right. Not yet. Not now. Sam was dealing with a lot and he needed time to process everything. And, as much as she liked him, Clare needed some time too, to think about what was happening and work out what she was feeling.

Pulling a sheet of paper from the pile under the coffee table, she got a pen from a pot on one of the bookshelves, then wrote a quick note, thanking Sam for the evening and telling him she'd speak to him in the morning. She set it on the table, propped up against the empty wine bottle so he would see it when he woke.

Before leaving, she blew him a kiss, not wanting to wake him by touching him, rubbed Scout's head, then put on her coat and gloves and headed out into the night.

Chapter 24

December had arrived, bringing frosty mornings and wintery showers that temporarily covered Little Bramble in a dusting of snow as fine as pure white icing sugar. It had been a week since Clare had gone to Sam's and they'd talked and held each other. They had spoken and met for coffee, lunch and dog walks a few times since then, and had arranged to meet this evening, the first weekend of December, for the turning on of the Christmas lights. She knew that she liked him a lot, that she felt good around him and that she cared about him, but she was also aware that she still had a way to go in terms of working out her own issues and that she didn't want to rush anything. Everything from here on in would be on terms that she was comfortable with and there would be no sacrificing herself anymore, not for anyone, however lovely they were.

Clare was getting ready after dinner, wrapping up in layers, aware that the temperature would be minus something this evening, when there was a knock at her bedroom door.

'Hold on a moment.' She went to open it.

'Clare . . . ?'

'Yes, Mum?'

'Do you think that these jeans go with this jumper?'

Clare looked at her mum's indigo skinny jeans and yellow turtleneck jumper.

'Anything goes with jeans. And you look lovely. That jumper is such a happy colour.'

Her mum smiled. 'Really?'

'Yes, but the vicar won't see that because you'll have a coat on over it.'

Elaine patted her hair that she'd styled in soft beach waves – had she borrowed Kyle's straighteners? – and laughed. 'He'll see it afterwards.'

'He will?'

'Yes, darling. I'm going back to the vicarage for a drink later on.'

'OK. Lovely.'

Clare nodded, hoping her smile would cover up her uncertainty. Why was it that Kyle could accept Clare having a man in her life, but Clare was struggling with Elaine having one? She was worried that her mum would get hurt and didn't want to see her newfound happiness marred by a relationship going wrong, but it was more than that and she knew it.

She was feeling a bit put out for her dad. It wasn't that she'd expected her mum to stay single for the rest of her days, of course not. She wanted to be happy for her, in fact she was, but it would take some time to adjust to the vicar being a part of their family, even though he'd always been a family friend.

'Right, I'll go and find my new boots then we can leave in about ten minutes. Does that sound OK?'

'Brilliant. I'll be down soon.'

When she'd pulled on a thick jumper and socks, Clare stuffed her feet into her soft black leather boots and wound a scarf around her neck. Her gloves were downstairs in her coat pockets. She turned off the bedroom light, then crossed the hallway and knocked on Kyle's door.

'You ready?' she called.

'He's already gone, Clare,' her mum said from the bottom of the stairs. 'He just left, said he's meeting someone there.'

'Kyle?'

'Yes, dear, that's your son's name.'

'Who's he meeting?'

Elaine shrugged. 'No idea, but he had a very nice after-shave on.'

Clare rubbed her eyes, then padded down the stairs. First her mum, then her, now her son. Was romance in the air in Little Bramble this season?

'Come on, let's get going.' Elaine clipped Goliath's lead to his collar, then opened the door. 'We don't want to be late!'

They made their way to the village green, the evening air icy on the exposed skin of their faces, the frost crunching beneath their boots. Even Goliath was wearing his fleecy coat and he seemed proud to have it on, his head held high as they walked. Clare wondered again at how attached she had become to the dog, at how often he made her smile and gave her comfort, at what an important part of her life he was now.

As they neared the green, she scanned the crowds, searching for people she knew. Jenny was there with Martin and the girls, so she waved at them and Jenny waved back.

'I'll just go and say hello to Jen, Mum.'

'OK, love. I'll take Goliath to see Iolo.'

Clare walked over to Jenny, looking back to see her mum and the vicar embracing openly in front of everyone; they clearly had no intention of hiding their relationship.

'Hey, Jen, how're you feeling?'

It was automatic now, checking to see how Jenny felt.

'I'm all right, actually.' Jenny smiled from beneath a bright red bobble hat, her eyes bright in the streetlights, her breath puffing out in front of her. 'Today, for the first time in weeks, the nausea has eased. It's probably because I haven't stopped stuffing my face, but I'll do whatever I can to banish that awful queasiness.' She gestured behind her at Martin and the twins. 'The girls have been baking all day . . . mince pies, cakes, pastries, so I've sampled everything.' She wrapped her arms around her belly and Clare smiled; Jenny was definitely filling out.

'How are things with you and our gorgeous vet?' Jenny winked twice and nudged Clare, making her blush.

Clare hadn't seen Jenny for a few days, but they'd talked on the phone and she had filled her in about Sam. Not what he'd confided, of course, but the fact that they'd talked for hours, kissed and cuddled.

'Oh, you know . . . all right. He'll be here this evening, so I'm looking forward to seeing him.' Clare couldn't help herself then, she looked around, her eyes scanning for Sam.

'I'm so pleased. I'm crossing everything that this works out for you.' Jenny held up her hands to prove her point.

'What are you wishing for now?' Martin slid an arm around Jenny's waist.

'For Clare to have a Christmas romance.'

'Stop it, Jen.' Clare shook her head, but Martin laughed. 'I see. Well, Mr Wilson hasn't had a relationship in the three years he's lived here, as far as I know, so I'm crossing everything for you too.'

Clare laughed, her cheeks burning in spite of the cold.

'Talking of vets . . .' Jenny pointed behind Clare, so she turned and there he was.

Tall. Broad-shouldered. His handsome face smiling at her from under a grey beanie. Clare turned back to Jenny, but she mouthed *Go get him,* so Clare nodded.

'See you later.' She blew kisses at Jenny and Martin then went to Sam's side.

'Hello, beautiful.' He leant forwards and kissed her cheek, and his scent washed over her, sandalwood and citrus with darker notes of cracked black pepper. *Delicious.*

'Hi, Sam.' Shyness stole over Clare, making her feel like a self-conscious teenager on a first date. This gorgeous man liked her; had kissed her and told her his secrets. She felt as if she should pinch herself to check she wasn't dreaming.

'Would you like a drink?' He pointed at the stall at the end of the grass closest to The Red.

'Yes, please.'

He took her hand and they walked over to the stall.

'Where's Scout?' she asked, realising that the dog was absent.

'She rolled in something on our walk today, so she had to have a bath and it always wears her out. I asked if she wanted to come but she preferred to stretch out on the sofa.'

'Oh, love her!' Clare giggled. 'Baths can be incredibly relaxing.'

'Mulled wine or cider?' he asked.

'Wine, please.'

He nodded, then paid for two mugs and handed her one. The pub landlord provided a stall with mulled drinks every year for the turning on of the lights and provided eco-friendly glass mugs which had to be returned to the stall when drinks were finished.

'I guess we know it's really Christmas then.' He clinked his mug against hers.

'We do.' She sipped her wine, savouring the berry notes enriched with lemon, orange and spices. 'This is scrummy.'

'I don't know why I don't make more mulled wine,' he said. 'I really like it, but it seems strange to think of drinking it anytime other than Christmas.'

'I know what you mean. Jason wasn't really a fan though so I never –'

Clare winced. She'd mentioned her ex-husband and wasn't sure if that was OK.

Sam smiled. 'It is OK to speak about Jason, you know. You did have a whole life before we met.'

She nodded. 'It's just a bit strange not to be with him, and it's taking me a while to get used to it, I suppose. I was saying that he didn't like mulled wine, so I didn't bother making it just for me.'

'Well, now you can have as much as you like.' He clinked his mug against hers again. 'I love it.'

Clare hugged herself inwardly. There was so much to learn about Sam, so much she didn't yet know, and she was excited to get to know him better. It was like starting her life over again, but from a better vantage point; this time she was older, wiser and (hopefully) stronger.

'Good evening!' The loud voice, sent out around the area by an amplifier in the boot of a car, caused all heads to turn to the Norwegian Spruce where Iolo Ifans was standing with a microphone. 'Thank you all for coming to the special turning on of Little Bramble's Christmas lights.'

There were a few whistles and whoops and Sam chuckled at Clare's side, then he stepped closer and slid his arm around her waist. A jolt of excitement shot through her.

'Can we have a countdown, please?' Iolo asked. 'From ten? Get ready . . . go!'

As the villagers counted down from ten to one, the tiny hairs on Clare's arms stood on end beneath her layers of clothing. She'd attended this annual event so many times and she was engulfed in waves of nostalgia, picturing herself as a small girl holding her dad's hand, as a teenager stealing sips of his mulled cider, as an adult one Christmas when she'd brought Kyle to visit. There was such an air of magic about this event, the combination of the freezing air, the frosty ground, the gathering of the villagers, the spiced cider and wine and the knowledge that Christmas was just weeks away. And this year, there would also be the show. Anticipation bubbled in her belly, and when the countdown ended and the village green was suddenly illuminated by thousands of colourful fairy lights, the huge tree glowing in the darkness, she gasped like a child on Christmas morning.

'It's so beautiful,' she said.

'I agree,' said Sam, but when she turned to him, he was gazing at her and not at the tree.

Sam was waiting for Clare to return from the drinks stall. Even though it was extremely cold, he felt warm inside. He'd come to the annual switching on of the lights every year that he'd been in the village and enjoyed the event, found watching Alyssa's joy in it uplifting. But this year was different; it was special, because he was with Clare. His feelings for her had deepened since he'd told her about his past, his fears and his overwhelming guilt, as if he'd needed to offload everything in order to move on with his life. It made sense, though, and was why so many people went to see counsellors and therapists. Sam had held it all in for years, but now, with each day that passed, he felt the weight lifting and hoped that one day soon, he would shake it off altogether.

There was still something bothering him, though: Alyssa. He hadn't seen her since the evening of her audition and although he had tried phoning and texting her, she had only replied once with a brief *I'm fine. I just need some time.* Sam had spoken to Clare about it, asked for her advice, and she'd told him that Alyssa probably did need some time to clear her head. She had been through so much: losing a child, being injured in a horrific accident and having to adjust to a new way of life. Now she had a new partner, a stepchild and a baby on the way. *Be gentle and kind towards her*, Clare had said to him, and he knew she was right. So, he was going against the grain, taking a step back and letting Alyssa get on with her life without trying to intervene. If she needed him, he would be there; if not, he would still be there whenever she wanted to see him. It was incredibly difficult, but he knew he had to do something to try to heal the rift between them. Not all siblings were close, a lot barely had any contact, but he and Alyssa had been close for most of her thirty-four years. He couldn't deny that he missed her, but mainly, he hoped that she was happy.

'Here you are.' Clare handed him a fresh mug of mulled wine.

'Thank you.'

'My pleasure.' She smiled up at him, her eyes shadowed by the bobble hat that was pulled down over her eyebrows.

'Is that Kyle?' Sam pointed at two figures over by the tree, gazing up at the lights.

'Yes, it is. He left earlier than us for the switch-on and didn't even say goodbye to me so he must have been keen to get here. Who's he with?'

Sam squinted at the figures. 'I think it's Magnus.'

'Of course! From here he looks like a Viking with that big golden beard.'

Sam laughed. 'I can see why you'd say that.'

'Kyle seems to like him.'

'It looks mutual.' Sam watched as his colleague and Clare's son nudged each other flirtatiously in front of the tree, their eyes locked, their body language revealing their mutual attraction.

'Goodness!' Clare shook her head. 'Kyle doesn't waste any time.'

'Is he fresh out of a relationship?'

She nodded. 'I can't keep up with him to be honest, Sam. My son is a warm and generous person, he would give anyone the shirt off his back, but he falls in and out of love with startling speed. Although, admittedly, it's not him who does the leaving.'

'At least he's giving love a chance.' Sam cleared his throat. 'Until you came to Little Bramble, Clare, I'd never met anyone I cared about like this.'

Her mouth fell open and he wondered if he'd said too much.

'I'm sorry . . .' He shook his head. 'I'm not very good at this. I haven't had much practice.'

She laid a hand on top of his where it cupped his mug.

'I don't have much experience either. I was married to a man who barely knew I existed most of the time and, apart from that, I'd had a few boyfriends when I was at school and they were hardly serious relationships. However, I think you're doing just fine. We're kind of learning together.'

'He was a fool to let you go, Clare.'

'Maybe, but I'm glad he did because there's so much life to live and I had no idea until now.'

He leant forwards and kissed her gently, tasting the cinnamon and cloves on her lips, feeling the warmth of her breath and the cold of the tip of her nose.

'You're cold,' he said, rubbing her back with his free hand.

'I'm OK. I have over six foot of gorgeous vet to keep me warm.'

He hugged her to his side. 'Indeed you do. Not that I think I'm gorgeous – I just meant that you have the vet to keep you warm.'

She giggled. 'Shall we go and socialise a bit?'

'Why? Am I boring you, Clare, by keeping you all to myself?'

'Not at all, but I'd like to see what's going on with Kyle and Magnus and to find out what Mum's plans are. She said something about going to the vicarage after this, but who knows with her? She's probably got her toothbrush stuffed up her sleeve.'

'They're that serious now, are they?'

She rolled her eyes. 'Who knows?'

'I'd never have guessed there was anything going on between them.'

'There wasn't until recently, I don't think. Iolo has been a family friend for as long as I can remember, but as for romantic interest, I think that's more recent. And they seem so happy.'

'Are you happy?' Sam held his breath.

'I really am.' Clare smiled. 'Happier than I thought I would ever be again after my marriage ended. Happier than I thought possible before I returned to Little Bramble.'

'Then all is well with the world.' His heart soared. 'Let's go and socialise for now, but I get to walk you home.'

'Deal.' The glance she flashed him was warm and something sparkled in her eyes as they caught the reflection of the Christmas tree lights. It fanned the flames of the fire inside him and he hoped she could see in his eyes exactly how much she had come to mean to him, this wonderful woman called Clare.

Chapter 25

A week and a half later, the afternoon of the dress rehearsal for the show had arrived. In the time since the turning on of the Christmas lights, Clare had settled into her new routine even more. She spent the days with her mum, Kyle and Goliath, doing Tai Chi, walking and baking, and some of the evenings with Sam. She had been to the pub quiz with him again twice, along with Magnus and Miranda – they made a good team. Her mum, Kyle and Iolo had also come the previous Friday and Clare had spent the evening smiling as her family and the man she was falling for laughed and joked, ate and drank, and she had been able to picture a future in Little Bramble, one with all the people she cared about the most.

She had also been back to Old Oak Stables and had an informal interview with Verity. They had discussed what the role involved, what the possibilities of future work would be after Briony returned from maternity leave, and then Clare had gone for her first ride in years. It had been nerve-wracking, exciting and wonderful. She'd been cautious at first getting back on to a horse, but as they'd trotted out of the stable yard, then cantered across a field, Clare's heart had soared. She had missed the exhilaration of being on a horse, the adrenaline rush that came as they galloped across the grass, the wind in her face, the muscles of her body taut and strong, and she felt herself becoming one with the magnificent beast. When they'd finally returned to the stables, Clare had felt alive, brimming with enthusiasm for her new job and for what it would bring to her life. Verity had told her to return whenever she wanted over the next two months to get to know the horses and other staff before she officially started work there, and so Clare had already been twice more, unable to resist now that her love of riding had been rekindled. It had taken her a few days and several hot baths to soothe the ache in her thighs and abdominals after the rides, her body being unused to riding after so long, but she was confident that it would soon adapt and that she would be stronger and the post-ride aches would ease.

'Are we ready for this then?' Elaine asked as they took their seats in front of the stage to watch the dress rehearsal. The acts were all backstage but had been told to take seats in the hall when they had performed to give everyone a sense of what it would be like with an audience.

'Absolutely!' Clare nodded, and Kyle did too.

The lights dimmed, then Slade's 'Merry Christmas Everybody' started to play and the spotlight came on the stage. There were a few whoops and whistles as the free-running firefighters trooped onto the stage, all wearing Christmas jumpers with jeans and red Christmas hats. Clare gasped and sighed as she watched their routine. It seemed even more daring than the one they'd done at their audition as they hopped on and off tables, somersaulted over one another and were as light as rabbits on their feet, as agile as cats.

The next act was Iolo in his Lycra – this time green and red with rubber elf ears attached to his head on a band – and as he bent himself into positions that made Clare's eyes water, her mum hooted and clapped and Kyle expressed his awe.

'He's teaching me, you know,' Elaine whispered as Iolo bowed at the end of his performance. 'What with that and Tai Chi, I'll be the most supple grandmother in Little Bramble.'

Kyle snorted and even Clare laughed; it was just too funny not to.

The lights went down again and Pavarotti's voice singing 'O Holy Night' filled the hall, making goosebumps rise on Clare's arms. The spotlight on the stage found the large fawn and white bulldog Mr Spike and when the dog began howling along, Clare actually thought she might start to cry. Mr Spike hit the high notes with the talented singer and seemed to really enjoy his performance.

'That's going to be a firm favourite with the audience,' Kyle said as Amanda King led Mr Spike off the stage, his small tail waggling as Clare, Elaine and Kyle clapped and whistled.

Next up were the salsa dancing ten-year-olds, whose fast and furious performance was wonderful and had everyone clapping along, then came the teenaged boy, John, and his girlfriend, Milly, who performed 'Rockin' Around the Christmas Tree', him on acoustic guitar while Milly sang and shook her tambourine.

When Miranda Fitzalan took to the stage, Clare sat up, keen to listen to the woman's clear, calm voice as she read 'A Visit from St. Nicholas'. As the words floated out from the stage, she was transported into the scenes, seeing the night before Christmas, the tree, the stockings by the fireplace, the family safely tucked up in their beds.

'Your dad used to read this to you,' her mum whispered.

'I know.' Clare nodded. It had been his Christmas Eve tradition and, even now, she could remember the excitement as he'd opened the book with its beautiful illustrations, as he'd turned the pages and pointed at the scenes, as the words had created far more detailed images in her mind than the pictures ever could. That had been a special tradition and one she had tried to recapture with Kyle, reading the same poem to him and savouring his youthful awe and excitement. Little traditions like that were special, to be treasured, and she hoped that they were creating a new one as a family.

When Miranda had finished to a round of applause, she left the stage, then Alyssa Wilson took her place. Wearing a red sparkly dress with black boots and a headband with reindeer antlers holding her hair off her face, Alyssa started to sing her *a capella* version of 'All I Want for Christmas is You'. Her voice was clear, beautiful and the words made Clare think of Christmases gone by. Once upon a time, she had wanted Jason, had danced to this song on Christmas morning with a baby Kyle in her arms, had sung it with the staff from the library at the Christmas party but now the words swirled around her, wrapped her up in their joy, made her think of Sam and what he meant to her, about what they could have ahead of them and anticipation filled her.

When Alyssa fell silent, it took everyone a few moments to compose themselves. Clare noticed Elaine dabbing her eyes and Kyle sniffing and she couldn't blame either of them for being so moved.

The penultimate act was an elderly gentleman named Greg Patrick. He'd lived in the village all his life and, along with his wife, Dawn, had been involved in the drama society. Dawn had passed away three and a half years ago, aged eighty, which Greg had told them at his audition, but Clare had already been aware as her mum had told her when Greg had applied to audition. He walked slowly across the stage in grey slacks, a red jumper and stripy red and green scarf, then stood in front of them and offered a small smile, the spotlight catching on his glasses as he moved his head to peer out at the audience.

'I would like to thank you again for letting me be in the show. It means a great deal.' His voice was quiet but clear. He cleared his throat. 'I am dedicating this song to my beautiful wife, Dawn, who I miss every single day.'

The opening notes of 'White Christmas' floated from the speakers, and Greg began to sing. His voice was as warm and full as Bing Crosby's, his frail-looking frame belying how well he could sing. Clare was right there with him, singing along in her head, when suddenly he fell silent, raised a hand to rub at his brow, then coughed nervously. The music continued, Marcellus, who was operating the stereo, seemingly unaware of eighty-four-year-old Greg's distress. Kyle got up and hurried to the back of the hall where Marcellus was, then the music stopped.

Greg stared out at the audience, his brow furrowed.

'I . . . I forgot the words. Can I start again?'

'Of course you can,' Elaine said, then the song began again.

Greg got through the first few bars, then his face fell and he seemed to crumble in front of them, hunching over and holding his stomach. Clare turned to her mum to ask what they should do, because she hadn't been prepared for this, but Elaine was already making her way onto the stage, Alyssa hot on her heels.

Elaine held up a hand and the music stopped, then she took Greg's arm and Alyssa took his other hand.

'From the top, Marcellus!' Elaine said, and Clare's heart swelled with love and pride.

With the support of the two women, Greg sang through 'White Christmas' without hesitation, and their three voices filled the air, harmonising perfectly, so that when they finished singing, Clare couldn't see for tears.

This was what family, friends and community was about. Coming together, supporting one another and creating some good old Christmas magic.

The final act was the school choir's Christmas medley, accompanied by their head teacher on piano and Elaine singing. So that was her surprise act, then, Clare realised. And as her mum stood on stage with the children, she smiled broadly, her face glowing in the way that Clare remembered from years gone by. The children stood proudly on stage, in equal numbers either side of Elaine, in their festive jumpers, red hats, faces lit up with excitement and enjoyment. The audience clapped along, the children and Elaine swayed from side to side and the dress rehearsal came to a cheerful end.

'If the actual show goes as well as the dress rehearsal, then the villagers are in for a real treat,' Clare's mum said after she had come down from the stage.

Clare nodded. She couldn't speak because she'd found the whole thing extremely moving. It had been a wonderful afternoon and she had enjoyed the acts, enjoyed seeing her mum regaining her former zest for life and enjoyed being part of a community once more.

The only thing missing was her dad, but she had felt during the rehearsal that he was there in some way, and even if it was only in her heart and her memories, then that was enough, because she knew she would always carry him with her. He would never be far away.

✻

The next few days leading up to the show were busy with selling the rest of the tickets, building the finished set (which the village primary school helped with) and confirming the final list of volunteers to run a raffle, sell tickets, provide hot and cold drinks and snacks and to clear up afterwards. There was a very small village hall committee, but people had been lax in their duties because the hall hadn't received the same love and use as the previous one. However, Clare had sensed a shifting in the village over the past few weeks, as if the community had started to embrace the new hall and this had breathed life into the place.

Similarly, the preparations for the show had definitely helped Elaine come through the low mood she had been in when Clare had first got to Little Bramble. Things between them were still stilted at times and Clare wanted to find a time to have a proper conversation about the past with her mum, but she kept putting it off, fearing she'd upset her and garner her disapproval. Elaine's relationship with the vicar was also having a positive effect upon her, and she did seem far happier, as if she too had shut herself off from life and was beginning to wake up – just like the village hall.

Sam had been busy with the surgery. It seemed that as winter set in animals were more prone to injury and he had to be on call more regularly during the nights. He and Clare hadn't yet spent a night together, but they had talked about it, and Clare was happy to take things slowly. She wanted to get to know Sam better first, for them both to be sure about each other before they sealed their relationship on a physical level. Besides, she was enjoying the time they spent together, kissing and cuddling, acting like teenagers and savouring every moment.

Today, Clare was going Christmas shopping with Jenny and she was really looking forward to spending the day with her friend. There was a shopping centre thirty minutes from Little Bramble and they had planned to go early because it was likely to be busy.

Martin had offered to drive them, so he could go off and do his own shopping, then he'd meet them at the end of the day to bring them home, so Clare was waiting on the front doorstep for him and Jenny to arrive. She checked her watch to see if she had time for one more psychological wee, just in case they did get stuck in traffic, and saw that she had five minutes to spare.

When she came back downstairs again, Goliath was waiting by the front door.

'Oh no you don't, mister! Come on, back to the kitchen with you.' She ushered him back through the house and he looked up at her with what she'd have described as disdain if he'd been human. 'And stop looking at me like that, you big oaf!'

He blinked and guilt coursed through her. How did dogs do that? They definitely had facial expressions and she felt certain that Goliath had more than most.

'Shall I get you a treat?' she asked him, hating the thought that he might think she didn't adore him, and his ears pricked up. 'How about one of those chewy kebab things that you like?' She opened the cupboard where her mum kept his food and located an ostrich kebab, then turned back to him. 'Now, if I give you this, you have to promise to love me.'

'Oh, I see, Mum, buying a man's love now, eh?'

Kyle was standing in the kitchen doorway in his dressing gown, his hair sticking up as though someone had turned him upside down and used him to mop the floor. He had come down first thing for Tai Chi, then gone back to bed.

'Ha! Ha! I felt bad because he wants to wait for the post just so he can terrorise poor Marcellus David, but I made him come back out here. The treat was also, I'm afraid, my attempt to buy his love, but what can I say?'

Kyle closed the door and trudged to the fridge. 'You've really taken to that dog, haven't you?'

Clare held the kebab up and said, 'Sit!'

'Sorry?' Kyle frowned.

'I was talking to Goliath.' The dog was sitting in front of her, drool trickling from his jaws. 'And paw?'

Goliath held up a paw and Clare shook it.

'You really have him trained, eh?' Kyle came to stand next to her as Goliath gently took the treat from Clare's hand and carried it to his bed.

'He's a good dog.'

'You'll miss him when you leave this cottage.'

Clare started. 'What?'

'Well, Mum, this isn't a long-term arrangement, is it? I mean, you can't live with Nanna indefinitely, can you?'

Clare knitted her brows together and exhaled slowly. 'I-I haven't been giving it much thought this past few weeks, but no, you're right, I can't live with Nanna for ever.'

'So, what will you do?'

'If I decide to stay in the village permanently, I'll rent somewhere or buy a place of my own.'

'So you might stay?'

'Perhaps. I do have the job at the stables lined up and there's a chance it could turn into something more than maternity cover. The impression I've got from Verity is that she needs as much help as she can get. What about you?'

Kyle ran a hand through his hair, but it bounced straight back into the crazy bedhead style.

'I'd like to stay around until the start of the next academic year. I'm enjoying being with you and Nanna . . . and Goliath.'

'And someone else?' Clare raised her eyebrows.

'Sorry?' Kyle turned back to the fridge and feigned interest in its contents.

'A certain veterinary nurse from Norway?'

Kyle snorted with laughter, so Clare went to him and hugged him. 'Just be careful, my baby boy.'

He turned in her embrace and grinned at her. 'Don't worry about me, Mum. I'll be just fine.'

'But you've been hurt before and I don't want to see that happen again.'

'I don't want to get hurt, but I also think that life's too short to be afraid to love. However many times I get hurt, I still want to be able to love freely, without restriction, without worrying about what could go wrong. Don't you think that's a good way to live?'

Clare nodded. He was right. Life and love were scary things, but to be able to love without fear would be liberating.

'Just don't rush things.'

'I promise I won't.' He turned back to the fridge. 'You hungry? Because I could eat an elephant!'

'I ate earlier, thanks, and I'm off shopping with Jenny.'

'Ah yes, that's right. If you see something for Nanna, would you pick it up for me and I'll give you the money later.'

'OK.' Clare smiled, knowing that this happened most years and that Kyle would offer the money and she'd probably decline it or tell him to use it to get something he needed. It was how they'd gone about getting Jason's gifts most years. 'Will do. See you later.'

Clare checked on Goliath, who was chewing away on his kebab, content to stay where he was for the time being.

'And don't worry, Mum, I'll walk the dog today.'

'Thank you.'

She closed the kitchen door behind her, then went into the hallway. The post had arrived and lay on the mat remarkably unscathed, so she picked it up and placed it on the hall table. There were always ways to work things out, whether that was saving the postman from your mum's giant dog, advising your son about how to behave in affairs of the heart, or how to resolve long-standing issues with your mum. Clare knew that she would have to speak to Elaine soon, but she wasn't sure when that would be or how she would initiate such a discussion. She certainly hadn't wanted to do it before the show and risk ruining it for everyone, so it would have to come later, perhaps at the weekend when things had quietened down and they had a week until Christmas.

She would find a way. But now she was off for a day of retail therapy with her oldest friend and she was looking forward to it enormously.

A car horn beeped outside, so she grabbed her bag and let herself out of the cottage, then practically skipped down the drive. Kyle was right, life was for living and Clare felt as if she was finally living hers.

'That is dusty!' Sneezing, Sam put the cardboard box down on the landing and wiped his hands on his jeans. He turned as if to smile at Alyssa, expecting her to be waiting at the bottom of the stairs with a big grin on her face, but she wasn't there. Of course she wasn't. He was home alone – as he usually was these days.

He climbed the ladder again and took hold of another box and carried that one down. When he had four large boxes, he went back up to turn the attic light off, but something caught his eye. It was a small suitcase that had belonged to his father. After his father had passed away, Sam had sorted through his belongings and given what he could to charity, then binned the rubbish, but he had kept a few things that he thought Alyssa would want one day. This suitcase was one of them; it didn't contain clothes but photographs, letters, postcards and other mementoes of his father's life. He reached for the suitcase, pulled the cord to turn the light off, then descended the ladder.

Ten minutes later, in the lounge, he looked at the boxes, each one clearly labelled in Alyssa's looped handwriting: *tree decorations, ornaments, lights, outdoor*. Every year, they went to town with Christmas, decorating every surface, every window, every branch of the tree. This year, as he would be alone, he'd keep it minimal. There didn't seem much point in decorating the whole cottage just for himself, although he was wondering if he'd get to spend some time with Clare over the holidays.

He had placed the small suitcase on the coffee table and now looked at it. He hadn't opened it in years, not since before they'd moved to Little Bramble, but he knew what was inside and was overcome by an urge to look again. At least once more. Then he would give it to Alyssa. They were her memories too.

In the kitchen he made a coffee. With it being the last Friday before Christmas, they'd closed the surgery except for emergencies, so the staff could go Christmas shopping. Sam and Miranda were on call, but Miranda had seemed to want to go shopping as well, so Sam had told her that he'd take any calls that came.

He took his coffee into the lounge and smiled at Scout. She'd taken a seat on the sofa and now wagged her tail, thumping the cushion rhythmically.

'It's OK, girl, you can sit there.'

He put his mug on the coffee table, then opened the suitcase and was hit by the smell of old papers, mint and coffee. All scents he associated with his father. Strange how time couldn't erode someone's individual scent when it was ingrained in papers, the satin lining of a suitcase and on things they had held over and over again.

The photographs were in a large envelope, so he got that out and emptied it onto his lap. Memories that he often put away, whether consciously or not, were evoked as he pored over the photographs, some black and white, some a fuzzy faded colour from old film that his parents had used in the seventies and eighties, some brighter as the years passed and his dad got a better camera, higher-quality film. He gazed at his mum and dad on their wedding day, understated clothing for a registry office ceremony, their witnesses strangers off the street. But their smiles, the glints in their eyes showed their utter joy at having found each other.

Then there was a photograph of his mum wearing a smock top and baggy jeans, cupping her belly proudly. The edges of this photo were well-thumbed, as if someone had looked at it many times. Next were some of Sam as a small boy, either with his mum or dad, the other presumably behind the camera. He smiled as he looked at his knobbly knees in shorts, his full Afro – much longer than he kept it now because his mum had loved it that way and it was the fashion at the time. Then there were some photos from after Alyssa arrived; as he flicked through them, it hit him exactly how much she'd missed out on in never knowing their mum. There he was, holding her next to a small white Christmas tree when he was around fourteen, Alyssa a toddler. She was reaching for something on the tree. Goosebumps rose on his arms and a lump stung his throat. His sweet sister had relied on him and their dad from the moment she was born, had never known their mum's loving hugs, her throaty laughter that could fill a room or her adoring gaze filled with love and pride. Alyssa deserved to be happy, to build a family of her own, and Sam wanted her to have that. She would make a wonderful mum; she had all their mother's best qualities as well as a whole load of her own love to give. From now on, Sam determined that he would support his sister in her decisions – no matter what.

He had been on a steep learning curve recently and it hadn't been easy, but he felt sure that from here on, things would improve.

❄

'Ooh! I like this one. What do you think?'

Clare looked over at Jenny and smiled. 'Definitely.'

The bright lights of the department store gave everything a shiny appearance, glinting off mirrors and Christmas decorations that swayed in the warm air. They had both removed their coats as soon as they'd come inside, knowing that with Jenny's pregnancy hormones and Clare's perimenopausal ones, they'd soon get too hot.

'It's funny, right?' Jenny giggled as she held the T-shirt up against her, smoothing it down over her bump. 'Maternity wear has progressed so much since I had the girls.'

The white T-shirt had the slogan *In the Christmas Pudding Club* across the chest and a cartoon image of a huge Christmas pudding that would sit over the baby bump. It was very cute.

'I like this one too.' Clare held up a black nightdress with a picture of a red hat complete with fluffy white pompom. The slogan on this one said *Santa Baby*.

'I like that one too.' Jenny took the nightdress from Clare. 'Which one shall I get?'

'Both.'

'Really? I'm supposed to be shopping for gifts for my family.'

Clare shrugged. 'You're going to need some bigger clothes, so why not get them now?'

'I guess you're right.' Jenny chewed at her bottom lip. 'I'm getting a bit nervous now.'

Clare placed a hand on Jenny's arm. 'Why, sweetheart?'

'I'm going to be huge, aren't I?'

'You'll get bigger, yes, but you've done it before.'

'I know, but I was so much younger then and everything just kind of pinged back into shape. This time I could be left with a jelly belly.'

'Jen, you have nothing to worry about. You will always be beautiful.'

'I feel just dreadful worrying about stupid stuff like that when I should be grateful I'm pregnant again and the only thing I should be worried about is whether my babies will be healthy.'

'Stop being so hard on yourself. It's perfectly normal to have a million worries as a pregnant mum. Just take some deep breaths and focus on looking after yourself.'

Jenny nodded. 'You're right. Thank you. Oh God, Clare . . .'

Unease filled Clare as she watched Jenny's eyes fill with tears. 'What's wrong? Are you feeling rough again?'

Jenny shook her head and waved a hand in front of her face, then blinked rapidly. 'No . . . I'm OK. It's just . . . just I'm so glad you're here.'

As fat tears rolled down Jenny's cheeks, Clare enveloped her in a hug and rocked her gently. 'It's OK, Jen. I know exactly what you mean. I'm so glad I'm back too.'

Jenny looked up, her eyes red, her face wet. 'These bloody pregnancy hormones are playing havoc with me. And to think I thought it was the menopause!' She started wailing then, so Clare held her tight as other shoppers glanced at them curiously, shuffling warily past, laden with bags, sweating in their hats and winter coats.

'Why don't we go and get something to eat? Your blood sugar is probably a bit low and we need to keep your strength up.' Clare kissed Jenny's forehead and she nodded.

'OK. Th-thanks.'

'I bet you'd like a gingerbread hot chocolate, wouldn't you?'

'That sounds amazing.'

'Come on, then. Let's pay for these and then find a café.'

Clare led her friend towards the counter, swallowing hard against her own welling emotions. She was incredibly glad that she'd come back to the village and rekindled her friendship with Jenny. Theirs was a bond that time, distance and a temporary failure to see eye to eye had failed to destroy. And now she was certain that it would last a lifetime.

❄

Sam unfolded the branches of the artificial tree he'd purchased the previous day at the supermarket, then tilted his head. He wasn't sure the branches were even and wished he had someone to ask for a second opinion. He usually took Alyssa to a Christmas tree farm to buy a real tree, but this year he'd decided to get one that would last a few years and, if he was being completely honest, because he couldn't face going to the tree farm alone.

The morning had passed quickly as he'd looked through the photographs, then moved on to the letters from his mum to his dad and back again. They were love notes filled with tenderness and adoration, written even though his parents were married by then, but they perfectly captured the bond his parents had enjoyed. It was a love that had united them and that they had aimed to share with their children. Sam had been able to savour the warmth of loving parents, whereas Alyssa had not so he would tell her to read the letters when she had some time. After their father had died, she'd been too upset and distracted to read them, then the years had passed and the suitcase had been tucked away in a cupboard. When they'd moved to Little Bramble, the suitcase had gone into the attic, along with lots of other things, to make as much space as possible for the building work that needed to be carried out. But now Alyssa should read the letters, look at the photographs, and maybe one day she could share them with her child too.

The tree looked about as good as it ever would, so he opened the box of tree decorations and looked through them. This was usually Alyssa's job; she would unwrap each one, then choose the spot to hang it on the tree while Michael Bublé and Frank Sinatra crooned from a laptop and Sam and Alyssa sipped eggnog or mulled wine. This year, however, it was very different, and Sam was struggling to summon his usual enthusiasm.

Scout came in, wagging her tail, then dropped into a little bow. Sam looked from the decorations to the dog, then shrugged.

'Let's go for a walk, shall we? This can wait.'

A brisk walk in the fresh air would help to clear his head and hopefully he'd come back feeling ready to decorate his Christmas tree for one.

❄

'That was a wonderful day. Thank you so much for coming.'

Clare smiled at Jenny. 'I had a fabulous time too.'

After they had gone for hot chocolates, they'd hit the shops again before stopping for lunch, and after another two hours of shopping, they were both exhausted.

'Let me carry some of my bags.' Jenny held out her hand, but Clare shook her head.

'You have two and that's plenty. I'm fine with all of these.'

'I'd forgotten about your superhero strength.' Jenny laughed.

'Not so strong these days, but I'm certainly not letting you carry too much in your condition.'

They made their way through the shopping centre's ground floor, the strains of carols floating through the air from the speakers outside shops. Everywhere they looked, there were people with bags, pushchairs, rosy cheeks and happy smiles. It was very festive and they'd had a lot of fun shopping together.

'I wonder if Martin has bought much.'

'Well, he hadn't when we saw him earlier, but then he did say he was taking his time to decide,' Clare replied. They had seen Martin just after their hot chocolate break, outside a craft beer shop, browsing the array of cans in the window. He'd looked slightly guilty at being caught looking at beer, but then explained that he'd had a good look around for gifts and was about to head back to purchase his favourites.

'I bet he's got something for the babies.' Jenny adjusted the strap of her handbag on her shoulder. 'He won't be able to resist.'

'He's a sweetie. Are you sure the outfit I bought for the show is OK?' Clare asked, doubt filling her now that they were done for the day.

'It's beautiful and you look incredible in it. I'm jealous of your slim figure and flat tummy.' Jenny patted her bump. 'Only a little bit though, because these two are worth being fat for.'

The automatic doors swished open and the chilly air outside hit Clare like a wave. She enjoyed the cooling rush over her cheeks and neck, feeling it washing away the heat of the shopping centre.

'Let's go and find the car and meet Martin then, shall we?' Jenny looked around them. 'I can never remember where I've parked at the best of times, but since I got pregnant, it's even worse. I swear I have pregnancy amnesia.'

'It's OK, I know where it is.'

They headed across the car park, Clare leading the way, her fingers burning from the handles of the bags, but her heart filled with Christmas joy.

❄

'What was that?' Sam jumped awake on the sofa. There had been a noise in the kitchen, he was sure of it.

Scout stirred at his side, then hopped off the sofa and went to the door.

'Hold on, girl,' Sam said, not wanting her to head out there alone, in case someone had just broken in. Not that there were many cases of burglary in Little Bramble – in fact, there hadn't been any during the time he'd lived there, but you never knew at this time of year if someone passing through might try their luck. What were those opportunistic burglars called? That was it: creeper burglars. Sam was pretty good at locking doors but sometimes, if he was home, he forgot or didn't see the need, but he had dozed off on the sofa after lunch and it was already getting dark out.

He paused in the kitchen doorway, gathering his wits, then the back door swung inwards and Alyssa was there.

'I didn't know you were coming home,' he said, crossing the kitchen to greet her, as Scout bounced over to say hello.

'I just came to get some things. I could see that the lights were off and I thought you might be at work, but I tried the door and it opened, so I wanted to check that you hadn't just forgotten to lock up.'

His heart sank. She hadn't come to see him then, just to get some of her stuff.

'Is there anything you need from in here?' He opened his arms and gestured around the kitchen. 'Utensils? Tins? Wine?'

'No, I'm fine for all that.'

'You sure? You can take whatever you want.'

'Honestly, Sam, I don't want any of it. It's very kind of you to offer, but Sebastian already has everything we need.'

'Right, OK.'

'Look, I did come to see you too. I wanted to make sure that you're all right.'

'Oh . . .' He swayed suddenly. 'I think I got up too quickly.' He gripped the kitchen worktop to steady himself.

'Have you been sleeping?'

He nodded. 'We gave the staff the day off for Christmas shopping and I'm on call, but it's been quiet so far. I got the decorations down and put the tree up . . . then I got side-tracked.'

'You put the tree up on your own?'

'Yeah . . .'

Alyssa's face contorted and her bottom lip trembled. 'I'm sorry, Sam. I don't like to think of you having to do all that alone.'

'It's fine, it is what it is.'

'Please don't do that.'

'Do what?'

'That dismissive thing that some men do. It's not you and it doesn't suit you.'

'Sorry.' He hung his head. He hadn't meant to be dismissive, had, if anything, been trying to affect a nonchalant air as part of his new attitude towards Alyssa's life choices. 'It's hard to get this right.'

'I know.' She nodded. 'Look, Sam, I love you. You're my big brother and I know you've only been looking out for me. I got really upset yesterday and finally spoke to Sebastian about everything. He said that it sounds like you're just a very protective older brother and you clearly love me and want the best for me. He also said that if he had a younger sister, he'd be wary of any new man in her life. It seems that I've been hasty in getting so angry at you. I mean . . .' She held out her hands. 'Well, not exactly hasty, because you have always been this way, but I reacted strongly too, and I could have been more understanding of your feelings. Seb thinks you're a great guy.'

'Oh . . . right. Nice to know.'

'You'd really get on if you gave him a chance.'

'I want to get to know him, Alyssa. I want to be the brother you want . . . I promise there will be no more overbearing big brother from me. Instead, I'll be supportive and here for you if you need me.'

'I will *always* need you, you dolt! You're my best friend. Don't you know that?' Tears ran down her cheeks, leaving glistening streaks in their wake and she opened her arms to him. 'Come here, for goodness' sake!'

He knelt down and hugged her, waves of relief leaving him breathless.

'Do you have to get straight back?' he asked.

'No, I have some time.'

'I don't suppose you fancy helping me with the tree, do you?'

She started to laugh, then squeezed his shoulders.

'Of course I'll help you decorate the tree. I wouldn't have it any other way. Also – do you have anything to eat? I'm *starving*.'

'I'll make some food and hot chocolate and we can have our typical festive evening of tree decorating.'

'That sounds perfect.'

She high-fived him and Sam felt as if he would burst with happiness.

Two hours later, it was pitch-black outside, but in Sam's lounge it was warm and cosy. He had made dinner for Alyssa, they'd had two hot chocolates each, and the tree looked amazing. White fairy lights twinkled on the branches and it was hung with ornaments from over the years, including a snowman that

Sam had made from clay in primary school and a tin fairy on the top of the tree that Alyssa had made in Design and Technology.

'Your artistic talents were definitely evident when you were still at school,' Sam said now as they relaxed on the sofa, Scout between them.

'Yours weren't.' Alyssa giggled. 'That snowman looks like he's melting.'

'Hey! I was six and I'll have you know that Mum said it was the best snowman she'd ever seen.' He winced, realising what he'd said. Alyssa had never been able to present their mother with one of her creations. 'I'm sorry.'

'What for?' Alyssa turned to face him.

'Well, you didn't get to give Mum your angel.'

'No, but I gave it to you, and you said it was the most amazing angel *you'd* ever seen. I was so proud. Dad liked it too.'

'He did.' Sam nodded. 'It sat on top of the tree for years.'

'And now it's here.'

'You should take it with you,' he said, sitting upright. 'To your new home.'

'Sam, I haven't *officially* moved in yet, because we want to wait until the New Year, but Seb has told his daughter that I'm staying over Christmas.'

'Well, when you're properly settled, take it.'

She shook her head. 'No. I want you to keep it.'

'Really?'

'Of course. I just can't bear to leave the wonky snowman alone with all the other lovely ornaments.' She winked at him. 'He'll feel so unattractive and old.'

'Shut up!' He laughed. 'Another hot chocolate?'

'Go on then. Just one more, though, because Seb's picking me up in half an hour.'

Sam made the drinks, then returned to the lounge.

'So you're really happy then?' He watched her face, admiring the shine in her eyes and her easy smile.

'I am. I know that things could go wrong.' She cradled her flat belly. 'I know this might not last. Not all pregnancies are viable, and it is incredibly early days, but even so, I have hope.'

'Hope is important.'

'Extremely important.' She reached across Scout and took Sam's hand. 'You always gave me hope, Sam.'

'I did?'

'When I was lying in that hospital bed after the accident, dosed up on painkillers and waiting for the scan to see if I had lost the baby, your words gave me hope. Even after I'd found out that the baby was gone and that I'd probably never walk again, you promised me that my life wasn't over, that it could go on, just differently.'

'I don't remember a lot from that time.'

'I'm not surprised. You were functioning on no sleep, worried out of your mind and rushing from work to the hospital and back again. You were exhausted, but you were always there. You are amazing, Sam, and I'm so grateful to have you as my brother.'

'I-I haven't always been as supportive as I could have been, though, have I?'

'You've tried, and that's what matters.'

'Look, I have to tell you something. I can't keep it to myself any longer. When you were born, and we lost Mum? Well, I resented you sometimes. I hate myself for it now, but I did.'

'But that's natural, Sam. I hated myself for it over the years as well, so of course you would and Dad must have too. You're only human, you know, though I suspect you'd have been a superhero if you'd had the choice.'

'I'm so sorry for that resentment.'

'Sam, you were twelve! Just a boy! You lost your mum and gained a squawking baby. Your dad fell apart. I'm not surprised you felt some resentment towards me, but what matters isn't that you had feelings like that but the good ones you had and the good things you did. You took care of me when Dad couldn't, you were there for me, have been there for me all my life.'

Sam sipped his wine and gazed at the tree. Alyssa's artistic flair was evident in the way she'd carefully selected ornaments and hung them to create a beautiful effect. She'd also had him lift her up so she could drape lights around the windows and the doorways and now it was like being inside a fairy cavern or Santa's grotto.

'I'm also sorry for arguing with you that day.'

'Again, don't. What's done is done and it wasn't your fault that I stormed out and got on my bike. I blamed myself for that too, but ultimately, we can't carry blame for the rest of our lives. If we're being completely honest, after the accident there were times when I resented you for being able to walk. Feelings are natural, but they come and go. We are good people, Sam, and we both deserve to be happy. And on that note, before Sebastian arrives, I want you to tell me more about the lovely Clare.'

Sam lowered his gaze to his glass, feeling his cheeks warming. Could he tell Alyssa about Clare? Could he share the feelings he had for her that were so new and confusing, so delightful, exciting and hopeful?

'We're just really good friends.' He smiled shyly.

'Sam, I'll forgive you for everything else, but you had better tell me what's going on with you and Clare or I'll never forgive you. A sister has a *right* to know.' She gave him a teasing glare.

'Your tune has changed.' He laughed.

'You'd better believe it, big brother. Come on, tell me everything.'

'OK . . .'

And he told her about how Clare had come into his life, had rocked his world and how he was crazy about her. It felt good to share his feelings with his sister and to see her obvious delight that her brother had, at last, found someone else to care for.

Chapter 26

Clare woke suddenly as if emerging from under water. She sat up in bed and looked around the room. What had woken her? She grabbed her phone off the bedside table and peered at the screen.

Five a.m.

What the . . . ?

Her heart raced and she tried to shake off the sludgy feeling of the dream she'd been having. Something about a dog chasing her and a snarling feral cat scratching at her ankles, then hiding in a huge melting welly.

So weird.

It was probably show-related anxiety that had prevented her from sleeping well. She took a drink from the glass of water on her bedside table, then swung her legs over the edge of the bed. She was still getting used to sleeping in a single bed, even though after Jason had left, she had stuck to her side of their double, unable to spread out because it didn't feel right. Now, though, she felt as if a bit more room would be a good thing.

Standing up, she stretched, hearing some of her joints click, then went to the window. She opened the curtains and gasped, because in the street light just outside her mum's cottage, she could see that everything was white. The forecast had predicted a possibility of snow but not a *heavy* snowfall.

This was certainly heavy – and it was still going.

'Damn it!'

Snow made getting to the shops difficult, yes, but she'd done her Christmas shopping yesterday with Jenny, and she'd planned on doing the big food shop in the week, getting some of it at the local farm shop. Her mum had already ordered a turkey from the farm and they were also going to deliver a veg box.

But today was the Christmas Show! The day that she'd planned and worried about for weeks. The show that Kyle, her mum and many other people had put a lot of effort into preparing, that had cost money to organise, that was meant to be the highlight of the festive calendar.

'Double damn it!'

Would the snow stop the show?

Of course not, it was a village show and most of the performers and people coming to watch it were local, but it might alter the proceedings a bit. There might be a few people coming to watch from outside the village who'd be affected. However . . . her thoughts started to race . . . two of the acts didn't live in Little Bramble. The singing bulldog and his owner, Amanda, lived a fifteen-minute drive away, and then there was Alyssa with her beautiful *a capella* version of the Mariah Carey hit. Sam would be devastated if Alyssa couldn't make it. And what about the ice sculptures that were meant to be delivered that afternoon from the sculptor Clare had found in Richmond? As a special touch, she'd commissioned two ice sculptures to stand outside the village hall. One was of Santa Claus in his sleigh and the other was of a snowman. Clare had thought people arriving could have photos taken with them and it could be a new tradition for the annual Christmas show. It had been sparked by something Sam had said to her about a book he'd read and she hadn't told him about it yet, thinking it would be a nice surprise for him too, something they could enjoy together.

There was a gentle tap at her door.

'Hello?'

The door swung slowly open and Elaine stood there in pyjamas and a silky dressing gown, her hair sticking out in waves, as though she'd plugged her finger in an electric socket.

'Clare!' Elaine rushed over to the window and they both stared out at the fat white flakes that drifted towards the ground, adding to the depths of the snow that had already fallen. 'Look!'

'I know. I had no idea we were expecting this. What are we going to do? Will we have to cancel?'

Her mum pushed her shoulders back and lifted her chin.

'Absolutely not! We are not cancelling this evening come hell or high water. Far too much is riding on this event.'

'But how will people get there? The roads will be blocked and it will be cold – and you know how it is whenever it snows in England, Mum. Things come to a standstill.'

'Not here, my darling daughter. People can wrap up warm and walk if they're local. A few flakes of snow aren't going to ruin things, not after all your hard work.' Her mum squeezed her arm. 'Whatever happens, Clare, the show must go on!'

Clare nodded, drawing strength from her mum's conviction. This was the strongest, the most positive she had seen her since she'd returned to the village. Whether it was down to the vicar, the show, or having Kyle and Clare around, she didn't know, but whatever it was, Clare was grateful for Elaine's strength right now.

'Come on, let's get the kettle on and have some breakfast, then we can start phoning around.' Elaine met Clare's eyes. 'Don't look so worried, Clare. Your old mum is here and I promise you that I won't let you down. Not today!'

She turned, her silky dressing gown billowing around her legs like the skirt of a Flamenco dancer, then strode across the hall and down the stairs. Clare took one more glance out of the window, then hurried after her mum, relieved to hand control over to someone else for a change, to be the one being rescued and not the rescuer.

❄

The village resembled a scene on a Christmas card. Everything had a thick white covering of snow and, as Clare and Kyle trudged towards the village hall, she experienced a flash of excitement. It was, she knew, linked to childhood joy at any amount of snowfall.

'It's so pretty,' Kyle said, panting with the effort of lifting his legs high to plough through the drifts.

'I just hope they can get a snowplough or a tractor out to clear some of it.'

'What? Where's your sense of adventure, Mum?'

'Oh, it is still there, just not today. Why couldn't it have snowed tomorrow instead? I do love snow, Kyle, I really do, but this could ruin the whole show because people might not want to come out in it. A lot of the villagers are elderly and their family members coming from outside the village to watch won't be able to get here and –'

'It'll be OK.' Kyle reached for her hand and squeezed it.

'I hope so. It would be such a shame if it all went wrong now.'

They neared the green and Clare paused. She had to admire the view, even though the snow was badly timed.

The morning was dark, the thick clouds blocking the sunlight, but someone had thought to switch the tree lights on and they glowed prettily and colourfully at the centre of the green as snowflakes drifted down. Fairy lights strung from trees and lamp posts surrounding the green twinkled, making the whole scene incredibly festive; it reminded her of a scene straight out of a Charles Dickens' novel.

'See . . .' Kyle nudged her. 'Isn't that just beautiful?'

'It is.'

'I feel so Christmassy! I can't wait for this evening.'

He leant forwards and grabbed a handful of snow, then patted it into a ball. Clare looked at him, then at the snowball.

'You wouldn't!'

He gave her a wicked grin, his eyes widened, then he raised his arm.

'No!' Clare started to run, or at least she tried to, but the covering of snow on the ground made it very difficult to move quickly. Her feet slipped and she lurched from side to side, giggling with excited fear as Kyle closed in on her.

When the snowball hit her back, she squealed and turned, then grabbed a handful of snow and shaped it between her hands.

'You are *SO* in for it now!'

Kyle shrieked and tried to run in the opposite direction, but he lost his footing and faceplanted into a snowdrift. Clare hurried over to him and patted his shoulder.

'Kyle? Are you all right? Kyle?'

He rolled over, his eyes and mouth filled with snow, which he scooped out with his fingers.

'Are you hurt?' Panic was tingling at Clare's edges now, but Kyle started laughing as he sat up and relief flooded through her.

'That was fun!' He accepted her outstretched hand. 'Let's go again.'

Clare was about to flee, but he hit her in the chin with a snowball before she could extract her wellies from the snow.

'Kyle! I can't believe you did that.'

'Truce?' he asked, his cheeks red, his eyes bright.

'I think so, don't you? Or we'll never get to the hall.'

They trudged on together, laughter making them breathless. Everything felt surreal because the snow muffled all noise; it was as if a thick blanket had been thrown over Little Bramble with plumped-up cold white pillows plopped onto roofs and treetops. If Clare hadn't known it was 11 a.m., she would have thought it was late afternoon and that it would soon be completely dark.

When they reached the village hall, they kicked their boots against the bottom step, trying to dislodge snow from the treads. Lights glowed inside and she breathed a sigh of relief, glad that at least one person had managed to get there to put the heating on and to open up.

Kyle shrugged out of his backpack. 'I'll go and put the kettle on, shall I? And make us one of those instant hot chocolates that you had the foresight to pack?'

'Please.' Clare nodded.

After their snowball fight and the exertion, she felt clammy and knew that it would soon turn to cold. Time to get inside and see what they could salvage of the show.

❄

The snow had been falling all day and Sam couldn't help worrying about how Alyssa would get to Little Bramble. She'd sent him a text around lunchtime, which he'd answered as soon as he'd finished his examination of a local cat brought in by its concerned owner, Gladys Treharne. The cat had been gaining weight, in spite of not being fed more, and the elderly lady who owned it was concerned that her darling *Claw*dius had a tumour or some other horror growing in his belly. However, Sam had soon diagnosed late pregnancy, something that was quite unusual for the time of year, as kitten season tended to run from spring to late autumn, and told her to take the cat home and keep her warm and rested. It looked like there would be kittens within days, so he promised to check in on them after the weekend. Magnus had helped the lady home, carrying the cat carrier, and Sam had been left shaking his head, amazed that Gladys had trekked through the snow to the surgery and that she'd thought her cat was male. Apparently, a friend had given her Clawdius to care for while she went on holiday, then decided to move to Spain, so Gladys had happily kept her, unaware of her gender.

Sam washed his hands, then peered out of the surgery window as he dried them. Flakes of snow drifted down, swirling around like feathers on the breeze that had picked up as the day had worn on. The street lights were on, appearing like dim yellow spheres floating in the air as they battled with the elements. It would be completely dark by four at this rate and, to his knowledge, the council had yet to send out a snowplough or tractor to try to clear some of the roads.

In spite of the conditions, they'd opened for Saturday morning because he had agreed with Miranda that they should run morning surgery just in case.

He replied to Alyssa, telling her not to try to get to the village unless the roads were clear, and she'd confirmed that she wouldn't. With the whole afternoon stretching out ahead of him, Sam's thoughts turned to Clare and all the work she'd done to prepare for the show. He sent her a text to ask if she needed any help, then turned off the lights in the examination room and went through to reception.

He pulled on his coat and hat and swapped his Crocs for wellies. He'd woken in such a good mood that morning, buoyed up by the evening he'd spent with his sister. They had spoken at length about everything that had been bothering them and promised to be open and honest going forwards, with Sam being supportive and not overprotective. He'd carried tension in his shoulders for years and after Alyssa had gone it suddenly drained out of him and he slept better than he had done since he was a child. It was an incredible feeling.

Then he'd seen the snow and worry had crept back in. How would Alyssa get to Little Bramble? Would Clare manage to forge ahead with the show?

He was about to turn off the lights when they flickered, plunging the room into darkness. It only lasted seconds and then the lights came back on. Thankfully, they didn't have any in-patients at the surgery at the moment, but if they had there was a portable backup generator in case of such emergencies.

He checked his mobile phone to see that Clare had replied, asking him to go to the village hall when he could. She said that she'd appreciate any help he could offer.

As he locked the front door to the surgery, he smiled. Clare needed him, so he would be there. Just thinking about seeing her made his heart swell and he marched through the snow, his long legs ploughing through the drifts almost effortlessly, tilting his face upwards to catch a few flakes on his tongue. Childish perhaps, but there was always joy to be found in freshly falling snow.

❄

Clare couldn't believe they'd done it, but they had. The hall was ready. The stage was set with props in the wings, the hall was warm and dry, the seats were set out in neat rows and the volunteers who had offered to cater for the event were in the kitchen adding last-minute touches to refreshments. Marcellus David was on the door behind a desk, ready to collect tickets and Kyle had performed a sound and lights check.

Sam had arrived not long after she had replied to his text, appearing out of the snow like a knight in shining armour, but his armour had been a covering of snow. He'd dusted himself off outside, then climbed the steps and come to her side, asking what he could do to help. To her dismay, she had choked up, so he'd hugged her tightly until she could speak again. There was something so wonderful about being held in his strong arms, about knowing that he was there for her, come what may. And today it was a blizzard and freezing conditions, with forecasters now threatening more heavy snow for the next week, with odds of a white Christmas highly likely.

A proper white Christmas! Clare hadn't seen one of those in years and Kyle had been like a child at the news. It was amazing how simple things like that could turn a grown man into a child again and it had made her smile to see her son so excited.

Elaine had stayed at home to get ready and to do some last-minute baking for the refreshments stand, promising to arrive in good time for the start of the show. Clare had told her mum not to worry about this, as other villagers were already sorting out the food, but in years gone by her mum and dad had made mince pies, gingerbread and mulled wine for the Christmas show, and it seemed that Elaine wanted to resurrect that tradition this year. Of course, Clare and Kyle needed to be at the hall so couldn't help, but Father Ifans was with Elaine and had promised to help her transport the baked goods in his sledge.

Ten minutes after six, Kyle called Clare to the front door. Elaine and Father Ifans were trudging towards the hall, pulling a large sledge behind them, laden with Tupperware and clinking with glass bottles.

'Here we are!' Elaine exclaimed. 'Bearing delicious provisions!'

Father Ifans started unloading it, handing bottles of wine and Tupperware containers to everyone who came to help.

Clare took her mum's hand to help her up the slippery steps. They had sprinkled grit on them, but the snow kept coming and as soon as a few people had climbed them, it became impacted and started to turn to ice.

'I hope you've been all right without me this afternoon, Clare, but with it being a Christmas show, I wanted to bring something special along. Besides which, who knows what the catering team will produce.' Her mum rolled her eyes. 'Probably a few stale custard creams and watery coffee.'

'Mum, I'm really grateful and I think it's lovely that you've done this, but the volunteers have been working in the kitchen for hours, so they do deserve credit for their efforts too.'

'Yes, darling, but I've done this before and know what to expect from some of our villagers. Also, there was something about this year, with us being together again as a family and the new hall and your incredible efforts with the show that made me want to do this. It kind of – this might seem silly – but it made me feel closer to your dad again. He would have loved to be here this evening and he'd have been so proud of you and Kyle.'

Clare tried to blink back the tears. Her dad *would* have enjoyed being here and it seemed so unfair that he wasn't, but it helped a bit that her mum was thinking of him too, that they were united in their love of him – and that was comforting.

Unable to vocalise her feelings, she gave her mum a quick hug and nodded, feeling that Elaine understood. Before heading back inside, Clare looked at the empty spaces where the ice sculptures would have stood if the company had been able to deliver them, and swallowed a sigh of disappointment. Hopefully there would be another opportunity next year.

In the central hall, some of the seats had already been taken by early arrivals, but there were a lot of empty seats. In the small dressing room backstage, the six acts who'd managed to get there were preparing to perform, even if to a very small crowd. Only Alyssa, Mr Spike and Amanda and Greg Patrick were missing. Concern for the latter in particular filled Clare, but she knew his daughter was visiting from London so he wouldn't be alone this evening.

It wouldn't be the extravaganza that Clare had hoped for, but it would still be nice.

As the clock was about to strike seven, Clare was standing on the doorstep, peering into the snow, hoping to see more people approaching, when everything went dark. She turned to the hall, but couldn't see inside and the windows had turned black. She made her way down the steps carefully and out into the street to see that the entire village was in darkness.

'Mum?' Kyle had come out of the hall and was at the top of the steps. 'What's happened?'

'Power cut.' She forced the words out through gritted teeth.

'What're we going to do?' Kyle's voice was laced with dismay and she shook her head, then returned to the steps and ascended using the handrail to avoid sliding.

'Honestly, Kyle? I have no idea.'

And as she shuffled back inside, where the darkness was as thick as smog and the air was still, as if all the people inside were holding their breath in shock, she felt depleted. She had tried to do something good, to prove to her mum that she was capable of helping out and bringing something wonderful to fruition, but her efforts had been in vain.

Time to pack up and go home, then lick her wounds. Although, of course, it wasn't actually her home. She didn't have a home of her own anymore.

How could she ever have thought that she could live successfully on her own, carve out a new path and live her life for herself, when she couldn't even get this one thing right?

Chapter 21

'Candles!'

Sam peered through the darkness trying to work out who had spoken.

'We brought some on the sledge. Iolo, what did you do with them?'

'Hold on, my dear . . .'

There was a shuffling of feet, then the noise of a bag being unzipped (at least Sam hoped it was a bag), a clunk as something was placed on the floor of the hall, then suddenly, there was light. At first, it was the glow from a lighter, but it grew as a thick candle was lit, then another, until there was a row of five fat candles near the stage.

'Well done, Iolo, you are such a good man. I wouldn't have thought to bring candles.'

Sam could see now that it was Elaine speaking and that she was standing in front of the stage with the vicar, who was grinning broadly, basking in the praise, but because the glow from the candles only reached to his nose, his eyes were dark hollows and it was quite eerie.

Sam's mobile buzzed in his pocket, so he pulled it out, realising that if enough of the people now at the village hall had phones, they could use the torches on them, as well as the candles, to light the stage. He read a text from Alyssa and breathed a sigh of relief. She wasn't going to try to get to Little Bramble, said that as much as she wanted to be in the show and to support Clare, she wasn't prepared to take the risk that the journey there posed.

Light spread through the room as Elaine and Iolo picked up the candles and put them on the front of the stage. The glow didn't reach to the back of the large room, but it created enough light to see to the doors. A small light glowed in the hallway where Marcellus had turned his phone torch on.

A fussing from near the windows, young voices, and the sound of someone crying was interrupted by a calm and commanding voice: 'Children, it's fine, calm down.' It was the primary school head teacher, Daphne Dix. She had ten of the pupils with her, along with some of their parents, but the rest of the village school choir hadn't made it, presumably deciding it would be better to stay indoors on this snowy evening.

Sam scanned the hall, realising with a lurch that Clare was missing. Where had she gone and when? He'd been showing people to their seats when the lights had gone out. He hurried out to Marcellus.

'Have you seen Clare?'

'She was outside with Kyle.' He stroked his salt and pepper beard. 'But she just went through to the kitchen, I think. It was dark, see.'

He held his phone up to light the way, but Sam shook his head. 'It's fine, thanks, I have my own phone.'

Sam flicked the torch back on, then followed the circle of light to the kitchen area. Kyle was there holding up a phone while Clare was looking in a cupboard.

'I thought there would be some here, somewhere. Fear not, everyone! I have candles.'

Clare appeared, her face semi-lit by Kyle's torch, her hair messy from where she'd been peering into the cupboard. She set a box on the counter, then went to the gas hob and turned one of the rings on. She lit some candles, handing them in turn to the various people milling around in the kitchen, until there was a circle of light.

'There. That's a bit better.' She offered a reassuring smile to everyone and Sam experienced that familiar feeling her kindness roused.

'Clare?' He approached her. 'Anything I can do?'

She looked at him and shook her head. 'I think we're OK, thanks. Best thing we can do now is get everyone safely home.'

'What?' It was Kyle, one hand holding his mobile aloft, the other on his chest. 'We can't just give up because of a little power cut, Mum.'

Clare looked at her son, then back at Sam, and his heart went out to her. She didn't want to give in, he could see that, but she wasn't sure what else to do.

'Clare.' He beckoned. 'Can I speak to you for a minute?'

'Of course.'

He held out his hand and she took it, then he led her into the hallway.

'We have candles, food and mulled wine. We could set something up in the main hall in front of the stage and sing some carols or something. At least that way the whole evening doesn't need to be written off.'

She sighed and pushed a hand through her hair. The thick cardigan she'd been wearing fell open and Sam gasped because beneath it was a beautiful black sequinned dress. In the light from his phone it sparkled from Clare's chest to just above her knees, hugging her curves and making him feel suddenly very warm.

'What's wrong?' she asked.

'Your dress is beautiful.' He smiled.

'Oh, I forgot I was wearing it, to be honest. I brought a thick cardigan and wore jeans and a jumper to walk over here in my wellies, but I changed about ten minutes before the lights went out. Silly, really.'

'Not at all. It's a very nice dress.'

'But not with my wellies!' She laughed, but it sounded more desperate than happy. 'I can't believe I forgot to bring my shoes.'

'Clare, you are the cutest person I have ever met.'

'Cute?' She met his eyes, holding his gaze. 'I'm in my forties, Sam, how can I possibly be cute?'

'You are, believe me. Cute. Sweet. Intelligent. Gorgeous. Adorable. Kind. Loving. Caring. Funny. Capable. Adaptable . . . I could go on all night.'

'I don't know what to say.' She cleared her throat. 'You really see me like that?'

'I do.'

'But this evening is ruined.'

'No, it's not. Come with me and you'll see.'

He led her back to the main room and, as they walked in, she gave a small cry of surprise. Candles burned on the stage and around the hall came the glow from lots of mobile phones. As they stood there, Kyle followed them in holding more candles, and he went around and lit them all so that soon the room was awash with a cosy glow.

'There you are, Clare.' Elaine walked up to her daughter. 'Iolo and I will bring the food and drink through, then we can at least enjoy some refreshments before everyone heads home.'

'Elaine, it doesn't need to be the end of the evening,' Sam said. 'We can eat, drink and sing some carols.'

'What a good idea, Sam! You're not just a devastatingly handsome man, you also have brains.' Elaine cupped his cheek, then gave it a gentle pat. 'Come on, Iolo, let's get to work.'

❄

The hall was filled with the sounds of glasses and mugs clinking and appreciative murmurs as people tucked into the mince pies and gingerbread that Elaine had made, along with the sandwiches and mini pizzas from the catering volunteers.

They had cleared away the chairs and everyone now sat in a circle, the food and drink spread out in the middle so they could help themselves to whatever they wanted.

'Cheers!' Elaine held up her glass and around them everyone responded. 'What a start to Christmas, eh?'

Clare realised that her mum sounded a bit tipsy, but she could feel a slight buzz herself and she'd only had a few sips, so she suspected that the mulled wine had been topped up with a generous amount of brandy. It was delicious, but she'd been taking her time, aware that getting drunk would not be conducive to getting home easily in the snow.

'It's a shame that it didn't work out as planned, little Clare – sorry, *Clare* – but there's always next year.' Marcellus smiled at Clare from the opposite side of the circle and she smiled back. Would she be here next year to help? A shy glance at Sam at her side made her hope she would be.

'Perhaps . . .'

'You know . . .' Marcellus hung his head. 'In the spirit of Christmas, and because we have a man of the cloth amongst us, I have a confession to make.' He sighed long and low and shook his head. 'I think this is the right time for me to get this off my chest. It's a weight I've carried for two years and I need to say the words now.'

'A confession?' Iolo sounded puzzled. 'Whatever could you have to confess?'

'Did you pull the post from Goliath too hard and rip another letter apart?' Elaine giggled, then snorted. 'Oops! Sorry.'

'I do find that whole scenario rather amusing,' Iolo said. 'A modern-day David and Goliath.'

Marcellus laughed softly. 'How did I never make that connection myself?'

'Isn't that story a bit questionable now?' Kyle muttered to Clare. 'I read something about the story being interpreted wrongly because the giant was actually the injured party as he was so big and slow, and David was a very accurate warrior with a slingshot? And also, in the case here, Goliath always wins.'

Clare smiled at her son, admiring how he thought so deeply about things. 'I think, in this case, we can take it as a harmless comparison,' she whispered.

'As I was saying,' Marcellus continued, his drawn-out vowels emphasised by the high ceiling of the hall and, Clare thought, by the strong wine. 'I have a confession, but it's not about the lovely Goliath. That dog is my nemesis, but there's no malice in him. We just enjoy a morning battle for the post.' His head bobbed gently. 'But what I have to say might anger some of you, so I'm apologising now and asking for your forgiveness.

'Two years ago, when I went home after the Christmas show, I found myself out of milk. The village shop was, obviously, shut, but I wanted a coffee badly. I couldn't bear to drink it without milk, so I wracked my brain . . .' He tapped the side of his head. 'Where could I get milk that late at night?'

'Where?' one of the children asked from Daphne's side, her soft lisp sending a hush through the room.

'From the old village hall, my dear.' Marcellus held up his hands. 'It was foolish of me, don't I know it now, and I have thought of it every day since. But I had the key to the hall, so I made my way over there and let myself in. I found a bottle of milk in the fridge, then I saw a box of eggs. I was hungry too, I realised, and on the gas hob was a clean frying pan. I thought . . . fool that I am, see . . . that I would make my food there, then go on home and no one would be any the wiser.' He shook his head. 'I washed up and intended to replace the eggs and milk the next day, but, see, I must have left the gas on – those old knobs were difficult to turn – and, well, we all know what happened next.' He gave a small shrug. 'I am so dreadfully sorry. It was an accident, but even so, I have lived with that.'

'No!' A voice came from the periphery of the circle. It was Martin Rolands. He'd arrived just before the power cut to tell Clare that Jenny would be staying home because of the weather, but must have stayed on after the lights went out. 'You can't blame yourself, Marcellus.' He crouched at the edge of the circle and rested his hands on his knees. 'If anyone's to blame, it's me. That night, I was in the dressing room dropping some costumes off – ones for the twins for the show – and the main light wouldn't switch on. There was a problem with the wiring, if you remember. Anyway, there was an old lamp in there that had been used as a prop, and I plugged that in to see what I was doing. When I got home, I realised I'd left it on. It must have blown the circuits or something, or perhaps even sparked the gas.'

This pattern of confessions went on for ten minutes, with various villagers confessing to having been at the old village hall that night after the show and it seemed that at least eight local people thought the fire had been their fault. Finally, Elaine raised her hands.

'Please . . . all of you, don't blame yourselves. I am categorically certain that none of you are to blame.'

'Mum?' Clare sat upright. 'What do you mean?'

'Oh, Clare, darling. Why do you think I have been so glum?' Her mum got up and paced the outside of the circle, her hands clasped in front of her as if she was about to deliver a dramatic monologue on stage. 'It was my fault . . .' She sighed, then placed the back of a hand to her brow. 'It was just after the anniversary of my dear husband's passing and I was incredibly sad and missing him dreadfully. I'd had a few drinks after the show, and I sat on the stage and lit some candles. Just like this.' She gestured at the stage. 'It was so pretty, and it made me feel closer to my husband because he'd spent so many hours at the hall too. That night, I was also missing my daughter and grandson terribly. I wondered, as we sometimes do when something suddenly hits us, what had happened over the years to create such a distance between us and if we would ever be close. I needed the loo, so I left the hall for just a few minutes and when I returned the stage curtains were ablaze!'

Gasps shot around the hall like bullets being fired from a gun.

'I know!' Elaine held up her hands. 'And I am so very, very sorry. I burnt down the old hall and I should be punished for it. I ran to the phone box and made a call, disguising my voice as best I could, then I ran off into the night. I couldn't face watching the blaze or risk being caught.' She held her hands out as if to have them placed in handcuffs.

Clare pressed a hand to her chest as sadness and confusion choked her. After all this time, her mum had admitted to missing her and Kyle, to wondering why they were distant, not just physically but emotionally. For years, Clare had wondered if her mum even cared, but she did, she had, and she had suffered because of it.

Suddenly, someone laughed and then that laughter spread around the room like a circle of dominoes being knocked down, filling the hall.

'Why is that so funny?' Elaine had adopted her teacher voice and it cut through the laughter, dimming it to a gentle chuckling. 'I am to blame. I should be punished – although I *have* punished myself ever since that night.'

'Mum!' Clare stood up and went to her mum, then wrapped an arm around her shoulders. 'Please don't. I'm so sorry you've been suffering.'

'Elaine, lovely lady,' Marcellus stood up too. 'It's not your fault.'

'Indeed, it is not.' Iolo walked around the circle until he got to Elaine, then he took her hand and raised it to his lips. 'I have listened to the many confessions here this evening and I'm fairly certain that the old village hall burning down was a combination of things. It was a terrible shame, but the verdict at the time was that the fire was accidental, caused by faulty electrics and a gas leak – and, goodness only knows, it could have been far worse. The important thing is that no one was hurt. And now, look at how we have progressed. Here we are, in our lovely new hall, with good food, drink and company. We cannot change the past, but we can appreciate the present and do our best to ensure that the future is filled with smiles and good times.'

'I have an idea.' Sam stood up. 'I don't know why I didn't think of it sooner. I could go and get the generator from the surgery. We could use it here for the show.'

Clare looked at her mum and they both smiled, then shook their heads.

'Sam, we couldn't possibly allow that.' Clare's mum placed a hand over her heart. 'It's incredibly kind of you, but what if you need it there? If there was an emergency this evening or tomorrow and you had no power, how would you and Miranda manage? No, we may not have electricity, but we can still perform some of our acts.'

'Yes, we can.' Clare nodded. 'How do you feel about singing for us?' She directed the question at Daphne and the teacher looked around the hall at her pupils, who nodded enthusiastically.

'Let's get the Christmas show started, then.' Clare went to the stage and moved the candles so they wouldn't be a risk to the children, then they climbed the steps to the stage with Daphne and she arranged them into two lines before descending the steps and opening the lid of the piano. Her mum hugged her then went to join the children.

Clare thought, as she looked at her mum standing there on stage, with the golden glow of the candlelight on her face and her shadow flickering on the wall behind her, that she looked like a Christmas angel. And if she squinted just a bit, she could picture her dad up there too, his arm around her mum, his face lit up with love and pride.

There was a cough from in front of the stage and Sam raised a hand. 'Just wondering . . . I'm a bit rusty, but I could join in, if that's all right? I'm not as good as my sister, but I can carry a tune.'

'Wonderful!' Daphne said, and Sam hopped up onto the stage, standing exactly where Clare had pictured her dad.

The rest of the people in the hall gathered together near the piano, and Clare was conscious of Kyle at her side. As the opening notes of 'Have Yourself a Merry Little Christmas' filled the air, emotion flooded though her and her vision blurred.

She blinked hard, then glanced at the window and goosebumps rose on her skin. She was with her loved ones, at the heart of the village community, celebrating the start of Christmas and outside the snow was falling softly, turning Little Bramble into a picturesque winter wonderland. What could be more perfect than this?

Sometimes, she mused, plans went awry, things didn't work out as you expected them to, but it didn't mean that everything was over. In fact, sometimes, it was just the beginning.

Chapter 28

'Right, that's all locked up then.' Marcellus pocketed the keys to the hall. 'Goodnight to you, Clare, and to you, Sam.'

'Goodnight, Marcellus.' Clare kissed his cheek and he chuckled.

'Thank you, sweet one.' He pressed his hand to his cheek, grinned, then made his way gingerly down the steps and off through the snow.

'I guess it's goodnight to you too, Sam.' Clare smiled at him. 'Thank you for helping to make what could have been a disaster into a wonderful evening.'

The power had gone on and off a few more times as they'd sung, but then it had come on again, just in time for everyone to leave. Kyle and Elaine had left twenty minutes ago and everyone else had gone an hour ago, but she'd wanted to stay to clean up. And, if she was completely honest, to make the evening last as long as possible. It had been a triumph, an achievement, evidence of what could happen when people pulled together as a community. It was a shame that lots of people hadn't made it, but it was the start of something, and as they'd tidied up, her mum had said that it would be lovely if they had something to look forward to in the summer, possibly a summer fete. It seemed like a good idea and one that Clare would love to be involved with.

Sam stepped closer to her and lifted his hand, then gently brushed her cheek. Something inside her unfurled gently, as if there had been a tightly coiled rope in her belly and now it was relaxing. Her knees weakened and she was surprised by the longing that flooded her whole body. Could one person want another so much?

'You had a snowflake there.' He held her gaze and she felt as if he could read her thoughts, see into her heart. It was scary, but also liberating, to feel that someone could truly see her, know her and still want her. 'And thank you, Clare. You made it wonderful. *You* are truly wonderful.'

He slid his arms around her waist and pulled her to him, his expression changing. There was longing and unsated desire in his eyes, and her heart sped up. He was holding her so tightly, tighter than she'd ever been held by a man. Her body was aflame, and everything tingled from the roots of her hair to the tips of her fingers.

Sam lowered his head to hers and their lips met. His kisses were soft at first, then firmer, growing harder with urgency, and she moaned as he kissed her the way she'd always wanted to be kissed. Everything around them faded away; the cold, the snow, the twinkling lights, the village hall, the muffled silence of the wintery night.

When Sam finally pulled back and looked at her, she felt sure that her face must be glowing, her eyes shooting hearts in his direction. This was what she'd read about, heard others talk about, and what all those books and songs were about.

This . . .

She knew that she could lose herself in this man, that she could become one with him and devote herself to a relationship with him. She could move back to Little Bramble permanently and see Sam every day, perhaps move in with him and love him and take care of him as she knew he would take care of her.

She could do all of this!

But . . .

That would mean surrendering her heart and her life to another man as she had done with Jason, giving up her newfound freedom, her fragile sense of self that was developing as she came to know who she was and what she wanted. She wasn't quite there yet and didn't know how long it would take, or exactly what it would take for her to know the woman she was meant to be. She had lived, but she had so much more she wanted to do, to experience, to enjoy. If she gave herself to Sam, which she felt sure that committing to falling in love with him would lead to, then surely, she would be relinquishing herself once more?

How could she live for herself if she was living for another person?

'Clare?' Sam's eyes widened as he gazed at her and a tiny line appeared between his brows. 'What is it? Are you OK?'

'I . . .' She slipped out of his embrace. 'I'm not sure.'

'Clare . . .' He reached for her again, but she went to the steps and descended, gripping the handrail tightly. 'Please don't go. Come home with me.'

He jumped the steps and landed next to her, his face unreadable as the snow fell faster. It covered his hat, his coat, his feet and Clare thought that if they didn't move soon, they'd be frozen there, locked in that moment, ice people outside the village hall like the sculptures she had commissioned.

'Clare . . . I love you.'

She shuddered as if ice had pierced through her ribcage, sharp and cold, severing her heart from her head.

'You love me?' she whispered. 'Oh Sam.'

'I can't help myself. I've never felt this way about anyone before, Clare.'

She opened her mouth, tried to reply, closed it again and looked around as if searching for an appropriate response. This kind, funny, caring man loved her – and she was standing there flapping her arms as if she would fly away.

'I'm so sorry, Sam. I just – just I can't do this right now.' She shook her head, raised her hand to touch him, but lowered it again. If she held him now, she would never let go and that thought terrified her. 'I have to go.'

She turned and started stomping her way through the snowdrifts, feeling ridiculous with her exaggerated movements, but the snow was so deep now that she had to lift each leg, then stamp it down before she could move forwards.

'Clare!' His voice broke and she knew, in that moment, that she was the worst person in the world. 'Let me at least see you safely home.'

She waved a hand, not turning around, because she couldn't bear to see the pain on his face and she knew, deep in her heart, that she loved him too.

❄

Sam watched Clare trudging through the snow and he wanted to follow her, but she didn't want him. She'd said as much; she couldn't do this. He had been foolish, had opened his heart to her, told her everything and she had rejected him.

The pain in his chest was raw. Every breath felt as though he'd inhaled copious amounts of smoke and burnt his lungs and when he exhaled, he coughed raggedly. He felt damaged, as if he would never escape the crushing weight of this rejection.

Everything had been going so well and he had let his guard slip. No, he had chosen to open up, to share himself with Clare and to confess to Alyssa the things he had held inside for so long. It had been a relief to get those things out in the open. Clare had been so kind, so supportive and so understanding and he admired her for that.

But he also loved her. How could he not love her when she was such a remarkable woman? He'd read somewhere once that, to truly love someone, you have to make yourself vulnerable; it was the only way to love someone openly and without hesitation.

He took a deep breath, watching as he released it into the night air, a puffy cloud that dispersed as snowflakes took its place. Everything around him sparkled as if diamond dust had been sprinkled over Little Bramble. It was magical. Festive. Perfect.

This village was special. This moment was special. What had grown between him and Clare was special. That could not be denied.

So why was his heart breaking?

Sam shook himself. He would not be sad that he had opened his heart to love. It had been a long time coming and falling for Clare had brought him so much joy. He would never regret that.

Now, though, he would head home and cuddle Scout. He would let the pain in and feel it because he'd pushed everything away for so long and he knew how it could eat away at him. He wouldn't make that mistake again.

So, even though he was devastated, he had learnt lessons that would stay with him for the rest of his days. He had given himself to love and it was, even in its darker moments, glorious to feel with such intensity.

He tucked his hands into his pockets and walked towards the green, doing the same funny walk that Clare had done because the drifts were so deep.

Nothing in life was easy, but there was always another way to view a situation. Clare had said that she couldn't do this now. Perhaps that meant that there was hope; perhaps one day she would be able to love him as he did her.

Sam was going to cling to that hope. It was all he could do.

Clare virtually fell through the front door of her mum's cottage along with a pile of snow. She was cold and wet, her coat and jeans heavy with water, and her bones ached from exhaustion after her walk back from the village hall. But all of that was nothing in comparison to how dreadful she felt for leaving Sam behind like that.

There was no way that Sam would ever deserve such treatment and no way that she could ever forgive herself for hurting him. It would be another thing she had to carry around every day, like a necklace of guilt and failure.

She sank to her knees and buried her face in her gloved hands. This had to be the worst she had ever felt. As tears mingled with the melting snowflakes on her cheeks, a cold nose pushed through her hands and a long tongue licked from her chin to her hat.

She lowered her hands and met Goliath's big blue eyes.

'Hello, boy.' She sniffed, but the tears kept falling, turning the dog into a blurry silver blob.

He licked her face again, then gave a low whine, as if sad to see her upset.

She flung her arms around his big neck and sobbed into his fur. They stayed that way until she'd cried herself out, then she pulled a tissue from her pocket, wiped her eyes and blew her nose.

'The best kind of friend has four paws and a wet nose, right, Goliath?'

She kissed his nose, then stood up, kicked some of the snow back outside and closed the door. When she'd removed her wellies, socks, coat and jeans, she carried her rucksack with her dress and other bits through to the kitchen and placed them on a chair. She'd empty the bag tomorrow and sort everything out; she was just too tired right now.

Goliath was right behind her, watching her as if he was afraid to take his eyes off her. She pulled her cardigan tighter around her chest, glad that it fell to mid-thigh, then made a mug of tea. Padding back through to the lounge with Goliath she saw that the downstairs of the cottage was empty. From upstairs she could hear the sound of a tap running, so either her mum or Kyle was in the bathroom.

Sinking onto the sofa, she pulled one of the soft blankets over her and patted the seat next to her. Goliath jumped up and placed his head on her lap. Such unconditional love made tears well up in her eyes again and she stroked his soft head, knowing that she would miss him if she did decide to leave the village or if she moved out of the cottage. The thought that he wouldn't understand where she'd gone started her off crying again, so she swallowed hard and tried to empty her mind.

She must have dozed off, because the next thing she knew, her mum was gently shaking her. 'Clare, dear? Don't lie like that . . . you'll have a bad neck in the morning. Why don't you go up to bed?'

'I can't feel my legs.' Clare shook her head, trying to wake up properly.

'That's because you have a large dog lying on them. Goliath, move a bit for Clare, won't you?'

Clare watched as Goliath shifted, sitting upright like a statue, but he didn't get down, staying next to her like a bodyguard.

'Ah, that's better. There's feeling rushing into them now . . . but ooh!' Clare rubbed her legs. 'I have pins and needles.'

'Do you want another mug of tea?'

'Yes please, Mum.' She sat up. 'Shall I get it?'

'No, it's fine. You stay there and I'll make one.'

Clare gazed into the fire, watching the red-amber glow of the logs, looking for faces and other images the way she used to as a child. It was a game she had played with her dad and he always agreed that he could see whatever creature she named, although now she knew he probably hadn't been able to. But he had done that for her, wanting to share that with her. She missed him deeply and the longing to see him was like a physical pain, one more sharp ache to pile on top of the rest. If he'd been here right now, he'd have sat with her, cuddled her and smoothed her hair back from her forehead. He'd have told her that it would all work out all right in the end and she'd have believed him, because dads knew these things. Dads were rocks for their daughters. Their job was to nurture and protect. Or so Clare had always believed, but she also knew that not all dads were like hers had been and some weren't very good at the job. Just like mums. After all, she'd had a dad she could lean on but her mum . . . it was a completely different dynamic.

When Elaine returned to the lounge carrying a tray, she handed Clare a mug of tea, then set a plate of gingerbread cookies on the coffee table.

'I thought you might be peckish.'

'Thanks.' Clare nodded, but she didn't think she'd ever be able to eat again. Her throat was tight, her stomach closed over with grief, and the thought that Sam had enjoyed some of her mum's baking earlier that evening brought fresh tears to her eyes. Would he ever enjoy it again?

Her mum sat on the other sofa, cradling her mug between her hands.

'What's wrong, Clare?' she asked finally. 'I thought you'd have been with Sam tonight. You two looked so happy this evening that I didn't think I'd see you until tomorrow.'

Clare sniffed. 'I could say the same about you and Iolo.'

'Oh, I sent him home alone. He has things to sort out tomorrow and I needed a night alone in my own bed. I'm shattered after this evening, but it was a lot of fun. Well done, my darling.'

Clare met her mum's eyes. 'Thanks.' She cleared her throat. 'It was a joint effort, though.'

'But you started it and put in a lot of work. You have done wonders for village morale.'

Clare forced her mouth into a smile, but it fell away quickly.

'Anyway, Clare, you evaded my question.'

Clare sipped her tea, wincing as it scalded her tongue, but glad of the physical pain as a distraction from the churning inside.

'I . . . I don't know, Mum. I don't know what to do.'

'Don't you like Sam?'

'Yes. A lot. But it's complicated.'

'Love always is.' Her mum nodded, then sighed. 'But it's worth it.'

'That's debatable.'

'In what way?' Elaine tucked her legs underneath her and turned to give Clare her full attention.

'I thought I'd got it right with Jason but look how that turned out. I failed to make my marriage work.'

'Darling, that's not true. You did your best with Jason. I know you did, I saw how hard you worked at your marriage.'

'And if that much hard work leads to failure, what would less effort lead to?' Clare shifted on the sofa, then finished her tea and placed the mug on the coffee table. 'How will I ever know if I'm going to get it right?'

'Love is always a chance.'

'But you had a happy marriage to Dad.'

'Not always.'

'What?' Clare bristled. How could this be true? 'But you two loved each other!'

'We did, but there were difficult times. Every relationship has ups and downs.'

'When were there difficult times?'

'After I had you.'

Clare pulled the throw up to her chest, digging her fingers into the plush fabric, feeling suddenly cold.

'I love you, Clare, and I always have done but I never wanted children. I had no maternal urges at all, and when I fell pregnant, I was devastated. I loved my job, was climbing the ladder in my career, which wasn't at all easy for a woman to do back in the seventies, then suddenly I found myself with morning sickness and swollen ankles. Along with anaemia, I had low blood pressure and I had to take time off work. It affected my career for quite some time because I had to have sick leave followed by maternity leave. Taking that much time away from school was frowned upon by management and it damaged my career.'

'I thought you always loved your job and were happy at work?'

'I did love it, but I was never more than head of department. I wanted more . . . to be a deputy head teacher, possibly even head.' She sounded wistful, as if her life was playing out before her eyes on a film.

'I'm sorry.' Clare gripped the throw tighter. 'For ruining your life.'

'No, no, Clare, that's not what I meant at all. You brought so much joy – but it was your father who loved you as you should have been loved. I think I failed you in that respect.'

'You resented me?'

'Not resented, more . . . wished things had been different.'

'That sounds like pretty much the same thing.'

'Semantics perhaps, but sometimes it's difficult to explain away a lifetime of feelings.' Elaine rubbed her eyes. 'Feelings are fluid too, so it wasn't as if I felt the same way every day. I loved you, certainly, but I always felt guilty for not loving you in the way that mothers should love their children.'

'I've always known.'

'I'm so sorry.'

'And yet, with Kyle, you're different. Warmer, somehow. I'm so glad of that.'

'With Kyle it's different. His arrival didn't take anything away from my life. That sounds dreadful, doesn't it? But having you ruined my career and left me with enormous guilt because I felt that I had failed you. Kyle has simply added value.'

'Did your own childhood affect you, do you think?' Clare held her breath, asking a question she had always wanted to ask before.

'Very much so. I'm convinced of it.'

'Will you tell me about it now?' Clare's exhaustion had numbed to a gentle nausea that drifted around, polluting her mind and body like a hangover. Her head felt woolly and her eyes stung but she wanted to hear more, to finally understand her mum's behaviour.

'I will.' Elaine nodded, the dark shadows under her eyes were like halfmoons, her skin pallid and her chest rose and fell rapidly. 'I know I owe you that much at the very least.'

'Thank you.' Clare hugged herself, already hurting at having what she had suspected her whole life confirmed: her mum had never really wanted her and that had made it difficult for her to love herself.

'My mother wasn't really my mother. What I mean by that is that the woman who raised me was actually my aunt. My biological mother got pregnant with me at seventeen, which was very young to have a baby and, at that time, single mothers were frowned upon. My mother's sister was married with two children, both boys, one just a year older than me and the other three years older. Her husband was a kind man, who understood his sister-in-law's predicament and who would have done anything to support his wife. My grandparents were already dead, so my aunt and uncle claimed me as their own. Not long after my birth, my mother disappeared from the small Welsh mining town where we lived and, to my knowledge, she was never seen again.

I called my auntie Mam, not knowing any better until I was sixteen, when she told me the truth. They were good parents, but money was tight. My uncle lost his job when the mine closed – there were a lot of pit closures in the sixties – and it hit him and the town hard. My aunt worked, my eldest cousin left home and went away to work, but the cousin who was a year my senior was a lazy lout who spent most of his time in the pub. I left school at sixteen, feeling that I was a drain on the family finances and finding the small terraced house claustrophobic. My aunt and uncle were arguing more and more, my cousin made things worse, and I needed to escape. So I did.'

'What did you do?' Clare was intrigued by the story, even though she was incredibly hurt. A small part of her had hoped for a different confession that would reassure her that her mum had loved and wanted her.

'I headed for London.'

'At sixteen?'

Her mum nodded.

'Why have you never told me this?'

Elaine shrugged, her face haggard in the firelight.

'I didn't want to remember, I guess. My aunt and uncle were good people, but they were trapped in their life, and although I knew they cared about me, they didn't love me as they would have if I'd actually been theirs. There was always a hesitancy in their attempts at affection, always something withheld. Perhaps they were like it with their sons too, I never noticed, but I remember feeling empty and alone for most of my childhood.'

'That's so sad.' Clare picked at the throw, trying not to think too hard about her mum as a sixteen-year-old girl, lonely and lost.

'I believe that it toughened me, made me resilient and resourceful. But sadly, it also made me reserved when it came to my own child. I don't think I actually knew *how* to love, you, Clare. I saw other mothers who were besotted with their babies, but for me it was different. You were so needy, as babies are, and you took up so much time and effort at a stage in my life when I wanted to be at work, proving that I was as good as any man in the school, that I was senior management material and that I deserved to be promoted.'

Clare didn't respond; it was too painful. Times were different now, but gender equality issues were still there, not always as prevalent perhaps, but for her mum, back then, it would have been an uphill battle. 'So – so how did you manage in London?'

'I found work cleaning pub toilets and the owner had a small bedsit he let to me. Soon, I was pulling pints and saving my pennies. I realised that I couldn't do that for the rest of my life, so I started using the library to study and then gained qualifications. I continued to work in the evenings while training to become a teacher then, when I qualified, I left bar work behind.'

'How did you and dad meet?'

'I thought we'd told you that.'

Clare shook her head.

'It was nothing dramatic or romantic. A mutual friend set us up on a blind date. I didn't expect to like your father, wasn't even that interested in finding someone, but when I saw him, I just knew he was the one for me.'

'He always said you were the only one for him.'

'We were lucky. We fell in love and had a good marriage. We were also very lucky to have you, even if you were an accident.' Elaine pushed her hair back from her face, but it swung forwards again, so she tucked it behind her ears. 'I'm so sorry for not being a good enough mum, Clare. I just think that I didn't really know how. My aunt was kind and she did all the things necessary to look after me – feeding me, making sure I ate my vegetables, all that functional stuff – but the emotional preparation just wasn't there.'

Clare thought of her own childhood, of the gaping hole that her mum had left by not giving her the attention she craved. But then she thought of the love and time she had received from her dad, her paternal grandparents and Jenny. Though she had lost out, her own relationship with Elaine being more functional than affectionate, she had found a balance of sorts in the love from others around her. She had then gone on to have Kyle and done her utmost to make him feel loved, probably too much at times. Kyle had never been afraid to fall in love.

But Clare had . . .

'I know that you felt there was a gap in your life; I felt that in mine too. I think it's because we expect our mothers to be heroes, believe that they should love us above all others. But that's not always how it works, Mum. You were abandoned by your mother, who was little more than a child when she had you, then raised by her sister, who had her own reasons for remaining reserved. You didn't want children and I was a shock. I'm not surprised you found it difficult to love me.'

'I always *loved* you, Clare, but I don't think I loved you enough. Goodness knows I beat myself up about it regularly, but I tried to be good at everything else. I was a good wife, I think, and I was a good teacher, took the ones who needed extra support under my wing. I knew how they felt. Sadly, the irony of it is that while I was doing all that, I was neglecting my own daughter. And, then, of course, the relationship between you and your dad was tough for me; not because I resented how much he loved you, but because I knew you and I could never be that close. When you cried as a baby, it should have been me you turned to for comfort, but it was always your father. It was as if you knew from the moment you were born that I wasn't going to be enough for you.'

They sat in silence, gazing at the fire, the ticking of the clock on the mantel and Goliath's snoring lulling them with their consistent familiarity.

'I think that our relationship sent me searching for a kind of replacement.' The revelation hit Clare like a lightning bolt. 'I never felt like I was enough for you, so I went looking for that kind of fulfilment elsewhere. That's probably why I fell for Jason. I wasn't even sure that he really loved me, but I'd have taken anything, just to feel accepted and wanted.'

Her mum emitted a small cry like a wounded animal.

'I'm so sorry.'

'No, don't be. I'm glad I can finally understand it. Jason wasn't a bad man, but he was never the *right* man. I settled rather than waiting, instead of having time alone to work out who I was and what I wanted from life. However, none of it matters now because I had Kyle – and I would never be without my son.'

'You are a wonderful mum, Clare. Truly wonderful. Kyle is very lucky to have you.'

Clare smiled, the compliment precious and welcome.

'He's so happy and contented with himself and who he is. I'm very grateful for that.'

'And what of you now, Clare – and Sam?'

Clare shook her head. 'I can't do it. I can't be in a relationship with someone until I've found myself. I can't surrender more than I have to give. I tried to do it with Jason for years and it just left me depleted. I barely had the energy to exist outside of home.'

'Clare, darling, you don't have to surrender anything. You can be yourself and live your life for you as well as having a fulfilling relationship. It's not all or nothing, and you are far stronger than you realise. You are resilient and adaptable, and you deserve to be happy.'

Clare swallowed, letting the words sink in.

'But – but I told him I couldn't be with him. He was so upset. He'll never forgive me for that.'

'I am sure that if you rang him right now, he'd be overjoyed to hear from you.'

Heart racing, blood whooshing through her ears, Clare stayed very still, trying to envisage if she had the strength to apologise to Sam, to explain to him everything she had just been told and to convey to him exactly how much it had all affected her.

What if they could slow down a bit, be together, but cement their friendship, allow her to continue her own journey while getting to know each other better? Neither of them had to make huge sacrifices, to give up the things and people they cared about. They could learn and grow together. Surely that was what made a good relationship?

She reached for her phone on the coffee table.

It was late. There was a chance that Sam would already be asleep.

She'd ring him and leave a message if he didn't answer.

She glanced at her mum and Elaine nodded, then got up and left the room, but not before she'd blown her daughter a kiss.

Clare swiped the screen, found Sam's number, then pressed *call* . . .

Chapter 29

Turning the postcard over, Clare looked at the picture again. It was one of those photo cards that could be made using photos from a mobile phone, and it showed Jason in a yoga tree pose, his arms above his head, hands clasped, one leg bent with the foot touching the inner thigh of the other. He was tanned and toned and his face beamed at the camera.

He was happy.

Clare had seen the postcard when it arrived a few days earlier, landing on the mat from where Kyle quickly rescued it. Jason had addressed it to Kyle, Clare and Elaine, which Clare appreciated. He had never been a cruel or bitter man, and there was a part of her that would always care about his welfare. She was just glad that they had both been able to find their way in life, even if it had taken until they were in their forties.

She read the postcard again, smiling at the brevity of the message. Typical Jason. He was having fun, relaxing, making the most of his time in Vietnam before heading somewhere else in the New Year. He wasn't sure where yet, but would be in touch. He was free.

Clare placed the card back on the mantel next to the Christmas cards and went out to the hallway. In the mirror, she checked her appearance. In the sparkly black dress that she'd bought for the show, paired with black boots, she felt good. All the walking, Tai Chi and horse riding had toned her up, but she'd kept her curves and she liked them. She was a woman in her mid-forties and that was OK. She was finding peace with herself, looking for the positives rather than the flaws and it certainly helped to silence that critical inner voice.

The cottage was filled with delicious aromas as Christmas dinner cooked – a joint effort, this year. Her mum and Kyle had insisted that Clare stay out of the kitchen and allow them to do everything. She was told to take a long bubble bath with the luxury bath foam her mum had bought her for Christmas and to use the clay face mask that Kyle had popped in the stocking he'd prepared for her. She'd done as they'd instructed, then slathered herself in scented moisturiser, blow-dried her hair into soft waves that accentuated the highlights. Along with a small amount of make-up, the overall effect was quite eye-catching. Of course, the glow in her cheeks and the sparkle in her eyes helped.

Goliath came to her side and rubbed his head against her hand. He had become her shadow, unwilling to let her out of his sight when she was home, and she had wondered how she would ever be able to leave him, if and when she found a place of her own. But then her mum and Iolo had made an announcement: Iolo was retiring and they were buying a campervan and were going to travel through Europe in the New Year. Her mum said she had considered taking Goliath, but seeing how attached he'd become to Clare, she thought he'd be happier staying with her – as long as Clare was happy with that. The delight Clare had felt had brought tears to her eyes; she loved Goliath and knew that he loved her, so of course she would stay with him. She had also agreed to look after the cottage while Elaine was away, which apparently would be anything from six months to a year, and Kyle was staying on with her too.

Not wanting anyone to spend Christmas Day alone, and having a turkey the size of an ostrich, her mum had told her and Kyle to invite as many people as they could think of. A glance at the clock told her that their guests would soon be arriving and her stomach flipped with joy and excitement. Their guest list included Iolo, Marcellus, Magnus and Miranda from the surgery, Jenny, Martin and the twins, and Clare's guest of honour, Sam.

When Clare had phoned him after the show, he had picked up almost immediately and they had talked until dawn. There had been tears, but plenty of kind words and lots of understanding. Since then, they had met three times in the week leading up to Christmas for coffee and cake, and although it was a challenge to hold back, they were doing their best. Clare liked to think that when they did, finally (and she was certain it would happen in the New Year), spend the night together, it would be all the more special. Sam was a wonderful man and they were learning that they had many things in common.

There was a knock at the door and Goliath barked, making Clare jump; she took a deep breath then went to answer it, holding Goliath's collar tightly as she let their guests in. There were hugs, kisses and bellows of *Merry Christmas*, then everyone filed through to the kitchen to repeat the process with Elaine and Kyle.

Everyone except for Sam.

He released Scout from her lead and she trotted through to the kitchen with Goliath, then he removed his coat and hat and hung them on the bottom of the banister before turning to Clare.

'Merry Christmas,' he said, as his eyes roamed over her, making her shiver with delight.

'Merry Christmas.'

He opened his arms, a question in his eyes and she nodded. This was fine, this was acceptable. In fact, as she slid her arms around his waist, she thought that it was wonderful. He smelt of clean washing, citrus and spice, and his hug was filled with affection and warmth. It was like finding her safe place after years of floundering, like coming home after being lost in a snowstorm. It was like nothing she had ever imagined possible. And it was real. She didn't feel like she was sacrificing anything to be with Sam, more that he enhanced her life and added to it with his kindness, intelligence and handsome presence.

'I have something for you.' He released her, then pulled an envelope from his pocket.

'What is it?' she asked.

'Open it and find out.'

She fumbled with the envelope, then pulled out a card. Inside was a voucher for an experience day. 'Which one am I going on?'

'That's up to you.' He smiled. 'You get to choose whatever it is you want to do, Clare. You get to follow your own path.'

'And live my life for myself?' she asked, thinking of the day two and a half months ago when she'd driven to Little Bramble and heard Cory Quincy say that exact same thing on the radio.

'That's right.' He nodded, then gently brushed her cheek with his lips, making her sigh.

'And do I go on this experience day alone?'

'That, my dear, is entirely up to you.'

She looked down at the voucher and toyed with her bottom lip, then raised her eyes to meet his and grinned.

'I don't want to do this without you,' she said, sliding her arms around him again.

'I was hoping you'd say that.' His voice was husky, his hands buried in her hair as he lowered his head to kiss her.

When they finally broke apart, Clare placed a hand on his chest, right above his heart.

'I'm not just talking about the experience day, Sam.'

'I was hoping you'd say that too.'

Holding hands, they made their way into the kitchen to celebrate Christmas with friends and family – and Clare knew although Christmas came at the end of the year, this time it signalled a brand-new start.

Acknowledgements

My thanks go to:

My husband and children, for your love and support.

My wonderful agent, Amanda Preston, and the LBA team, in particular Hannah for patiently answering my emails and Alison for the Tweets.

The amazing team at Bonnier Books UK, with special thanks to my fabulous editor, Claire Johnson-Creek, and to the lovely Jenna Petts for her support and enthusiasm.

My very supportive author and blogger friends, especially (and in no particular order) Jules, Sarah, Bella and Phillipa for the friendship, writing support and motivation; Ann, Wendy and Kate for being such good friends; Holly for being a wealth of writing knowledge and more; Laura for being so kind and inspirational, Annie, Laura K and Andi for the chats, and Ian for the support and enthusiasm on social media.

Sarah, Dawn, Deb, Sam, Clare, Yvonne, Emma, Kelly and Caryn for always being there.

All the readers who take the time to read, write reviews and share the book love.

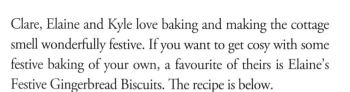

Elaine's Festive Gingerbread Biscuits

Clare, Elaine and Kyle love baking and making the cottage smell wonderfully festive. If you want to get cosy with some festive baking of your own, a favourite of theirs is Elaine's Festive Gingerbread Biscuits. The recipe is below.

Ingredients:

150g dark brown sugar
180g black treacle
145g unsalted butter, softened
1 teaspoon vanilla extract
1 large free-range egg
400g plain flour, plus extra for rolling out
1 teaspoon baking powder
Pinch of salt
1 tablespoon ground ginger
1 tablespoon ground cinnamon
½ teaspoon ground allspice
½ teaspoon ground cloves

To decorate (optional):

Piping icing/buttercream, small sweets, chocolate buttons

Method:

1. Melt the butter, brown sugar and treacle in a saucepan. Cool to room temperature.
2. Beat the butter until soft and fluffy then stir in the cooled treacle mixture. (You can do this by hand, with a wooden spoon or with an electric mixer.)
3. Add the vanilla extract and egg and beat until smooth.
4. In a separate bowl, combine the flour, baking powder, salt, ginger, cinnamon, allspice and cloves then mix with the wet ingredients.
5. You will now have a thick and sticky cookie dough. Divide the dough in half then wrap each half in clingfilm and press out into circles. Chill for 2–3 hours or up to 2 days.

6. Preheat the oven to 170°C and line two large baking trays with non-stick baking paper.
7. Flour a worksurface then remove cookie dough from the fridge and roll out until 5mm ¼ inch thick. Cut into shapes – circles, trees, Christmas jumpers, people or shapes of your choice. Place cookies on baking paper with plenty of space between them. Repeat until all the dough has been used.
8. Bake for around 8–10 minutes, depending on cookie shape.
9. Cool for 5 minutes on the tray then transfer to a wire rack and allow to cool completely. Decorate with piping icing / buttercream and sweets of your choice.

Enjoy!

Return to the village of Little Bramble with Cathy Lake's next book . . .

The Country Village Summer Fete

Emma Patrick's life is spiralling out of control. On the cusp of her 50th birthday, she suddenly realises that she doesn't have many meaningful relationships in her life. She's single, successful, living alone and thinks she's loving it, but being so focused on work and always online means she's lost any real connection to people.

When Emma gets a call to say her ageing father is becoming increasingly confused, she decides that she should go back home to the countryside to spend some time with him. But returning to Little Bramble, the village she grew up in, after all these years is filled with complications of its own and people she'd rather avoid.

As Emma starts to settle in to her childhood home, she finds herself loving village life – much to her surprise. When the opportunity to get involved in the running of the summer fete comes her way, before she knows it she's embracing jam making, cake baking and bunting. And with romance brewing, Emma begins to doubt the glamorous life in London that she worked so hard to build . . .

A feel-good, uplifting summer read, coming May 2021